Platinum Widow:
Who Killed Jean Harlow's Husband?
A Porter Down Hollywood Mystery

By
Gregory William Mank

Platinum Widow:
Who Killed Jean Harlow's Husband?
A Porter Down Hollywood Mystery
By Gregory William Mank
Copyright © 2023 Gregory William Mank
All Rights Reserved. No part of this book may be used, transmitted, stored, distributed, or reproduced in any manner whatsoever without the writer's written permission, except very short excerpts for reviews. The scanning, uploading, and distribution of this book via the Internet or by any other means without the publisher's/author's express permission is illegal and punishable by law.

Published in the USA by:
BearManor Media
1317 Edgewater Dr #110
Orlando, FL 32804
www.bearmanormedia.com

Perfect ISBN 979-8-88771-169-0
Case ISBN 979-8-88771-170-6
BearManor Media, Orlando, Florida
Printed in the United States of America
Book design by Robbie Adkins, www.adkinsconsult.com

Dedication:

For My Barbara
My loving companion on all those many research adventures in Hollywood…
This novel pays tribute to them – and to you.

Table of Contents:

Dedication iii

Prologue (September 5, 1932) ix

Part One – "All Out for Sex" (May 25 to June 18, 1932) 1
Chapter One: The Platinum Poisoner 2
Chapter Two: Yaqui Crest 7
Chapter Three: Fan Mail 13
Chapter Four: Ars-Gratia-Artis 16
Chapter Five: A Bagel and A Gable 20
Chapter Six: Billee's 23
Chapter Seven: 1353 Club View Drive 31
Chapter Eight: 9820 Easton Drive 41
Chapter Nine: Balthazar 50
Chapter Ten: Fargo Street 55
Chapter Eleven: Lights! Camera! Action! 60
Chapter Twelve: The Ambassador Hotel 68
Chapter Thirteen: The Fox Theatre 77
Chapter Fourteen: Room 625 82
Chapter Fifteen: Castellammare 85
Chapter Sixteen: The Cove 93

Part Two – Dear Dorothy (June 18 to July 2, 1932) 95
Chapter Seventeen: One Morning 96
Chapter Eighteen: Noon 102
Chapter Nineteen: That Night 111
Chapter Twenty: San Francisco Caper 116
Photo Gallery 125
Chapter Twenty-One: A New Scenario 133
Chapter Twenty-Two: Summer Reading List 135
Chapter Twenty-Three: Hiding Place 142
Chapter Twenty-Four: Angel from Heaven 147
Chapter Twenty-Five: The Phoebe 151
Chapter Twenty-Six: Opening Night 156

Chapter Twenty-Seven: Down Mexico Way 161
Chapter Twenty-Eight: Pilgrimage 167
Chapter Twenty-Nine: Falcon Lair 170
Chapter Thirty: Approach of the Nuptials 181
Chapter Thirty-One: The Wedding 191

Part Three – The Baby (August 26 to September 5, 1932) 198
Chapter Thirty-Two: Phone Call 199
Chapter Thirty-Three: Travel Plans 207
Chapter Thirty-Four: Saturday Night Date 210
Chapter Thirty-Five: West and East 213
Chapter Thirty-Six: The Father Confessor's Confession 217
Chapter Thirty-Seven: Impending Visit 226
Chapter Thirty-Eight: Temper Tantrums 231
Chapter Thirty-Nine: Hiding Place 235
Chapter Forty: Pick-Ups 239
Chapter Forty-One: Countdown 242
Chapter Forty-Two: The Audition 247
Chapter Forty-Three: The .38 251
Chapter Forty-Four: Aftershock 255

Part Four – "Frightful Wrong" and "Abject Humiliation" (September 5 to
    September 26, 1932) 260
Chapter Forty-Five: Labor Day Morning 261
Chapter Forty-Six: Suspects 267
Chapter Forty-Seven: The Aftermath of the "Suicide" 272
Chapter Forty-Eight: Walnut Grove 279
Chapter Forty-Nine: Coroner's Inquest 284
Chapter Fifty: San Luis Obispo 289
Chapter Fifty-One: Night Flight 291
Chapter Fifty-Two: The Funeral 295
Chapter Fifty-Three: Paternal Affection 302
Chapter Fifty-Four: The Weekend 309
Chapter Fifty-Five: "Dorothy Millette's Ghost" – A Horror Movie 313
Chapter Fifty-Six: Lake Arrowhead 320
Chapter Fifty-Seven: Wrap-Up 324
Chapter Fifty-Eight: Farewell Cruise 329

Chapter Fifty-Nine: A broch tsu dayn lebn................... 330
Chapter Sixty: Flying East.................................. 335

Epilogue.. 338

Author's Note... 342

> Dearest Dear/
> Unfortunately this is the only way to make good the frightful wrong I have done you and to wipe out my abject humiliation/ I love you.
> Paul
> You understand that last night was only a comedy

Paul Bern's alleged "suicide" note left to his widow Jean Harlow, September 5, 1932.

Prologue

Monday, September 5, 1932

When Jean Harlow, Metro-Goldwyn-Mayer's "Platinum Blonde," played a sex scene in the movies, she had two rituals: she rubbed ice cubes on her nipples to create a more provocative effect, and she dabbed Mitsouko perfume between her breasts.

Mitsouko, in the Japanese language, means "mystery." This perfume had been created in 1919, a mixture of peach and oak moss, lush, earthy and richly sensual. In addition to using Mitsouko professionally, Miss Harlow favored it as her personal perfume as well.

At dawn on Labor Day, 1932, her husband's naked corpse reeked in it.

Paul Bern, MGM producer, lie dead upstairs in the house he'd shared with Harlow, his bride of 65 days, high in Benedict Canyon. The Bavarian-style hideaway, with its turret and leaded glass, quaintly resembled a fairy tale house...the type where the Witch hoped to eat Hansel and Gretel, or the Wolf to devour Red Riding Hood. Yet even the most nightmarish fairy tales lacked a nude body with its brains blown out by a .38 pistol, and a suicide note citing "abject humiliation."

Diminutive but distinguished in life, Bern looked dwarfish and grotesque in death, his mustached face turned sideways toward the camera as studio security photographed the cadaver. Downstairs in the living room, Louis B. Mayer, the chief of MGM, paced beside the unlit fireplace, sweating and moaning. His studio manager Eddie Mannix and publicity director Howard Strickling noted their boss's rising hysteria.

"God will be good to me," Mayer fervently repeated, over and over, as if it were a prayer, his eyes wet behind his spectacles.

Outside by the pool, Irving Thalberg, Metro's "Boy Wonder" producer, sat on a bench, weeping. The dead man had been his most trusted associate, his amusing, literate friend. The frail, 33-year-old Thalberg had warily regarded the balding, 42-year-old Bern marrying the sexpot, 21-year-old Harlow, but he'd never anticipated this tragedy.

No one had yet notified the police, and the widow was not on the premises.

The Depression public had fallen in love with unlikely attractions, including Dietrich's demonic Blue Angel, Karloff's soulful Frankenstein Monster, and Harlow's platinum vamp. Now, as a real-life vixen, Harlow might spark the most explosive Hollywood scandal of all time.

"God will be good to me," said Mayer again. Then suddenly the phone rang. A guard Mayer had posted by the gate was calling from the servants' quarters down the hill.

"He's here," said the guard.

Mayer led the strapping Mannix and the slender Strickling through the door. Thalberg saw them and stood poolside. As the sun rose over the ridge, a stocky figure in a white sailor's uniform and round Navy hat emerged through the trees, marching like a puffin up the 75 hillside steps. The sun seemingly spotlighted him, transfiguring him, at least in the eyes of Mayer, who believed the information the man brought might herald the salvation or damnation of MGM.

He was close now, but Mayer, whimpering in anxiety, could wait no longer. He lost control, running to the man and grabbing him by the shirt.

"This is the most horrible moment in the history of our company!" shrieked Mayer.

"Wanna' let go of my shirt?" said the man.

Mayer slapped his face. The man slapped him back, hard. Mayer fell into the damp grass.

"You son of a bitch!" barked the dog-faced Mannix as he and Strickling raised the squat mogul to his feet. "I swear, Down, when this is all over, you'll be fucking dead too."

"You got me all-a-tremble," said the man. "Get Mayer in the house. I got no time for his hambone act."

While Thalberg stayed forlornly by the pool, the other men entered the house and sat in the living room. Strickling brought Mayer a glass of water. And Porter Down began his story, noting, as he had in the night, the musky scent of Mitsouko...now mixed with the fetid smell of death.

Part One
"All Out for Sex"

Metro-Goldwyn-Mayer slogan, 1932.

Chapter One
The Platinum Poisoner

Wednesday, May 25, 1932

Effie Abigail McCoo was to die by hanging at midnight.

Since her first-degree conviction for having killed three husbands for insurance – two by arsenic, and one by a lethal cocktail of perfume and shoe polish – McCoo had ardently wooed the press. Many reporters saw a vague resemblance between the hip-swaying murderess and Hollywood's new sex sensation, Jean Harlow. It was all in the platinum blonde hair dye. McCoo was tall, gangly, and old enough to be Harlow's mother, yet she'd loved the comparison and embraced it passionately.

She was known, infamously, as "The Platinum Poisoner."

"I'll sashay up onto that gallows, boys," she promised reporters, "and stick my head right into that noose. And I'll be wearing a negligee and high heels when I do it!" She also claimed that, just before the fatal plunge, she'd deliver Harlow's notorious line from *Hell's Angels*:

"Would you be shocked if I put on something more comfortable?"

San Quentin's Warden James B. Holohan, alarmed by these *Police Gazette*-style promises, decided McCoo's execution would be neither a burlesque show, nor a movie star homage. Of course, McCoo would be wearing neither a negligee nor high heels as she met the hangman, but Holohan went beyond that: He announced there would be only two witnesses at the execution. One would be a member of the Los Angeles police who'd participated in McCoo's arrest and conviction. The other would be a reporter, selected by lottery. Holohan had personally visited the cell of the condemned woman to inform her of his decision.

When he had, she spat in his face.

*

San Quentin was on the north side of San Francisco Bay, 441 miles from Los Angeles. Lt. James J. O'Leary, LAPD, rail-thin, bespectacled, and clad in a three-piece suit, hated air travel. Nevertheless, considering the distance, he was *en route* tonight to San Quentin via a Stinson Tri-Motor Airliner, complete with toilet facilities and room for ten passengers. Rain, lightning and thunder rocked the plane as it neared the Bay.

In the sleazy melodrama of Effie McCoo, O'Leary would have been first to admit he was only a supporting player. It had been Porter Down, his longtime P.I. pal, who'd really delved into the case, actually grave-robbing Effie's third victim for damning evidence that the coroner hadn't previously detected. Yes, it had been Down who'd delivered the goods over a year ago, before the sensational trial and its anguished appeals, with Effie's lawyer describing his client as "a poor, lost woman, crucified by this hellish Depression until she'd lost her moral compass."

But...it was O'Leary, an official face of LAPD, who was Warden Holohan's personal choice to witness tonight's hanging. So, here he was, squinting through his thick wire-rim glasses out his plane window, seeing San Quentin and its lighthouse aglow on the Bay.

I'm comin,' Effie, thought O'Leary.

*

The airliner landed at 11:10 P.M. delayed 40 minutes by the storm. O'Leary put on his hat and raincoat, grabbed his overnight bag and boarded the car waiting to drive him to the prison. At 11:32 P.M., a guard admitted O'Leary through San Quentin's gates, and about ten minutes later, Warden Holohan met him in the main building and shook hands.

"Thank you for coming," said Holohan, wearing a hat and raincoat. "Follow me, please." Then he led O'Leary outside to the death chamber.

*

The San Quentin death chamber was a separate building that resembled, inside and out, a huge warehouse. There were large windows near the high ceiling and lightning flashed above them. There, in the death chamber, O'Leary beheld the dominant, Calvary-esque gallows on its scaffolding. Although he'd seen it previously, he froze for a moment and swallowed.

"The lady from the *Los Angeles Illustrated News* has already arrived," said Holohan. There were several rows of seats about 20 yards from the scaffold, and O'Leary saw a woman sitting in the middle row. She was young, blonde, and wore a dark blue dress and a matching cloche hat. Her raincoat was neatly folded on the chair to her right.

"Miss Maggie York," said Holohan formally, "this is Lt. James O'Leary of the Los Angeles Police Department."

"How do you do, Miss," said O'Leary in his soft Virginia accent.

"A pleasure to meet you, Lieutenant," smiled the lady.

"As you two are the only witnesses tonight," said Warden Holohan, "we'll dim the lights where you're sitting during the execution. It's best that Miss McCoo not focus on either of you." He looked at the reporter. "I regret if this handicaps your taking any notes."

"I won't need any notes," said Maggie York. "I'll remember vividly what I'm about to see."

Holohan walked away. O'Leary placed his hat and raincoat in the row behind him and sat to Maggie's left. The lady's lips were full, her grin pleasant, and she wore a light perfume.

"I read a fine story by M. S. York in last week's *News*, about the Olympics comin' to L.A. this summer. Forgive me, but I figured 'M. S. York' was a man."

"That's the idea," said Maggie. "I try to cover it all." She paused. "I wasn't sure what to wear. Black seemed extreme, so I wore navy blue. How many executions have you witnessed, Lieutenant?"

"Too many," said O'Leary.

They made small talk for a while, and then suddenly, the lights dimmed out above them. The two witnesses heard thunder, and then several floodlights lit the gallows and scaffolding. A small parade led by Warden Holohan came around from the rear of the gallows. A guard followed Holohan, a matron followed the guard, a Salvation Army woman in uniform followed the matron, and then appeared the lady of the hour...followed by another guard.

Effie McCoo looked all of her 47 years. In the year she'd spent on Death Row, her roots had grown out, and her hair was a fright wig of dirty blonde, gray and a few defiantly surviving strands of platinum. Tall and horse-faced, she wore gray prison sackcloth and, of course, none of the flashy clothes and accoutrements she'd favored in her courtroom appearances. Her face turned slowly toward the shadows where the two witnesses sat, and her eyes, long deprived of false eyelashes, stared eerily.

She was silent as they slowly led her up the steep stairs onto the gallows, where the hangman awaited her. Effie stood flanked by a guard and the matron on either side. Thunder sounded. The Salvation Army woman opened her prayer book.

"Pray with me, Effie," said the woman softly. "'The Lord is my Shepherd...'"

"I know you're out there," said Effie McCoo, staring into the shadows.

O'Leary felt a chill. He noticed Maggie was very still.

"I know you're out there in the dark," said Effie. "Holohan told me you're not, but he's lying. Stand up so I can see you...you pigeon-toed bastard!"

"Please, Effie," said the Salvation Army woman. "'The Lord is...'."

"Shut up!" shrieked Effie, trembling violently. "Stand up, Porter Down! I bet you're wearing that sailor suit of yours."

The guards and matrons tensed for a possible struggle. The Salvation Army woman wept and retreated.

"Think you're so smart!" shouted Effie. "*You* put me here tonight! You came to see me die! Well, *fuck you!*"

The hangman proceeded with his ministrations.

"You came to see me go to Hell?" howled Effie. "Well, *you* go to Hell!" She seemed to laugh...and then, suddenly, horribly, took on the vampy manner she'd used in court.

"Come on up, big boy," cried Effie, her seductive voice quavering. "Stick your neck in the noose with mine. *Neck* with me. *Die* with me. We'll go to Hell together. I'll *blow* you when we get there!"

The hangman slipped the noose over her head, then covered her face and hair with a hood. She dropped the vamp act, livid and terrified, crying, gasping, trembling. Holohan, the guards and the matrons moved to their final positions.

"Don't you laugh me!" Effie shouted, sobbing. "Porter Down, you mother fucker...*Don't you dare laugh at me!*"

Warden Holohan gave the signal. The hangman moved into position.

"*Would you be shocked,*" howled the voice under the hood, "*if I put...!*"

There was a gothic midnight explosion of thunder, cruelly drowning out the woman's curtain line. Lightning flashed at the windows as Effie Abigail McCoo fell through the trap door, her neck violently snapping, her body grotesquely jerking....and her hips provocatively swaying.

*

After a moment, the lights came on over the witness rows. O'Leary and Maggie were silent for a time. Then they stood, their backs to the gallows. The last female reporter that O'Leary had sat next to at a hanging had – to his embarrassment and certainly her own – thrown up all over him and herself. Maggie seemed relatively composed.

"I shouldn't say this to a police officer," said Maggie, "but where can a girl get a drink in this town? And...who's Porter Down?"

"I'm sure we can find a speakeasy in San Francisco," grinned O'Leary. "My driver will know where to find one, I'll bet. Follow me in your car. I'm buyin'."

He ignored her second question for now.

Chapter Two
Yaqui Crest

Wednesday, June 1, 1932

The last time Lt. James O'Leary had seen his pal Porter Down had been New Year's Eve in Hollywood. On that date, the State of California had officially suspended Down's license as a P.I. The charge had been manslaughter.

In that case, Down's victim had been an accused murderess who'd claimed to be a witch.

*

It was the first day of June in 1932, and O'Leary figured he was the only man in the Mojave Desert this perilously hot morning who was wearing a three-piece suit. A friend on the force had loaned him his convertible, advising O'Leary he'd be damn glad he was driving it once he hit the blast furnace heat. He glanced at the brown, slag-pile mountains, a few tinged with snow.

Desolation, he thought.

Based in L.A. for the past 12 years, O'Leary still nostalgically missed his home state of Virginia. He was driving about 45 miles northeast of Palm Springs, a new trendy spot for movie stars who desired a hothouse escape 110 miles from Hollywood, passing gnarled, twisted Joshua trees. Ahead was a battered green aluminum sign with orange letters:

Twentynine Palms, 3 Miles

He was worried about his friend. Porter Down had taken his payment from his last job at Universal Studios, paid despite the manslaughter charge, and vanished into the desert. He'd said he was buying a "ranch," but O'Leary feared what he might find... Porter living in a teepee, or in an old kiln, or maybe in his plane. Or, based on Porter's demons, he just might come crawling out from under a pile of bootleg liquor bottles.

Desolation, thought O'Leary again, looking at the desert. *Goddamn desolation.*

A large rattlesnake stretched across the road, hit by traffic, bleeding but moving. O'Leary, wincing, couldn't avoid striking it. Yes, his friend was somewhere out here, in the fulcrum of the Santana winds, amidst the heat, the slag pile mountains, and the rattlesnakes. He had no phone number and no specific address to find him. It might be a hell of a challenge.

Then, off to the left, O'Leary saw a biplane. It was a Spad, that had seen battle as a fighter plane in the Great War. It soared straight up into the blue sky, performing a dazzling loop, plunging into a nosedive, leveling dangerously close to the ground, and soaring again. As it ascended, O'Leary saw the black sketch profile of a wolf and the painted-blue words *Timber Wolf* on the plane's fuselage, below the cockpit.

"Porter, ya' son of a bitch," he chuckled.

*

The two men stood on a solitary hill, outside an adobe house with a thick, squat tower. Five months ago, it had been in virtual ruins. Now it had a new roof, plumbing, and was starkly but realistically habitable. The redwood deck offered a 360-degree view of the desert's dusky mountains, yellow flats, and green-brown forests of yucca trees. A tall, solitary palm loomed over the house and *Timber Wolf* sat far below, outside its barn-like hanger. There was a fresh scent in the air, a faint breeze stirring on the hill.

"Anyway, Doc," said his host, "before 1932's over, I'll have a seedless grape business. And every egg, vegetable, piece of fruit and pound of poultry I eat will come off my own land."

Porter Down had nicknamed O'Leary "Doc" long ago because, as he put it, he "looked more like a dentist than a cop." Down had doffed his flyer's cap and goggles and wore his customary white sailor's hat and crumpled white uniform, the shirt unbuttoned, his amulet hanging on a chain around his neck. The man's handsome, "Arrow-Collar" profile looked incongruous on his stocky, powerful, 5'8" frame.

"At sunrise," said Porter, his bright eyes always reminding O'Leary of an eagle's, "the desert changes colors...sunset too. And one night, it snowed."

"You've done a hell of a lot in five months, Porter," said O'Leary, admiring the house, the terraced fruit trees, the vegetable garden, the chicken and turkey coops.

"Long John loves it here too," said Porter, pointing at the road-injured, one-legged jackrabbit he'd recently adopted. The rabbit careened around the deck and sipped water from its bowl. "This is Long John's old stomping grounds," said Porter. "The lady jackrabbits climb up here to visit him. My guess is the fuzzy-tailed bastard gets laid every night. Want a Coke?"

"Sure."

On the deck was a wooden tub filled with melted ice and at least a half-dozen chilled bottles of Coca-Cola. O'Leary was relieved to see no alcohol. Porter pulled out two bottles and used his pen knife to yank off the caps.

"Pearls in your oyster," said Porter, handing a bottle to his guest.

O'Leary took a sip. "Damn, that's refreshing," he said.

They sat on wooden benches facing each other. "So," said Porter, "You're still wearin' your dogcatcher hat. That means you're on formal business."

"Well, I wanted to tell ya,' in case you hadn't heard…Effie McCoo went to the gallows last week. Your name was on her lips."

"I'm glad it was only my name on her lips. And you're not here just to tell me that. My guess is you came to pitch a mission. The answer's no, so take off the damn hat."

"I've driven three hours to get here, fella," said O'Leary. "How about two minutes?"

"Remember me?" asked Porter. "I'm the boy that the Great State of California slammed down last December. Two years' probation for manslaughter…or in my case, *woman*slaughter."

"Your prospective employer sees your 'notoriety' as a point in your favor," said O'Leary. "That, along with the fact that poor ol' Effie went out screaming your name. *The Illustrated News* played it up big, by the way. Fine reporter. Got a copy of her story for you in my car."

"Keep it. And who's the 'prospective employer?'"

"Metro-Goldwyn-Mayer. Remember? 'More Stars Than There are in Heaven.'"

"Yeah, and more freaks than there are in the circus. Forget your two minutes."

"Okay. How about two words?"

"Try me."

"Jean Harlow."

Porter gave a long wolf whistle and pushed back his sailor cap over his chestnut hair.

"Your *Hell's Angels* co-star," grinned O'Leary. "Didn't you stunt fly on that movie?"

"Yep," said Porter. "For that jackass Howard Hughes."

"Well," drawled O'Leary, "Harlow's getting married."

"Who's the ridiculously lucky guy?" asked Porter.

"Paul Bern. A producer. Remember him from Metro?"

"Yeah. He's in charge of all of Bigfoot's pictures."

MGM proclaimed Greta Garbo as "La Divina," but to Porter, who'd extricated her from a potentially career-destroying near-scandal, she was, due to her large feet, forever "Bigfoot."

"Bern's 42," said O'Leary. "Exactly double Harlow's age. Remember the star, Barbara La Marr? They called her 'The Girl Who Was Too Beautiful'?"

"Yep. Five husbands. Dead from drugs at 29. Why?"

"Bern had proposed to her. When La Marr turned him down, he tried to drown himself in his toilet. His maid found him with his head caught in the seat."

"Sounds like quite a guy," said Porter.

"I had the honor of rescuing him," said O'Leary. "We don't know if Bern was really that heartbroken, or if he just wanted the maid to find him like that…if ya' get what I mean."

"Yeah, I get it," said Porter. "Harlow's marrying a sex creep."

"Maybe he's a sex creep – he's definitely a power figure. He convinced Thalberg to give Harlow an MGM contract. But there's a lot of mystery about the guy. People can't decide if he's a great lover of women, or of men. Or a eunuch. Or… well, something else altogether."

"Something else like what? A hermaphrodite?"

"Actually, that's one of the stories goin' around, yeah."

"Spooky," said Porter. "Anyway, wrap it up, before only Long John's listenin' to you."

"Harlow was involved a while ago with an old acquaintance of yours...Abner Zwillman."

"Good old 'Longie,'" grinned Porter wryly.

"Yep. Capone's old pal and the U.S.A.'s most powerful mobster, now that 'Scarface Al's' behind the wall. Your background with Zwillman could be helpful here, naturally."

"Naturally."

"As for Bern," sad O'Leary, "he allegedly has a relationship with a lady who's a Hollywood pornography star. An *artiste*, who directs her own films. Big here and in Europe, especially Berlin."

"This gets better and better," growled Porter.

"Different topic, sort of," said O'Leary, changing bait. "But Metro, the only Hollywood studio makin' a Depression profit, will offer a big payday for protection. So, there you are, Porter. The most powerful film studio in the world, the sexiest lady in the Movies, the most dangerous gangster in the U.S.A., a porno star, and what might become the nastiest scandal in Hollywood history...just waiting for little old you."

"And Mayer wants little old me to jump into the lions' den," said Porter.

"At feeding time," said O'Leary.

Porter downed his Coke. "Well, it just so happens that I've been thinking about a pool...my own little oasis, near that group of Joshua trees down there. Got paper and a pencil?"

O'Leary had both in his inside suit coat pocket and handed them to Porter, who scribbled a figure and shoved the pad and pencil back across the table. "For four weeks' work," said Porter.

"That's one hell of a big pool, fella," chuckled O'Leary. "More like a reservoir. And I doubt Mayer pays that rajah's ransom in four weeks to Miss Garbo."

"Yeah? Well, I'm prettier than Miss Garbo. At least first thing in the morning."

"Well, we'll see," said O'Leary, placing the pad and pencil back in his jacket pocket. "I know Mayer's impressed that you were a Lafayette Escadrille pilot...and appreciates what you did for Garbo...and admires how you handled that affair at Universal last fall... and he liked that *Illustrated News* story. I'll give 'em your terms and let you know. Thanks, Porter."

They shook hands. "Hey, stick around, Doc. I'll barbecue steaks for lunch. You can tell me about what's new with Charlotte and the girls. But only if you take off that damned hat."

Long John had loped over and Porter picked up the crippled jackrabbit. He stood, cradling the pet under his arm, leaning again on his rail, looking out at the silent desert.

"Really is a hell of a view, isn't it, Doc?"

O'Leary, who'd removed his hat and suit coat, joined him at the rail, taking another look at the vista. Porter had rescued these ruins in the desert desolation, like he always rescued everything... or tried to. Seeing him in his little oasis, sober, peacefully raising fruit and fowl, made O'Leary feel relief. Porter's last job, the previous fall, had virtually saved Universal Studios, but it had also almost destroyed Porter. And he knew the date of the murder of Porter's wife – the fifth anniversary, he believed – was later this month. O'Leary wondered if perhaps he should have just allowed his violent, broken friend this new idyllic life.

It was quiet, the desert almost mystically still, the only sound the chickens and turkeys, pecking along the hillside. Then O'Leary noticed Porter's amulet. It was very old and he knew Porter never removed it. The chain draped over the rail, the amulet dangling over the drop. O'Leary saw its baroque image...Saint George battling the dragon.

"Yeah, it's a hell of a view, Porter... a swell place ya' got. You're a damned lucky fella."

O'Leary wished he'd never made the trip.

Chapter Three
Fan Mail

Wednesday, June 15, 1932

Metro-Goldwyn-Mayer Studios in Culver City, southwest of Hollywood, had several back lots. Lot Two featured the jungle compound and lake of *Tarzan the Ape Man*. In the fenced-off lake swam crocodiles.

Close to this site was a small stucco building with two floors and an orange tile roof. A flock of ducks strolled on its lawn. It was here that this morning the Culver City post office had delivered Jean Harlow's three teeming sacks of fan mail for the day. Most Metro employees who responded to star fan mail were on the main lot. Harlow, however, was new to the studio and receiving an avalanche of letters – especially since the publicity about *Red-Headed Woman* and her engagement to be married – so the Publicity Department had afforded her this space. Only a few carefully-screened letters ever actually reached the star herself.

A trio of ladies responded to the fan mail. The "boss," more or less, was named Lu, a middle-aged, still attractive woman who'd formerly led an All-Female band. Mary, bespectacled and pretty, was the best writer of the three, and had come to Hollywood from Illinois, hoping to write scripts. The third woman, who called herself "Lona," was the "sex baby" of the bunch, and still dreamed of becoming a starlet.

None of the three women had ever met Jean Harlow.

This morning was very hot. The ladies' isolation allowed a certain informality. All three had removed their high heels and Lona, who frequently worked hot afternoons wearing only her silk slip, had already semi-stripped due to this morning's temperature. They turned on the electric fan and divided up the mountain of mail. They had learned to forge Harlow's signature, or actually her mother's, since Harlow's mother usually signed her publicity pictures and the signatures had to match.

Polite and adoring letters, such as the ones rhapsodizing about Harlow's hair and beauty, received typed and forged personal responses and a "signed" picture. Then there were the nasty letters, the ones from the bitter, jealous folk, who wrote that she couldn't act any better than Betty Boop and mocked her "albino" hair and "dustpan" figure. Some claimed they could tell she was really evil, just like the "tramps and whores" she played on the screen, and hoped she knew she belonged in Hell, for it was Hell where she'd surely be going, in the foul region reserved for all Jezebels throughout the ages. These letters they tossed away.

Also tossed, usually, were the violent ones. All three secretaries would likely open letters today from men describing to Harlow, in crudely vivid detail, their fantasies of raping her. All these came daily, in addition to the bevy of pornographic photos, sketches and various other items that had provided Lu, Mary, and Lona a rather startling education.

They rarely shared what they read and saw. This morning, however, Lona asked the other two to listen to a just-opened missive. The person who sent it had perfumed it, and the perfume was evidently expensive, smelling of peach and oak:

> *Dear Miss Harlow:*
>
> *I adore you. Please find enclosed $150.00 in cash, so you may send me a pair of your silk panties, and a pair of your high heel shoes, both preferably black.*
>
> *This is more than enough money to pay for these items and necessary postage.*
>
> *Please wear this specific apparel at least one more time before mailing them.*
>
> *Love and kisses.*

"No signature or address," said Lona. "Just a post office box in Santa Monica. Should I forward it to security?"

Lu shook her head as she continued typing. "There's no threat," she said. "Just mail back the cash. No letter."

"She certainly writes well," said Mary.

"It might not be a 'she,'" wisecracked Lona. "Anyway, 'she' or 'he,' I have a spooky feeling about this one…"

Suddenly there was loud squawking outside...the ducks had flown over the chain-link fence to the lake, and a crocodile had snared one of them in its jaws. As the ducks wildly screeched in mourning, the trio of ladies, startled by the noise, looked up, but none of them glanced out the window. There was an uncomfortable silence, and then Lu spoke.

"Okay, ladies. Back to work for little Miss Harlow."

The three ladies resumed typing and forging.

Chapter Four
Ars-Gratia-Artis

Wednesday, June 15, 1932

Metro-Goldwyn-Mayer, with its "More Stars Than There are in Heaven," was actually the ugliest studio in Hollywood.

The main entranceway at 10202 W. Washington Boulevard in Culver City boasted impressive Corinthian columns, but behind the gate was another story. MGM's Leo the Lion logo stood atop a large glass soundstage on the main lot, with its Latin trademark, "Ars-Gratia-Artis." If a stranger in this strange land didn't know it translated as "Art for Art's Sake," he might have figured he was visiting a factory producing cheap shoes or ball bearings. It didn't matter. With most studios suffering Depression losses – and Paramount and RKO facing bankruptcy and receivership – MGM was hoping for a 1932 profit of $8 million.

It was a hot-as-hell Wednesday, June 15, 1932. Porter Down was angrily second-guessing his decision to accept this four-week deal as he drove up to the MGM gate and regarded the lot.

Even the damn water tower's ugly, he thought.

He gave his name to the uniformed gateman. "Please pull right over there, sir," said the gateman. "We've reserved a parking place for you. I'll phone Mr. Strickling that you're here."

Porter was irritable about having to pay a neighboring Twentynine Palms rancher to tend to his crops and feed and water Long John, his chickens and his turkeys, even though the money would come from his expense account while he began this 28-day joyride in L.A.

Who needs a pool? he thought. *I can get just as wet in the shower...*

Of course, Leo and all that the mighty beast symbolized failed to impress Porter Down. Nor was he impressed, or had let on that he was, when the studio had delivered to his L.A. address a brand new 1932 Ford three-window coupe, somber black with butterfly opening hood, red spoke wheels with white walls, and a rumble seat with pearl gray interior. It was his for the duration of his MGM stay. Dressed in his usual sailor suit and cap, Porter parked in his VIP spot, got out, and leaned sullenly against the Ford, watching the various limousines entering the gate, some with curtains over the windows, protecting whatever deity rode inside from the stares of the commonality. The gateman effusively greeted them all.

Nobody's as happy to see anybody anytime, thought Porter, *as that guy is to see everybody all the time.*

"Well, well, well…Porter!"

It was Howard Strickling, Metro's publicity chief, eagerly trotting toward him with outstretched hand. "How really *swell* to see you again!"

"Yeah, swell," mumbled Porter, shaking Howard's hand.

Strickling had the fresh, open face and manner of a young, small-town banker. In fact, he was MGM's "Fixer" – fulsomely promoting the Metro stars while simultaneously paying off male and female prostitutes, back-alley abortionists, axe-to-grind spouses, blackmailers of all variety and, on one occasion, an aghast zoo-keeper.

Howard, looking especially small town this morning in his three-piece suit with bow tie and knickers, lowered his voice confidentially.

"Porter, when you worked here previously, we appreciated the low profile you kept while providing your services. However, your clothes have become something of a… trademark. Since you're here undercover, Mr. Mayer has approved that you report today to wardrobe and be measured for three new suits and any and all accessories. Our expense and yours to keep."

"Okay," said Porter.

"Also, this time, we think it best that you work under an alias, just in case someone questions your presence on the lot. We thought that since you'll be associated with Mr. Bern, we might perhaps present you as a writer."

"Call me… Patrick Killarney, the Irish vagabond poet," said Porter. "'Patty' for short."

Strickling took a pad and pen from his pocket. "How do you spell 'Killarney'?" he asked.

"Surprise me," said Porter.

*

As Strickling and Porter walked across the lot, Porter noticed a particular oddity about the MGM factory that he remembered from his last job here: Fire escapes and catwalks overstocked the buildings. A marble bridge ran over the front gate, and studio insiders called it MGM's "Bridge of Sighs," evoking the historic site in Venice where prisoners enjoyed one last look at the world before dark imprisonment.

It seemed a maze of secrets extended above the streets, adding an aura of clandestine intrigue to Hollywood's most powerful studio. Porter knew some of these secrets all-too-well.

*

Suddenly, a solidly built man with an angry face under his snap-brim hat came marching toward them. He whistled sharply at Porter, as if disciplining a dog. The man was Eddie Mannix.

In Metro mythology, Irving Thalberg was the "Boy Wonder," Paul Bern the "Father Confessor," Howard Strickling the "Fixer," and Eddie Mannix the "Bulldog." Porter always found it amusing that the "Tiffany" of Hollywood studios had as its general manager a swaggering thug from New Jersey who'd once been a Palisades Park bouncer.

Strickling knew that part of Porter's arrangement was that he'd never have to deal with Mannix. He also stuttered when he was nervous. "Eddie," said Strickling, "I b-believe you know P-P-...?"

"I'd have known him a mile away," said Mannix. "That sailor hat and pigeon-toed walk. L. B. told me yesterday, Down, that you don't even want to see my face."

"Who would?" said Porter.

"Watch your mouth, jackass," said Mannix loudly.

Porter figured Mayer had ordered Eddie to behave himself, but Eddie could be a rebellious shit. His voice carried, and craftsmen came out from workshops and secretaries peered from office windows to see the "Bulldog" do what he did best...kick ass.

"So, Eddie," asked Porter casually, "what do you hear from 'Bubbles'?"

Mannix recoiled. "Bubbles" was Mary Nolan, a blonde, wildly promiscuous ex- Ziegfeld girl, ex-MGM star, and ex-Mannix paramour. He'd nearly beaten her to death in a fit of jealousy several years ago and Porter, alerted of the danger, had saved her. Mannix knew it. And Porter also knew that Mayer had paid Bubbles half-a-million dollars to keep her mouth shut and save Eddie from the slammer.

"I'll never forget the night," said Porter casually, "I got a tip that some pig had pounded poor Bubbles to a pulp and dumped her in Griffith Park..."

"You think you're hot shit, Down," hissed Mannix. "I think you're just plain shit."

Porter began whistling *I'm Forever Blowing Bubbles*.

"Cocky bastard!" roared Mannix.

"Eddie, p-p-please," pleaded Strickling.

"Down," growled Mannix, "you got to the count of three to stop that Goddamn whistling."

Porter whistled away like a bird.

"One," growled Mannix. "Two..." and he swung. Porter deflected his punch and his right fist slammed Mannix square in his face. Mannix reeled, and then came back with a left that Porter dodged. The P.I. regained his balance, took aim and, with a roundhouse from the right, KO'd Eddie Mannix.

The man fell like a redwood.

"Will s-somebody please call the inf-f-firmary?" shouted Strickling, kneeling over Eddie.

The "Fixer" recruited some onlookers to tend to the "Bulldog" and a moment later they heard the studio ambulance siren. The crowd gawked at Porter, who remembered he was supposed to be Ireland's vagabond poet, Patrick Killarney. He looked at the unconscious Mannix, shrugged, and decided to try for an Irish accent.

"Faith and Gomorrah!" he cried out. "Shit. I mean, Faith and Begorrah!"

Chapter Five
A Bagel and A Gable

Wednesday, June 15, 1932

Howard Strickling, having just seen the unconscious Eddie Mannix driven away in an infirmary ambulance, escorted Porter to the commissary. He'd said he wanted a bagel.

Porter put in his order and Strickling rabbited off. A waitress brought Porter a bagel with jelly. He also ordered orange juice and coffee. It was a slow time in the commissary, and quiet, but then came a rustle. Porter saw why: Clark Gable strolled in, carrying a script.

Gable was Metro's new superstar. The star sat at his accustomed table and an agog waitress instantly brought him coffee, surely brewed precisely as he liked it. Gable joked breezily with the waitress, sipped his coffee and saw Porter. He raised both eyebrows, smiled his crooked smile, stood and approached Porter's table.

"You look to me like a pretty unpopular character," said Gable in his famous baritone.

"Patrick Killarney," said Porter.

"The name I've heard is Porter Down," grinned Gable, lowering his voice. "But glad to meet you…Pat." He sat at Porter's table. "You know, Eddie Mannix and Howard Strickling are friends of mine. I wouldn't be where I am right now without them."

His ears really are big, thought Porter.

"I need the help of those guys," said Gable, his voice confidential. "But you know what? One day, I might need your help too." He lit a cigarette. "I hear you're here to help Harlow. Jean's a great gal."

Porter wondered how many other MGM high profilers were aware of his presence and his mission. Metro's top male star took his wallet, removed a card, wrote on the back of it and handed it to Porter. "Here. Be my guest tonight. Have a nightcap." The card read simply *Billee's* and there was a West Hollywood address. Gable stood. "Relax and enjoy yourself."

Clark Gable returned to his table, opened his script, looked again at Porter and winked. Porter winked back at him. He'd heard of Billee's.

*

Gable had left, Porter had ordered another coffee, and now Howard Strickling returned to the commissary. He carried Porter's new MGM employee card, bearing the name, "Patrick Killarney," as well as a packet of recent "More Stars Than There are in Heaven" Metro publicity releases.

"For you, sir," smiled Strickling, handing Porter his name card and the PR packet. On top was a flier for *Grand Hotel.*

"Have you *seen* that?" asked Strickling. "It's wonderful! Garbo, John Barrymore, Joan Crawford, Wallace Beery, Lionel Barrymore, Lewis Stone, and Jean Hersholt."

"Wow," deadpanned Porter.

"Just think, Porter," said Strickling – *"They all work here at MGM Studios!"*

And they all use MGM toilets, thought Porter.

Strickling flipped a page and showed Porter a full-length portrait of Jean Harlow in *Red-Headed Woman*, a sex comedy in which she'd worn a red wig. The film was about to be released and there was a cartoon of Leo the Lion ogling Harlow's picture. The copy read:

MGM's Going All Out for Sex in 1932!

"How about that motto? asked Strickling.

"My pulse can hardly stand it," deadpanned Porter.

"We're officially announcing the motto later this summer," said Strickling as they prepared to leave the commissary.

"By the way, Porter," said Strickling a bit uneasily as they strolled away from the commissary. "I've checked in with Miss Harlow and Mr. Bern. Their schedules are very busy today and they're attending a premiere this evening. Miss Harlow has requested you meet her at her home tomorrow at 10:00 A.M. Mr. Bern has asked if you'd call on him at his home tomorrow around 7:00 P.M."

They're stalling me, thought Porter. *Waiting to see if Mayer fires me for belting Mannix.*

"They're both eager to welcome you into their homes," said Strickling.

I bet, thought Porter.

Strickling accompanied Porter to Wardrobe. "Just c-c-call me if you need anything," said Strickling, leaving Porter to the tender mercies of a tailor who meticulously measured him for his three new suits, as well as checking his hat size and shoe size. Considering how often Porter dressed up, this new wardrobe would probably last him through 1950.

With his suits measured and his meetings with Harlow and Bern cancelled, thus ended Porter's first day at MGM. He was glad to get out before lunch and briskly headed for the gates, enjoying the gawking stares of people passing him. The news of a guy in a sailor suit slugging Eddie Mannix had surely spread all over the lot. He took a little detour and, thinking about Harlow, walked past MGM's star dressing room compound. It was a white, two-story, barracks-style wooden building, with a veranda on the first floor, and a balcony running across the length of the second. Garbo, Norma Shearer, Joan Crawford, Myrna Loy, and Jean Harlow had dressing rooms in this building, which the occupants had nicknamed the "Bordello."

Porter felt eyes on him. He turned quickly. One of the first-floor doors was cracked open and he saw a glimpse of a face before whoever it was saw him looking back and quickly shut the door.

Porter saw little of her face, but the hair was platinum blonde.

Chapter Six
Billee's

Wednesday, June 15 and Thursday, June 16, 1932

The HOLLYWOODLAND sign stood on Mount Lee, its thousands of light bulbs aglow on the 50'-high letters, a monolith in the violent night storm. Porter sat in Musso and Frank's Restaurant on Hollywood Boulevard, enjoying a late-night turkey dinner.

He had the place almost to himself. The lightning, thunder, and wind, along with the almost tropical gales of rain, were gothic in their own right, but instilled true reasons for fear in L.A. residents: Devastating mudslides, lightning-inflicted fires, and houses tumbling into canyons or the ocean.

It had been a busy afternoon. He'd driven downtown to the Broadway movie house district, where an old acquaintance named Saul Lestz had a tiny office high in the rear of the United Artists Theatre. Saul, whose official business was bail bonds, also made the best skeleton keys in L.A. Porter figured there'd be some places at MGM nobody would want him to visit. Old Saul, grizzled, dyspeptic, wearing a yarmulke, and partly doubled over from a gall bladder operation that had gone badly, provided Porter a ring of six small keys.

"At least one of them works any lock," promised Saul. "I guarantee it."

Early evening, Porter had driven to Eagle Rock to the bungalow home of Maxwell Tyler, a former cop whose specialty was firearms. Max had customized a Remington Model .95 derringer with .41 rimfire – easy to conceal, but packed with extra caliber power. Porter, aware that he'd soon be dealing with the mob, figured he'd need it. He'd jawed with Max, a recent widower and no doubt lonely, and had left with a prized, well-oiled weapon.

Porter finished his dinner and left a lavish tip courtesy of his MGM expense account, ventured back out into the intensifying storm, and decided to take up Gable on the nightcap.

*

The address on Gable's card led Porter west and into the steep hills. Rainwater cascaded down the street. Porter heard various sirens.

Hell of a night in Hollywood, he thought.

He knew about Billee's. It was nothing new. Whorehouses with girls made up to look like movie stars had been around for years. Porter had visited a cat house in New Jersey eight or nine years ago where the star attraction was "Mary Pickford," wearing blonde sausage curls and prancing around in bows and bloomers. And there'd probably been enough cat house "Clara Bows" in the late 1920s to fill the Ambassador Hotel for an "It Girl" Hooker Reunion.

Of course, if Gable gave him this treat, he could likely trust the girls were clean and up-to-snuff...so to speak.

The two-story house was high up King's Road, a Tudor-style English manor looking, as did most architecture in Southern California, that it belonged someplace else. There were lit candles in the diamond-paned windows and Porter, glancing up and down the street, realized the storm had knocked out the power. Smoke rose from the house's chimney. Porter rushed through the gate amidst the lightning and thunder, around a fountain that was overflowing in the storm, and rang the bell. A tall, imposing butler looked through a grilled window in the door.

"Yes?" he asked formally. Porter handed his card through the bars and the imperious butler unlocked the door, leading Porter into a large candlelit living room with a blazing stone fireplace and handsome oaken furnishings. An aged pianist was playing classical music on a polished baby grand Steinway, topped by a lit candelabrum. Perfume was in the air.

Gable, you dog, thought Porter.

"I'm Peter," said the butler, whose powerful frame made Porter suspect he doubled as a bouncer. He took Porter's pea coat and cap. Porter stood by the fire and looked at the pianist.

"How's it hangin'?" Porter asked.

The pianist nodded his old gray head and kept playing.

"Well, hello there!"

Porter turned to see a rather stately woman, wearing a silk robe sashed at the waist. She wore high heels and was fastidious in her make-up and grooming. "I'm Billee," she said, shaking Porter's hand. Her facial features were large and the look in her eye was unmistakable – the arch, teasing, "Aren't-you-something" look of a high-class madame.

"Naturally, any friend of Mr. Clark Gable is a *special* friend of ours," grinned Billee, pulling a bell cord three times. "Have a seat by the fire. Wine? Beer? Whiskey?"

"How about a Coca-Cola?" asked Porter, sitting by the hearth.

"Coming right up," said Billie, going to the bar. "We were afraid we'd all be lonely tonight. It's like the end of the world out there!" She crossed the room with a tray, one glass, and a bottle of Coca-Cola.

"But *you're* here," said Billee, placing the tray beside Porter. "And *we're* glad."

Porter sipped his Coke by the fire, Billee bullshitted about the weather, the pianist tickled the ivories, and several minutes passed. Then Porter heard footsteps on the staircase. The lightning flashed, the thunder crashed, and a tall woman who was a dead ringer for Greta Garbo appeared on the stairs, dressed as Garbo had been in the opening of *Anna Christie* – complete with the brim-up hat and the tight black skirt. As she came down the stairs, what impressed Porter most were her black high heels.

She's even got the size 12 feet, he marveled.

The hooker eyed Porter from under her spidery "La Divina" false eyelashes – spooky, he thought, in the candlelight. The old pianist played strains from Beethoven's *Seventh Symphony*. *GARBO TALKS*, MGM had proclaimed of *Anna Christie*, Garbo's sound debut, but this Garbo wasn't talking. The dummy knew a hell of a lot of other tricks, no doubt, but talking didn't appear to be one of them. She just stood there, a morbid mannequin, staring at him.

Christ, thought Porter.

More high heels came a-tapping on the oaken staircase. There followed "Joan Crawford," adorned in a copy of the dark, sleek secretary-for-hire frock Crawford had recently worn in *Grand Hotel*. The pianist segued into *The Blue Danube Waltz*. The room was soon rich in the perfumes of MGM's dueling deity copycats. At last came "Jean Harlow," a peroxide blonde, wearing an outfit inspired by one of Harlow's popular pin-up poses – a low-cut, black velvet jacket, black stockings, high heels and nothing else.

More whores than there are in Heaven, thought Porter.

*

Billee stood there, beaming at her brood, like a proud Catholic mother watching her kids in a May procession. Peter entered and summoned her to the telephone.

The storm raged outside, the fire glowed and Porter sat amidst all the fabricated pulchritude, each and every one of the ladies in the Leo the Lion harem silently eyeballing him. The pianist had finished up with the *Blue Danube* and was now playing classical chords that Porter recognized as Wagner. The painted and perfumed women just kept staring and posing, like figures in a wax museum. He stared back and sipped his Coke.

Silence. Then Billee, even more arch and joyful than she'd been upon Porter's arrival, returned from her phone call with a note in her hand.

"Oh, girls," chirped Billee. "Fortune smiles on us again! Would any of you like to perform a little freelance film work next week for our dear friend… 'Luscious Custard'?"

For a moment the three girls eyed each other slyly, their waxy countenances slowly cracking into tiny smiles. "Garbo" giggled, and then "Crawford" laughed through her nose, and then suddenly all three exploded into laughter. Any and all sex goddess vestige was gone, they were shrieking, and Porter looked at them in the firelight, cackling like witches, the whore trio seemingly growing hysterical.

"Pose, girls, pose!" laughed Madame Billee, beginning an outlandish pantomime, as if cranking a camera. The girls screamed even louder.

"Oh, *please*!" cooed "Garbo," lifting her skirt almost to her pubic hair. "Do film *mine* from its *best angle*!"

The girls howled anew.

"Powder puff!" cried "Joan Crawford," bending over, yanking up her dress, showing her stockings, garters and bare ass. "I need a powder puff!"

Billie playfully slapped "Joan's" exposed bottom and the cacophony of shrieks, screams and cackles filled the house, backed up by the storm's lightning and thunder, the ancient pianist now adding to the gaiety with Offenbach's *Can Can*.

Porter wished he was back in the desert with Long John.

"*La, la-la-la!*" sang the girls, joining together for a few *Can-Can* high kicks. "Garbo" took the middle spot, singing the loudest and kicking the highest – after all, she was "Garbo." Madame Billee kept aiming her imaginary camera as if filming the show. Finally, "Garbo," forsaking any effort to appear divine, kicked so high and provocatively that one of her huge high heels flew off, hit the bar, and struck a crystal decanter that shattered loudly to the floor.

"Ohhh!" wailed Billee.

A new shrill scream of hilarity arose from the coven, despite the madame's obvious distress. "Jean Harlow," seizing the moment, grabbed Porter's hand. Snaring what would likely be the stormy evening's only client, she led him up the candlelit staircase.

*

The sex had been fast but fine. "Jeanie" knew her business, and Porter had been alone in the desert a long time. Now they lie in bed, propped up next to each other under the sheet as lightning flashed at the rain-streaked window. The wind howled and the thunder roared.

"Jeanie" was proud of the passion she'd just inspired, and a bit giddy at how much she'd enjoyed it too. The light of two candles played on her peroxide hair. An occasional whoop still sounded from below, along with the now mournful, classical piano flourishes.

"I've heard I'm the best piece here," said Jeanie proudly. "They say 'Crawford's' only good with the guys who want their balls busted. And 'Garbo'" – she grinned vindictively – "they say she has gas in bed."

"That's very interesting," said Porter. He imagined the marquee – *GARBO FARTS.*

"So," said Jeanie, "I bet I know what you're wondering. Yes, I'm over 21, and yes, we all get checked every month."

"Actually," said Porter, "I was wondering what the odds are that MGM gets wise to this place and shuts you ladies down?"

"MGM set us up. Saves the actresses there from being bothered…keeps the guys off the actresses' backs." She mussed the hair on Porter's chest. "Off their fronts, too."

"Don't tell me Mayer comes here?"

"Hell, no. But some of the others do. Like Mr. Mannix. By the way, I hear you slugged Mr. Mannix. Good for you."

"You don't like him?"

"Hell no. But he's good to us, I guess. Took us all to a party at Metro last Christmas Eve." She smiled mischievously. "The three of us drank and fucked guys in Thalberg's office…on his desk. Thalberg wasn't there, of course. He'd gone home to Norma."

"Tell me you didn't screw Mannix," said Porter.

"That ugly mutt? Never," said Jeanie. "We tried to get into Mayer's office too, but the door was locked."

Porter wondered if Mayer or Thalberg knew what Mannix had done, but it was a moot point – "Eddie" knew too many secrets, assuring his place in the studio hierarchy.

"We're safe here," said Jeanie, sipping her drink. "We have protection. And we meet sweet guys…like you."

She kissed his ear, rose from the bed, and picked up a bottle of Irish rye whiskey. He declined a glass and she poured herself one. Jeanie stood naked before Porter, her pubic hair as *faux* platinum as the hair on her head, and downed the shot. The lightning flashed and the wind sounded as if it had penetrated the garret above the ceiling. Jean picked up her pair of black stockings and sat on a chair. Having stripped for Porter almost an hour ago, she now began dressing in front of him. He watched from the bed as she began sliding a stocking up her leg.

"Tell me," he said. "What was all that hilarity downstairs about… 'Tasty Pudding?'"

"'Luscious Custard!'" laughed Jeanie. "She's a crazy bitch who makes stag movies – smokers – and stars in them herself. The real *nasty* smokers. The ones the *gangsters* watch!"

"You ladies seem to derive a certain joy from her."

"You *bet* we do!" said Jeanie, laughing again. Her face took on the joy of a teenage girl who knew a juicy secret as she pulled the stocking up her thigh.

"The bitch stars in her own movies, right? But she's a cat-faced hag. Only looks good from far away. So, she hires us, or whomever she can get, and when she zooms in close for boobs and pussy? She shows some *other* gal's boobs and pussy. Her own goods are old and nasty. Nobody wants to see *that*. Her face, too…I hear she only comes out at night now. They say she's got the rot!"

Jeanie stood, wearing just the one stocking and smoothing it along her leg. "You know how a cowboy actor uses a *stunt* double?" asked Jeanie, reveling in her naughty humor. "Well, Annie uses a *cunt* double!"

"More than one?" asked Porter.

"Sure," said Jeanie. "Depends on what color wig she's wearing in the movie."

"And she really and truly calls herself 'Luscious Custard'?" asked Porter.

Jean sat and began putting on the other stocking. "That's just the title of one of her movies. She played a nympho stripper in it, and that was the character's name. She hired us for it. But when we saw it, we realized what she'd done – filmed close shots of us, and cut 'em in with herself! Of course, we could tell whose boobs she used, and whose ass, and whose…"

"Yeah," said Porter. "So you're tellin' me that 'Luscious Custard' isn't very luscious?"

"I'm bettin' on rancid," said Jeanie.

"She got a real name?" asked Porter.

"Annie Spry. But we all call her 'Luscious Custard' for laughs. She lives out by the beach. Makes all kinds of smokers… even ones with animals…snakes…spiders. Of course, we refuse to do those.

Anyway, she makes movies for whatever your twist is…and whatever *her* twists are."

She stood in front of Porter, adjusted the other stocking, and placed her hands on her hips. "I have a guess what *yours* is," she smiled.

"Does Paul Bern ever come here?" asked Porter.

Jeanie laughed derisively. "Everybody knows he's queer. He's marryin' Harlow because he thinks she can cure him."

"Of what?"

"Of his queerness!" she said, as if he'd asked a totally asinine question.

Porter seriously doubted that there was a "cure" for that proclivity, but he felt it significant that the prostitute spoke so confidently on the *raison d'etre* for the marriage. Jeanie came around the bed and, wearing just her stockings, crawled under the sheet.

"I didn't see a 'Norma Shearer' downstairs," said Porter. "I'm guessing that's because the real Norma is Mrs. Thalberg. What happens to you when the real Jean is Mrs. Bern?"

"Who the fuck knows, and who the fuck cares," said Jeanie, kissing his ear.

If Porter had hit a nerve, the prostitute didn't show it. She nestled against him and he noticed something he hadn't before – Jeanie's right ear had apparently been cut at some point. There was no ear lobe, and a thin scar ran the length of the ear. Porter wondered if a jealous customer might have attacked her at some point. She seemed to sense he noticed the minor disfigurement and fluffed her dyed hair over the scarred ear.

"Relax, baby," she said, stroking his chest. "We have all night."

It was quiet downstairs now. The rain and wind in the late night were the only sound. Jeanie kissed his chest. Yeah, he'd been in the desert a long time…and it was bad form in Hollywood not to take full advantage of a gift from Clark Gable.

Chapter Seven
1353 Club View Drive

Thursday, June 16, 1932

Thursday's dawn was cold but beautiful in Malibu, the storm having blown up the coast.

Porter had arrived only a couple hours ago after his night at Billee's where he'd provided Jeanie a generous tip. As he sat in his shorts and cap on the trawler's deck watching the sunrise, he saw the second trawler come into sight, heading back to the marina after the night's catch.

"Hi, Luke!" shouted Porter. "Good catch tonight?"

"Hi, Porter! You bet!"

Three-and-a-half years ago, Porter had shot and killed the man who'd murdered Fred Foster, Luke's LAPD veteran father. Luke, whose mother Phoebe had died of grief shortly after the death of his dad, had taken the sizeable life insurance payment, finished high school, and started his own marina at Venice Beach with one leaky trawler, *The Frederick*, named after his father, and one narrow dock. Six weeks ago, he'd moved up the coast, beyond Malibu's trendy area, north of "the Colony," where the stars paid sky-high rentals on what was virtually a land-lease ragtag row of beachfront shacks and cottages. Porter, admiring the boy's dream and work ethic, rented space on Luke's trawler whenever on a case in the L.A. area.

Luke idolized Porter. He would have let him stay for free, but Porter always insisted on paying rent, helping Luke's one trawler operation grow to two. Luke had named this second trawler *The Phoebe* after his mother. MGM's expense account had allowed for prestigious lodgings, but Porter was paying the money to Luke for a cabin on *The Phoebe* with a shower, bunk, one closet, and a two-way radio. It was a long drive to town, but there was an airfield nearby for his plane, and he enjoyed the ocean.

Porter helped Luke carve up the catch. Then he squeezed under the trawler's shower. Having spent a very cozy night with a fake Harlow, he'd have to freshen up this morning to visit the real one.

*

On May 27, 1930, *Hell's Angels* had premiered at Grauman's Chinese Theatre, complete with sweeping searchlights, biplanes flying over Hollywood Boulevard, and a record-breaking street crowd of 75,000 spectators. The evening's true sensation had been Jean Harlow, the film's platinum blonde star, proving more spectacular than *Hell's Angels*' dogfights (which had killed several stunt pilots) and exploding zeppelin (color-tinted in the release print).

Harlow's escort that evening had been Paul Bern.

Porter had done his research. Harlow was actually Harlean Carpenter, from Kansas City, Missouri, daughter of a dentist. She was an alumna of the upper-class Ferry Hall School for Girls in Lake Forest, Illinois. Her parents had divorced, and the mother had brought her breathtakingly blonde daughter west to crash the movies. Harlean – who took her mother's maiden name of "Jean Harlow" as a stage name – eventually became a beautiful stooge in Laurel and Hardy comedies, such as 1929's *Double Whoopee*.

There'd been complications. In 1927, 16-year-old Harlean had impetuously embarked on a 20-month marriage to Charles McGrew, socialite. McGrew blamed the mother for being nuts on advancing her daughter's movie career, the mother blamed McGrew for disapproving of that career, and the press reported that on one occasion at the St. Francis Hotel in San Francisco, a drunken McGrew had thrown bottles at his platinum-dyed wife... and hadn't missed.

Jean's mother had also acquired a new spouse a few months before her daughter's doomed marriage – a swarthy, mustached dude named Marino Bello. From all Porter had learned, Bello was a cheat and a gigolo, allegedly pimping his stepdaughter's services at the studios.

Then came Harlow's big break. Eccentric young millionaire Howard Hughes had prodigally squandered $2,000,000 on *Hell's Angels,* only to double the cost by reshooting the film in Sound. The leading lady, blonde Norwegian Greta Nissen, had to go due to her heavy accent. Harlow tested for and won the coveted part of "Helen," thanks to her hair and figure. James Whale, who Porter had come to know all too well last year at Universal during the horrific shooting of *Frankenstein*, had been Hughes' "ghost director" on the Sound version. The London homosexual and the Kansas City blonde hated each other. He ridiculed her attempts to act, while she begged him for coaching on her now-infamous "Would you be shocked if I put on something more comfortable?" seduction scene.

"My dear girl," Whale had archly told her, "I can tell you how to be an actress, but I cannot tell you how to be a woman."

Harlow won overnight stardom in *Hell's Angels*, but Hughes had no follow-up for her. He refused Bern's overture to sell her contract to MGM, preferring to loan her out carelessly to other studios, where she played roles she described as "sex vultures." Mother Jean and Bello booked their meal ticket on a personal appearance tour in the east, where Harlow visibly trembled onstage. The crowds blew raspberries at her. She was so mortified that she collapsed.

A gangster had come to her rescue. Marino Bello, who idolized mobsters, personally invited underworld kingpins – including Capone – to squire (and, rumor claimed, screw) his movie star stepdaughter. Eventually she met Longie Zwillman. It was Zwillman who arranged for her to escape the traumatic tour and sign a two-picture contract with Columbia, sealing the deal for his mistress by providing Columbia Pictures' chief Harry Cohn a $500,000 loan. She starred for up-and-coming director Frank Capra in the Columbia comedy *Platinum Blonde*, and the film's title became Harlow's professional *soubriquet*. Her second Columbia film: the already-forgotten *Three Wise Girls*.

Then, in the spring of 1932, Hughes had finally acquiesced to Bern's request – he'd sold Harlow's contract to Metro. Bern had provided professional coaching, paved the way for her to win the widely-cherished title role in *Red-Headed Woman*, and was now set to marry her. Porter wasn't sure when Longie Zwillman had jumped off the bandwagon.

Longie might still be on the bandwagon, he thought.

The mob connection could be a death kiss, Porter knew, literally and figuratively. What Zwillman might conceivably do to the producer who'd stolen his mistress – and to the mistress herself – was staggeringly dangerous.

A fanatical stage mother. A pimp of a stepfather. A shafted gangster. And the screen's most overt *femme fatale* who, within 60 days of setting up quarters at MGM, had triumphantly sunk her nails into one of the studio's most powerful men…but one who'd once gotten his head stuck in a toilet seat.

Hell of a Goddamn case, thought Porter.

*

1353 Club View Drive was between Wilshire and Santa Monica Boulevards, east of Beverly Glen. The impressive stone domicile sat above the drive. The right wing was a towering A-frame with a giant window, almost ecclesiastical in appearance. Porter climbed the steep steps, amused that this church-like house was the lair of the peroxide Platinum Blonde "sex vulture."

An attractive but snooty maid, who called herself Claudette, was trying very hard to look French, complete with spit curls, frilly black uniform and black hosiery. Claudette closed the door in Porter's face after he announced his name but opened it again a moment later. A tall, blonde, elegantly-dressed woman posed behind her.

"Welcome, Mr. Down. I'm Jean Bello. The Baby's mother."

Porter looked around for a baby, or a crib or bassinette. The woman, attractive but definitely too long in the tooth to be the mother of a baby, kept smiling widely, as if someone had wedged a coat hanger into her mouth.

"I'll tell The Baby you're here."

Porter was wondering why in the hell this smilin' *grande dame* would tell a baby he was here when he remembered… The Baby she referred to must be Harlow. The nickname "The Baby" struck him as weird, but so did this smiling, toothy poseuse who'd moved to the dark oak staircase.

"Mr. Down?"

The voice came from above, from a balding, thickly mustached man in sartorial splendor, posing on the upper area of the staircase.

He looked as if he were ideal casting for the part of an Italian seducer or a Sicilian gangster.

"I am Marino Bello. Harlean's stepfather."

Mrs. Bello ascended the staircase, Bello descended, and as they passed Bello wrapped her in a Valentino-style embrace, gave her a passionate kiss and released her. He smiled, she sighed rapturously, and then she trotted up the remaining stairs. Porter, figuring he'd just seen a Hollywood show staged for his benefit, feigned a yawn.

Bello came down the stairs, walked across the room and offered his hand. Porter shook it. "Nice spats," he said, indicating Bello's shoes.

"Did you come from the docks?" asked Bello, critically assessing Porter's sailor suit.

"Actually, I did."

"That is fine. Follow me, please." Bello led Porter through the expensively decorated house. They passed the ooh-la-la Claudette, who grinned flirtatiously at Bello as he brushed insinuatingly past her. Porter followed Bello through the rear-entrance French doors and out to a stone patio. From an upstairs window, Porter heard a record playing "I Found a Million Dollar Baby in a Five and Ten Cent Store." He glanced up, guessing the room was Harlow's.

"Do sit," said Bello. Both men sat under an umbrella on the patio. Bello took a sterling silver cigarette case from his coat pocket. He lit up, not offering a cigarette to Porter.

"Despite whatever you might hear," said Bello, "I am Harlean's business agent, and my personal authority is supreme."

"You finished yet?"

"Also, I can provide protection without the services of some sailor-suited gumshoe."

"Are you finished now?"

"Last, and most importantly, I love my wife and stepdaughter like a tiger and I will protect them like a lion." He blew out a jet of smoke. "That includes protecting them from you. I already know much about you, Mr. Down…including that your investigator's license is suspended because last year you caused a woman's death. Out of sensitivity for Harlean, I haven't told her this fact. Why Mayer hired you mystifies me, but no matter. Finish your job, go home to your hermit's life in your Redskin hut...and resume feeding your turkeys."

Porter imagined Bello had paid some cheaply-hired detective to dig up a Porter Down dossier. The man glowed knowingly.

"You see, you don't impress me, Mr. Down. I know professionals."

"And you don't impress me, Mr. Bello. You have bird shit on your spats."

He didn't really, but Bello looked anyway. Porter had burst his bubble. Bello's eyes darkened, and he stood, again smiling challengingly.

"Good day," said Bello. "Remember what I said." He swaggered into the house, still doing his Sicilian gang lord act.

Clotheshorse creep, though Porter.

*

The music upstairs had stopped but Jean Harlow hadn't shown. Porter decided he'd give her two more minutes. Meanwhile, he cynically reviewed in his mind trashy trivia he'd learned in his research. For example, Harlow insisted her platinum blonde hair was natural, but in fact, every Sunday was peroxide day, complete with a special formula of Lux flakes, Clorox, and ammonia. With that weekly ritual, Porter wondered how soon the "Baby" would be slick bald.

Maybe that's why she's hiding upstairs, thought Porter.

The crazy stories had seemed endless. Harlow had played in *The Public Enemy*, the Warner Bros. gangster saga that had made James Cagney a star. The film's director, "Wild Bill" Wellman, was a Lafayette Escadrille veteran too, and had told Porter that Harlow had been so hopelessly vapid that he'd cut her part in half. The salty Wellman had also shared with Porter another tidbit: Harlow prepared for sexy shots by rubbing her nipples with ice cubes. Porter glanced again up at the window.

Maybe she's icing her nipples, he thought.

Porter stretched in his chair, looked at his watch, figured he'd give her one more minute, and then heard high heels on the patio. "I'm so sorry I kept you waiting."

Porter sat up. Jean Harlow stood before him in a white bathing suit with black sash and silver-colored heels, her platinum hair shining in the morning sun. Without realizing it, he got directly to his feet and respectfully removed his cap.

"I'm Jean Harlow," she said, smiling and offering her hand. "Please call me Jean."

"Porter Down," he said, taking her hand. "Please call me Porter."

There seemed a glow about the woman, a presence, even if she was, Porter guessed, barely over 5'3" tall, even in the heels. Adding to her allure was a rich perfume.

"I didn't think," Porter said, regarding her bathing suit, "there's a swimming pool here."

"There isn't," smiled Harlow. "But I'm aware of all the trouble Paul and I are causing, so I just wanted to look nice for you."

She said it without any sense of vamping, with what struck Porter as genuine sincerity. From what he'd seen of her on the screen, she wasn't a good enough actress to fake it.

"Please sit down," she said. Claudette appeared in her *parlez-vous Francais* way, silently providing a pitcher of lemonade and some crackers and cheese on a small table beside Porter. She also placed on the table a cigarette case, ashtray and lighter before prancing back into the house. Harlow sat across from Porter under the umbrella and crossed her legs.

"Paul and I are both so grateful for your help," she said, a bit shyly, or so it seemed. "We're very fortunate to have you. A war hero…"

"That's alright, Miss," said Porter, habitually non-receptive when his war service was mentioned. He poured two glasses of lemonade.

"I understand you were one of the stunt pilots on *Hell's Angels*," she said.

"Yep," said Porter. He offered her the cheese and crackers.

"No, no. I'm on a diet. I'm *always* on a diet."

Porter sipped his lemonade, surprised by the stunning effect she'd had on him. "Paul and I will of course do everything to cooperate with you," said Harlow.

"I hope so," he said. "You'll have to be honest. No acting."

"Everyone knows," she smiled, "that Jean Harlow's no actress."

Damn right, he thought, but he had to grin.

"I know many people are suspicious of my love for Paul," she said, "but it's genuine. I've never met a man like him. He loves me for myself."

Clunky line, thought Porter, and she seemed to realize it, even if Porter believed *she* believed it. She paused to drink her lemonade. A breeze stirred and he caught another whiff of her perfume. He decided, before going moonbeam again, to cut to the chase.

"Miss Harlow… Jean… what do you hear from Abner Zwillman?"

Porter thought the question might pop the bubble, unleash the vampire who sat before him, cloaked in a patina of MGM How-To-Act-Like-a-Lady drama school finesse. He looked at her eyes and they didn't darken.

"My relationship with Mr. Zwillman ended months ago," she said. "He was very generous to me and my family. He's also aware that, in his field, it would be a mistake for everyone concerned if he ever married a so-called public figure."

Zwillman had his own code of honor. Porter knew that personally.

"Also, your stepfather was here…acting like he was auditioning for a sequel to *Scarface*."

Now her eyes darkened. Harlow restlessly uncrossed her legs and for a moment appeared to be conjuring up one of her tart-mouthed floozies of the movies. "He *embarrasses* me," she finally said, simply and rather sadly. She sighed, took a cigarette from the case and lit up. She'd become comfortable with her caller and jumped to a new topic.

"Do you read often, Porter?"

"Yeah."

"Paul sends me books along with flowers. He's heard the joke going around about me. You've probably heard it too. The joke goes that somebody asks Jean Harlow, 'Would you like a book as a gift?' And she says, 'No, thank you. I already have one.'"

She smiled, clearly a good sport, but didn't laugh. Porter grinned but didn't laugh either. And he found it interesting that she had referred to herself for the second time in the third person.

"Paul has asked me to read *Hamlet*. Of course, I'd read it at Ferry Hall. When you came today, I was reading a soliloquy I especially liked."

"Were you reading it while listening to 'Million Dollar Baby'?" asked Porter.

Harlow laughed. "The speech began, 'Now I am alone…'"

"'O what a rogue and peasant slave am I,'" said Porter.

"Yes! Do you know more of it?"

Porter, a bit embarrassed, went on:

> *Is it not monstrous that this poor player here,*
> *But in a fiction, in a dream of passion,*
> *Can force his soul, so to his own conceit,*
> *That through its working, all his visage wanned…*

"Mr. Down, you're full of surprises," smiled Harlow.

Aren't we both, thought Porter. He might have told her of his near-total memorization of much of the Bible and Shakespeare, but didn't.

"Tell me what you believe the speech means," she asked.

"Well," said Porter. "Hamlet's saying that it seems unfair that actors show fake passion, while people in real life sometimes never show *real* passion."

"Maybe they're afraid to show it," said Harlow softly, extinguishing her cigarette in the ashtray. "Or don't know how to…or they just…can't."

Porter sensed an intimacy in her words. She broke from her reverie, tossing off her mysteriously sudden, somber mood. "Well!" she said, standing. "This meeting we discussed Shakespeare. Next time…how about if we shoot craps? I've got a lucky rabbit's foot."

"That's funny," said Porter, also standing. "I've got a pet rabbit that's missing a foot."

He briefly told her the history of Long John and she enjoyed the story of the rabbit's rescue. She was close to him, and asked, with just a hint of her screen siren persona, "Any more questions for now?"

"Yeah. What perfume do you wear?" Porter was surprised he'd asked the question.

"It's called Mitsouko," said Harlow. "I have several bottles upstairs. Would you like one to take home to your wife as a gift from Jean Harlow?"

"Thank you, no, Miss. I'm a widower."

"Oh…I'm so sorry. And you're such a young man. Do you have a girlfriend who might like the perfume? No… I'm sorry. That was very poor taste… to ask you about…"

"Baby!" cried her mother, standing sternly at the door with Marino. "You've been talking to that man for far too long."

"Harlean," said Bello sternly.

"Goodbye for now," said Jean Harlow. "I like you."

"I'll show you out, Mr. Down," announced Bello.

Porter gently took Harlow's hand before going inside, leaving her alone on the patio, resplendent in her platinum hair, white bathing suit and silver heels, hoping she hadn't upset or disappointed the man.

She really did like him.

Chapter Eight
9820 Easton Drive

Thursday, June 16, 1932

The sun was setting as Porter Down drove up Benedict Canyon.

Running north of Beverly Hills, Benedict Canyon featured some of the movie colony's most palatial addresses. High on Tower Road was "Bella Vista," the home of John Barrymore. "The Great Profile's" spread boasted a tower, various pools, an aviary, and a 29'-tall totem pole Barrymore had brought home from an Alaskan cruise, possibly "cursed" (or so brother Lionel had warned him) due to the ashes of several Indians entombed inside it. Bella Vista's gate bore Barrymore's self-designed coat-of-arms, revealing both his ego and repellant self-image...a serpent wearing a crown.

However, as far as Benedict Canyon's perverse sites, Falcon Lair, up on Bella Drive, was the topper. It had been the home of Rudolph Valentino who, Porter knew, had erected the house to impress his bride. She was some ball-buster with a Russian name, a phony diva who'd finally given him the shaft, and the rejection had contributed to his death. For the past six years, Valentino's residence had been Hollywood Memorial Cemetery.

Movie folk, thought Porter. Despite all their blessings and money, they were the most unhappy, self-pitying *kvetches* anywhere. God had laid it in their laps and they blew it all away. He hoped Jean Harlow, who'd impressed him today, was different. Then he saw the street sign…Easton Drive. He turned right and the road steeply scaled the canyon hillside. At the top on the right was a gate. The number was 9820.

Yeah, this was it, thought Porter – the hideaway home of Paul Who-Got-His-Head-Caught-In-a-Toilet-Seat Bern.

*

There was a two-story house on the left inside the gate. A radio upstairs was playing "Star Dust" and Porter banged at the door. A plain, heavy-set woman, totally opposite the spit-curled chorine who'd answered at Club View Drive, came down the stairs and opened the screen door.

"I have an appointment with Mr. Bern. My name's Porter Down."

"I'm Mrs. Carmichael," she said. "Mr. Bern's housekeeper." Based on Bern's artsy reputation, Porter imagined his servants would have been a pair of gazelle-like ballet dancers, leaping all over the damn place, cleaning house while in tights and on point. Mrs. Carmichael looked more the polka type.

"My husband, Mr. Carmichael, is the butler," said Mrs. Carmichael. "You'll find him and Mr. Bern up at the house."

She pointed up the hill and toward a thicket of trees, indicating a path of steps. "That's the house. This is the servants' quarters, kitchen and garage."

"Kitchen? There's no kitchen up at the house?"

"No. Mr. Bern doesn't want the smell of cookin' food in his living room. Anyway, the house is up there...75 steps."

"Swell. Thanks." Porter squinted up into the woods and now saw a timbered roof and a window. He began hiking up the steps, pissed off all over again. As a man who enjoyed his food, heartily, he wondered about anyone keeping his kitchen 75 steps down the hill and through the woods. What the hell happened when you wanted a midnight snack?

Birds sang as the sun set across the canyon. Gradually, Porter could see more of the house, looming through the trees. The Grimm Brothers effect was inescapable. It was Bavarian-style, a fairy tale hunting lodge of stone and timber with a turret and a sharply sloping roof. The house sat on a square of white stones that buttressed it on the hillside. The home was nestled in this woodsy glen, and a hill ran up to the east, another across the drive to the north. A wooden bridge ran over a stream and Porter crossed it. Yeah, the place was private. Damn private. The home's quaint look and isolated location made it seem one of the last places where, at night, a cinema sex goddess would lay her head, or anything else.

One of Porter Down's only possessions as a child had been a fairy tale book with rather lavish illustrations. Being the one book he owned, he'd read it day and night. Now, in his angry but suddenly fanciful mood, Porter pictured Harlow in this story book glen, dressed as Snow White, in black wig and flouncy dress, dancing around and smiling, the singing birdies twittering around her as, all the while, she iced her nipples. And capering about and below her was Paul Bern, one of the dwarfs, playing a flute and wearing a toilet seat as a hat as he and Harlow merrily danced their way up and down these 75 Goddamned steps.

Snow White and the Father Confessor Dwarf, thought Porter. No, that wasn't nice. He really was in a shitty mood. Or maybe, he admitted to himself, after the undeniable impact Harlow had on him today, he was feeling jealous about her.

*

He came up to the house, its leaded glass sparkling in the evening light, some of the windows open. Stone steps ran down from the house to a small swimming pool and a patio with a tiny table and two chairs. A large, bear-like man in a white servant jacket and black trousers stood at a table beside the pool.

"Good evening, sir," he said, his voice gruff. "I'm Carmichael, Mr. Bern's butler."

Porter shook his hand and introduced himself. The man looked cockeyed, and Porter wondered if one of his eyes was glass.

"Mr. Bern is on the telephone," said Carmichael. "He'll be with you shortly."

Porter regarded the table. It held a pewter cigarette case, a bottle of wine, a carafe of ice water, and two glasses. Then a pleasant, cultivated voice flowed from the house's darkness.

"Mr. Down. How *very* good of you to come!"

Porter stood. Paul Bern, still in his dark double-breasted suit from work, emerged from the shadowy house, smiled easily, briskly trotted down the stone steps and firmly shook his hand. He was shorter than Porter, his mustache neat, his hair receding but impeccably groomed, and his face, if not handsome, certainly distinguished and animated. His instant charm made Porter feel a tiny bit guilty about his Snow White and the dwarf flautist fantasy.

"Please sit down, sir, and be my guest. Jean called me this afternoon and you've impressed her totally. You're her new champion, which makes me your unconditional admirer."

Bern sat and offered his open cigarette case. Porter declined and Bern lit up. "Would this 1899 Benedictine be satisfactory?" asked Bern. "I confess that I enjoy boasting about my home's modest wine cellar. It's completely at your disposal."

"I'm fine with ice water."

Bern looked a bit hurt that Porter had refused his Benedictine. "Carmichael, please," he said. Carmichael poured ice water for Porter and the Benedictine for Bern. The butler glanced at Porter's clothes. "You a Navy man, sir?" he asked Porter.

"No. I was at Annapolis for a while."

"Mr. Down is a war hero," said Bern. "He was a decorated pilot with the Lafayette Escadrille. That will be all, Carmichael."

"Yes sir," murmured Carmichael, and went up into the house.

"I'm so sorry," said Bern.

"That's alright," said Porter, removing his cap. "The Navy clothes are an eccentricity of mine, I admit."

"No man you'll ever meet is more indulgent of eccentricities," said Bern. "My personal life is a museum of them. By the way, have you had any supper? I'll be happy to have Mrs. Carmichael prepare a meal for you."

"In the kitchen? 75 steps down there?" said Porter, indicating with his thumb.

"You see? One of *my* many eccentricities." Bern smiled and raised his glass. "Thank you for being here for Jean and me," he toasted. They both drank.

Much had been made about Bern being twice Harlow's age, but he had a youthful quality, an upbeat energy that dovetailed nicely with his sophistication. Porter could imagine the producer quickly winning over actors and writers, just as he was winning him over tonight.

"I do hope you had no trouble finding your way here," said Bern. "This house is so isolated that, when I first built here two years ago, I felt obliged to post a large sign down below, with an arrow pointing up this hill and the single word, 'Bern.' Then I realized I was treading precariously where mere mortals shouldn't go. The only personage in Hollywood billed simply by a surname is Garbo… although I've learned that Karloff is about to join her."

Porter knew Bern was aware of his work for Garbo, which is when he'd first met him briefly. He also knew Porter was familiar with Boris Karloff, since Porter had investigated behind the scenes of *Frankenstein* the previous summer. Bern, thought Porter, probably considered this a groundbreaker. Porter, however, made no reply.

"So," said Bern. "Isn't Jean an angel from Heaven?"

The words, albeit florid, suited the man who said them. Paul Bern was elegant without being effeminate, sophisticated without being pretentious. Porter knew Bern was a Jew from a poor background – his real name was Levy – who had a degree from the Academy of Dramatic Arts in New York City, a versatile background in theatre, and a dynamic reputation as a writer/ director / producer in the Movies. Yet personally, in a hyper-invasive world where everybody eventually knew almost everything about nearly everybody, this man was an enigma. Porter had heard a shitload of crazy, unsubstantiated stories, but they were just that.

"Miss Harlow's a lovely lady," said Porter.

"It's quite marvelous," said Bern, "that you and Jean spent part of your first meeting exploring the depths of Shakespeare. It's typical of the class of my employer that when Leo the Lion engages a private investigator, he finds one with the good looks of a matinee idol, the fine physique of a pugilist, and a scholar's knowledge of the Bard."

And a revoked P.I. license for manslaughter, thought Porter, wondering if Bern were yet aware of that fact. "Miss Harlow understands Shakespeare very well," he said.

Bern sipped his Benedictine and his tiny mouth smiled its tight-lipped smile. "Yes," he said, and began reciting:

> *Yet I, who am not made for sportive tricks,*
> *Nor made to court an amorous looking glass…*

"That's *Richard III*," said Porter. "Jean's reading *Hamlet*."

Bern looked startled, and then grinned again. "My apologies. If you see Jack Barrymore at Metro, please don't tell him I made this mistake. He'd never forgive me. He played Richard *and* Hamlet, you know. I saw him as both in New York. Perhaps that's why I confused them."

Porter was suspicious. His guess was that Bern had recited the wrong quote to try to catch him up, to see if Porter knew his Shakespeare as well as Harlow had apparently reported.

"Jean and I discussed the 'Now I am alone' soliloquy," said Porter.

"Ah, yes," said Bern. "'What would he do, if he had the motive and cue for passion that I have?'"

"Yep," said Porter.

The sun was just below the west ridge of the canyon. "You know," said Bern, "as for my mistaken quote…" The evening shadows were falling on his face and doing strange things to it. His eyes seemed darker with circles under them Porter hadn't noticed previously. He also saw how nicely the man's expertly tailored vest covered his potbelly.

"I imagine you're finding many people in our colony who dismiss Jean as merely 'an amorous looking glass?' And who claim that I'm not 'made for sportive tricks?'"

Now Porter was angry. The misquote was not only a trick to catch him up – it was a contrivance, he believed, to broach this topic. There was self-pity suddenly obvious in the man and the morbid expression he now wore. Porter didn't like crybabies.

"First of all, Mr. Bern," said Porter, tensing in his chair, "this is 1932 Depression America. You're earning, I hear, $75,000 a year. Tell that to a family man in a soup line and see how fast his tears splash your custom-tailored suit."

Bern blushed. "My dear Mr. Down, I merely…"

"In hardly any time at all, you've brought up Jean Harlow from being a sex freak that your own boss, Mr. Thalberg, called 'a mantrap,' to a star who, from what everybody says, is gonna' carry a major movie. Millions of gals in theatres will wish they were her. Once you're married, millions of guys will wish they were you."

Bern showed his dime-slot grin.

"So, stop feeling sorry for yourself. At 42, you're no graybeard. And as for your matinee idol good looks, or your perceived lack of them…"

Bern chuckled. "Please, Mr. Down…"

"I have to tell ya," said Porter, "that as a man who once saw Karloff in full Frankenstein Monster makeup and costume, late one night at Universal, pissing in a bucket in the moonlight because his fancy-pants director wouldn't allow him a break to walk to the latrine…you don't look scary to me at all."

Bern appeared genuinely aggrieved. "I'm so sorry," he said. "Apparently, I've provoked you and I sincerely apologize. May I please refill your glass?"

"Sure."

Bern was quick to pour Porter's water and move to a new topic. "You mentioned Jean's remarkable transfiguration as an actress," he said. "We've scheduled a final sneak preview of *Red-Headed Woman*. Tomorrow evening. We would both like you to be there. You're a part of the MGM family now…and, more importantly, Jean and I consider you a part of *our* family."

If Bern were bullshitting, he was damn good at it. "Okay," said Porter.

"The Fox Theatre, Pomona, 9:00 P.M." Both men drank and Bern looked reflective in the darkening light. "As for the 'Now I am alone' soliloquy…may we please revisit it for just a moment?"

"Alright."

"It's truly a fascinating study in the human mind and soul, isn't it? The common man – which Hamlet is, even if he's a prince – tormented that stage actors can *pretend* passion that he can't *display*. Of course, there's the other side. Sometimes the actors, or people in the arts, envy the common man – or woman – for they can truly *feel* passion that a man of the arts might only be able to *simulate*. Do you think Shakespeare ever pondered it that way?"

"He's one of the people I want to look up in Heaven," said Porter, downing his glass of water. "If I get there, I'll ask him."

"A charming notion," smiled Bern.

Porter stood. Bern stood too. "Thank you," he said, "for being here for Jean and me at this most magical time of our lives. You'll receive our honest cooperation."

"In that case, I have one more question tonight, and it's a two-parter. Mr. Bern, are you now involved intimately with anyone else besides Miss Harlow…and are you now involved, intimately or otherwise, with a Hollywood pornographer?"

Bern looked at Porter with sad eyes, as if genuinely sorry he'd had to ask such a distasteful question. "No and no," he said softly.

Porter extended his hand. "Thanks for the ice water."

"You're very welcome," chuckled Bern, shaking his hand. "Good night, sir."

"Good night."

"Oh, Mr. Down."

Porter turned. Bern offered his hand again, clasping Porter's hand with both hands. "Jean mentioned to me the loss of your wife. I'm so very sorry. I can only assume, based on your youth, that her death was an especially tragic one. My own family has a history of early and tragic deaths and, as such, I have the deepest empathy for your loss."

Bern's eyes were wet in the twilight. "Thanks," said Porter.

"If you need to talk at any time about whatever happened, you know where I am."

He released Porter's hands, watched him go, and walked up the steps to his house.

*

Carmichael had lit several lanterns that hung on tree branches along the 75 steps. The candlelight added to the fairy tale milieu as Porter reviewed what had just occurred.

Maybe Bern was preoccupied with death. Or maybe he was a genuinely kind man, truly Hollywood's "Father Confessor," and Porter was being too cynical about him. Or maybe some of the rumors were right and Bern simply enjoyed the excuse to hold Porter's hands.

As Porter opened the gate, something was bothering him. How much of this puppy dog act Bern displayed, Porter wondered, was an act? If any man in America had the chance to get laid early and often, it was Paul Bern – the only unmarried power figure at a studio that was "going all out for sex" this 1932 A.D., where gals with stars in their eyes would flip their panties in the air for even a crack at collecting a paycheck with the Leo the Lion logo on it.

The man worked with the word "sex" in front of him every day – how to script it, how to cast it, how to market it. Now he was probably going to marry Hollywood's sexiest star, yet he moped about his looks, called his fiancée an "angel" when a "succubus" was more appropriate (at least her screen image was), and actually gave a Goddamn about what the gossipers said.

The man of the arts envies the common man… Simulated passion…I am not made for sportive tricks…

Maybe it was his act, his *shtick*; maybe all that sad-eyed angst was the "Father Confessor's" tried-and-true way of slipping under the sheets fast…

As he walked up the drive to his car, he saw headlights. He instinctively ducked into the trees as the car reached the top of the drive and made a U-turn. The driver, a man, jumped out, ran to the gate of 9820, put something large in the milk can, jumped back into the car and headed down Easton, turning south at Benedict Canyon.

Porter emerged from the trees, went to the gate, opened the milk can and removed a heavy round case – a canister of film. He had an immediate instinctive suspicion, despite what Bern had told him: Pornography.

Chapter Nine
Balthazar

Thursday, June 16, 1932

The moon, two nights away from being full, was high over MGM as Porter drove through the gate, showed his employee badge and asked for directions to the screening rooms.

Many directors worked late, so the rooms were available to view "rushes" until midnight. It was 10 o'clock now. Porter parked outside the building, strolled in with his purloined can of film from Bern's house, and found a thin, horse-faced man in red suspenders, playing solitaire.

"I'm Al," said the man, seeing Porter's I.D. and offering his hand. "Is this a tech check?"

"Yep," lied Porter. There were about twenty seats in the screening room and Porter sat in the middle. Al ditched the lights and entered the projection booth. The silver glow hit the screen, the decreasing numbers flickering to a blackout, and up came the title, accompanied by some piano flourishes on the soundtrack:

AS Productions
Presents...

This should be swell, smirked Porter. *They can't even spell "ass" right.*

Cave Canem!
Te Necet Lingendo

Porter recognized the Latin expression: *Beware of the Dog! He might lick you to death.*

The film opened on a chateau with a high tower – a convincing, well-lit miniature. The camera smoothly tracked up to the tower's arched window, "dissolved" though the window and into a boudoir, and glided across a four-poster bed. There was a long shot of a woman at a vanity mirror, her back to the camera.

Mademoiselle Poppy LaRue always wanted to look her most attractive, proclaimed the silent film's card.

Although there was an accompanying piano score, there was no recorded dialogue. As the piano tinkled seductively, the camera beheld "Mademoiselle LaRue," seated at her vanity in tight white corset and high, black-laced boots. The actress had a vague resemblance to Marlene Dietrich but a rather feline face. She touched up her false eyelashes, placed a black top hat atop her blonde coiffure, stood in her lingerie, picked up a riding crop, and paraded before her mirror, striking poses.

Al, not hearing any dialogue, curiously peered through the booth, just in time to see the vainglorious Mademoiselle LaRue, in cocked top hat, placing one leg on her vanity chair, sensually stroking her thigh with her riding crop.

"Well, hello there," said Al.

Every day, read the card, *Mademoiselle provided her dog Balthazar a spirited run in the park.*

Mademoiselle LaRue, now fully dressed in a dark riding jacket, tan tight skirt, and black boots, descended a "stone" chateau staircase with her riding crop and a considerable swagger. In the first gaffe Porter had noticed, the stone wall, painted (quite convincingly) on canvas, swayed a bit as she made her way.

"Did you see the stone wall?" asked Al, watching from the booth. "It's wiggling."

"So is she," said Porter.

Although there'd been no close-ups, Porter noticed "Poppy LaRue's" bright intense eyes. Porter wondered if she was fantasizing that this opus might cop her an Academy Award.

Best Performance by a Floozy in a Smoker, thought Porter.

Mademoiselle entered an archway gate, and into a dark, cavernous kennel. There in the shadows was a large dog, only it wasn't a dog. The close-up revealed a man in a dog suit, wearing a partial mask, mugging merrily for the camera, his tongue lolling out the side of his mouth.

Reminds me of Eddie Mannix, thought Porter.

The "dog" rubbed playfully against Mademoiselle's legs and she smacked him with her crop.

Behave, Balthazar! Naughty! read the card.

"Balthazar" slinked behind Mademoiselle and, in dog fashion, sniffed her tail. "Mademoiselle LaRue" did a comic "take," popping her eyes, pursing her lips, and hitting the "dog" again with her crop...hard. The crop smacking went on, the trussed-up lady in the top hat getting progressively violent, the dog cowering, the woman shouting at him.

"I think she just called him 'a son of a bitch,'" said Al.

"Literally," said Porter.

There was a fadeout, then a shot of the dog, its muzzle severely constricted by a leather strap.

Dissolve to a park – obviously a soundstage set, but with convincing trees, flowers and bushes. The grand bitch, still sporting her top hat at a jaunty angle, strolled behind Balthazar, one hand grasping the leash, the other flourishing her riding crop. She swatted the hapless beast on the rear and laughed.

Your laughter might soon haunt you, Mademoiselle! read the card.

Then followed a close-up of the pseudo-canine. His face had changed. Replacing the partial mask was a grotesque, full-head mask, the hair wild and teased, the teeth sharp and elongated. Porter guessed the grotesque morphing of "Balthazar" was supposedly a consequence of his sadistic treatment. A close-up revealed the monster dog's muzzle, shredding the leather strap with his fang-like teeth.

Revenge is a treat best served cold!

And now, with the piano music turning wildly dramatic, the beast suddenly attacked his mistress, snapping at the crop-waving Mademoiselle. She fluttered her eyes, viciously swinging the crop like a whip, fighting with unfeigned ferocity as the dog ripped off her skirt with his teeth.

Naughty, Balthazar, naughty!

Porter again noted the actress's raw emotion. As she looked up and into the camera, her eyes terrified, Porter knew she was truly screaming, even though this atrocity had no sound.

"Jesus," he mumbled.

The "smoker" now became increasingly violent and sadistic. The dog knocked the feline-faced woman to the soundstage ground, his teeth tearing off her remaining clothes until she was down to her lingerie. Then came a shot of the corset, panties, and boots flying into the air, followed by a close-up of the dog/actor dangling his tongue:

Te Necet Lingendo!

He repulsively licked the woman, her face, her thighs, and the film played on, a simulated but fully repellant version of a bestial rape. In a sudden costume change, "Balthazar" was now naked from the hips down, wearing an apparatus that gave him both a giant phallus and a long tail, crowned by a black ball of hair. He was standing, a horrific hybrid of man and dog, leering and snarling as the lady cried in terror.

No, Balthazar, No!

"Mademoiselle LaRue" sought escape, crawling away on all fours, the camera following her bare ass. "Balthazar" humped her, then lifted his leg and pissed on her. The actor appeared to be genuinely pissing. The piano music was wildly triumphant now – Liszt, thought Porter. There was a long shot of the naked woman in the grass, the dog-man capering around her.

Balthazar!

Then suddenly, jarringly intercut into the film, came close-ups of a real dog, a huge Doberman, eyes ferocious, mouth frothing as it attacked the jerking and twitching camera.

Bow-wow-WOW!

The scenes now switched back and forth between the enraged, snarling Doberman and close shots of breasts, buttocks and vagina, the piano's pounding classical music thunderously exhorting the attack. A close-up showed the dog ripping some animal to pieces – a rabbit, guessed Porter – standing in for the mangled woman. Its flesh and sinew hung from the dog's bloody, salivating jaws. The next close-up beheld the woman, her face streaked with prop blood, crazed with fear, her wild eyes looking up into the camera, her arms pleading:

"Oh God and Jesus, help meeeee!"

In a startling shot, Mademoiselle LaRue appeared a mutilated pulp, so spattered in fake blood and gore that only her hair, now long and unloosed, gave a clue to her sex. Balthazar, in monstrous standing form again, grabbed his naked, bloody prey by her feet, dragging the carcass behind a bush as the piano hit a crescendo and the scene faded into darkness.

The *denouement* showed "Balthazar," once again in a partial mask and pasted whiskers, smiling in close-up, the music antic and happy. He now wore the lady's top hat and was merrily munching on a skeletal bone. There was a final flourish of music, and the card read:

After all...Every dog has his day!

The End

*

The lights came up. "Don't say you want to see it again," Al said from the booth.

"I'd go blind," said Porter. "Maybe just the opening."

"It's your funeral." Al rewound the film and it soon began again. Porter thought he remembered something regarding the credits, and there it was:

AS Productions

AS, he nodded, remembering the hysteria at the cathouse: *The initials of Annie Spry... The pornography producer and star...also known as Luscious Custard.*

Al rewound the film. A few minutes later, he handed Porter the reel back in its can.

"Put you in the mood to go home and pitch woo to the wife?" asked Porter.

"I'm sure in hell not takin' the dog for a walk," said Al.

Chapter Ten
Fargo Street

Thursday, June 16, 1932

Cave Canem....a foul piece of garbage made by a sadistic loony for the tantalizing of other sadistic loonies. And it had been personally delivered to the estate of Paul Bern, who'd just lied to Porter's face this very night that he had no dealings with a pornographer.

There was no address on the film can. However, in the car, Porter had torn off the lid a taped slip of paper that had Bern's address printed on it in pencil. Now back in the car, he looked at the slip, turned it over and saw it was written on a diner receipt – Fred's, on Glendale Boulevard. The receipt had the words FATS penned on it and the sum of $5.00. Also scribbled on the back of the receipt was a number on Fargo Street. Porter recognized the address.

Often these kinds of ragtag clues burned up days and nights of wild goose chases. Porter had no idea that this one would pay off within hours.

*

Fargo Street, in the Echo Park section of L.A., was the steepest street in L.A. It plunged into what appeared to be virtually a straight drop between tree-shrouded residences. The Olympic Games were set to open in Los Angeles on July 30, and Porter had heard that local Olympic aspirants trained by running up Fargo. None were here tonight.

Close to Fargo, not as perilously steep, a road dead ended at the top of the hill. Overlooking Silver Lake, behind an open gate, was a Spanish-style house. It was, Porter knew, a Ma-and-Pa style speakeasy, housed in the private home of Olive and Buck Jackson. Former vaudeville song-and-dance partners, they were now husband-and-wife alcoholics who ran their speakeasy with monastic devotion. Porter had known them for years. He let himself in the gate, heard the piano accompanying Olive's slurred singing, and peeked in the door. There was burly Buck in his tux, tickling the ivories, and aging Olive in her mane of dyed brown hair and too-snug evening gown, singing "Dream a Little Dream of Me" under a dim light for a numb crowd of four.

Porter sat at the garden patio that overlooked Silver Lake, heard Olive skid flat on her last note, then rang the little bell on the candlelit table for service. A moment later, Olive came outside to take the order.

"Why, Porter Down!" she said.

"You look swell, Olive," said Porter. *Actually, she looked like hell, but why tell her?*

"Thanks," said Olive. "You still have those pretty eyes. Still have that cute walk?"

"Just for you."

"You're sweet. Wait." She went inside, and then came back with a tray holding three glasses, a bottle of hootch and, remembering Porter's beverage of choice, a bottle of Coca-Cola. The hootch bottle was unique – tall with a long neck, personally designed by Buck to offer the patron a bargain shot. Olive sat across from Porter.

"Bucky says hi," said Olive, pouring Porter's Coke and her hootch. "He'll be out later. Meanwhile, the Coke's on the house."

"Thanks," said Porter.

"Have you heard?" asked Olive. "If that Roosevelt bastard wins, he'll end Prohibition."

"It doesn't look like business is booming anyway, Olive."

"Yeah. You're Goddamned right. Bucky says we might have to go back to vaudeville."

"Well, here's to breaking a leg on the Orpheum circuit," toasted Porter. They both drank. "Actually, Olive," said Porter, "I came with a question."

"I love it when detectives ask me questions," said Olive. "Makes me feel sexy."

"A real long shot. All I've got is a receipt from a diner down the hill with your address penned on it. You notice any unusual actresses or show business types in your place lately?"

Olive snorted. It wasn't becoming. "All the studios around here died. The only one left is on Hyperion. That Disney guy...and his

Goddamned smilin' mouse." She gulped her drink. "The movie people go west for their booze now, out to the beach. We get mainly a local crowd who drink because they're out of work and are trying to get up the courage to blow their brains out."

Lighting a cigarette, she poured them both another drink. "Actually," said Olive, "a funny thing happened a few Friday nights ago. Good crowd, almost like the old days, lots of laughs. I was in great voice."

I bet, thought Porter.

"Late in the night, after everybody's been drinkin,' all of a sudden, this young gal comes in – you'd have sworn it was Jean Harlow. The platinum hair…everything."

Porter paid close attention.

"Of course, it wasn't Harlow," said Olive, "but for a minute she sure in hell had me fooled. Everybody's starin' at her, even after the word goes out, she's not really Harlow. Anyway, she gets up at some point to go to the can and after a minute, some bitch – a blonde, but not a platinum blonde, an ash blonde – gets up and follows her inside the can. The latch on the door was broken. And the ladies' room in there's hardly bigger than a closet."

Olive took a break for a belt, and then continued. "So, suddenly we hear these screams from the can – Jesus! The door crashes open, the Harlow babe storms out, she's crying that the ash-blonde bitch insulted her, the bitch runs out behind her and heads for the door, the Harlow boyfriend goes after the bitch, Bucky has to keep the guy from breakin' the bitch's neck, everybody's yellin'…"

She paused, savoring the memory with lip-smacking relish, and then drank again.

"I figure the bitch was a lady queer," said Olive, "who put the make on the Harlow babe while the babe was sittin' on the throne. Later, the Harlow babe claimed the bitch had asked her to be in movies she made. She presumed they were dirty movies – they probably were. But by that time, Bucky had kicked the bitch out. Literally. Told her if she ever came in again, he'd throw her down into Silver Lake."

"Why do you keep calling her 'the bitch'?" asked Porter.

"Because she *was!*" said Olive, as if the question were ridiculous. "She told Bucky, 'Keep your fucking hands off me!' She was lucky he didn't kill her on the spot. She's never been back, but there were a couple men with her…I think they've been back. Bucky sells them a case now and then. Most of our business these nights is carry-out."

Porter grinned. "Did this lady maybe have a vague resemblance to Marlene Dietrich?"

Olive gave an epic snort. "Who…the bitch? Not even in her dreams! She looked like a pissed-off cat."

*

Fred's, on Glendale Boulevard, not far from Olive's, was a 24/7 diner. Porter ordered a cheeseburger, a piece of cherry pie *a la* mode, and a cup of coffee. As he ate, he chatted with Fred himself, who was running the place tonight assisted only by the cook, Gunther. Fred, burly and middle-aged, still had his tie on at nearly midnight, despite the fact he only had one customer in the whole damn place. Gunther, stringy and taciturn, wore a towering chef's hat as he grilled a hamburger with onions, presumably for Fred or himself. Porter respected their work ethic. The radio was playing – Kate Smith singing "When the Moon Comes Over the Mountain."

"Business seems slow," said Porter. "Don't the Fargo Street runners come in here?"

"Burgers and pie are off their diet," grinned Fred. "We used to be busy this time of night until the Crash. Right, Gunther?"

Gunther nodded and flipped the burger. Porter took the receipt from his pocket and showed it to Fred. "Can you tell me what 'fats' are or who 'Fats' is?" he asked.

"I had a feeling you were a cop," smiled Fred. He pointed down into the glass counter and Porter saw a carton of Fatima Cigarettes. "We don't sell many. They're long cigarettes. Expensive. Anyway, that's Gunther's handwriting. How about it, Gunther?"

"I seen the same lady buy 'em here a few times," said the cook.

"What she look like?" asked Porter.

"Looks like an actress," said Gunther, sprinkling salt and pepper on the burger. "Maybe a whore. It's hard sometimes to tell 'em apart."

"You watch her go?" asked Porter.

"She just heads down that way…toward the old studio."

"The Mack Sennett studio," said Fred. "It's all shut up. When I first opened this place fifteen years ago, Chaplin would come up here. Fatty Arbuckle. Mabel Normand. The Keystone Cops. After working all day getting pies in the face, they'd all come up here at night and *eat* pie. Hell of a sight, wasn't it, Gunther?"

Gunther grinned nostalgically.

"Now, it's a 20-acre ghost town," said Fred. "I hear fly-by-nighters go in there and rent by the week, sometimes by the day. But the street's a morgue. The only studio making it in this part of town is up on Hyperion, the mouse guy…"

"Disney," said Porter.

"Yeah," said Fred.

"So, Gunther," asked Porter, realizing he was tossing out a leading question. "This lady look anything like Marlene Dietrich? Or a cat?"

Gunther smirked. "Well, she ain't no Dietrich. If I had to choose between her lookin' like Dietrich or a cat, I'd go with the cat."

The cheeseburger had been a medium-rare masterpiece, there'd been no pits in the cherry pie, the ice cream and coffee had been delicious, and the information was enticing. Porter left a tip that exceeded the total bill. "Split it with your master chef," said Porter.

"Thank you, sir," said the surprised Fred. Porter exited, Fred handed Gunther his share of the tip and grinned. "So, you watch that lady go, huh, Gunther?"

"Yeah," said Gunther, preparing to eat the burger himself. "But if I'm remembering her right, she's a real bitch."

Chapter Eleven
Lights! Camera! Action!

Thursday, June 16 and Friday, June 17, 1932

It was about midnight. Porter felt adventurous.

He strolled down Glendale Boulevard. Up ahead on the left he saw the old Sennett lot, dark and seemingly mournful under the nearly full moon – ironic, thought Porter, for a studio that had specialized in slapstick. In its heyday, the Sennett studio had competed with Hal Roach's lot as Hollywood's "fun factory," but this night, the neglected property appeared foreboding and sinister.

Not a Keystone Cop or a Bathing Beauty in sight, thought Porter.

To Porter, the place looked like a coffin factory – appropriate, as Forest Lawn was just a few trolley stops away. Then he actually heard a sound from the lot... like a ghostly cheering, as if a spectral crowd was in a haunted stadium. Silence followed, but then he heard again what sounded like cheers, now with a blast of trumpets.

He'd have to scale the locked Sennett studio gate – it wouldn't be easy, and Porter had a primal male fear of straddling sharp objects – but he did it. Descending the other side, he fell the last few feet, caught his balance and righted himself. The cheers and trumpets were louder now and he followed the escalating sound.

The large, barn-like soundstage stood against the hillside. There was a glow of light seeping under the door and out the roof vents. The intensity was unmistakable – they were klieg lights. Somebody was shooting a movie and playing sound effects and music. Technicians usually dubbed in these effects after a film was shot, so Porter presumed the director intended the trumpets and cheers as inspiration for the actors.

*

The red light was spinning above the stage door, the signal that shooting was in progress. Porter saw about a dozen or more cars parked behind the stage. The stage-left door was locked but tumbled under the first probe of a Saul Lestz skeleton key.

Porter crept into the soundstage. Although more compact than anything he'd seen at Universal and, of course, MGM, it was nevertheless fully equipped. The overhead lights glowed from rickety catwalks, a small crew huddled in the darkness behind the light line and Porter, behind them all, quietly stepped up on a wooden crate to see the scene.

"Action!" cried a female voice. Records played of a crowd roaring and trumpets blasting, and Porter – not easily amazed – was wide-eyed at what he beheld.

The female appeared naked. She was apparently playing a Christian martyr, with cascading platinum blonde hair and only a boa of laurel draped around her body, languishing against a Roman pillar. She gasped and moaned, struggling vainly against her bonds, epically writhing before a splendidly painted backdrop of the "Games" of Ancient Rome. There was another trumpet fanfare, and emerging stage left came a gorilla – a man in a suit – ambling up to the woman, beating his chest. As the woman cast her eyes heavenward, Porter looked at her feline face and knew exactly who she was...Mademoiselle LaRue from *Cave Canem*!

Holy hell, he thought. *It's Luscious Custard*.

The gorilla's mouth actually stretched into a smile of lechery, and the martyr turned her face away, looked beyond the camera...and saw Porter Down.

"*CUT!*" she shrieked. "Who the *FUCK* is that?!"

The blonde viciously burst the bonds of her pillar. The gorilla retreated. One of the light operators swung the arc light around, shining it accusingly on Porter, balanced atop the crate.

Porter squinted, then tipped his cap. "Hi ya', folks," he said.

*

Less than a minute later, the lights were on and the company was packing up for the night. Porter's presence had been just one of the problems that had caused Annie Spry to wrap. It had, after all, become very late, and the cameraman was running low on film.

Nobody accosted Porter. He figured they likely thought him a sailor on the prowl, eager for a peek at a smoker-in-the-works, basically harmless, probably drunk. The exhausted crew ignored him as he moved toward Annie, who'd shouted for an assistant to bring her shoes and kimono. She stood on a raised platform, the camera on the stage floor having shot upward, as if to create an exalted vision. This close, two things were evident to Porter: The woman was wearing a wig, as well as a body stocking, complete with red rosy nipples and a small nest of platinum blonde pubic hair.

Annie, standing, impatiently squeezed on her black heels as Porter approached her. His face was about at the level of her hips.

"May I have your autograph, Miss Spry?" asked Porter.

"No," she said. "And you mayn't sniff my quiff, either."

Annie Spry grabbed the kimono, turned with a flourish, and imperiously hurried away. She dragged the kimono behind her as she vanished into a dark nether region behind the set.

*

Porter was about to pursue Annie Spry when a tall young man in wire rim glasses and a clean but inexpensive suit came up to him.

"I'm Joe Westbrook, production manager," he said somberly. "We're finished for the night, sir, so please leave the premises now."

Porter showed him his old P.I. license, figuring the man wouldn't check to see if it were still in effect. He didn't. Westbrook immediately took an envelope from his inside coat pocket. "If we're under investigation, everything's legit," he said, handing Porter the envelope. "These are the papers and the studio rental contract. And nobody here is underage."

Porter glanced at the contract. "Also," said Westbrook hastily, "what you saw tonight is not pornography. Cecil B. DeMille is preparing to film *The Sign of the Cross* at Paramount and Miss Spry is providing him concepts for the Coliseum scenes."

"She can't just tell DeMille about them?" asked Porter.

"Film is a visual medium," said Westbrook.

"You work for Saint Babycakes often?" asked Porter, handing back the contract.

Westbrook shrugged. "We take what we can get. Most of the crew here are layoffs from Paramount and RKO. I was an assistant production manager at Warners until their last round of cuts three months ago. Miss Spry's company and MGM might be the only two in-the-black studios operating in Hollywood tonight."

"Then why ain't I been paid?" The accented voice came from behind Porter, who turned to see the young actor playing the gorilla. The man, who appeared to be a Filipino, held his ape head at his side but otherwise was still in his pelts.

"I was not paid last night," said the actor. "And I don't leave tonight till I *do* get paid."

"Why hasn't this *artiste* been paid?" asked Porter.

"There have been...artistic differences between Miss Spry and Mr. Gemora," said Westbrook uncomfortably. "She's not satisfied with his performance."

Gemora looked at Porter. "She wants me to feel her up in her movie," he snorted. "Imagine a gorilla doing that."

"Or wanting to," said Porter.

"I get paid," said Gemora. "Tonight. *Pronto!*"

"I'll speak to Miss Spry about it," said Westbrook, but went in the opposite direction of where Spry had gone.

"She went that-a-way," said Porter to the "ape," pointing to the rear of the stage. "Come on, Cheetah. Let's get your dough."

As they went behind the stage, Porter noticed a burly, slovenly man with a broom, sweeping the floor. He looked familiar, and then Porter realized why...

Balthazar.

Annie must have cast this janitor in *Cave Canem!* because he was dog-faced, or maybe he was the only guy willing to take the job. The man seemed tired, bored, and sullen. Porter decided against asking him for an autograph.

*

Charlie Gemora, with gorilla body and human head, strolled with his new pal Porter behind the painted canvas Coliseum backdrop, following a long, dark corridor that led to an exit. Outside the soundstage, about 20 yards from the stage door, was a small building that once had probably been a storage facility or garage. Light glowed dimly through a small window above the door. They assumed this served as the star dressing room bungalow of Annie Spry.

The door was locked. Porter knocked. No answer. "Do you think she's already gone?" asked Gemora.

"No," said Porter. "She's in there. I can feel the magic."

Gemora sized up the door and loosened up his right arm in his gorilla suit, packed with metal pieces and armatures. Suddenly a dog barked behind the door. It sounded like a big dog.

"Are you afraid of dogs?" asked Gemora.

"I'm not even afraid of gorillas," said Porter. "Go ahead."

Gemora powerfully swung, smacking the door right off its handles so it crashed into the room. The two men stepped through the shattered doorway one behind the other, Gemora first.

"Helen ... *GO!*"

At Annie Spry's scream, a huge black Doberman suddenly leaped, lunging for the throat of the nearest man, Gemora. He instinctively raised his costume arm to protect himself and the dog viciously sank its teeth into it, ripping through the thick pelt, biting at the metal pieces. The man shrieked in terror and Porter pulled his pistol, aiming at the shadow by the back door.

"Call it off!" shouted Porter over the growling. "Or I'll shoot you *and* the dog."

The shadow hesitated only a moment. "Helen, *come!*" it said, and the dog immediately ceased its attack, returning to its mistress, sitting obediently beside the shadow.

"You alright?" Porter asked Gemora.

"It tore through my suit," said the man, staring at the ripped arm, dazed by the attack.

"Pay this man his money," said Porter to the shadow by the door.

Annie Spry slowly came from the darkness, the light from the exposed overhead bulb falling on her face and its strange, challenging grin. She stood staring at them, her platinum wig on her vanity table, a stocking cap over her own hair, her full-length red silk kimono sashed at the waist, her hands on her hips. Although recognizable from *Cave Canem!* and her Christian martyr portrayal, she also looked oddly, totally different, and Porter remembered what "Jeanie" had said at the whorehouse:

A cat-faced hag...

Annie's face was indeed fiercely feline, and all the starker due to the stocking cap. The "hag" was more accurate as to her grin than her features, and her makeup, effective under the klieg lights, was grotesquely heavy here. There also was an austerity in her face, like that of a strict and foreboding schoolteacher. "Jeanie" had referred to Annie as "old," and she was – in "Jeanie's" eyes. Porter guessed she was at least 40.

Her eyes flashed as if she were enjoying the standoff. Porter again brandished his pistol. "One last time," he ordered, "pay this man."

Annie sighed, opened a drawer of her vanity, removed an envelope and started counting out cash. Meanwhile, Porter noticed a strangely familiar smell. He turned and saw Annie's body stocking, hanging on a hook behind him. It reeked of sweat and perfume. He noticed the clammy stocking was designed with both tight rubber and sculpted padding in the appropriate areas, and its nipples were perky.

When wouldn't they be? thought Porter.

Annie handed the wad of money at arm's length to Gemora, who took it and counted it himself. "You will also pay me for this damage," he said, indicating the torn costume. She handed him several more bills and then he was gone. Annie, still standing, looked at Porter, who lowered his pistol.

"What do you want?" she asked.

"I'm here," he said, "regarding a screen test you dropped off at Paul Bern's house."

Annie's face morphed into a smile worthy of her Christian martyr, now beatified. "Oh, well, how do you *do*!" she said, elegantly extending her hand. "I'm Annie Spry."

"I'm Porter Down." He didn't take her hand.

"So sorry," said Spry. "When I first saw you out there, I thought you were just a sailor boy. Silly me." She sat at the vanity, with its illuminated makeup mirror, showing and crossing her bare legs. "Would you care for a cigarette?"

"Nah," said Porter, looking at the packet. It was Fatimas.

"Would you care for a drink?"

"Nope," said Porter, noticing the high-necked bottle on the vanity. It was from Olive's.

Annie lit a cigarette and filled a shot glass from the bottle. "So," she grinned. "You represent the celebrated Mr. Bern."

"I do." He glanced from Annie to the dog, panting in the shadows, its eyes flashing back and forth from him to Annie.

Cat-faced Annie dragged on her cigarette. "I'll be delighted to talk with you," she said, blowing out a jet of smoke, "but not tonight. I'm all-in. Maybe tomorrow evening?"

"How about tomorrow morning?"

"I look my best at night," she flirted.

"Then I'd hate to see you tomorrow morning," said Porter.

Annie sipped her drink. "Tomorrow night... say midnight? I'll look nice for you."

Porter remembered he had the *Red-Headed Woman* preview early tomorrow night. He also recalled what "Jeanie" at the cathouse had said about Annie: *Her face... they say she only comes out at night now...*

"OK, late tomorrow night," said Porter. "The stroke of twelve. Where?"

Annie took a pen and pad, jotting down an address. Porter noticed she was left-handed. She tore off the piece of paper, stood and held it toward him, so he'd have to come to her to get it. As he moved toward her, the Doberman growled, but ceased when Annie made a "kiss-kiss" sound in the dog's direction.

"There you are, Sailor Boy," said Annie. "Come in a pumpkin coach and bring me a glass slipper."

For a moment, Porter hesitated taking the paper. Her sudden transformation – from a screaming, dog-siccing Hyde to a flirty, cockteasing Jekyll – was so sudden and so freaky that it spooked him. She seemed damned jolly and oddly victorious, as if she'd long-looked forward to this night and to meeting an emissary from Paul Bern. Porter immediately suspected her game, of course – blackmail.

Their fingers touched as he took the piece of paper. He looked her in the eye, and remembered how she'd looked in *Cave Canem!* screaming in horror, her face dripping with prop blood.

"Good night," said Porter. "To you and your hellhound."

Annie still wore her grin of triumph. Porter turned to go. Again, he noticed the smell. He regarded the body stocking, tickled a rubber nipple, and looked at Annie.

"Don't feel bad," said Porter. "Sarah Bernhardt had a wooden leg. Sweet dreams."

"Nighty-night," grinned Annie.

*

As Porter made his moonlit after-midnight ride up the coast, he realized he'd been on the move with no sleep the previous night. It had been a marathon stretch, but he'd learned a lot.

He thought of Harlow, how gorgeous she was, yet so intimidated by that toothy fool of a mama and that jackass Mafia-wannabe stepfather. For a moment, he could swear he still smelled her perfume...Mitsouko, she'd called it.

He thought about Paul Bern, his charm, his duplicity, his fairy tale house in Goddamned Benedict Canyon...his pornography. He'd have to confront Bern about it... maybe before the *Red-Headed Woman* preview tomorrow night. If not, as soon as possible afterwards.

And he thought of Annie Spry. Her bloody face in *Cave Canem!*... her eerie grin in the dressing room. Learning he was Bern's man, Annie had almost preened – yeah, like a cat – but her face also reminded him of some other animal. Maybe a vulture...eyeing him as if he, Bern, and maybe Harlow were delectable dead meat, all laid out for her succulent dining pleasure.

Annie...the real *sex vulture*, thought Porter.

Blackmail, sure...but what the hell *else* might she be up to? He took a deep breath and smelled the salty ocean, but in his growing fatigue, he could swear he still smelled Harlow...her scent. Then Porter thought again of Annie, and her rank body stocking, and it suddenly hit him.

Harlow and Annie wore the same perfume...Mitsouko.

Chapter Twelve
The Ambassador Hotel

Friday, June 17, 1932

The Ambassador Hotel, 3400 Wilshire Boulevard, was where MGM had originally offered to base Porter Down. It was posh and luxurious, the highest profile hotel in L.A. Among its amenities were the Coconut Grove nightclub and the Fiesta Room, the latter already booked to host the Academy Awards ceremony in November. Across the street was the Brown Derby, actually built like a derby, with its famous "Eat in the Hat" sign.

The telegram had been awaiting Porter when he'd arrived back at the marina last night. *Lunch tomorrow Ambassador Hotel Noon Zwillman.*

Porter had figured Zwillman was in New Jersey. He wasn't surprised, however, to learn that "Longie" was wise to his investigation...and was in L.A. to look into things personally.

*

An Ambassador valet parked Porter's Ford and the P.I., dressed in his sailor suit, sauntered into the lobby, filled with elegantly dressed guests from all over the world promenading about on this late morning. Porter rode the elevator up to the penthouse.

*

It was his impressive 6'2" height that had officially won Abner Zwillman the nickname of "Longie," although some claimed a different inspiration for it. Another *sobriquet* was "the Al Capone of New Jersey." Like "Scarface Al," "Longie" was young – only 27 – having started a numbers racket in his teens. Also, like Capone, Zwillman saw himself as a folk hero. It was Zwillman who'd offered major assistance and a giant reward for the rescue of the Lindbergh baby, whose kidnapping in March of '32 had shocked the world, and whose body had been found May 12.

Porter personally knew the "heroic" side of Longie Zwillman. After learning of Porter's wife's brutal murder, Longie – an antagonist of

Porter, who nevertheless admired his courage – had fed Porter leads to the assassin, who worked undercover for a Chicago mobster Zwillman despised. The widower made the final discoveries, taking revenge on his own, but thereafter had respect for "Longie" while having no illusions about his character. Zwillman remained one of the most dangerous, intelligent, and wealthy mobsters in the world. He had a tributary of bootleg liquor from Canada and other gambling, racketeering and prostitution interests.

It was hardly hyperbole to call Longie Zwillman an underworld king. Jean Harlow could have reigned as his queen.

*

"Well, Porter! It's fine to see you again!"

The greeter at Zwillman's suite was Nick Kirk, Longie's majordomo and personal bodyguard. Nick was a towering, broad-shouldered, Perth Amboy guy who looked like he could have been both a football and basketball star. He dressed impeccably in expensive suits and had the gentleman touch Longie wanted in his operation, even though the story went that Nick could – and on several occasions had – snapped a man's spine.

"Been a while since those nights back east, hasn't it?" smiled Nick, powerfully pumping Porter's hand.

Porter grinned, noticing Nick's two physical idiosyncrasies: He had the most epically broken nose Porter had ever seen, and he wore a toupee that looked like a black, parted-on-the- side roof shingle. You could tease Nick about his nose but not his toupee. Porter wondered why Nick, on the money Longie was surely paying him, didn't spring for a better rug, but Nick seemed to think this one looked dandy and never went without it. Porter imagined Nick put on his toupee if he got up in the middle of the night to take a piss.

Sensitive, spine-snapping Nick, thought Porter as he followed him into the suite.

You could have driven a truck through the enormously spacious penthouse. Nick led Porter through the living room where there were three glamorous women, including a blonde – but not platinum blonde – who was reading *Vanity Fair*. She peeked at Porter above the cover. There were balcony views, including from the dining room. There stood the host, awaiting his guest.

"Ha! I knew you'd be early," chuckled Abner "Longie" Zwillman, adorned in a handmade brown suit. He shook Porter's hand. "Porter Down, always 15 minutes early. So, I had the lobsters *timed* 15 minutes early. How about *that*?"

Zwillman was a handsome man in a coarse, large-featured way – big eyes, nose, mouth, shoulders, even ear lobes. He was well groomed with full, slickly oiled brown hair and a direct, no-nonsense look; in a movie, he might have played a tough, sympathetic prosecutor.

"I'll let you two catch up on news," said Nick. "Great to see ya,' Porter."

"You too, Nick."

"Hell of a guy," said Zwillman, indicating Nick as he walked away.

The formal waiter appeared, pulling back the chairs for each man. The lobsters on the two plates were among the biggest Porter had ever seen, at least three pounds in size with a giant baked potato and a vat of melted butter.

"I got the coldest Coca-Cola and beer in L.A. to go with them," boasted Zwillman.

An ice bucket held three bottles of Coca-Cola. The waiter poured Porter's Coke and Longie's beer, then tied a lobster bib around Porter's neck, and then Zwillman's.

"You won't want butter on that ten-year-old sailor suit," said Zwillman.

"Thanks," said Porter, sporting his bib.

"Can I do anything more for you now, gentlemen?" asked the waiter.

"No, thank you," said Zwillman. The waiter bowed and retreated out of sight.

"I know a good 'Jew boy' isn't supposed to eat lobster, but I'm not always a good 'Jew boy,'" Zwillman said as he diligently attacked his lobster with the tiny fork and tools. Porter knew Longie's act – he tried hard to appear the gentleman and eschew the gangster image. It usually didn't last long. Zwillman looked at Porter.

"You know what?" said Longie. "Fuck the fork."

"Congratulations, Longie," said Porter. "I was here a full minute before you said 'fuck.'"

"Yeah? Well, fuck it," Longie laughed. "Let's pull these monsters apart and eat 'em with our bare hands." He demonstrated, ripping the tail off the lobster shell, dunking it in butter, taking a huge bite and chasing it down with a swig of beer. Porter ate likewise.

"The guy who sells me lobsters has a motto," said Longie chewing heartily. "It goes, 'The seafood that you eat today, slept last night in the Avalon Bay.'"

"Catchy," said Porter.

Longie stabbed his baked potato. "Are the potatoes you grow this big?" he asked.

"I'll know when I dig 'em up next month," said Porter.

"You surprised I know about your place in the desert?" asked Longie.

"No," said Porter.

"You forget how to have a conversation with a pal?" asked Longie.

"No," said Porter.

"You tryin' to piss me off with one-word answers?" said Longie.

"No," said Porter.

"You want me to throw my fuckin' potato at you?" asked Longie.

Porter chuckled. "You were born too late, Longie. You should have been a pirate."

"Look who's talkin'," said Zwillman.

"Yep," said Porter. "I can see us two swordfightin' over pieces of eight."

"Yeah," said Zwillman. "Except now we're gonna' fight over one piece of ass."

"You get right to the point, don't ya,' Longie?"

"Goddamn yes." Zwillman chomped heartily and looked intently at Porter. "You still wear that charm around your neck? That St. George and the Dragon?"

Porter opened a button and pulled the amulet out so Zwillman could see it. "Ever since the War, right?" asked Zwillman. "Well, I wear an amulet now too. A locket, actually." He impatiently tore off his bib, opened his collar and pulled out a solid gold locket, holding it in a buttery hand. He popped the clasp. Under a crystal covering, like a relic, was a strand of platinum blonde hair.

"And it ain't off her head," said Zwillman.

"You're bullshittin' me, Longie. I'm guessin' you got that hair off some wanna-be Harlow chorus girl…or a white rat."

"Fuck you. By the way, I hear you met Harlow yesterday."

"Your spies tell you?"

"No. *She* did."

Porter finished chewing. "She told me you two don't talk anymore."

"She lies, like most broads. We don't fuck anymore, but we do talk." Zwillman swigged some beer. "And I call her. She doesn't call me."

"You mind closin' the locket?" asked Porter. "It's distracting while I eat."

"Fuck you," growled Zwillman, but he closed the locket.

"You keepin' tabs on Harlow? Looking out for her welfare? Sorry, Longie. I know you wanna be the good guy knight in shining armor here, but…"

"But what?" demanded Zwillman.

"But I don't think they make codpieces that big."

Zwillman gradually smiled, then shook with laughter. "You're a funny son of a bitch, Porter, you know that?" He calmed and concentrated a moment or two on his food. "You and me got a history," said Zwillman quietly, trying the gentleman act again, but mixed with genuine sincerity. "I respect you and you know it. If I didn't like you…"

"Yeah," said Porter. "Instead of feedin' me lobsters, you'd be feedin' me *to* the lobsters."

"I liked the codpiece joke better. No, I respect you. So…get off this case."

"Why?"

"Because I'm already on it."

"Maybe MGM doesn't want you on it. Maybe they're uneasy with the mob."

Zwillman laughed, spraying bits of lobster and a shower of butter. "Longie," suggested Porter, "maybe you oughta' put your bib back on."

"Fuck the bib. Porter – you remember Frank Orsatti? One of Capone's guys. A pimp, a bootlegger and a douche bag. Well, he's now the big shot agent at MGM. Two years ago, Frank beat a major rap. And you know who pulled the strings to get him off? Louis B. Mayer!" Zwillman chewed and chortled. "Hollywood's a jungle shithole. Harlow needs somebody who knows the jungle shithole."

"And Paul Bern," said Porter, dropping the big name, "doesn't know the jungle?"

Zwillman stiffened. "As for your friend Mr. Bern…You know my pal, Johnny Rosselli?"

"Yeah," said Porter. "And I'm disappointed you consider that sleaze ball your pal."

"You're breaking my heart. Johnny does the investigation like nobody does the investigation – except you, my friend. And you know what he learned?" Zwillman sat back and actually stopped chewing before continuing. "Bern's a pansy. The worst kind of pansy…the kind of fuckin' phony pansy who likes having pretty gals around him all the time."

"Rosselli give you names? If so, give me one."

"Yeah, I'll give you one – Barbara La Marr! She turned down Bern's marriage proposal. Ya' know why? She told somebody… the little freak is sexually deformed!"

"La Marr's been dead for six years," said Porter. "If she's talkin,' she's yellin' through the wall of her crypt."

"What the hell's the matter with you? Nobody's word good enough for you anymore? You know what they're tellin' Rosselli? Paul Bern is… a *hermaphrodite!*"

Zwillman, spat out the word with relish, even if he placed the accent on the first syllable and ended the word with a long *e*. "Longie," said Porter, "before you call somebody a hermaphrodite, learn how to pronounce it."

"You think I want that freak touchin' Harlow?"

"That's her decision."

"What the fuck are you takin' up for *him* for?" roared Zwillman. "He hurts her in any way, and I swear by Jesus Christ Almighty, I'll hang his hermaphrodite body off the MGM water tower! The HOLLYWOODLAND sign!"

Zwillman was so furious he swept his lobster and beer crashing to the floor. He stood. "What in the *hell* is the matter with you, Down? You suddenly a 'gentleman' since they took away your investigator's license after that manslaughter charge? You think I don't know all about that?"

Porter waited for the storm to calm. Zwillman kicked spasmodically at the wreckage of china, crystal, and crustacean that had fallen near his feet. He sat down in disgust.

"I'm telling you two things, Longie," said Porter, aware he couldn't let Zwillman know about the startlingly cruel pornography he'd found at Bern's house. "Yeah, I did a lot of digging before I clocked in at MGM. I heard the same stories Rosselli did. And not one of them proved to me Paul Bern ever had sex with anybody, male or female, in his life."

"See what I mean? He's hiding it! He's a hermaph…"

"Maybe. Or maybe he's impotent. Or deformed. Or a hermaphrodite. Or maybe he's an impotent, deformed hermaphrodite."

"Now you're talkin' sense."

"No, Longie. The sense is this; if Harlow's happy with him, that's all that matters. Have you talked this over with Harlow?"

"Yeah. I told her what Johnny found out. And you know what she said?" Zwillman shook his head in sad amazement. "She said… it didn't matter."

"Maybe," said Porter, "Harlow's just tired of guys clawin' and pawin' after her."

"She can't help it," said Zwillman defensively. "Hell, you saw how gorgeous she is. Everybody wants to get in her pants…except she doesn't wear any pants…"

"So I've heard."

"She's had a lot of lovers, but they're nothin' to all the ones she has to fight off."

"Yeah," said Porter. "It's a different relationship than what you and she had, Longie. My bet's that Bern's not wearing any locket.

But if it's the life she wants, and the husband she needs …well, what the hell can you do? Just respect her right to have it."

Zwillman shook his head again. His voice was hoarse now.

"I didn't mean what I said a while back, Porter. Like I said, I respect you. I respect the way you work. I always did. I especially did after what happened…to your wife. I know you went nuts for a time and you got that bastard. I respect the way you came out of it. I'd have never come out of it. And I respect the way you got off the booze."

Porter was silent. He wiped his mouth with his napkin. "I'll step aside," said Longie resignedly. "I'll call off Rosselli. If you need my help in any way, call me. But if Bern hurts her…in any freaky, Goddamn way…all promises are off."

"By the way," said Porter, "Harlow's stepfather, Marino Bello, claims he's got connections."

Zwillman snorted. "That pop-eyed spaghetti-bender's a joke. Yeah, he's got connections – with the bottom of the barrel crowd. I wouldn't give Bello the skin off a grape and he knows it. He tells everybody that he introduced me to Harlow. That's bullshit. He introduced Harlow to Capone and Capone introduced Harlow to me. Bello's another one – if he ever hurts her…"

The two men were silent. Porter looked at Zwillman, covered in shell, butter, and splashed beer. "Longie… you're a hell of a mess."

Zwillman had to laugh. "Looks like you got two pounds of uncracked lobster left," he said. "I'll have the waiter wrap it up. You take it with you."

He pushed himself away from the table and motioned Porter to follow him to the balcony. Porter stood beside him and they looked out at L.A. from its most continental hotel. Below in the hotel gardens a few young, elegantly dressed women were strolling and talking. Zwillman noticed them, watched them awhile, and chortled.

"Have you heard the joke, Porter – why do women wear makeup and perfume?"

"Yeah," said Porter. "Because they're ugly and they stink."

"You *have* heard it," said Longie. He ruefully looked out again at the city. "You know," he said, "Capone used to say there was a lot of good in some folks' lives because of him. There's a lot of good in Harlow's life because of me. I made great deals for her when she was on contract to that screwball Howard Hughes. But we were right. A movie star can't marry a guy like me."

"She's grateful," said Porter.

"Yeah, she oughta be," said Longie Zwillman. "And you know why, Porter? Because – along with everything else – I gave her what's likely gonna' be the best Goddamn fuck of her life."

Spoken like a man named Longie, thought Porter Down.

Chapter Thirteen
The Fox Theatre

Friday, June 17, 1932

At 7:30 P.M. this Friday night, the marquee of the Fox Theatre in Pomona read:

MAJOR HOLLYWOOD SNEAK PREVIEW TONIGHT!
ADULTS ONLY!

Having returned to the marina that afternoon after his lunch with Longie, Porter discovered that MGM had delivered the first of his three custom-made suits. It was navy blue with a white shirt, blue-striped tie, a white snap-brimmed hat, and black shoes. He decided to wear his new ensemble to the premiere that night.

I'll look like a movie-star myself, thought Porter

He watched the long line at the box office. Howard Strickling was there, naturally, with members of his publicity department, and gave Porter his pass. The theatre was filled to capacity.

At 7:50, Strickling, his stutter under control, took to the stage and announced this was indeed "a major preview." As such, no one else would be admitted and once the film began, no one allowed to leave. The crowd called out "What is it?" and "Who's in it?" but Strickling just grinned – a mix of choirboy smile and snake oil peddler charm.

7:59. The Fox manager came down from the booth and made a quick inspection. At precisely 8 P.M., the houselights dimmed, the excited audience applauded, and a newsreel began. Only seconds later, two limousines glided in front of the theatre. A black chauffeur/bodyguard in uniform held the door and Jean Harlow and Paul Bern ran inside, laughing like adolescents. Bern was in a long dark coat despite the summer night. Harlow wore a pretty but rather simple beige frock, a beige hat with a brown hatband, and white and brown spectator pumps. She looked fresh and very young rather than glamorous.

"Porter!" said Bern, and he came to him and shook his hand. Harlow hugged Porter and kissed his cheek. Once again, he smelled the Mitsouko.

"I'm terrified," she whispered, looking into Porter's eyes as if that were a confidence.

Three people from the second limo followed them into the lobby, escorted by another chauffeur/bodyguard. "Come," said Bern, ushering Porter over to the trio in the lobby. "Let me introduce you. Porter Down, may I present Miss Norma Shearer."

Porter was surprised Bern hadn't used the "Patrick Killarney" tag – but then again, these people knew who he really was and why he actually was there. Norma Shearer, MGM's "American Beauty Rose" and winner of the Academy Award for 1930's *The Divorcee*, was tiny but compelling, strangely glamorous. She seemed to Porter to be squinting to hide the cast in her eye, and laughed charmingly as she shook his hand. "So very nice to know you," said Shearer.

An actress all the way, thought Porter.

"This," said Bern, "is Anita Loos, who wrote the script for *Red-Headed Woman*."

Porter recognized the name – she'd also written the novel *Gentlemen Prefer Blondes*. Loos also was small, attractive, and wrapped up this warm June night in what looked like a raccoon coat. "Hello there," said Loos, flirtatiously.

"And this, of course," said Bern, "is my very good friend, Mr. Irving Thalberg."

Porter had seen MGM's "Boy Wonder" only in quick sightings as the man rushed to and from various Metro triumphs and crises. Like Bern, he wore a long dark coat despite the summer night. Thalberg's face was lean and handsome, his eyes bright, and there was both a princely power and fragility about him as he shook Porter's hand. "Good evening," said Thalberg.

The chauffeurs went outside and the Thalbergs, Loos, Bern, and Harlow stood there, a quintet of Hollywood aristocracy. They all were small in stature but their presence, Porter had to admit, filled the lobby.

Porter bet himself none of the five would buy popcorn. He won his bet.

*

The back row was empty, secretly reserved for the celebrities. Porter sat on the aisle seat, next to Loos. Bern and Harlow were on the other side of the Thalbergs. Leo the Lion roared on screen and Porter wondered about Harlow's nerves, especially after a racy cheer sounded as her name and the wildly publicized title filled the screen.

Red-Headed Woman, scripted by Loos and based on a novel by Katharine Brush, was the sex saga of Lil Andrews who, as *Time* magazine expressed it, "cooed and screwed" her way up in the world. The novel's novelty was that Lil's carnality went unpunished, and MGM retained this twist in the film. Garbo's vamps – roles she had described (while still perfecting her English) as "bad womens" – usually received censor-thrilling comeuppances. Now, "Going All Out for Sex in 1932," MGM was telling Depression America that, yes indeed, adultery can pay.

The audience applauded Harlow's first close-up; a towel removed from her hair. She wore a red wig, but the studio had publicized it as a temporary dye job. "So 'gentlemen prefer blondes,' do they?" she smiled, and Porter realized Miss Loos, grinning smugly beside him, had plugged her famous book in the film's first line. Hollywood was jam-packed with self-homage.

"Yes, they do!" purred Harlow, concluding her opening line. The crowd loved it.

The "Baby" had a baby face and looked incongruous in her red wig, Porter thought, even in black-and-white. Harlow's Lil Andrews was sexy as hell as she sashayed through the movie, shamelessly seducing her boss (played sympathetically by Chester Morris). In one episode, Porter suspected Bern's direct input – Morris slapped Harlow, and she responded joyfully.

"Do it again!" gasped Harlow. "I like it!" So did the crowd. They cheered again.

As the film proceeded, it dawned on Porter why Harlow was pulling this off – it was the same basic decency he'd responded to when he'd first met her. Lil Andrews, as played by Joan Crawford or (God forbid) Garbo, would have been horrific. Harlow was adorably sexy in her fishnets and red wig but, in a strange, contradictory twist, her Lil was a make-believe hoot – and as lethal as the Easter Bunny.

Also, this was a different Harlow than Porter had seen in *Hell's Angels*. She had timing, credibility, and star power. Maybe, thought Porter, Paul Bern was a magician.

*

As THE END flashed on the screen, the audience applauded lustily. The manager rushed the half-dozen denizens of the last row out into the lobby. He stationed ushers to guard the doors to prevent anyone seeing the film's star in the lobby and causing a riot. Strickling was on the stage, solemnly impressing upon everyone the critical necessity of staying seated and filling out completely his or her preview card. Porter stood apart from the little band in the lobby. They were hugging and congratulating Harlow, who was expressing her joy in a strange way.

"It really wasn't me up there," she kept saying. "It was Jean Harlow, so I didn't mind it."

She looked at Porter and walked directly to him. Before he could say "Congratulations," she kissed him on the mouth. "Thank you for coming tonight," she sighed.

The limos were waiting. Bern, who'd watched the kiss, rather brusquely whisked Harlow away from Porter and out the door. The Thalbergs and Anita Loos followed, as did Porter. "I need a drink!" he heard Harlow laugh as the black, broadly smiling uniformed chauffeur opened the car door for her. She smiled at least as broadly at him as she ducked into the limousine.

"Good night to one and all!" said Bern, and he joined his fiancée in the back seat. Thalberg watched the car drift a few yards down the block, allowing his limo to pick up its passengers precisely where they stood, before offering his own candid judgment.

"You know," said the "Boy Wonder," looking at the limo of Bern and Harlow, "that girl's so bad she just might be good."

Shearer smiled and Loos laughed. Then everyone saw the same sight. Through the rear window of the first limousine, one could see Paul Bern and Jean Harlow, spotlighted by the headlights of the Thalberg limo, passionately kissing.

Everyone was silent as if seeing something shameful and disturbing. It was Anita Loos who finally spoke.

"I still can't believe she'll marry that German psycho," she said.

Chapter Fourteen
Room 625

Friday, June 17, 1932

The Plaza was a quiet but world-class hotel, overlooking Union Square in San Francisco. It had seven stories, a European-décor, and a management that prided itself on the privacy and discretion it afforded its guests and long-time residents.

The violent storm that had struck Los Angeles Wednesday night had moved up the coast. A bellboy, dressed in the red and black uniform of the Plaza's staff, rode the elevator to the sixth floor. He carried a rolled copy of the *San Francisco Examiner*, bagged due to the rain. The late edition promptly hit the streets at 9:45 P.M. The bellboy was delivering the copy to Room 625 at precisely 10:00 P.M., as the occupant demanded.

The bellboy had never seen the woman in 625, nor had any of the other bellboys who performed this nightly task. She never answered the door. Her strict instructions were to place the paper on the floor by the door, knock, and leave. The manager was most definite on these points, as communicated by the guest, and the bellboy carried out this duty exactly as directed.

After the bellboy left and departed on the elevator, there was silence. Then a faint sound came from inside the door, the sound of several locks being unlocked. A moment passed, the door opened only a sliver, and then a hand jutted from behind the door, a small, dainty hand with pale nail polish and long fingers. The fingers clutched the paper, snaring it back into the room, and the door promptly shut.

There was the sound of locks put in place, and then silence.

*

The only light was a small antique lamp by the chair and sofa. On the Victrola a record played of Tchaikovsky's orchestral work, *Romeo and Juliet*.

The woman had let her reddish blonde hair down for the night. She was petite, and wore a pale negligee and a pair of pink slippers. She took the newspaper to the kitchen, for the bag was still wet, the bellboy having failed to dry it properly. Tomorrow she'd telephone the front desk and register her complaint.

She dried the paper thoroughly and returned to the living room. She pulled back a corner of her closed curtain and looked at the storm over Union Square, the theatre district, and Chinatown. The thunder was loud, she winced at the lightning, and then she went to her sofa. The woman placed the Friday night paper in her lap, put on her reading glasses, and immediately turned to the Arts section, always augmented for the weekend editions. She quickly read down the news regarding new cinema productions, but didn't see what she hoped to find. Then she turned the page and saw an article titled "Upcoming Releases." A photograph dominated with this caption:

> *Chester Morris and Jean Harlow in* Red-Headed Woman, *which opens June 24th at Los Angeles' Loew's State Theatre.*

The photograph showed Harlow, sitting so her legs were in Morris's lap. She wore a red wig and fishnet stockings, with a garter visible.

The woman looked for a long time at the photo, the *Romeo and Juliet* love theme playing on the Victrola. Then she looked at a framed photograph on the desk beside her chair. It had been taken 12 years ago. She gazed at the image of her younger self, and then at the image of the diminutive man beside her...his small mouth, his deep, sad eyes, even when he was smiling. The love of her life...

For a moment she sat very still, staring at the framed photograph. Then she reached for a fountain pen on the desk, looked again at the newspaper photo, and with her dainty hand, crossed out one letter in Harlow's name. She added another, so the caption read:

Jean Harlot

Her oval face grinned, mischievously adding horns to Harlow's head, a goatee to her face, and then a long, pointed devil's tail. For a moment she admired her work, then suddenly sobbing, viciously stabbed the fountain pen point into the paper, ripping apart Harlow's image, plunging the pen again and again until she realized she had stabbed through the paper and her robe and had cut into her thigh.

She dropped the pen to the floor, watching her blood stain the torn and shredded paper scraps in her lap where the photo had been. The thunder was loud again, lightning flashed behind the curtains, and the woman looked at the eviscerated paper.

"Whore!" she said, crying. "Rotten, filthy whore!"

Romeo and Juliet's love theme climaxed on the Victrola, and the woman's sob sounded like the moan of an animal.

Chapter Fifteen
Castellammare

Friday, June 17 and Saturday, June 18, 1932

After the *Red-Headed Woman* preview, Porter had another appointment that Friday night...Annie Spry. He headed west, enjoying his MGM Ford. He also decided to get comfortable and removed his tie, opening the top buttons of his shirt. Some of his chest hair showed below his collar.

Cat-faced Annie will purr with pleasure, smirked Porter.

*

Castellammare was a colony of whitewashed stucco homes with red-tiled roofs, high above the west tail end of Sunset Boulevard, overlooking the Pacific. The area had never fully caught favor with the big money film crowd, possibly because of the steep hill that, in an earthquake, might have provided the houses a roller coaster plunge right down into the ocean.

It was 11:45 P.M. The moon was almost full. Porter drove near the crest of the hill and found the house, a miniature castle, hanging on the hillside. It had a baroque sense of style – a 30'-tall white tower at its center, a tall arched first floor window, and a large iron gate. It amused Porter that the star of *Red-Headed Woman* and the star/producer/director of *Cave Canem!* both had houses that looked like Tyrolean churches.

The precipitous setting meant Porter parked beneath the house. He started up the steps, continuing up the front of the tower to a second-floor balcony, which apparently offered the only entrance and exit. It was one hell of a lot of steps but at last he reached the balcony.

There on a table awaiting him, just as at Bern's, was a lit candle, a bottle of wine, and two crystal glasses. There was a cigarette case too, this one silver-plated. There was also a folder. Suddenly Porter heard loud, vicious barking and a large, black Doberman appeared behind the panes of the French door. *I'll be dammed!* thought Porter. *It's the same dog I saw in* Cave Canem.

A "Shh!" sound hissed inside, the barking stopped, and the French door opened.

"Good evening," said Annie Spry.

She was dressed in a pale blue negligee that looked silvery in the moonlight, sashed at the waist and fashioned of light, almost diaphanous silk. She looked willowy and wore blue high heels, her high cheek-boned face framed nicely by her ash-blonde hair, a lock of which fell over her left eye. The feline look was still there, but she appeared young, fresh and, Porter had to admit to himself, actually quite alluring. Her Mitsouko perfume was seductive in the breeze off the ocean.

"Well, well, Annie," said Porter, eyeing her negligee. "I'd have never guessed you were a vestal virgin."

"You look rather attractive yourself," said Annie.

"I do," said Porter.

"Please sit," said Annie. She sat too, poured a glass of wine, and offered it to him.

"No thanks," said Porter.

"Oh, yes," said Annie teasingly. "You *can't* drink. I mean...you *don't* drink."

Porter realized she'd learned about his alcoholism. Annie sipped the wine herself. "Incidentally," she said, "we've been together at least two minutes, and you haven't pulled out your cute little pistol and pointed it at me."

"And you haven't told me," said Porter, "that I mayn't sniff your quiff."

Annie had settled so the night shadow partly shrouded her face. Still, her eyes were bright and they laughed at Porter as she sipped her wine. She crossed her legs, and Porter heard her silk stockings swish against each other.

"You're looking at me very strangely, Mr. Down."

"When I was a kid," said Porter, "I had a fairy tale book. *Pinocchio* was in it. After seeing you as Mademoiselle Poppy and the naked Christian martyr, it's weird seeing you as the Blue Fairy."

"That's sweet. Maybe if you're nice, I'll turn your friend Mr. Bern into a real live boy." She sipped her wine. "I've been trying ever so hard for some time, you know."

"Personally?" asked Porter. "Or through your cinematic masterpieces like *Cave Canem?*"

"My films *are* personal," said Annie. "However, Mr. Bern is merely a client, fan, and admirer."

"No doubt you'll tell me," said Porter, "that Bern, as a 'fan and admirer,' has offered you an MGM contract, but that you're too much an *artiste* to accept."

"I know my craft, Mr. Down. As an actress, I have a range of talents. For example, I can imitate perfectly the sounds of a dozen different animals, plus various birds. It served me quite lucratively when I was a radio actress."

"Do you take requests?" asked Porter. "How about a trumpeting elephant?"

The large black dog was growling and glowering behind the panes of the French door. "Helen!" said Annie crisply, and the dog obediently retreated.

"Oh, yeah... Helen," Porter said. "Your canine co-star. Got a real gorilla in there too?"

"I fear you're not aware of the significance of what you saw the other night, Mr. Down. I'm creating that film for a very special personal client. His name is Cecil B. DeMille."

"Yeah, so I've heard," interrupted Porter. "So, C.B.'s a fan of yours?"

She took a sip of wine, reached into the folder on the table and removed a check. It had DeMille's name and Laughlin Park address stamped in the corner and his bold, flamboyant signature on the payee line.

"Are you set to recreate your Christian martyr for DeMille?" asked Porter.

"Maybe," said Annie.

"Like hell," said Porter. "Ten to one he hires the gorilla but not you."

"I have my compensations," said Annie.

"Like screen credit?" asked Porter. "'Advisor on sick and depraved Coliseum scenes – Annie Spry'?"

"No," said Annie, refilling her glass. "But I do have a library of my work that circulates...world-wide."

"So I've heard. Classics like *Luscious Custard, Her Fall and Rise*."

"I'm so happy that title tantalizes you, Mr. Down. *Luscious Custard* is a very popular entry internationally. I probably earned more last month via rentals of that single film than your little Miss Harlow has received since joining MGM."

"But she works for a real studio. In real movies."

"Yes. Wearing a red wig and fishnets. She's so above me. Cigarette?"

"I don't smoke."

Annie laughed faintly, as if what he'd said was funny, opened the case and lit a cigarette. Porter noted again the brand – Fatimas. The smell of the cigarette mixed in the night air with the Mitsouko.

"Well," said Porter, easing toward the Paul Bern topic. "I kinda' doubt MGM is planning to make any movies this year with a raping gorilla."

"Oh, they already have," said Annie. "Did you miss my contribution to *Tarzan the Ape Man*? The pygmies placed Jane in a pit with a huge gorilla that was about to rape her. He was a hybrid, actually – had teeth like a crocodile. That was my idea, too. Anyway, Tarzan saved Jane."

Annie blew a smoke ring.

"I've had a nice run recently with gorillas. I must say my pride and joy is Marlene Dietrich's upcoming film, *Blonde Venus*. She'll perform a musical number titled 'Hot Voodoo' while dressed as a gorilla. Marlene adores the concept."

"I bet she does," said Porter.

"Paramount starts shooting next month," said Annie. "And, also for Paramount...the studio is in the early stages of blueprinting a version of H.G. Wells' *The Island of Dr Moreau*. I'm working with them developing a concept not in Wells' novel...a 'Panther Woman'...a female created by Dr. Moreau from a panther."

"Bet you've got your eye on that role for yourself," said Porter.

"I believe I'd do it justice," winked Annie.

She smiled...then suddenly screamed wildly like a panther. It was shrill, piercing, and so completely unexpected that Porter jumped. The dog inside bellowed and Annie's eyes crinkled as she laughed.

"You look startled, Mr. Down," purred Annie. "And rather uncomfortable. Did you just piss your pants?"

She's nuts, thought Porter, but for now concealed his apprehension. She'd clearly enjoyed unleashing her freaky yowl, but now her face darkened. "Paramount has a totally asinine idea of having a Panther Woman Contest, and selecting some fucking starlet-wanna-be for the role...some provincial teenage ninny who couldn't begin to understand..."

She cut herself off. Porter, having just had a peek into Annie Spry's insecurities, stared at her in silence. The night was still. The surf pounded at the beach.

*

"So," asked Porter finally. "When do you make a sequel to *Cave Canem?*"

"*Cave Canem! Te Necet Lingendo*," said Annie, "is actually an evocation of what's called zoomimic masochism, Mr. Down. People debased, hurt, killed by animals. It has its disciples, many of them. We expect that film to be very popular too, especially in Berlin. Will there be a sequel? Maybe."

"I guess you go to MGM movies," said Porter, "to coo at the sight of Leo the Lion."

"Actually, Mr. Down," she snapped, "I'm unique in this town in a way you haven't realized. I'm a successful female producer and director. There's only one other female producer, Mary Pickford. There's only one other female director, Dorothy Arzner."

"Yeah? And you call what you produce a credit to your gender?"

"Look out at the moon over the Pacific, Mr. Down. This house and view speak for me. Can you truly argue with success...or giving the world public what it desires?"

"Tell me," said Porter. "How did a pretty pink-and-blue lass like you grow up to be Hollywood's bestiality queen?"

"Oh, I'm actually quite...ecumenical," said Annie. "I have various fascinations. We are what we are, Mr. Down. Sex is our biggest part…more than heart, mind or soul. Our sexual appetite *is* our soul, Mr. Down. It's what we feel most intensely, most powerfully. It defines *us*. We don't define *it*. If we did…if we *could*… your Mr. Bern would be a far happier man."

"Yeah," said Porter. "Maybe it's time I cut to the chase."

"I warn you," said Annie, smiling faintly. "'Hell hath no fury like a woman scorned.' And I think you and Mr. Bern are preparing to scorn me."

"And I think," said Porter, "you're about to show me another one of your autographs."

Annie slipped from the folder a check. There in the candlelight was Paul Bern's signature. The amount was $300 and marked, *Advisor's fee*.

"Could be a forgery," said Porter, realizing it was a feeble parry.

"If so, I have dozens of forgeries. Dating from 1928."

Helen was back at the door, whining strangely. Annie held up the commanding finger again, but this time she winked at the dog, and made "kiss-kiss" sounds. The dog became still.

Jesus, thought Porter.

"A man with Jean Harlow as a wife," he said, redirecting his thoughts, "won't be needing your services anymore."

"Maybe he will."

"Bern can claim it was all 'research,' just like DeMille can."

"This type of 'research' would have never passed the censors," said Annie.

"You've got DeMille, Dietrich, and your 'world-wide' fan club. You don't need Bern."

"Maybe my vanity does. So, if he decides to 'scorn' me, it'll cost him $75,000."

"One question," said Porter. "Intellectual to intellectual. Has it ever occurred to you that Bern has the protection of the most powerful film studio in the world? And that Harlow not only has MGM looking out for her, but also has a still-smitten ex-boyfriend who's one of the most powerful mobsters in America?"

"So?"

"So… have you imagined Bern and Harlow siccing one of their buddies from the playground to beat you up?"

"But they didn't, Mr. Down. They sicced *you*. A war hero...a man with *honor*." She laughed scornfully. "So much honor that he's on two years' probation for causing a woman's death. And as such, you can't dare risk causing as much as a tiny rip in a lady's silk stocking."

Annie sipped her wine, her eyes laughing at Porter. "See how much a girl can learn in a day?" she asked. "And be aware...I have protectors too. And their guns are so much bigger than yours."

"I seriously suggest," said Porter, "you forget all about blackmailing my client."

"And I seriously suggest," said Annie, "that you go fuck yourself."

They were silent. The moonlight now fell on Annie's face, which had been more attractive in the shadows. Porter noted the steel will in her eyes, but also an odd strain in her countenance. He saw her suddenly shiver almost convulsively in the night cold. He thought of what "Jeanie" at the whorehouse had said about Annie:

A cat-faced hag...they say she's got the rot...

The ocean wind rose, mixing with the scent of Mitsouko. Porter looked at Annie, her ferocity lit up by the moon, as if seeing her fully for the first time. The skin was very tight over her face and made Porter think of a skull. Her eyes glared.

"Well," said Porter, standing. "Thanks for a night I'll always remember as bewitching."

"I'm so sorry it had its tense moments," said Annie, composing herself, also standing. "At any rate, we understand each other now."

Porter looked at her, a faint grin on his face. There was a confidence about him that confused Annie and that she found instinctively threatening.

"I doubt we'll meet again," said Porter. "But I'll make you a promise. If you get the Panther Woman part in *Island of Lost Souls*, I'll go see it. If the Panther Woman has any provocative shots – rolling over for a belly rub, or whatever – I'll know it's the 'provincial ninny' winner of the Panther Woman Contest, serving as your double. *Adios*."

"Nighty-night," said Annie, controlling her temper. "Love and kisses."

Annie watched him go down the steps. She heard him start his car. After a few moments she was calm again, a bit drained by her anger, but relishing the battle to come. She refilled her wine glass, then let her dog onto the balcony. Helen nestled against Annie, who gently petted the dog's head.

"Do you want to look at the moon with me, darling Helen?" she asked softly.

Chapter Sixteen
The Cove

Saturday, June 18, 1932

There was an area Porter knew north of Malibu and Luke's marina, a cove where the breakers were rough and swimmers rarely came. He drove there and parked on the beach. It was after 1:00 A.M. and nobody was there. Porter stripped off clothes, tossed them into the car and, in his shorts, dove into the cold waves. He swam furiously out into the breakers, desperate for the challenge. The waves pounded and he swam over them, under them, his powerful arms working as if fighting an enemy.

It was Saturday now. The fifth anniversary of Mary's murder was 10 days away.

He'd come home to their Chicago apartment that rainy night five years ago and found her on their bedroom floor, a needle beside her, her death staged by an assassin to look like suicide or accidental overdose. He could see it all again in his mind as he battled the waves in the moonlight and felt the sharp, driving night wind. He remembered her open eyes and the clothes she was wearing. He remembered the private funeral and the burial. He'd learned who his friends were and there'd been some surprise ones, such as Longie Zwillman, who'd been an enemy until a rival mob boss had ordered this unthinkably cruel and spiteful hit. It was revenge on an agent hailed a hero in the beer-and-blood wars, by a monster that knew Porter loved his wife more than life itself.

Most of all, Porter had learned about himself. He'd been surprised that he could actually enjoy killing someone – he never had in the war. He could still savor the sensations of having tracked down and killed both the man who'd murdered Mary and the man who'd ordered her death. He'd never fully recovered from her murder and had come west to escape the reminders, fading back into P.I. work, long a member of the walking dead, drinking himself into a stupor every June 28, finally pulling out of his nosedive only because he knew how sad she'd be to see his self-destruction.

As he swam far from the shore, he realized how easily he could lose control, as evidenced by his manslaughter charge last fall. He'd made a new life in Twentynine Palms but now here he was again, working for a movie star who gave strands of her pubic hair to a gangster, and a producer pervert who watched "zoomimic masochism" pornography...dealing with it all only days away from the hardest day and night of the year.

He plunged under the water again, finally succeeding in exhausting himself.

*

It was 4 A.M. by the time Porter returned to the marina.

Luke was asleep in *The Frederick* and Porter checked in the shack for a snack and a Coke. There were his remaining two MGM suits, shirts, ties, shoes, and haberdashery, obviously personally delivered by studio messenger earlier in the day. Yeah, Strickling was trying damn hard to impress him.

There were also two packages on the table, both addressed to him, also apparently delivered by MGM messenger. He sat aft on *The Phoebe*, took his penknife, and cut open the first package. It contained a very old copy of *Hamlet* with an engraved cover, presumably an antique and, he guessed, expensive. Inside was a business card – *The Dora Ingram Bookshop, Culver City*. The card had been placed on the page with the "Now I am alone" soliloquy and on the back of the card was handwriting:

Profound words, my friend. /Thanks for setting me straight and for being here for us/From a rogue and peasant slave/Paul.

Porter laid the book in his lap and opened the second package. It contained a rabbit's foot and a handwritten note:

This is for your poor bunny, Long John – but borrow it from him when we shoot craps – you'll need it. Love, from Me.

Porter realized Paul Bern and Jean Harlow had taken time on the day of a critical sneak preview to select these gifts, write these notes, and dispatch a deliverer to Malibu. He held the play script in one hand, the rabbit's foot in the other, and shook his head at both.

This was going to be one hell of a case.

Part Two
Dear Dorothy

Chapter Seventeen
One Morning

Saturday, June 18, 1932

Saturday was a working day in Hollywood. Many of the studios labored late into the night and past midnight into Sunday morning, resenting the Sabbath's traditional day of rest.

Early Saturday morning, Porter Down dressed in one of his three new suits, a brown, three-piece pinstripe that made him resemble, he thought, a Wild West gambler. He added a pair of brown shoes and a tan snap-brim hat, left Malibu and headed for MGM. He had to confront Bern about the pornography. He wished the hell he was back in Twentynine Palms. He'd had only three hours' sleep. It wouldn't be wise for anyone to trifle with him today.

*

He parked his Ford in the first available spot and marched to the Lion Building, a handsome, Spanish revival style structure that housed the offices of Mayer, Thalberg, and Bern. He carried the film can in a brown grocery bag. As he approached the door, it opened.

Out came Louis B. Mayer and Eddie Mannix.

Mayer, short, stocky, bespectacled, looked Porter in the eye. Mannix, standing behind Mayer's right shoulder with a black eye, glowered.

"Eddie," said Mayer, "stay here. I want to speak with Mr. Down a moment."

Mannix kept glaring. Mayer beckoned Porter and led him several yards away from the building. "Mr. Down, I'm a busy man, so are you, and I know you don't like me, so I'll come to the point."

He took a dramatic pause, staring into Porter's eyes. Porter stared back into Mayer's.

"Every empire that ever fell," said Mayer, "did so because of immorality. Ancient Rome, for example. The decay, Mr. Down, always comes from *within.* I'm sure we both understand that if Miss Harlow and Mr. Bern behave in an unacceptable way or associate with undesirable people...MGM's world-wide audience will stop attending our pictures."

"God forbid," said Porter.

"The victims hardest hit," continued Mayer, ignoring the sarcasm, "would be the people here who rig the lights, clean the costumes and paint the soundstages. I promise those people several times every year, at our parties and picnics, that if they work hard and show this company devotion, that they have a job at MGM for life. I'd hate ever to break that promise." There were tears in his eyes. "I need a *mensch* who will do whatever's necessary," said Mayer. "That's why I immediately accepted your terms. Is the car satisfactory? And your new suits from wardrobe?"

Porter indicated his *ensemble.* "Jim-Dandy."

"I'm glad we have a deal," said Mayer. He wiped his eyes and marched off, Mannix trailing behind him like the obedient attack dog he was.

*

Porter climbed the stairs to Paul Bern's quarters. The office was considerably smaller than the *sanctum sanctorums* of Mayer and Thalberg on the first floor. As Bern was known as Metro's "Father Confessor," his office had its own nickname: "The Confessional."

A young, baby-faced woman with honey blonde hair sat at her desk, briskly typing. She glanced at Porter as if she knew who he was, but said nothing. The typing continued. The brass nameplate on her desk identified her as *Irene Harrison.*

"Top o' the morning," growled Porter, half-heartedly offering his lousy "Patrick Killarney" brogue. "I'm here t' see Mr. Bern."

The secretary stopped typing, looked Porter directly in the eye, and crossed her arms. "I certainly hope you haven't come here to *hit* him," she said.

"Ya' mean," said Porter, "you're not buyin' that I'm Patrick Killarney, bringin' a bit of Gaelic poetry that your baldin' boss might fancy?"

"You're Mr. Down, correct?"

"Yep."

The woman stuck out her chin. Porter thought she'd be good casting at Warner Bros. as James Cagney's sister.

"I assumed, Mr. Down, that you'd be polite enough to make an appointment."

Although her face evoked Warners, Irene Harrison's voice was affectedly MGM – the I-work-at-the-Tiffany-of-studios-so-my-tail-never-stinks tone that many of the Metro upper echelon work force so carefully cultivated.

"Mr. Bern is developing a script treatment," said Harrison. "I doubt if he wishes to be interrupted."

"You'll know if you ask him," said Porter.

Harrison huffed, swiveled in her chair, rose, and briskly marched across the room, thought Porter, like a high school cheerleader with a John Philip Sousa tune pounding in her head. She tapped on her boss's door and entered, carefully pivoting so to block Porter from seeing inside the office. The door closed behind her.

The foyer was tastefully modest. Copies of *The New Yorker* were on the table by the reception room couch. An abstract painting was on the wall. Suddenly, Bern's office door opened. "Porter!" he said, almost running into the reception area, shaking Porter's hand. Irene Harrison stood sheepishly behind him.

"Irene, Mr. Down is always welcome here," said Bern, "day or night."

"Yes, Mr. Bern," said Irene, sullenly sitting at her desk.

"Incidentally, Porter," said Bern. "Did you see this?" He indicated a framed photograph on the wall. It was of Bern and Harlow, all dressed up and taken outside at night. Harlow's hair looked strange, and Porter realized she was wearing her wig from *Red-Headed Woman*. A small engraved plaque under the frame read:

Premiere of Grand Hotel
Hollywood
April 29, 1932

Thalberg had been *Grand Hotel's* producer, of course, but Bern had been the "supervisor" of what had been MGM's most acclaimed and star-studded film to date. "I'd never been so proud in my life as I was that evening," said Bern. "Proud of the film, of course... but even prouder to be Jean's escort. Please, come into my office."

*

Bern sat at his desk, covered with script pages he'd annotated in red ink. Porter slammed the office door behind him and locked it. The vigilant Irene, startled by the slam, sprang into action, turning on her intercom.

"What the hell's this?" the P.I. demanded, turning the grocery bag upside down, dumping the film can on Bern's desk atop the red-inked pages.

"Mr. Bern?" squawked Irene through the intercom. "Shall I send for security?"

Bern turned red when he saw the can. Recovering, he smiled his tiny smile. "I thought you were coming to thank me for the gift," said Bern petulantly. "Or express how much you enjoyed *Red-Headed Woman* last evening."

"The gift's swell. The movie's a pip. Now what about this smoker?"

"Mr. Bern?" demanded Irene, her voice so loud she didn't need the intercom.

"No, Irene, don't bother," replied Bern through the intercom. He took a cigarette, and then offered the box to Porter. "Oh...sorry. I believe you don't smoke?"

"Mr. Bern, you've got thirty seconds to tell me about this porno horror movie I found at your house. Shoot, pal."

"Well," said Bern, "this studio builds its output on sex. It's my job..."

"Yeah, I know all about that. Annie Spry filled me in last night about the advisory capacity she provides you and the studio. You looked me in the eye at your house and said you had no relationship with a pornographer."

"You saw Annie?"

"Last night. Perfectly charming woman. Too bad she belongs in a kennel."

"Porter, forgive me, but you might be too quick to judge admittedly 'different' people..."

"...who plan," interrupted Porter, "to blackmail you into the gutter?"

"Blackmail me? Since when?"

"Since last night. Listen... Mayer's paying me to run the undesirables out of your life and Miss Harlow's. Annie's jolly as hell, planning to do what she's long dreamed of doing... siphoning away a year of your salary."

Bern frowned and puffed his cigarette. "Perhaps if I spoke personally with Annie..."

"No. You never again see Annie, talk to Annie and, if you can help it, smell Annie." Porter pointed to the reception area. "Does Twinkletoes out there know about these movies?"

"If you're referring to Irene, she knows every aspect of my business dealings."

"Hooray for Irene. Get her in here. We're writing a letter."

Bern buzzed for his secretary and Porter unlocked the door. Irene marched in with her note pad and pen. "Take this chair," he said, "and take this letter."

Irene kept standing defiantly. "Look here, Mr. Down," she intoned. "Nobody comes into this office and dares tell Mr. Bern what to do, or dares tell me..."

"Do I have to spank you?" asked Porter.

"How dare you!" said Irene.

"Please do as he says, Irene," said Bern softly. She sat, crossed her legs, stuck out her chin, and sighed mightily in protest.

"Do you dictate it or do I?" asked Porter.

Bern said nothing.

"To Miss Annie Spry," said Porter. "Castellammare, Los Angeles. Dear Miss Spry: Effective as of today, June 18, 1932, any business arrangement of any variety between you and me is hereby terminated. No communication from you will be acceptable or tolerated. Any questions regarding this matter, while not welcome, can only be addressed if entirely necessary to Mr. Porter Down, care of Howard Strickling's office at MGM or, after July 13, at RD 1, Twentynine Palms, California. May you roast in Hell, Paul Bern."

Irene gave him a you-dirty-rat look. "OK," said Porter. "Just put 'Sincerely.'"

"Is there anything else, Mr. Bern?" asked the secretary. "Shall I call…"

"You're just itchin' to call security, aren't you, Sunshine?" said Porter.

"You're a *lout*!" said Irene.

"Irene, please prepare and mail the letter," said Bern. "Thank you."

She briskly left the room and closed the door. "You're at war with a blackmailer, Mr. Bern," said Porter. "Your fiancée needs to know it. If she doesn't already, tell her tonight on your Saturday night date. If I find out you didn't tell her, I will."

Bern nodded. He looked shrunken and close to tears. Porter, feeling no pity for him, nevertheless sensed a deeper degree of darkness in the man that alarmed him.

"You must understand, Porter," said Bern, suddenly launching into a defense. "I would hate for you to think the worst of me. I'm sorry I was untruthful with you, but I feared you wouldn't understand. I'm a *student* of sex, you see. Freud, for example…I researched his theories for *Strange Interlude*, a film that we're producing with Norma Shearer and Clark Gable. It's research…don't you see?"

"Frankly," said Porter, "most people would figure that having Jean Harlow for a bride should be all the sex research you'll need for a while. See ya'."

*

The timing was perfect. As Porter emerged from Bern's office, Irene Harrison, with an envelope in her hand, looked him in the face, blushed, and quickly stuffed the letter in a drawer.

What the hell's she hiding, wondered Porter. She hadn't had time to type the letter he'd dictated to her – this was something else. Irene defiantly kept eye contact, her chin jutting impressively.

"Tell me," asked Porter. "You ever hit anybody in the face with a grapefruit?"

"I beg your pardon?" said Irene.

"Never mind," said Porter.

Chapter Eighteen
Noon

Saturday, June 18, 1932

Irene Harrison was hiding something, thought Porter, and it had to do with that letter.

He looked at the mail drop in the executive building. A note on the bin indicated the postal collector came at 5:00 P.M. daily. Porter walked a block down the studio street to a mailbox. There'd be a pick-up at noon. It was about 11:50. Porter imagined that Irene Harrison, super secretary, would deliver this special letter to the street mailbox, giving it a five-hour head start on what was dumped down the mail drop. He moved into an alley and kept an eye on the executive building door. What the hell was she so spooked about with that envelope in her hand? Why, he wondered, did she look like he'd just walked in on her washing her panties?

11:53...11:54...and there she was. In her haughty, poker-faced, Sousa marching band way, Irene Harrison made her majorette maneuver to the mailbox, slid in a single letter, and followed her upturned nose back into the building. Porter considered his action. Mail theft was a major crime. LAPD wouldn't back him up and Porter knew there wasn't a judge in the state of California who wouldn't slam him in the cooler for what he now couldn't resist doing.

11:56...Nobody was on the corner. Within minutes, the mailman would be at the box and most of MGM would be in the streets heading for the commissary. Yet it was irresistible. Porter ran from the alley, ducked behind the mailbox, and pulled from his pocket his ring of Saul Lestz skeleton keys. The first one didn't turn. The second one stuck and he had to yank it to disengage.

Third's the charm, thought Porter, and it was.

Luck was on his side. The box was usually stuffed with mail. It was used by, among others, Joan Crawford's secretary, who three times a day dropped in 5"x 7" packets containing a facsimile autographed portrait in response to the star's letter-writing worshippers. But this Saturday morning, the mail was light. Porter quickly shuffled the letters and there it was: Bern's name wasn't in the return address but the building and office number were. He looked at the address:

Miss Dorothy Millette
The Plaza Hotel
San Francisco, Calif.

Porter shoved the other letters back up the chute, locked the hatch and stuffed his prize in his pocket. He figured he owed himself a celebratory lunch. He was so pleased with himself, he decided he just might invite Jean Harlow to join him.

*

Porter strolled over to the "Bordello." He learned that Harlow's dressing room was "A" on the ground floor. Playing inside the room, loudly, was Duke Ellington's "It Don't Mean a Thing if It Ain't Got that Swing." Porter tapped on the door. It opened. The woman looking at him was young, slender, and black with a large-eyed, animated face. She shouted over the music.

"My, my. I bet you the man who slugged Mr. Mannix!"

"I'm Porter Down, Miss."

"I'm Blanche Williams, sir." They were both shouting. Porter could see the room's vanity table and mirror and smelled the scent of expensive perfume. He pointed to the record, then to his ear. Blanche closed the door behind her to shut out the music.

"Baby's not here," said Blanche. "She's over at Stage Six. They doin' a test, and she's having lunch with the crew." She smiled a hell of a pretty smile. "You can go see her there. From what she tells me, she likes you."

"Thanks," said Porter. "Say, you're a looker. You ought to be in pictures yourself."

"Hattie and Louise got any parts for me sewn up for themselves," smiled Blanche. "And I'm too pretty to play maid parts anyway. So-long, Mr. Down!"

*

Porter figured he'd catch Harlow later, if only to thank her for the rabbit's foot. He headed for lunch at the commissary.

The dining room was full and Louis B. Mayer presided at the center of his personal table, flanked by guests and minions. Porter sat in a corner, ordering and quickly receiving a shrimp salad sandwich with a pickle. He took in the sights, watching actress Lupe Velez epically flirting with Johnny "Tarzan" Weissmuller at a nearby table with a lunch large enough to feed six people. Presumably things weren't proceeding in as spicy a manner as Lupe desired. After a tense moment, Lupe took a large breadstick, viciously and suggestively snapped it in half, and threw both pieces at the amused Johnny.

"Ox!" she screamed, and made her exit.

As Porter watched Lupe storm out, somebody came towards him from the center of the commissary. "Say, pal," said Clark Gable, smiling, his voice low and confidential, "I hear you made a hit with 'Jeanie.'"

Porter shrugged.

Gable sat, raised his eyebrows and spoke almost in a whisper. "From what I've heard, she'll be happy to see you any time…and on the house. Take my advice: Never look a gift whore in the mouth."

The star smiled, stood, and headed back toward his table. As he did so, Porter saw Marino Bello making the rounds. He was glad-handing various celebrities and now made a beeline for Gable, who introduced him to Weissmuller. Bello smiled and laughed easily, wore his elegant clothes with style, gestured with his cane with panache, and moved among these world-famous folk as if he too were a prince of the Hollywood blood. Nevertheless, Porter wondered why the hell Gable wasted his time with this four-flusher. They were chatting animatedly and Porter saw Bello toss back his head and roar with laughter.

Phony poseur bastard, thought Porter.

He finished his sandwich and pickle and turned his attentions to his apple pie as suddenly a young woman approached and sat at his table. "May I?" she asked, breathlessly.

She was pretty, with a rather broad face, yellow hair an MGM publicist might have described as "flaxen," and a vibrantly red dress. Porter was immediately suspicious. "You must have seen Clark Gable sitting at my table," he said.

"Oh! You truly *are* a poet!" she smiled.

Porter had to think a moment as to what was "poetic" about his previous remark. "Oh… yeah," he realized. "But I don't know Gable well, so you go to… Well, anyway, skip it."

"No, Mr. Killarney. I have to be true – I want to meet *you!* Oh! I made a poem myself!"

"No kiddin'," said Porter.

"I hear your verses are simply…aesthetic," she said.

"Then your literary taste must be…pathetic," said Porter. This was fun, but he doubted he could keep it up.

"I'm Yvonne," smiled the young lady. "Yvonne Carlson. First day here. Term contract."

She's lovely, thought Porter, but probably too lovely for the movies. Those sleepy-looking gals who appeared droopy and doped-up like Garbo and Dietrich were primarily in vogue. Yvonne looked like a hearty milkmaid. Hell, she could run a dairy farm.

"Let me guess," said Porter. "You're from…Iowa?"

"Nebraska." She placed a folder beside Porter's pie plate. "My portfolio," she announced.

Porter politely opened the folder as Yvonne took a pencil from her pocketbook, scribbled on a napkin, and then turned it over to write more. There were two pictures in the folder of Yvonne. One was a portrait, with an enormous smile that made Porter wonder if the gal had extra teeth. In the other she stood behind a giant sombrero, showing bare shoulders, bare legs, and dimpled knees. Her legs were shapely but large. Porter imagined she could kick a field goal.

"They're swell," said Porter. She really was attractive, he thought. Yvonne looked back with her lush-lipped grin and slid the scribbled-on napkin toward him. He guessed it had her phone number on one side and her address on the other. Instead, he read, in tiny letters:

LAPD

Porter's first thought was that somebody had seen him robbing the mailbox and this gal was either tipping him off or fingering him. He looked around for police, imagining his pinch being made right in the midst of the Metro family, but saw none. Porter glared at Yvonne.

"What's the matter?" she asked softly. "Lt. O'Leary said you'd be glad to meet me."

Porter was relieved to hear O'Leary's name. She flipped over the napkin. The message read: *Maggie York. LAPD. Posing as vapid MGM starlet.*

Porter chuckled at the adjective. She slid back the napkin and cautiously tore it up. "Perhaps I can help you," Maggie asked, "while awaiting my film debut? Maybe give you some editorial assistance with your writing? Perhaps help you with your 'Heroic Couplets'?"

Porter smirked. "My 'Heroic Couplets' are just fine, thank you," he said.

She grinned and Porter put it together. LAPD sometimes hired gals for investigative purposes, even if there were no female cops or detectives. O'Leary, he knew, had been on the look-out for such a gal. Yvonne/Maggie looked at him, her green eyes bright.

"We'll talk about this later, Miss… Carlson," said Porter, raising his voice a bit. "Yes, as we say here at MGM, perhaps I might be able to…use you."

She cooed flirtatiously. "Ooo, Mr. Killarney!"

"Don't ham it up," said Porter *sotto voce*. "You off at five?"

"Oh yes!" she said, and fluttered her eyelids.

"I'll pick you up at the east gate," said Porter.

"I will surely not be late," grinned Maggie.

He winked at her and she winked back.

*

Porter found the "Baby" on Soundstage 6. With *Red-Headed Woman* officially set for release this coming Friday, June 24, MGM was blueprinting *Red Dust*, a jungle sex saga, for Harlow's next vehicle. John Gilbert was set to co-star.

Gilbert was already a pathetic Hollywood living legend. Sound had emasculated MGM's great Silent Screen lover as women laughed at Gilbert's tinny voice in *His Glorious Night*. Making his downfall more melodramatic was the allegation that Mayer, who despised Gilbert (the antipathy was mutual), had sabotaged the star's critical first-released "Talkie," promising the director, the drug-addicted Lionel Barrymore, all the dope he needed if he'd participate in the Machiavellian plot and make sure the sound recording did its worst to Gilbert's voice. Gilbert was festering, occasionally vowing suicide.

Thalberg hoped Gilbert's *Red Dust* love scenes with Harlow might revive the man's dead-in-the-water career. It wasn't a sentimental decision – Gilbert still had a contract and the studio was paying him far more than they were Gable or Harlow.

Both stars were shooting test portraits, Harlow in a rain barrel. The script called for her to bathe in the barrel naked. Porter could see her bare shoulders. Photographer Virgil Apger and his crew were shooting the shots and a separate construction crew was working, tearing down old flats and setting up new ones. The sound of pounding hammers filled the soundstage.

"You missed it, pal," a technician murmured to Porter over the din. "Baby's really in her birthday suit. And it's one hell of a happy birthday."

The stage was stiflingly hot, yet Porter was amazed again at Harlow's lustrous star quality. Yes, "the Baby" was the perfect nickname – her face was oval, her skin pink, and her smile almost cherubic. She was a total departure from Garbo and Dietrich, those languishing bloodsuckers. And speaking of "bloodsuckers," Porter had always been amused that Geraldine Dvorak, one of MGM's Garbo doubles, had moonlighted at Universal as the tallest and spookiest of Bela Lugosi's vampire brides in *Dracula*.

Yet even more striking was Harlow's exuberance as she stood in the barrel. In Porter's eyes, she seemed exhilarated, as she had in *Red Headed Woman*, now wearing a sensual aggressiveness and confidence in her nakedness he'd never observed in their previous meetings. If she were truly nude, as everybody was whispering, there was no need for it – surely the studio could have provided a specially designed bathing suit that allowed the requisite peeks of bosom for these test shots. Yet she reveled in her sexuality, proudly, almost wantonly, and Porter took in this new, revealing in-person glimpse of her personality.

"I'll be damned," he said softly to himself.

Just then, Harlow suddenly stood on her toes in the rain barrel. "Yoo-hoo!" she cried, splashing the water in the barrel, and as everyone looked, Harlow gave the company, almost entirely male, a full look at her breasts. There was laughter, applause, even cheers. Harlow immediately ducked back into the barrel and now peeked again over it.

"I just thought you all might have been getting bored," explained Harlow.

"Encore!" shouted a crew member.

*

Only after the wildly appreciated peep show was over did Porter notice John Gilbert, whose Hollywood future was virtually riding on Harlow's bare shoulders. He appeared as pathetically insecure as Harlow looked brazenly assured. He seemed gaunt, and his costume of open shirt, puttee pants and high boots made him look like a seedy lion tamer. His makeup was overdone and effeminate and his once-wavy hair was plastered against his scalp, looking thin and almost painted. He was clearly highly-strung as a makeup man mopped his sweaty face.

The afternoon crawled as Gilbert, looking constantly and frantically in his mirror, delayed the still photos time and again. He bitched about the noise and the heat. The crew became restless with his constant delays. And as the hapless makeup man applied paint and powder one more time, Gilbert threw an epic tantrum.

"You're trying to sabotage me, you sons of bitches!" he shrieked. "*All* of you!"

The makeup man, who in the pre-Sound days would have kissed Gilbert's ass, got defensive as Gilbert erupted. The star stormed off the set and locked himself in his dressing room. A half-hour passed. Then an hour.

All the while, Jean Harlow stood in the rain barrel.

Porter was tempted to throw a tantrum himself as the heat soared and everyone awaited Gilbert's return. He imagined how Harlow was suffering in the barrel, not only standing all this while but trapped in water that must have been miserably hot after all that time under the lights. It was nearly 4 P.M. when Blanche Williams finally came up to the stage with a robe.

"You men pull Baby out, or I do!" she shouted.

Three men came and, surely enjoying their work, hoisted the genuinely naked Harlow out of the barrel. Porter couldn't resist looking. Yes, like "Jeanie" at the whorehouse, she bleached her pubic hair.

*

A few moments later, Harlow saw Porter and came up to him in her white robe and gold high-heeled sandals. "Don't you look swell!" she exclaimed, regarding his new suit.

"The rabbit foot's swell, too," said Porter. "Thanks."

Harlow beamed. "I'm so glad you like it," she said. Blanche held Harlow's pack of cigarettes. There was one left and Blanche lit it for her.

"Did you see my little peep show?" Harlow asked Porter. She suddenly seemed a bit shy, and he couldn't tell if she were being coy or was actually embarrassed.

Porter nodded. There was a pause. "I enjoyed talking with you on Thursday," she said. "How about if we chat for a while in my dressing room? Give me a half-hour? I've been curdling in that God-awful water and need a shower."

As Harlow left the soundstage, she tossed the empty cigarette pack into a nearly full trash can. Porter noticed the name brand: *Fatimas*. As he'd noticed Thursday night, Annie Spry smoked Fatimas. Annie also wore Mitsouko. Coincidence...maybe. Nevertheless, Porter suspected that Annie was more than Bern's blackmailer.

She was also an obsessed Jean Harlow fan.

*

At 4:30, Porter knocked on Harlow's dressing room door and Blanche Williams admitted him. *Saint Louis Blues* was playing loudly on the record player and Harlow was seated at her vanity, wearing tan slacks and a striped blouse, brushing her hair and drinking a glass of orange juice. She looked at Porter and smiled.

"Mr. Down," said Blanche, fidgeting, "would you like an orange juice too?"

"Sure, thanks."

Blanche poured him a glass and gave it to him. He and Harlow clinked glasses. "Okay," said Harlow. "You have your rabbit's foot, so let's shoot craps!"

She took a pair of dice from a drawer and knelt on the floor in front of Porter. He knelt opposite her. She shook the dice, smiling, seemingly joyous, like a child playing a game. Porter had to grin at her glow. Harlow adjusted on one knee and was about to toss the dice when she lost balance and fell backwards against a waste can. It tipped over and its lid fell off.

An empty fifth of whiskey rolled out onto the floor.

Harlow looked mortified. "I needed a pick-me-up after this afternoon," she said sullenly.

"Yeah," said Porter as he and Blanche helped her stand. "See ya'." He downed his orange juice, turned, and left the dressing room.

*

It wasn't the fact that Jean Harlow had drunk a fifth of whiskey, Porter ruminated as he walked across the lot. It was the fact that Blanche Williams felt she had to hide it. The orange juice, Porter guessed, was a precaution so Porter wouldn't smell alcohol on Harlow's breath.

Porter wasn't so much concerned that a movie star might have a drinking problem as the fact that a 21-year-old might have a drinking problem.

Chapter Nineteen
That Night

Saturday, June 18, 1932

It was 5 P.M. on the dot as Porter arrived at the MGM east gate. There, impossible to miss, waiting in her red dress and flaxen hair, was Maggie York, looking like the valedictorian from the graduating class of the Nebraska 4H Club School of Drama. He pulled up to the curb.

"It's the lady in red," said Porter. "Hop in."

"Hi," she smiled, climbing into the passenger seat and tossing her portfolio into the back seat. "Whew!"

Porter pulled out onto Washington Boulevard. "So, how's the 'vapid MGM starlet?'"

"Swell," said Maggie, taking off her high heels and rubbing her stocking feet. "I always wanted to spend the day walking on stilts and smiling till my mouth hurt."

"What did you do this afternoon?"

"Posed for publicity in evening gowns. I'll add them to my portfolio. Oh, by the way, remember that shot of me with the giant sombrero? I had a bathing suit on behind it."

"You're shatterin' my Tinsel Town illusions," said Porter flatly. "How about dinner?"

"Would you mind if we ate at my place? I am tired of being 'the lady in red.' I can change clothes and we can send out for food. I can't cook. 1922 North Highland."

Porter turned north. "Tell me about your job."

"It all happened very fast. Lt. O'Leary and I met at Effie McCoo's execution. He said he was looking for a female reporter who might want to work undercover for LAPD. I fit the bill. He called me late Thursday night and told me you could use somebody to do legwork. Then he phoned Whitey Hendry, MGM's police chief, who gave me a bogus contract and sent me to the still department for those portfolio pictures to prove I'm a starlet. I picked them up this morning. Those were the only two they could use. On the other 'come-hither' shots they posed of me, I'm laughing hysterically."

"Anybody else know about you other than Hendry? How about Howard Strickling?"

"I don't think so. By the way, Mr. Strickling addressed the new stock actresses today. He got very solemn about the significance of working for MGM, and then told us we're all to show up next weekend as hostesses at a studio barbeque for exhibitors. We're wearing cowgirl suits."

"What paper did you work for?"

"*The L.A. Illustrated News.* I had the *nom de plume* 'M. S. York.'"

"Very mysterious," said Porter. "Anyway, I got an ethics question. When you were a reporter, would you, or did you, ever open somebody else's mail?"

"Only when marginally necessary."

Porter grinned. "There's a picnic at your place tonight, Maggie," he said. "And it's all goin' on L.B. Mayer's tab."

*

1922 North Highland Avenue was the address of a Hollywood hotel that housed many starlets who settled into the movie colony. If the studio picked up their options, the favored ladies often moved to more plush quarters. If the studio dumped them, they usually vacated 1922 North Highland or, on at least three occasions, jumped out a window.

Of course, the hotel wasn't confined to only starlets, and adventurous journalist-turned-LAPD-snooper Maggie York had a top floor apartment, now rich in the smell of delicatessen sandwiches. She and Porter had called out for the "picnic" and ate a Saturday night spread of cold cuts, french fries, and Kosher pickles, washed down with a carton of Coca-Cola. Ice cream and a cherry pie awaited them in the icebox.

Porter had removed his jacket and tie and opened his vest. The hostess had changed to wide-cut brown slacks and a beige cotton blouse, comfortably standing in her bare feet in the kitchen. She was munching a sandwich while holding the purloined letter over a whistling teakettle.

O'Leary had given Maggie the basics about the Harlow and Bern situation. Now, Porter was candid about filling in details, aware that a former female L.A. newspaper reporter didn't require kid gloves treatment. Maggie was attentive, very interested, and didn't seem to shock easily. Nevertheless, he said nothing for now about Harlow's drinking.

Porter sat in the living room, savoring the corned beef on rye with provolone cheese and extra mustard. There were books everywhere, fiction and non-fiction. Porter was thumbing through Maggie's copy of the best seller *I Am a Fugitive from a Chain Gang*, by Robert Burns, as Maggie came from the kitchen, standing before him with her large-lipped grin, triumphantly holding the steamed-open envelope.

"*Voila*," she said.

Porter read the letter, typed on plain paper.

> *June 18, 1932*
>
> *Dear Dorothy:*
>
> *I am so pleased to hear from you and to know you are happily settled at the Plaza Hotel.*
>
> *Yes, I am very busy. The script for* The Sacrifice *is nearly complete, and of course tailored to your unique beauty and talents. We have been meticulous in its preparation. I'm entirely satisfied with depth of characterization and quality of story values.*
>
> *Thank you for your ideas regarding the casting of certain other featured roles. I will certainly take them under consideration.*
>
> *Thank you too for sending your new telephone number. No, I still have no phone at my home, but if and when I do, you'll of course receive the number.*
>
> *Yes, you can ignore what you read in the newspapers. Prattling gossip is the life's blood of their circulation and obviously, they do not check facts. You are wise in only reading the late edition and perhaps should consider eliminating that too from your habits – although I well recall how much you always enjoyed the late paper before retiring for the night. At any rate, much ado about nothing, my dear.*

The money will come in my next letter and please advise me if you require anything at all.

I, too, hope we may arrange a visit soon.

Paul

Porter handed the letter to Maggie. She curled up in a chair and read it. "So," nodded Porter. "The Father Confessor is just a run-of-the mill Hollywood phony."

"Connect the dots for me," said Maggie.

"It's typical casting couch crap. Bern's got this dame squirreled away up in a San Francisco hotel. He leads her on with promises he'll star her in a movie. He claims he has no home phone so she can't pester him...hell, he was on the phone the evening that I went up to his house. Then he launches into this holier-than-thou baloney – don't believe what she reads in the papers – because he knows the papers are reporting that he and Harlow will marry."

"He also refers to knowing she always liked the late paper before 'retiring for the night,'" said Maggie. "There's clearly a history there."

"She's got to be nuts to believe this man's claptrap!"

"Well, Paul Bern's the number two man, creatively, at MGM," said Maggie. "And the fact that he's set her up at the San Francisco Plaza shows commitment. That joint ain't cheap."

"Maggie, what's your work day like at MGM?"

"I clock in at 8. I'm one of dozens of ladies on new term contracts – I can slip right out again through the Overland Avenue gate and nobody would miss me."

"I'm going away for a day or two," said Porter tightly. "You say you're a good investigator?"

"I might surprise you," smiled Maggie.

"Good. This week, see what you can find out about Dorothy Millette. Any film credits, stage work in L.A., old addresses around town. If this dame Dorothy is newly settled in San Francisco, my guess is that Bern deported her there from L.A."

"What else?" asked Maggie, scribbling notes on a pad in shorthand.

"Next, see what's new about Marino Bello, Harlow's stepfather. I saw him working the bigwigs in the commissary at MGM today. Find out if he's a real thug or a thug-wanna-be. If he's a real thug, and he sniffs out that his prospective son-in-law has a floozy stashed in San Francisco, we might have a mess."

"What else?"

Porter was impressed by Maggie's eagerness. "Paul Bern might be hearing this week from a lady named Annie Spry. In addition to his dear Dorothy in Frisco, the Father Confessor has a longtime kinship with Spry...a Hollywood pornographer."

"Platonic?" asked Maggie, making notes.

"I'd hate to imagine it any other way. Anyway, she's going for blackmail. See if you can find anything that we can throw back at her. Wear your gloves when you dig *her* dirt."

Porter finished his sandwich. "So," he asked. "Does this stuff catch your fancy?"

"My fancy is definitely caught," grinned Maggie.

"Good," said Porter. "Now let's dig into that cherry pie and ice cream."

Chapter Twenty
San Francisco Caper

Sunday, June 19 and Monday, June 20, 1932

Porter joined Luke fishing on Sunday, each piloting a trawler to Catalina. They both made huge catches.

On Monday at dawn, Luke drove Porter to the airfield and Porter took off in *Timber Wolf* for San Francisco with a suitcase. He enjoyed the view of the cliffs, whitecaps and fishing boats, and for a time he almost forgot his festering anger at Paul Bern. Yeah, the man was a pig...pouting like a little boy when told to get rid of his porno queen, and sneaking off letters via his in-cahoots secretary to "Dear Dorothy" at a San Francisco love nest. The monthly rent there probably topped the annual income of most family men lucky enough in 1932 to have jobs. And all the time, the little schnook is engaged to marry Harlow!

He also thought about Longie Zwillman. Longie hadn't mentioned anything about Dorothy Millette during their lunch last week and apparently knew nothing about her. For Millette's sake, Porter knew it had better stay that way. Longie also didn't seem to know that Harlow had an alcohol problem. Porter wasn't about to tell him.

His thoughts turned to his new associate. She'd soon be clocking in at MGM and making a fast exit out a side gate to get on the case. He was a bit concerned about her pulling off her starlet stunt. Maggie as "Yvonne" was probably five or six years older than most of the gals in that crop, a bit taller, and more...well, bountiful. Nevertheless, as an investigator and an attractive, funny and damn smart woman, Maggie York had made one hell of a fine impression.

He was eager to see her again.

*

Porter was in San Francisco by early afternoon. His first stop after hailing a taxi at the airport was *The Lorayne*.

It was an art-deco hotel, somehow eluding official condemnation despite its notorious lack of city-approved earthquake supports. Porter still sent the $28.50 a month for his front top floor office even after most of the other tenants had fled. Hookers had moved in, and rumor claimed the wrecking ball had a date with *The Lorayne*, but the view was great of the bay and Alcatraz (the prison island now rumored to become a federal penitentiary), and the old aerie offered a lot of memories.

The platinum blonde clerk at the lobby desk gave him the eye as she handed him some mail that had come since his last visit. He shuffled through the stack as the old caged elevator rattled up the shaft to the top floor. Among the ads and magazines were a few letters and he saw the name on the return address of one – *Eve Devonshire*. She was a major player in his last Hollywood case at Universal, and it had cost her dearly. She'd left L.A. to start a new life in Sacramento.

The elevator jarred at its summit stop. Porter walked down the hallway and unlocked the door with its smoked glass window. There was little inside the office anymore – only some furniture, file cabinets, and books. He cranked open the casement windows, looked at the view, and glanced again at the mail, placing Eve's letter on top. He decided to save it for tonight, when what he had to do was finished. It would give him something to look forward to.

*

Porter changed from his sailor togs to the third of his new suits, a dark grey tweed, and left *The Lorayne* about 4:30. He planned to get dinner before heading for the Plaza. Waiting at a cable car stop, he saw the first evening edition of the Monday, June 20, 1932 *Chronicle*, tossed off a truck at the corner newsstand. He wandered over to look at the headlines. There it was:

It's Official!
Jean Harlow and MGM Producer Get Marriage License.

He paid for a paper and read the story. Yeah, Harlow and Bern had gone for the license this morning. There was a picture, with three people in it: Harlow, flashing her beauty queen smile; Bern, busy with the paperwork, looking over his shoulder with the expression of a trapped rat; and Marino Bello, smiling as if he were the bridegroom. Porter shook his head, realized a cable car was clanging, and hopped aboard for the trip to Fisherman's Wharf. Several people on the car were reading the story. Porter wondered if "Dorothy" had read the news yet and seen the picture. Then again, based on Bern's letter, she only read the late evening edition…

It could all add up to perfect timing.

*

The seafood meal at Fisherman's Wharf was delicious, all the more so considering MGM was paying for it. Porter munched the mussels and hatched his plan. He knew the late editions in San Francisco came out competitively between 9:45 and 10 P.M. With luck and maybe a little cooperation, his idea could work. No, Bern wouldn't go on hoodwinking Harlow.

Porter looked forward to setting off the dynamite.

*

He hopped off the cable car just before 8:30 P.M., arriving at The Plaza, glancing up at the hotel, savoring the fact that somewhere in that building was Paul Bern's mystery woman.

Probably reading a movie magazine and painting her toenails, thought Porter.

He'd formed a rather sharp mental picture of her – a drop-dead sexy looker with the morals of an alley cat and the brain and jaws of a T-Rex. She was so damn dumb she was buying Bern's line about a script "tailored" for her special talents, which Porter imagined extended no farther than providing private parts close-ups for Annie Spry.

Aware of the dignity and old-world sophistication of the Plaza, he knew it might take some time to find a partner-in-crime on the staff. In fact, it took five minutes. A bellboy named Timothy practically slobbered on the brass buttons of his red and black uniform when Porter slipped him a $50 bill – MGM "petty cash" – with the promise of more if Timothy could provide him information. By 8:55 they were in cahoots, riding up and down on the freight elevator as Porter hatched the plan. Young Tim had checked the file on Dorothy Millette. Yes, she'd moved there in May. Yes, her file had marked her request for the late evening paper, which Tim himself sometimes placed outside her door, delivered precisely at 10:00 P.M. No, Tim had never seen her. And sure, he knew her room number – 625. Facing out front.

"One of the really nice rooms, a suite actually," said Tim.

Porter and his new pal rode back down the freight elevator as Porter handed the wide-eyed bellboy another crisp $50 bill. "Wow!" exulted Tim. "When my girl sees I got all this money, she's gonna'…she's gonna'…"

"You bet she will," said Porter. "Now… want to make another $50, and look like a hero besides?"

*

At 9:52 P.M., Tim nervously stood at a lobby house phone, away from the eyes of the desk staff and bell captain. "You have a special messenger," he said stiffly and nervously to the woman who answered in 625. "He's from…from…"

Tim forgot his lines. "MGM," said Porter.

"MGM," said Tim. "He says his orders are to deliver a package personally and get your signature himself. Yes ma'am." He hung up the receiver. "She said to come up!"

"Good. You know what to do now. How soon you gonna' be on the 6th floor with the service elevator door open?"

Tim looked at his watch. "Eight minutes. No – *seven* minutes. 10:00. Sharp. I'll bring her the late newspaper as my reason for being there."

"Right."

Porter boarded the service elevator – the lobby elevator had a uniformed attendant – as Tim jittered back to duty. The P.I. held a San Francisco telephone book he'd placed in a paper bag Tim had provided. Inside the telephone book was the afternoon *Chronicle*, showing Bern and Harlow getting the marriage license.

*

Porter had busted up enough love nests to know the drill. Confront the lady in her lair. Lay down the law, let her know the party was over, and get out as she began squawking or screaming for the police or her lover or whomever. At any rate, once the little lady of these sagas knew the jig was up, so did her keeper, and everything usually ended in a hell of a hurry.

The elevator door opened. He strolled down the sixth-floor hallway, figuring Dorothy could never resist the "script" sent 400 miles by MGM special courier. He was spiffily dressed for a delivery boy, sporting his tweeds, but MGM had class, Goddamnit. He found Room 625 and knocked.

*

It was silent for a time on the other side of the door. "Yes?" finally whispered the voice, soft and feminine.

"Metro-Goldwyn-Mayer, Miss. Special delivery for Miss Dorothy Millette from Mr. Paul Bern. I need a signature."

There were at least three locks on the door and the woman took some time to unfasten each one. The door opened slowly and the woman stayed shielded behind it. Porter stepped into the room, dark, with only a small table lamp lit. The curtains covered all but a sliver of the view of Union Square, whose glow reached the 6th floor window, adding just a bit more light to the chamber. The room had a scent of flowery perfume and as the door shut, Porter turned around to see his hostess.

That she was a surprise was an understatement.

The woman was short, overweight, her moon face a bit wrinkled, with only a vestige of what might have been prettiness in her youth. She had taken her hair down for the night and it fell over the gray silk frock she'd put on after the call from the lobby. There'd been no time to pin up her hair which, in the near darkness, seemed to Porter to be a dark, reddish blonde.

"Good evening," he said, removing his hat.

"Good evening," she said formally. "You say you require a signature?"

"Yes. Mind if I sit a minute? It's a ten-hour ride back tonight."

The woman hesitated a moment, then reluctantly indicated the couch.

"Thanks," said Porter, sitting, still holding his bag.

The woman locked the door behind her and Porter noticed her strange walk as she moved to her chair. It was an affected, tippy-toe walk, and as she sat near the window to the side of him, she crossed her legs with a decided elegance. Her large eyes curiously focused on the bag on his lap and Porter sensed she was trying to hide her desire to grab it from his hands.

An old Victrola near the window, its volume very low, was playing an opera – Porter recognized *Nessun Dorma* from Puccini's *Turandot*.

"I'd offer you tea, but it's late," said Dorothy.

"That's fine," said Porter, still amazed by this tiny, round, wizened woman when he was expecting a Ziegfeld Follies dominatrix. *Well, appearances can be deceiving*, he thought.

"So," said Dorothy. "Mr. Bern is ready to produce *The Sacrifice*?"

"Seems that way." *The Sacrifice*, thought Porter. *Ah yes – the title of the phony script. Sure, he'll put it on a double bill with Red Dust.*

"Production to commence in September?"

"I believe that's when it commences, yes."

"I imagine everyone at the studio is quite excited."

"Oh, they're excited, you bet."

"The role of Eliana," she said softly, staring at the bag Porter held, "who sacrifices her life for the man she loves and the Lord she worships. She's the heart-breaking role I've dreamed of playing all my life."

The woman's voice was soft and a bit affected, and Porter noticed she pronounced all her *s* sounds like soft *c*'s. All the while he was taking in not only Dorothy Millette, but also her room. The dim light made the perusal difficult, but he soon saw something staring at him right beside the couch. It was a framed picture of Dorothy who, although obviously younger, still had her oddly oval face and plump elfin look. Beside her was a young man who, even without the mustache, was instantly recognizable to Porter due to the mournful eyes.

"So," he said. "You've known Mr. Bern for some time?"

"Yes," she said.

"I bet he'd like to see this," said Porter, pointing at the picture. "He could make a copy at the studio and send it back. May I…?"

"No," she said firmly. "Of course not. Anyway, I'm sure he has his own copy. That was a very special day for us."

"How so?" asked Porter.

"You're very impertinent!" snapped Dorothy.

"Sorry," said Porter.

She sighed and ignored his apology. "You say I must sign... something or other?" she asked impatiently.

"Oh...yeah." Porter took a piece of note paper from his pocket and handed her a pencil. "Here. This'll be fine."

Dorothy took the paper and pencil. She also took a copy of *The New Yorker* from the table by the couch and placed the paper against it as she signed. Porter studied her face in the dim light. At news of her caller, she'd apparently quickly added face powder and eyeliner – too quickly. And Porter's trained eye noted something else odd as Dorothy sat there with her legs crossed...her shoes. They were gray or light blue high heels, with very high spikes. Porter guessed they were especially made, probably to give the tiny round woman extra height, and it accounted for her tippy-toe walk. She and Bern surely would have sired no basketball stars.

"There you are," she said, handing him the signed paper and the pencil. "Incidentally, do you know if Mr. Bern has made a definite decision about the casting of the temptress?"

"You mean the temptress in *The Sacrifice*?"

"Yes."

"No."

Dorothy was still but there was suddenly a dark energy about her that struck Porter instantly. Her moon eyes became very bright in the shadows.

"I imagine," she said, "he'll take my suggestion and cast that awful woman...that platinum blonde."

Porter thought the room felt cold.

"Imagine those stupid newspapers," said Dorothy, "having the unmitigated nerve to link him with her romantically. Harlow," she said, with a tiny smile that reminded him of Paul Bern's. "The very name sounds like 'harlot.'"

Porter glanced at his watch. He had about 90 seconds.

"Oh," said Dorothy, seeing him looking at his watch. "I imagine you should receive a tip." She stood and reached for her purse on the table.

"No, no," said Porter, standing. "Mr. Bern tipped me up front."

"That's so like him," she said, promptly putting back the purse.

"Yeah, he's quite a guy," nodded Porter. He handed her the paper bag.

Here it comes, Dottie, he thought.

Dorothy's hands darted and she grasped the bag hungrily. "It's heavy," she said, clearly pleased with her star-making vehicle's epic scope. She sat again, placed the bag on her lap and put on her wire-rim spectacles. The tenor on the Victrola was approaching the climactic throes of *Nessun Dorma* as Porter looked at his watch.

One minute.

The woman reached in the bag with her dainty, delicate hands and long fingers and extricated what she recognized as a telephone book. She sat very still, looked up at Porter, then back at the book on her lap. Suddenly, at first very softly, she began whining, almost keening, like a tricked, humiliated child. She shook her head, and then saw the newspaper's edge jutting from the book. She ripped it from its place and studied the picture of Bern, Harlow, and Bello, its headline and caption.

30 seconds, thought Porter.

Now Dorothy Millette's mouth fell and the keening rose, a sharp, mournful, high-pitched wail. She stood. The book and the copy of the *Chronicle* fell from her lap and she looked at Porter over her glasses, her eyes suddenly enlarged, her tiny mouth wide-open.

"Liar!" she cried.

Porter put on his hat and made for the door.

"Liar!" she wailed, this time louder, standing, her glasses sliding down her nose, off her face and onto the floor. Porter fiddled with the locks, his back to her.

"LIAR!" she screamed now, and she was right behind him. Porter turned and saw her lined-and-powdered face, distorted and wet with tears.

"LIAR! LIAR! LIAR!" she screamed, raising her small fists, hitting him with surprising force. Porter forced the last lock and hurried to the hallway and around the corner, where Timothy, pale at what he heard, stood in the open elevator, holding the late edition of the *San Francisco Examiner*.

Porter ran into the elevator and slapped the third $50 bill into Timothy's hand. The bellboy pocketed the money as he ran past Porter and, as Porter descended to the lobby, Timothy rushed to Miss Millette's aid. As rehearsed, Timothy waited a full minute before calling for help from her phone. By that time, Porter was in Union Square.

Timothy had never seen a case of hysteria. It scared him so badly that, by the time the hotel doctor and security arrived, he wondered if it had all been worth the $150.

Among the numerous Pre-Code movies made containing "zoomimic masochism" flourishes, Cecil B. DeMille's 1932 The Sign of the Cross *is a prime example. The actor playing the gorilla is allegedly Charles Gemora; the unidentified actress is definitely NOT Jean Harlow.*

Jean Harlow, as Lil Andrews, in her break-through film, 1932's Red-Headed Woman. *She wore a red wig over her platinum hair.*

Jean Harlow married MGM producer Paul Bern on Saturday, July 2, 1932.

Dorothy Millette, common law wife of Paul Bern. What, if anything, would she have to do with the upcoming tragedy?

Mobster Abner "Longie" Zwillman, former paramour of Jean Harlow. What, if anything, would he have to do with the upcoming tragedy?

130   PLATINUM WIDOW: WHO KILLED JEAN HARLOW'S HUSBAND?

Jean Harlow with step-father Marino Bello and Mother Jean Harlow Bello. What, if anything, would Harlow's step-father have to do with the upcoming tragedy?

MGM "Bulldog" Eddie Mannix with Jean Harlow. What, if anything, would Mannix have to do with the upcoming tragedy?

The "suicide" house at 9820 Easton Drive, Labor Day 1932. Paul Bern's naked, perfume-drenched corpse was discovered in the Master bedroom along with his "suicide" note.

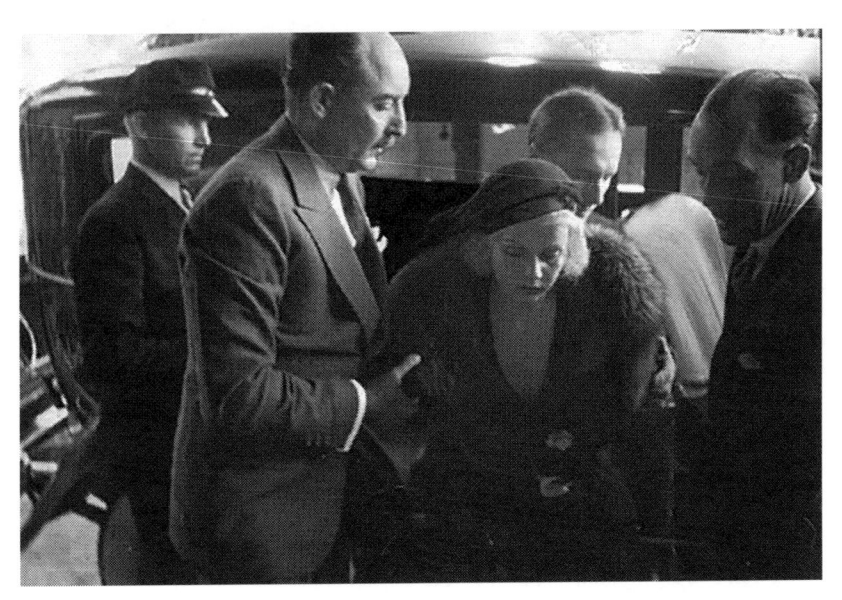

Supported by her step-father, Marino Bello, Jean Harlow attends her husband Paul's funeral.

Harlean Harlow Carpenter
AKA Jean Harlow
March 3, 1911 - June 7, 1937

Chapter Twenty-One
A New Scenario

Tuesday, June 21, 1932

When Annie Spry worked on one of her scripts, she wore only a pair of black silk panties and a splash of Mitsouko.

She sat at her desk on this sunny morning by the Pacific, a glass of gin beside her, a Fatima cigarette clenched between her lips as she tickled the keys of her typewriter. The current job was for RKO Studios, where David O. Selznick was producing a movie about a giant male gorilla and a blonde female human. The title: *King Kong*.

Beauty Kills the Beast, thought Annie, although in her own films, it was often more like *Bestiality Kills the Beauty*.

Selznick, aware of Annie's peculiar talents, had engaged her to write a few scenes to spice up the show. She was finishing an episode in which Kong holds the blonde, named "Ann Darrow," in his humongous paw, high on a cliff on Skull Island, her dress torn and tattered after various escapes from prehistoric carnivores. Annie typed:

> *Kong curiously, pruriently peels off a piece of Ann's now-raggedy and revealing dress. She writhes in his hand. Modesty? Passion? Kong treats himself to another piece of her dress and we see her lacy slip. Kong coyly tickles her. Her pungent female scent arises in the jungle air. Kong, still holding Ann, sniffs his fingers where he's touched her young, nubile body...*

She nodded in approval, then thought again of the important letter she was expecting. Her mailbox was at the bottom of the 70 steps that led down from her living area to her garage. She rarely ventured out anymore into the merciless daylight, for any reason, going out in the evening to get her mail. Nevertheless, when she heard the mailman calling to a neighbor, she was too exhilarated to wait to see if what she expected was in the box.

It must have arrived today, thought Annie.

Of course, her current attire wasn't acceptable for going out to get the mail, so she threw on a kimono – she liked kimonos – and this one was a very dark purple with a large, white orchid pattern. She added a pair of sunglasses and a large, white straw beach bonnet, put on a pair of black slippers, then ventured down the 70 steps...

And there it was...amidst bills and other letters. Complete with the MGM logo of Leo the Lion. No name on the envelope, but an office number.

Annie hurried up the stairs, tossed the other mail on her balcony table, and tore open the letter from Metro. It was dated June 18, 1932...last Saturday...the morning after Porter Down had been here. Yes, this was the kiss-off. There was Down's name. There was Bern's signature.

"Those god-damned sons-of-bitches," she said, almost singing the words to herself.

Annie placed the letter and its envelope into her kimono pocket, took a Fatima from the cigarette box on the balcony table, lit up, stood very still, and looked out at the Pacific. Yes, this was just what she'd expected. She'd already planned what her attack would be.

They'd scorned her ...and now, by Christ, she'd scorn them back.

Annie clenched her cigarette in her teeth as she ran into the house, trembling. She tore off the beach bonnet, the kimono, the sunglasses. She was exhilarated, she told herself, not intimidated. She kicked off the slippers, sat at her desk, downed a nearly full glass of gin and, her hand shaking, poured herself another one. She put a fresh piece of paper into the typewriter.

"Here it comes, you fuckers," she hissed, and she began typing furiously in a blistering white heat, trembling and perspiring, laughing but also crying, once again adorned in only her black panties.

"Get ready for an earthquake, Baby," she smiled as tears ran down her face.

Chapter Twenty-Two
Summer Reading List

Tuesday, June 21 through Thursday, June 23, 1932

It sure hadn't happened last night like Porter had planned it.

He was back at *The Lorayne*, sitting on the windowsill, looking out at the sunlit bay and Alcatraz. Usually in a case like this, the gal erupted, he ran while she threw high heels and perfume bottles at him, and everything burned out fast.

This one had been a shocker.

He guessed the events currently unfolding. Dorothy would have had Bern on the phone at MGM first thing this morning. Bern would know it was Porter who'd blown their cover. The producer would have to do damage control and he'd have to tell Harlow the truth, knowing damn well that if he didn't tell her, Porter would.

He's trapped, thought Porter. *The game's over.*

But again, this wasn't what he'd expected. This woman wasn't young or beautiful, so the bond likely wasn't superficial. Even considering her terror at the realization there was a stranger in her room who had duped her, her contorted face and pitiful screams had given indications of mental illness. And, there'd been Bern's picture with her.

"*LIAR!*" she'd wailed, and Porter wondered: *Was she calling him a liar, or Paul Bern…or both?*

Anyway, it was all their game to play.

Porter took Eve Devonshire's letter from his bedside table where he had placed it after opening and reading it last night. He sat back on the windowsill and read it again, appreciating her warm words, the news that she was well, and her personal sentiments to him.

He relaxed, placed the letter in his shirt pocket, and looked out again at the bay. He'd take his time flying back to await developments in the Metro melodrama. He decided to treat himself to a trip to the San Francisco Zoo before starting back.

Porter enjoyed a beautiful Tuesday evening flight, arriving at the airfield in Malibu around midnight. He expected some message at the marina from Bern, either a phone message or telegram, regarding the discovery at the Plaza and its repercussions.

There was no word.

*

Come Wednesday morning, there was still no word. No how-dare-you-you-son-of-a-bitch, nothing. Porter offered to help Luke and that afternoon they sailed out to the 12-mile point to fish. Surely there'd be a message, he figured, by the time they returned. They docked just before 1:00 A.M. There was still nothing.

Porter was decidedly pissed off. Had Dorothy Millette contacted Bern? Had Annie Spry responded to Bern's letter? Tomorrow morning he'd be at MGM and find out just what the hell was happening.

*

The congratulatory flowers so filled Paul Bern's office this Thursday morning that baskets of them had spilled outside the office door. Porter, casual in his nautical attire, had to maneuver around them. When he entered "The Confessional," it appeared to be a florist's shop. The smell of the banks of flowers was almost overpowering.

Irene Harrison was aglow as if she were the bride. Several fluttery writers or art directors or whatever-the-hell-they-were had just expressed their effusions to Bern in his office and were now falling all over Irene, the blushing secretary. The well-wishers finally departed and Irene saw Porter. Suddenly all her cooing stopped. She jutted out her chin and buzzed the intercom.

"Mr. Down is here," she said.

"Bring him into my office," said Bern's voice.

Irene led Porter into the office with her haughty strut, closing the door behind the three of them. Bern sat at his desk. He looked coldly at Porter.

"Well, Mr. Down?" asked Bern.

"You know what happened Monday night," said Porter. "I've been waiting over two days for a response from you." He indicated Irene. "Or at least from Brunhilde here."

Bern took a moment to light a cigarette. "Mr. Down, I'm a gentleman. When I fear I might succumb to anger, I try to avoid the person who's angered me until I'm capable of a civil response. With you, however, that will not be possible."

He inhaled his cigarette and blew out a jet of smoke.

"The Spartan shenanigans you employed in San Francisco Monday night," said Bern, "were shameful." He shook his head, closed his eyes, and pinched his temples. "How could you have done such a thing, Porter? And to someone as gentle and kind as dear Dorothy, who…"

"Who now knows," said Porter, "that your story about producing *The Sacrifice* with her as the star is total baloney."

"Irene and I have made our assurances to Dorothy," said Bern. "We claimed that you're a disgruntled ex-Metro employee who has had an axe to grind, ever since I had to fire you for unacceptable behavior. And what we told her is not so much deceitful as it is prophetic."

"You got me all a-tremble," said Porter. "And you still plan to marry Miss Harlow?"

"Yes," said Bern. "Precisely one week from Saturday."

"And Harlow's fine with you having a woman stashed away in San Francisco?" demanded Porter.

Bern looked at Irene, who now looked at Porter. "Mr. Down," she said, "perhaps you should learn here and now that as far as the topic of Miss Dorothy Millette goes, Miss Harlow knows all about her."

Porter was stunned. "I don't believe you."

"Ask her," said Irene.

"And you tell me I should be ashamed?" demanded Porter.

Bern and Irene clucked again, as if appalled by Porter's moral naiveté. "Mr. Down," said Irene, "I'm afraid MGM has been a bit too much for you…perhaps too worldly."

Porter tensed. "The woman I saw at the Plaza didn't seem very worldly. When I left, she was crying and screaming like a banshee."

"I'd cry and scream too," said Irene righteously, "if a brute lied his way into my home and tried to bully and terrify me." She stood, folded her arms and looked Porter in the eye. "And I'd especially cry and scream if he were a disgraced ex-private investigator... whose badge was revoked after he'd killed a woman."

"You see," said Bern, "Irene has done some expert investigating of her own. Bravo, Irene."

Silence. Irene Harrison stood there, looking proud as punch.

"I'll inform Irving this afternoon" said Bern, "that Jean and I no longer want or require your particular brand of Philistine service, especially since it's coming from a convicted felon, struggling to control an alcohol problem. Irving most certainly will communicate that news to Mr. Mayer." He paused. "Under other circumstances, I'd have sympathy for you, Porter. However, after your behavior in San Francisco...we have nothing more to say to one another."

Porter made no reply. He figured he'd allow the runt and his she-wolf secretary their temporary victory, imagining how Mayer would chew both their asses, and even Thalberg's, when they reported their discovery. This was MGM. Thalberg made artistic choices, but the almighty L.B. Mayer tolerated nobody butting into his business.

Irene, still standing and glowing, suddenly pivoted in her heels and regarded her boss with sparkle-eyed empathy. "May I get you anything, Mr. Bern? A coffee, perhaps?"

"No, dear lady, but how sweet of you to ask."

"May I go, Mr. Bern? The thank you notes for the flowers are an overwhelming job!"

"Of course, dear lady. What would Jean and I ever do without you? Go, go, go."

"Oh, one more thing," said Irene. "The Dora Ingram Bookshop called. Your new book order has arrived. Would you like me to go over on my lunch break and pick it up for you?"

"No, no, Irene. I'll pick up the books on my way home tonight. Now, go, dear lady, go."

Irene Harrison enjoyed a triumphant exit, ignoring Porter as if he weren't there. Bern seemed to lose a bit of bravado in her absence and focused on a script on his desk.

"I'd still like to hear your fiancée's opinion on all this," said Porter.

Bern didn't look up from his script. "She's quite busy," he said, his voice frosty. "The official opening of *Red-Headed Woman* is tomorrow and she's choosing the wardrobe for her personal appearance. Tonight, there's a party at Fredric March's home and I happen to know that Jean is also concerned about her attire for that affair."

Porter paused. At 5'8" he wasn't tall, but this day, standing over Bern huddled behind his desk, he felt towering. "You have nothing more to say for yourself?"

"No."

"No word from Annie Spry?" he asked.

"No. But as I've mentioned, none of this is of your concern anymore." He began briskly writing notes on a script page.

"And…just out of curiosity…what the hell happens when Dorothy Millette sees the newspaper coverage of your marriage to Harlow? And when she finally discovers there never was or will be a film vehicle, especially tailored by you for her, called *The Sacrifice*?"

"That is not your concern anymore!" glared Bern.

The two men regarded each other for a moment. "I enjoyed meeting Miss Harlow," said Porter. "I have a funny feeling I'll be seeing her again."

He left the office. Neither he nor Irene Harrison looked at each other as he exited through the maze of flowers.

*

Porter knew if he stayed on the lot, he'd punch somebody, or worse. He also knew that, despite his past battles with alcohol, he needed a drink. Just one, he told himself.

He walked stiffly out the front gate, crossing Washington Boulevard in the midst of blaring traffic, heading for the speakeasy down the block. He casually glanced in a bookstore window, the only kind of store Porter enjoyed, and noticed the name.

The Dora Ingram Bookshop

Yes, it was the shop where Bern had bought Porter's antique edition of *Hamlet*. Here it was, conveniently across the street from MGM. Irene Harrison had just said it had an order for Bern to pick up.

Porter had a hunch.

Dora Ingram's had a large, eclectic selection. There were the current best sellers, first editions, "rarities," and books in foreign languages. In the rear was a nook, as Porter expected, marked *Adult Readers Only*. A young, fastidiously dressed blonde clerk approached him.

"Hello," chirped the clerk. "I'm Paulette."

"Indeed you are," said Porter, going into his Irish act.

"May I help you?" she asked.

"Indeed you may," he replied.

"Are you in the Navy?" she asked politely, regarding his sailor suit.

"No more," said Porter. "I just don me nautical togs for old times. I'm Patrick Killarney. I work for MGM." He flashed his studio I.D. badge.

"Oh, my!" she said, impressed properly.

"I'm here for Mr. Paul Bern, the great MGM producer. Ya' know he's gettin' married."

"Yes, of course," smiled Paulette. "To Jean Harlow."

"Aye," said Porter, "a grand girl."

"I've never met Mr. Bern," said Paulette, "but when I came back last Friday from lunch, they told me he'd been here. If Jean Harlow ever came into the store, I'd just die!"

"The heavens forbid. Anyway, I'm here to pick up Mr. Bern's order for him."

"I'll get it for you right away," beamed Paulette, and vanished into the rear of the store. She promptly returned with what appeared to be two books wrapped in brown paper.

"These books have been charged to Mr. Bern's account," said Paulette, handing the package to Porter. "I do hope he'll enjoy reading them."

"Thank you," said Porter.

"Thank you," said Paulette. "And always remember what we say at Dora Ingram's – a book is not only a gift, but a compliment."

"And you're not only a clerk," said Porter. "You're a doll."

Paulette blushed.

Outside, Porter sat on a bench, took his pen knife and opened the package. Yes, there were two books. The first was titled *The Biological Tragedy of Woman*, which included analysis of Arthur Schopenhauer's credo that "sexual love...exacts sacrificial offerings, sometimes of life."

Porter thought of the title for Dorothy Millette's fantasy epic-that-would-never-be – *The Sacrifice* – and figured Bern had been beating this drum for a long time.

The second book was *The Glands Regulating Personality*. Porter thumbed through it and found in-depth coverage of "the Eunuchoid personality," which the book described as "a flabby freak...with the reproductive organs of a little boy."

Porter shook his head. "Poor Bern," he said to himself, then headed across the street to MGM.

*

Ten minutes later, Porter breezed back into MGM's Lion Building, carrying the two books. As he approached Bern's door, Irene Harrison stood, frowned and put her hands on her hips.

"Mr. Down, I'm calling security."

Porter made no answer as he walked directly into Bern's office. "Mr. Down!" shouted Irene. "How dare you!"

Bern looked up, angrily put down his pen, and Porter dropped the two books on his desk.

"I figured I'd deliver your pre-marital summer reading list," said Porter. "Seems you have a lot on your mind."

Bern, ashen-faced, pinched his temples and lowered his head in humiliation.

"Happy reading," said Porter. "See ya.'"

As he left, Irene Harrison had her back to him as she telephoned her distress call to studio security.

Porter couldn't resist. He slapped her ass.

Chapter Twenty-Three
Hiding Place

Thursday, June 23, 1932

Porter celebrated in the commissary with a huge lunch and two desserts.

At this point, he didn't really give a damn if Paul "Eunuchoid" Bern tried to get him fired or not. The man's pinched temple mortification was a vivid memory to be savored. However, Porter felt he better check on Harlow.

*

The sky was clouding as he walked to Harlow's dressing room. Blanche Williams, looking worried, told him to go to Stage 6. When he got there, it was suggested he'd find her in wardrobe. A designer there said she had been there, but had left at noon. Not knowing where a major star was at every moment was a truly odd situation at this particular studio.

Rain began falling. Porter tried the dressing room again. Only Blanche was there.

"Blanche, what's going on?"

Her eyes filled with tears. "Baby likes you. And someone else needs to know about this."

*

The jungle dock of *Tarzan the Ape Man* stood on MGM's man-made lake on Lot Two. Blanche drove Porter to the back lot in her 1929 Chevy. "I drove Baby here a little while ago," said Blanche.

She behaved like a spy behind enemy lines as she held her umbrella and hurriedly led Porter through the heavy rain. The *Tarzan* set was abandoned for now. "Baby?" whispered Blanche, hurrying into a native hut and coming out looking worried. "Baby?" she asked at another hut and she went inside. Her dark, thin face appeared at the window and she motioned to Porter.

Inside he saw Harlow, curled up on the mat floor. She wore a red and white striped outfit with casual white shoes and socks. There was a purse, a bottle, a glass, and a pair of dice beside her.

"Well, hi there, Toots," she said to Porter. "Bring your rabbit's foot?"

"No."

"I got mine." She reached inside her blouse and removed the rabbit's foot from between her breasts. She rolled a pair of dice and took a drink. Porter barely recognized her. With hardly any make-up, she resembled a high school kid, trying to look like Jean Harlow. Her platinum hair was uncombed and fell over one eye as she rolled her dice.

"Who's winning?" asked Porter.

"Me," she said sullenly.

"Please talk to her, Mr. Down," said Blanche. "Please? I'll make sure nobody come."

Blanche went outside with her umbrella and Porter squatted on the floor opposite Harlow. "I thought I'd find the blushing bride-to-be on top of the world," he said. "Throwing fairy dust from both hands."

"Yeah, I'm Floradora the Glad Girl," said Harlow, rolling the dice again. "You want to play? No… you *can't* play. I won't *allow* you to play unless you have your rabbit's foot."

"A film opening tomorrow," said Porter. "A wedding next week. The pressure's gotta' show."

Harlow took a drink. "You're sweet to care," she said. "I mean that. You really are."

She looked at him and in the dim light he detected something he'd only marginally noticed before…for all of Harlow's sensuality, she didn't appear entirely well. The eyes looked tired and there were dark rings around them that he didn't think were makeup. The Sunday-dyed platinum hair gave a perhaps freakish tinge to her face, but something wasn't right…and for a moment Porter thought he saw a sick girl under that albino halo. The irony struck him that Garbo and Dietrich, who worked like dogs on their makeup to purvey that wilting voluptuary look, might look healthier dripping wet in the shower than Jean Harlow did…at least today.

"I guess it hasn't helped," said Porter, "to learn your fiancé has a lady pornographer who's blackmailing him."

"Paul told me about her Saturday. He said you're handling that."

"I am. But I guess it was worse to learn about the other lady in San Francisco."

"So what."

Porter suddenly wondered. "When did he tell you about her?"

"I think last night. No…the night before."

So, Bern waited to tell her until Millette called him, thought Porter. *Harlow knew all about her, as Irene Harrison had said, because Irene knew Bern had just told her…*

"Just how much do you know about the lady in San Francisco?" asked Porter. "I met…"

"Don't say her name," said Harlow quickly, almost childishly. "When he started to tell me, I said I'd listen, but never wanted him to tell me her name."

Porter had figured Bern would never have told Harlow about Millette unless he'd forced him into it. This was proof of it. He looked at the drunken Harlow, rolling her dice again.

"So, if this woman has no name," he asked, "it's easier to forget she exists?"

"Stop it."

"You can still call off this marriage, you know."

"We already have the license."

"And *that's* why you'll still marry him?" demanded Porter, angry at her passivity. "After learning about the blackmail? And San Francisco?"

"He wants to marry Jean Harlow," said Harlow, reaching for her bottle. "Jean Harlow always does what everybody tells her to do."

"Everybody who?" asked Porter.

"Everybody," said Harlow, refilling her glass. "Paul, Mother Jean, Marino, Mayer, Thalberg, Mannix, Strickling, the directors, the makeup men, the dress designers, the agents, the dieticians, the columnists…"

"I see," said Porter. He watched her for a while, tossing her dice like a sad kid playing alone.

"I wish you brought the rabbit's foot I sent you," sniffled Harlow, downing her drink. "Then we could both play. Don't you like it?"

"Sure. I promise you next time we meet, I'll have it."

"When will that be?"

"Well, I'm not sure. Mr. Bern wants to can me."

It took Harlow a moment to focus on what he had said. "No," she said softly. "No, he can't. I won't let him. I feel safe with you."

"Well, that's between you two. As I'm sure he'll tell you, I'm on suspension as a P.I. and on probation for manslaughter..."

"I don't care! You're staying. I'll go to Mayer. I'll show Paul – you'll meet us at the party tonight. At Freddie March's house."

"I'm not much for parties."

"There are always lots of nice people at Freddie's parties. He invites the crew, so they're fun. Please?" She was silent a moment, her black-ringed eyes pleading.

"I always do what they tell me to do," she said. "Tonight, help me do *what I want to do*."

"OK," Porter nodded. "Put it that way and you got a deal."

"Also...I have to be at the opening of *Red-Headed Woman* tomorrow. Jean Harlow's making a personal appearance. I'll hate it, so you have to be there and hate it too."

"Swell, since you asked so nicely."

She laughed, then suddenly lunged and put her arms around his shoulders. He felt her breasts shoved up against him and smelled her perfume...Mitsouko. There was thunder and the rain fell now like a monsoon. It was very dark inside the hut.

"I like you," she sighed. "And I don't like to be alone in the dark."

It sounded like a come-on line and he had to resist his urges as she lushly nestled into his arms. Blanche ducked into the shack. She didn't seem surprised or embarrassed to see Porter holding Harlow.

"Baby, we gotta' go back...they gonna' be lookin' everywhere for you."

Harlow moaned but moved. "You'll be there tonight?" she asked Porter, the alcohol on her breath strong. "You won't run out on me?"

"I'll be there," said Porter.

"You promise?"

"Yeah, I promise. Now you return *two* promises. I'll handle the blackmailer, but it's up to you to tell Bern to get rid of the lady in San Francisco. Otherwise, you don't marry him."

"Alright," said Harlow. "What's the other promise you want me to make?"

"Gargle before you go to the party tonight," said Porter. "That bootleg liquor's a killer."

Harlow grinned, left the glass and bottle in the shack, placed the rabbit's foot back in her bodice and left with Blanche. Both huddled under the umbrella as they walked to Blanche's car. Porter followed them in the wind and pouring rain. Up ahead was one of the world's most famous stars, on the eve of the premiere of her new big picture, going tonight to a glamorous Hollywood party, one week away from marrying a major producer.

Yet Porter couldn't shake the uneasy feeling that, as he followed Harlow and Blanche in the rain, he was part of a funeral procession.

Chapter Twenty-Four
Angel from Heaven

Thursday, June 23, 1932

Fredric March was already the predicted winner of the 1932 Academy Award for his virtuoso performance(s) in Paramount's *Dr. Jekyll and Mr. Hyde*. He and his wife, actress Florence Eldridge, were popular hosts at their Beverly Hills home, where the couple graciously welcomed all levels of Hollywood society. Nevertheless, Porter Down hated *soirees* and wondered if Harlow, when she sobered up, would even remember she'd invited him…or that she'd requested he stay on despite Bern's decision.

Come 9 P.M., Porter arrived, wearing his dark grey tweed, this time avoiding his usual 15-minutes early routine. It was still pouring rain and the wind was severe. Fredric March, with his Barrymore profile, had a reputation in the movie colony as a "chaser" and Florence, presumably content to be wed to a major star, chronically forgave him while trying to look the other way.

"Make yourself comfortable," said Florence to Porter.

Porter got a glass of ice water and found a corner in the living room. There were shelves of rare books and Porter found a first edition of one of his favorites, *Oliver Twist*. He turned to the climactic chase after Bill Sikes, following Sikes' murder of Nancy, and read it again, although he knew it almost by heart.

As the various guests arrived, Porter glanced up now and then from the book. Many of the women were soaked by the storm, and after removing their "wraps," their brassieres and girdles showed through their tight gowns. "Freddie" was in his glory – stroking their straps, touching their tails, the women laughing shrilly, Florence meanwhile pointing out the living room's new paintings. The fondled women's escorts tolerated the molesting host, Porter imagined, because they were somehow complimented that a famous star found their women alluring enough to grope.

The party had three purposes: to toast Harlow and Paul Bern on their nine-day-away wedding, to *fete* east coast socialite Cornelius Vanderbilt Whitney, and to welcome actor Lionel Atwill to Hollywood. Atwill, a British matinee idol who looked to Porter as if he were going to seed, was the first guest-of-honor to arrive – a plump, cat-eyed, chain-smoking *poseur*. He'd triumphed in the Broadway play *Deburau* in 1920 and, as March told the guests, he'd been Atwill's understudy. Porter imagined March had learned more from Atwill than just acting, since the Britisher was at least the lecher March was, although he had his own little tricks. One was going up to the various ladies and whispering something in their ears that made each and every female he'd targeted whoop, screech and turn beet red.

I bet Atwill would get a kick out of Annie's movies, thought Porter.

Now Harlow – coiffed, made up and dressed to kill – arrived with Bern. Everyone applauded and March and Atwill practically had a foot race as to who would be first to get his hands on the satin-clad Harlow. Porter caught Bern's eye. The producer looked grim and potty in his dark suit and, although he cast a censorial glance at Porter, he said nothing. He had a look of defeat, almost violation, and Porter guessed that both Mayer and Harlow had thoroughly reamed him this afternoon after Bern's demand that Porter be fired. Meanwhile, Harlow extricated herself from both lechers and came right up to Porter, who stood to greet her.

"Thank you for being here," she said softly, and she kissed him on the mouth.

It was a hell of a great kiss. Porter almost felt the need to wipe his face as he said, "You're welcome." Harlow turned, defiantly looking across the room at Bern, who glared at her and Porter.

"Have you given him the ultimatum about San Francisco yet?" asked Porter softly.

"Not yet. But I told him he can't fire you – and so did Mayer. He knows he better not!"

As beautiful as Harlow was, Porter had the impression there might still be a residue of hooch in her system. Besides her gauntlet-tossing kiss of Porter, she seemed especially flirtatious, and Porter sat down again, watching her make the rounds, work the room, and help herself to the drinks. At length Cornelius Vanderbilt Whitney arrived, fashionably late. His "date" for the evening was Irene Selznick, daughter of L. B. Mayer and wife of producer David O. Selznick, who was otherwise engaged that night. The black-haired Irene, very visibly pregnant, distastefully watched as Harlow welcomed Whitney.

"Mr. Whitney!" she exclaimed, and kissed him on the lips. For a moment, Porter thought Whitney would faint...and that Irene Selznick would slap Harlow. Bern blanched but stoically maintained his milksop grin.

The house was large, there were many guests, the bootleg liquor flowed freely, and it seemed virtually everybody smoked. Harlow was flirting and slinking, March was groping and fondling, Atwill was whispering and chuckling, Irene Selznick went to the powder room, and Bern looked pathetically lost. Porter figured Harlow's blatant behavior might at least partially be a victory lap after her fight with her fiancé over Porter's retention.

What a zoo, thought Porter.

It was 10 P.M. now and the volume was rising. Harlow joined Whitney at the bench of the grand piano and draped an arm over his shoulders. He played badly, she sang very badly, and Bern watched forlornly. Amidst so many handsome men, beautiful women and assured sensuality – the full-bloom, off-key Harlow its sexpot centerpiece – Paul Bern was woefully out of his league. He appeared obviously and painfully aware of it.

"I'm going upstairs to take a nap," he announced.

It sounded so much like a spoiled child's "I'm taking my ball and going home" that the guests laughed. Bern petulantly made his way up the stairs as people whispered and chortled. Harlow flounced at the piano. Porter stayed in his corner with *Oliver Twist*.

"Yoo-hoo!" shouted Harlow, waving to Porter from the piano bench. "You're cute!"

"I know," said Porter, waving back at her.

Meanwhile, Irene Selznick returned from the powder room. She looked for Bern, and then loudly and irritably told Florence Eldridge she'd only come because Bern had insisted she come. Porter wondered why Bern would force a woman who looked as if she'd give birth any minute to attend a party where he wasn't even the host.

"Where is Paul?" demanded Mrs. Selznick.

"He's...taking a nap," said Florence.

"Taking a *what*?" shrieked Mrs. Selznick.

Not her father's daughter for nothing, Irene Selznick imperiously demanded that Bern be summoned to her. March went upstairs to retrieve him. Mrs. Selznick meanwhile glared at Harlow, who caught one of her Fury-like frowns and merrily stuck out her tongue at her.

At last Bern appeared at the top of the stairs with his host. March anxiously descended into the throng of the party, but Bern stayed on the landing, staring at his fiancée at the piano. He paled. Porter and virtually everyone else turned to watch him. The man was trembling. The crowd quieted. Whitney was still playing, Harlow still cooing, but now even they grew silent.

"She's an angel," Bern said, looking down at Harlow.

Irene Selznick, casting herself as the evening's heroine, came up the stairs to rescue Bern. She whispered something into his ear and took his hand. Then the crowd suddenly gasped as Bern grabbed the pregnant woman, almost violently spun her around, and held her so she had to look at his bride-to-be.

"She's an angel from heaven!" ranted Bern to Irene Selznick. "Always remember, no matter what happens.... *Jean is an angel from heaven!*"

Fredric March came back up the steps to calm his guest. He and Irene each took Bern by an arm and slowly led him down the stairs. As the guests silently relished the meltdown they'd just witnessed, Porter asked the butler for his raincoat.

*

The rain was still heavy. As Porter left the party he passed Bern outside, being consoled – actually hectored – by the still-loyal Irene Selznick, each of them standing under an umbrella. Porter, hurrying to his car, nevertheless heard the woman's voice loudly and clearly.

"You can't marry that tramp," she told Bern. "You'd blow your brains out."

Chapter Twenty-Five
The Phoebe

Thursday, June 23, 1932

Porter drove west, angry with what he'd seen tonight and the past week-and-a-half in general. For a time, he'd welcomed the sideshows as a distraction from what he feared would hit him soon and hard next week – the fifth anniversary of Mary's murder.

He didn't pity himself. *Man lives but a short time, and all his days are full of turmoil,* quoth the Bible. He was playing games now and he knew it, baby-sitting the rich and famous, saving their tails from trouble, and telling himself it was worth it because there were decent people whose lives depended on the mass opiate of the Motion Picture.

Where were they hiding at that damned party tonight? he wondered.

*

There was a mudslide on the northbound lane of Pacific Coast Highway. An emergency crew allowed Porter to pass on the southbound lane but warned him to get where he was going fast – the rain would surely launch more mudslides. He arrived at the marina in Malibu near midnight and saw the lit lantern swinging in the wind. The turbulent surf splashed the dock, there was a light on in the shack, and there was a car parked outside it. Porter opened the door, and there was Luke, playing cards with Maggie York. The overhead bulb lit up her flaxen hair.

"What are you doing here?" asked Porter.

"Thanks for the warm welcome!" she laughed. Luke laughed too. "I had some information for you," said Maggie, "and decided to take a drive out to the ocean."

"It's the end of the world out there," said Porter. "The PCH has mudslides. You'll never get back to Hollywood tonight. You and Luke can sleep in the two trawlers and I'll bunk here in the shack."

"Oh, no," said Luke. "The trawler cabins are nicer than the shack. I'll take the shack and you two take the trawlers."

Porter thought he detected goo-goo eyes on Luke as he looked at Maggie. He allowed the lad his chivalry. "OK. But I hope you two aren't startin' a game of strip poker."

Luke blushed.

*

After the game and a snack, Porter and Maggie bid Luke goodnight. Although it was only a walk of a few yards, both Porter and Maggie put on yellow slickers in the shack due to the force of the storm. Porter led Maggie across the wet dock and into *The Phoebe*. He noticed that she carried a folder.

They settled into the trawler's pilot house. Porter lit a lamp and they removed the drenched slickers. Maggie wore blue slacks, a white long-sleeved blouse, and flats. Porter noted that although her attire was casual, she appeared to have taken some time with her makeup.

"You can have my room," said Porter, indicating a hatch leading below. "I'll sleep in Luke's, on the other boat." They sat across from each other in the cramped quarters, their knees almost touching, and looked at each other for a moment. Porter went below, came back up with two bottles of Coca-Cola and handed one to Maggie. "So. What brings you out in this storm? Why didn't you just call me?"

"I did," said Maggie. "There was no answer. I guess…I got restless. And I'm anxious to tell you what I've learned about the case, and find out what *you've* learned."

"Okay." He relaxed. He really was glad to see her. "Ladies first. Batter up. Play ball."

Maggie opened her folder. "Well," she said, "as for Dorothy Millette, I struck out."

I didn't, thought Porter, but said nothing.

"Sorry to disappoint, Porter. I tried everything in L.A. – police files, legal files, casting directories, employment agencies, real estate records, the works. I searched for Dorothy Millette with every variation of the l's and the t's in her name…nothing. What did you find out about her in San Francisco?"

"I'll tell you later. What about Marino Bello?"

"Well, there I hit the ball. The man's a skunk, no doubt about it. I've got a full report here in the file for you. Bello's soliciting funds for a gold mine in Mexico – he always calls it a 'great, giant crevice of gold.' He's been harassing various big shots at Metro for money – Clark Gable's a favorite target. In fact, Metro's police chief is worried about Bello's friendship with Gable, which is how I got some of this information. Bello's planning a visit to his mine Monday."

"I'm betting the mine's got false eyelashes," said Porter.

"'Mother Jean' is a whole other story," said Maggie. "A textbook case of a woman living her dreams of stardom through her daughter. She answers Harlow's fan mail and signs her pictures. I've heard all sides this week: Some say Harlow cherishes her mother; others that she resents her controlling her life and sapping her money. Some say the mother adores her daughter, others say she's insanely jealous of her and would like to kill her Baby."

"Kill her baby? Oh yeah...her Baby."

"Oh, by the way – the Baby's platinum hair formula? Peroxide. Mixed with …"

"Ammonia, Clorox and Lux flakes," mumbled Porter. "Yeah, I know. Anyway, nice hit, Maggie. A run-driving double."

The rain was falling fiercely and the surf crashed up against the trawler, rocking at its mooring. It was growing cold and Porter turned up the small electric heater under the wheel.

"Now," said Maggie, "as for Anne Cynthia Spry."

"I'm all ears," said Porter.

"First," said Maggie, "I traced business records for 'AS' Productions. Miss Spry started her film company in 1929 with a man named Robert Jordan, a financier with various money interests in Southern California. He cleared the way for licenses and distribution in the U.S. and abroad, handling the business end of the enterprise while Miss Spry devoted herself to its 'artistic' nature. I had a chat with Jordan. He's quite full of himself, and told me that he and Spry worked together at AS Productions, as he put it, 'like Mayer and Thalberg at MGM.'"

Porter had to grin.

"Anyway," said Maggie, "it seems Miss Annie Spry got too big for her girdle and wanted more control. Jordan said she 'went crazy,' as he put it, and he was glad to pull out of AS Productions in April of '31. Ever since, he says, Spry has relied on underworld contacts to deal with any business problems."

"Swell," said Porter. "That means she probably has hired muscle...and professionals."

"There's more," said Maggie. "Jordan also said that, back in February, Spry came to see him and asked for a loan – said she'd been in contact with men in Berlin who wanted her to set up a studio there. You know about the type of decadent showmanship they have in 'Weimar Berlin,' Porter – bestiality, so on. It's where Marlene Dietrich became a star."

"Say no more," said Porter.

"Along with that, apparently the producers, 'hot for Annie's services,' are loyal members of the on-the-rise Nazi Party."

"Well, this just keeps getting better and better," deadpanned Porter.

"Jordan says that the Nazis wanted Annie to put up half the money for the studio," continued Maggie. "He also claims that, after he left AS Productions, the company has barely managed to stay in the black and that Spry hasn't the capital to make that investment. Her claim that she's making a fortune is a lie. She asked Jordan to put up the money. He told her to go fry an egg, and she told him she'd get the money somewhere else."

"Yeah," said Porter. "From Bern and Harlow. But that still doesn't add up. With their protection, they're two of the most dangerous people in California to blackmail."

"Maybe she enjoys the danger," said Maggie. "Or maybe she's a Harlow fan." She took a few more papers out of her folder. "Incidentally, she began as an actress. Annie had a strange specialty..."

"Animal sounds," said Porter.

"Yes. How'd you know?"

"Never mind," said Porter.

"She had a vaudeville act before the War," said Maggie. "Bird calls. Later she dubbed in shrieks and howls on radio and in some early Sound films."

"Why am I not surprised?" asked Porter.

"Finally, I know how old she is," said Maggie. "She's 43, although on recent records, she's claimed she's 35. At least ten years past the prime of ladies who usually star in her particular type of entertainment."

"22 years older than Harlow," said Porter. "And one year older than Bern."

"I consider myself pretty worldly," said Maggie, closing her folder. "But my eyes were wide as I investigated Miss Spry. Sometimes she uses animals in her movies, and characters often die in her films – horribly. I had a nightmare or two after researching Annie, and I usually sleep like a baby. I mean a real baby, not a Jean Harlow Baby..."

"Yeah, I get it."

"So," smiled Maggie. "Was that a triple?"

"Yep, and it drove in two runs," said Porter.

"By the way," said Maggie. "I got hold of one of Annie's movies. It was called *Medusa's Revenge,* starring guess who?"

"How'd Medusa get her head back on, after Perseus cut it off?" asked Porter.

"Oh, she managed," said Maggie.

"What about the snakes?" asked Porter.

"Annie was wearing a snake wig," said Maggie. "Those nasty puppets jiggled, had shiny fangs, and tongues that flicked. And where those snakes were biting Perseus…well, you don't want to know."

"Damn right," said Porter, getting them each another Coke. "Anyway, a home run, Maggie. A ninth inning grand slam."

"I told you I'd surprise you," said Maggie, winking.

"Yeah, but now you're scaring me," said Porter, winking back. They clinked bottles and his knees brushed against hers.

"Sorry," he said.

"That's alright," she said.

Chapter Twenty-Six
Opening Night

Friday, June 24 through Sunday, June 26, 1932

The news came Friday morning on the radio that Pacific Coast Highway was closed from Malibu south to Santa Monica due to mudslides in the night. The rain was still falling.

Maggie York, a bit embarrassed to be wearing the same clothes from the night before but high-spirited nonetheless, joined Porter and Luke for breakfast. Later they took one of the trawlers out to sea and Luke reveled in showing off his skills as a skipper and a fisherman. Porter brought along an old kite, found among the junk in the shack, and sent it sailing out over the rough ocean and high into the rain-swept sky.

The rain finally weakened, they cooked some of their catch for an early dinner, and the sun actually appeared, a pale red ball come late afternoon. The radio reported that PCH was clear and Maggie prepared to head home. Luke wandered along the beach to find her some seashells.

"What are you doing tonight?" asked Porter.

"Changing my underwear," said Maggie.

Porter chuckled. "I'd promised Harlow I'd show up at the opening of *Red-Headed Woman*," he said. "At Loew's State Theatre. Wanna' come along?"

"Sure."

"You drive home and change. I'll pick you up tonight at 8:30."

Luke returned with the bag of seashells, which he gave to Maggie. She made a fuss over them, and then got in her car, smiled and waved as she drove away.

"Wow, she's so nice and so pretty!" gushed Luke.

"Yeah," said Porter. "She sure is."

*

Red-Headed Woman, opening Friday, June 24, 1932 at Loew's, had a special bait for audiences: Jean Harlow would appear in person at 1:00 P.M., 3:30 P.M., and 9:15 P.M, along with a stage show, through July 1, the eve of her wedding.

Porter wore his "Wild West gambler" brown pinstripe suit. Maggie was attractively dressed in yellow, wore a cloche hat over her nicely brushed hair, and looked every inch an MGM starlet. In her heels, she was at least as tall as Porter, and he didn't mind at all.

They arrived at Loew's at 7th and Broadway at 9:05. The theatre was a sell-out, but Porter flashed his MGM pass and the uniformed usher escorted the couple into the balcony, where they watched the last few minutes of the movie.

The stage show began with a bevy of chorus girls, brazenly showing off their hosiery and their garters. Gilda Gray, who had popularized the "Shimmy," came out and performed a torch song. Following this came more of the chorus girls in a number titled "Ubangi," in which the all-white ensemble, led by the Caucasian Miss Gray, wore black tights with large flapping lips attached to their own.

"Porter, this is horrible!" whispered Maggie.

"You're telling me!" replied Porter.

After this number came the Crosby Brothers (no relation to Bing) who performed a furious tap dance to the "William Tell Overture." Then at last came Harlow, wearing a silver gown. There was no "act" – she just stood there, smiling and waving. The crowd cheered the way they did a game winning touchdown. The reception nearly drowned out the orchestra. Messenger boys ran down the aisles with flowers and placed them over the corner lips of the stage. The curtain came down and up again six times and Harlow threw kisses. Finally, she spoke.

"Ladies and Gentlemen, here's the lady who wrote the script for *Red-Headed Woman*…the famous author of *Gentlemen Prefer Blondes*…Miss Anita Loos."

Loos entered, took a bow, and she and Harlow exited together.

A violinist came up out of the pit, stood stage center and, as a finale, played "Oh, Promise Me." Hardly anybody noticed.

*

At this point Porter and Maggie started backstage. Gilda Gray and Leroy Prinz, the show's choreographer, had returned to the stage to host a "Snake Hips" contest offering a cash prize of $300 to the winner. "If you can shake a mean pair of hips," called out Prinz, "wiggle over here right now!"

A line was already forming.

"I'll be happy to wait," Porter told Maggie, "If you want to compete in the contest."

"You go to hell!" said Maggie good naturedly.

Backstage Porter and Maggie found Harlow surrounded by Bern, Marino, and Mother Jean, as well as Howard Stickling and a fleet of MGM publicity workers. Bern clearly saw Porter but pretended he didn't. Marino saw him and grinned challengingly under his mustache. Mother Jean, almost hysterical with excitement, appeared oblivious to everything except her "Baby."

Harlow broke away when she saw Porter and came to him. He introduced Maggie and the two women shook hands. "You're very lovely," said Maggie.

"So are you," said Harlow.

"We'll be going now," said Porter. "Thanks for inviting us. Congratulations."

"Thank you for being here," Harlow said fervently to Porter. She maneuvered him so her back was to her entourage, then she kissed him. Porter was startled that she did so with her mouth open. Maggie was too.

*

"That's an appreciative client you have," said Maggie.

She and Porter had gone to a diner after the show. Now he was walking her up to her apartment. She hadn't remarked about the kiss until now.

"Sorry," said Maggie. "I wasn't going to say anything, but obviously I couldn't resist."

Porter said nothing.

They'd reached her door and she took her keys from her purse. "I need to tell you something," she said. "About my having driven out to Malibu...It's true that Whitey Hendry had called me about us possibly no longer being on the case. And I was anxious to tell you what I'd found. But I really came because...well, Lt. O'Leary telephoned me. He's vacationing with his family in Virginia, you know. He said…this might be a bad weekend for you…that it was leading up to the anniversary of your wife's death…"

"So, he sent you out to babysit me?"

"Actually, he just suggested I call you. In my St. Bernard dog-in-your-lap way, I decided to drive out. Please don't be angry – I was concerned that…well, I thought MGM might be sacking you and me, and with this being such a sad time for you already…"

"That's fine," said Porter, and his voice softened. "Thank you."

She looked at him, her green eyes very pretty. "Pardon a nosey investigator question. What day is the anniversary? What will you do?"

"Tuesday. I have a….private way to mark it."

"If I can help in any way," said Maggie, "please call me. Good night, Porter." She kissed him, almost on the lips, and then went into her apartment.

*

Porter took the weekend off…sort of. Saturday, with the news that huge schools of fish were off Catalina Island, Porter and Luke each piloted a trawler to the grounds. By evening, both boats were teaming with fish. They packed the fish at the marina, loaded them into Luke's truck, and Luke left at 9:30 P.M. to drive downtown to the market and sell his mountainous catch. Sunday morning, they each sailed back to Catalina, returning late in the day with the trawlers loaded.

Luke made another night trip to the market and Porter sat on *The Phoebe*, under lantern light, catching up with the weekend newspapers. His favorite was the *Evening-Herald Express*, which had the most adventurous reporters. He was tempted to skip Friday's two-day old news but was glad he hadn't.

JEAN HARLOW GETS MANSION AS GIFT

The headline grabbed his attention and he read:

> *Paul Bern, motion picture producer whose engagement to Jean Harlow, the famous platinum blonde of stage and screen, was announced several days ago, planned to present Miss Harlow with a $60,000 home today, the house he built on Easton Drive in Benedict Canyon two years ago…*

Neither Bern nor Harlow had mentioned this to him. Porter suspected the man behind it was Marino Bello.

Chapter Twenty-Seven
Down Mexico Way

Monday, June 27 and Tuesday, June 28, 1932

Porter Down figured tagging along after Marino Bello on his trip to his Mexican mine – his "great, giant crevice of gold" – would be easy.

Harlow's swarthy stepfather, dressed as elegantly as any luminary in the MGM commissary that Monday, June 27th, lunched, hobnobbed, gestured flamboyantly with his cane, reiterated loudly that he was *en route* to check his gold mine, and then drove his red Cadillac touring car – or rather, his stepdaughter's – through the gate, heading south. He drove for hours, past Long Beach and San Clemente, Porter keeping a safe distance behind him. Only after they crossed the border did the chase become challenging.

Bello headed out to the desert and Porter lost him at a fork in the road. The sun was setting when he finally saw a woebegone cantina/gas station. He asked the man at the pump if he'd seen a fancy Cadillac stop in or drive by, and the Mexican responded with hoots of laughter.

"Gringo in spits! *Spits!*" he belly-laughed.

It took a moment for Porter to realize the man meant "spats." Yep…Bello. He was on the right track. Porter filled up his car and resumed the chase. Beside him on the front seat was a camera he'd borrowed from MGM. Porter was quite certain of what Bello's "gold mine" actually was and hoped she'd lie still long enough for him to snap an incriminating picture.

*

The stars were bright as Porter saw a small ranch off the desert road. He turned off the headlights and drifted down the drive to a handsome hacienda. There was the Cadillac.

The hacienda had two stories, the top floor offering a front and rear balcony. Porter got out of his car with his camera, snooped, and saw a fountain splashing on the patio. Aside from flickering candles, the entire house was in darkness.

Then from above, inside the open doors at the balcony, the moaning started. Porter recognized the sound instantly. The lady was in a mounting state of rapture, her volume rising, falling, and then rising again. It was tough, of course, to calculate how much time this would take – it always was – but Porter figured it best if he moved fast. A Saul Lestz skeleton key popped the back door and Porter tiptoed to the staircase.

The lady was approaching the operatic in her ascending ecstasy as Porter made his way up the staircase. He reached the door, saw the shadows bouncing and writhing on the huge bed, making, as Shakespeare had so quaintly put it, "the beast with two backs." He aimed the camera, and threw on the light. By the time he'd taken a picture, the large, black-haired woman had risen from the bed, screaming like a creature of the damned, grabbing a wine bottle from a table beside the bed, throwing the bottle at Porter. It crashed over his head against the doorframe, and then a basin hit him square in the chest. He somehow snapped another picture as she charged him, smashing into him as she and he together crashed through the door, wrestled atop the stairway, and finally tumbled down the steps in a commingled heap.

The woman didn't move. Porter realized she was unconscious. Her giant breasts trapped him in a stockade of flesh. He crawled out from under the Amazon and saw his camera was somehow still intact. The lights came on and Porter, still on the floor, looked up.

A naked Marino Bello was atop the staircase, aiming a pistol at him.

*

Almost a half-hour had passed. A bruised Porter, with a small cut on his forehead, sat with his host on the patio, the fountain cascading in the desert starlight. The revived, unhappy señorita, named Consuelo, had taken to her now solitary bed, nursing a violent headache from her stairway fall and a giant petulance from her sexual frustration.

Bello, sporting a red brocaded dressing gown worthy of a Silent Screen idol, elegantly smoked as he poured himself a glass of

Madeira wine. He regarded his "guest" with a mocking civility. Bello wore his smirk, Porter thought, as brazenly as his stepdaughter wore her hair. He also had his cane beside him – Porter would have bet any odds it was a sword cane.

"Gold mine," smirked Porter. "The only 'great, giant crevice' here tonight is Consuelo's."

Marino smiled. "So. Do you wish to tell me what you plan to do with your photographs?"

"Well," Porter began, "first of all, I'll probably print a thousand copies of the picture – the first one I took…you know, the one where you're wearing Consuelo's ass like a sombrero. Then I'll hop into my plane, fly over MGM, and drop 500 of them over the studio. I'll drop the other 500 over Club View Drive."

Marino grinned. "Suppose I began to refill my glass" – he did – "while suddenly, without warning, with my other hand, I pulled my pistol from my robe pocket and shot you right between your eyes?"

"I bet you scare yourself to death."

"Or perhaps, my Consuelo is at this very moment at an upstairs window with the hunting rifle that I keep here, primed, loaded and ready. Perhaps she has you in the rifle's crosshairs even now. And she's very tense. Most women, you know, are tense when they fail to get their prize."

"No, I don't know. You obviously have more trouble giving women a 'prize' than I do."

Marino blew his cigarette smoke through his nostrils. "Perhaps we both will shoot you," he said calmly. "I shoot you through the face, and she blows off the top of your skull. Nobody would ever find you, you know."

The man's beady eyes and full mustache gave him a feral look in the starlight, the cigarette smoke creating a cloud around his face. He proudly unsheathed his cane, touching its sword edge.

There it is, thought Porter.

"Consuelo and I would lift you," said Bello, "with your shattered face and blasted skull, wrap you in a blanket, place you in my Cadillac's trunk, and drive you out into the desert and the base of the mountains. The vultures would find you quickly, dine on your carcass, and shit you all over the mountains and valley. No more Mr. Porter Down. Just vulture shit. And perhaps, before I'd feed you to them" – he raised and brandished his sword cane – "I'd cut off your balls."

His voice had lost its suavity and his eyes were angry in the darkness. Porter grinned.

"It'll never happen," he said. "Not now. You have too much to lose, Bello. You and your perfectly charming wife have reached a personal pinnacle as far as pimping your step-daughter. She's marrying into MGM royalty and you both plan to stay aboard for every mile of the joyride. You can't risk fouling it up with a murder…at least not on the eve of the wedding."

"You make Harlean sound like a vampire," said Bello, more amused than angry.

"No. You and Mrs. Bello are the bloodsuckers. 'The Baby' wasn't at MGM three months before you had her engaged to one of the studio's most powerful men."

"Mr. Bern escorted Harlean to the *Hell's Angels* premiere over two years ago," said Bello. "Their picture was in all the papers. He's been smitten with her all this time."

"Yeah, but my guess is he'd have stayed smitten – the way he stayed smitten with Norma Shearer and Joan Crawford and all the rest – and never proposed marriage if she hadn't lit the fire under him. And she'd never have lit the fire unless you and Mrs. Bello gave her the matches. It's like an old country royal marriage… you're marrying into the kingdom. You and the wife plan to drain Jean Harlow's money, and Paul Bern's money, and anybody else's money you can leech onto at Metro. Bern's house is the first big acquisition."

"As the papers have reported," said Bello, "Bern is giving his house to Harlean."

"Yeah, and I bet within 90 days she signs it over to you. So…you won't be killing anybody tonight. You can't risk it."

Bello smirked, apparently proud of his perfidy. He raised his glass. "You're quite the philosopher, Mr. Down. Perhaps, in the depth of your thinking, you will understand that I, in turn, have no fear that you'll use those pictures to embarrass me in any way."

"Do tell. Do."

"You are a champion of Harlean! I've heard her talk of you. She likes you. I saw your eyes the day you met her…and I saw her eyes when she met you."

Bello lit a fresh cigarette. "You know how close Harlean is to her mother and how close her mother is to me. We are a unit, a force – an army, if you will. We guard each other, defend each other, honor each other. To embarrass me is to embarrass Harlean. You'd never do this."

Porter was silent. The son-of-a-bitch had a point.

"*Ha!*" suddenly laughed Bello, startlingly and triumphantly, pointing the sword at Porter's throat. "See? She has bewitched you too!"

His hyena laugh repeated and lingered. Porter stayed silent. Yes, he couldn't hurt her. It was her vulnerability. He batted away the sword.

"You have a long drive back to your dock," said Bello. "But as I told you before, I love my wife and stepdaughter like a tiger and I will protect them like a lion. Mr. Bern serves us now. If the day ever comes that he does not, we – our little army – simply march on."

"Over his dead body?" asked Porter.

Bello grinned but did not reply. He stood formally. Porter stood too. "By the way," said Porter, "did you ever imagine your stepdaughter might actually love Paul Bern?"

"Does it matter? Good night, Mr. Down. If you'll pardon me, I have a lady to console."

Marino Bello suggestively plunged his sword cane into his sheath and entered the hacienda.

*

It had been a long, hot drive back to Malibu. Porter was aware that midnight had passed and the date was June 28. The dreaded day had arrived, the anniversary of Mary's murder.

He parked at the marina, checked for messages, and found a telegram on the table in the shack. *Arrived after midnight*, Luke had written on the envelope. Porter tore it open:

I WANT A DATE WITH YOU TUESDAY NIGHT SAILOR BOY STOP FALCON LAIR 10 PM STOP BE READY FOR A BIG SURPRISE STOP LOVE AND KISSES ANNIE

Porter realized the game that Annie was playing. She knew about Mary and the significance of June 28.

This was going to be one hell of a day and night.

Chapter Twenty-Eight
Pilgrimage

Tuesday, June 28, 1932

Come early morning of Tuesday, June 28th, Porter decided to honor the occasion by wearing one of his new suits...the blue one. He put on the straw boater MGM had provided, looked in his mirror, frowned and shook his head.

I look like I'm gonna' do a Goddamn buck 'n wing, he thought.

He ditched the *Paddlin' Madeline Home* hat and put on the snap brim hat instead. Then he drove to the airfield, stowed the hat under his seat, put on his leather flying helmet and took off in *Timber Wolf* for Santa Barbara. The day was beautiful as he landed and took a cab to the Santa Barbara Mission.

Mary had been a devout Catholic and Porter, in her memory, had started two years ago coming to the mission for Mass on June 28. There were few people in the church this Tuesday morning, but even so, Porter sat at the back by himself.

Afterwards he went up to the altar to light a votive candle. He had been here last Christmas Eve and after the Midnight Mass, he'd lit two candles, one for Mary and one for Eve Devonshire's murdered friend Bonnie.

Porter knelt by the altar rail, lit the candle and, for a long time, watched the flame.

*

He'd flown for a while over the ocean and was back at the marina by mid-afternoon. A florist had made the delivery of a single rose. It had come in a glass vase with a few sprigs of baby's breath and a note:

This is in memory of your wife. I'm sure she was a wonderful woman. Maggie.

*

At the marina that evening, Porter swam out in the ocean. He'd just climbed back onto the pier when the phone rang in the shack. It was Maggie. "How are you?" she asked.

"Fine," he said, glancing at the rose she'd sent.

They were silent again. "Porter," she said finally, "I hope you're not angry that I sent the note and flower."

"No," he said. "Thanks. We'll...we'll talk later."

"Take care," she said. "Call me any time."

"Thanks," he said, and he hung up.

He looked at the rose for a moment, then dressed again in his navy-blue suit. He noticed Harlow's rabbit foot on his small dresser, picked it up and put it in his pocket. He suspected he'd need it tonight.

*

Porter drove downtown to Loew's before making the trip to Falcon Lair. *Red-Headed Woman's* weekend release and Harlow's personal appearances had been a smash. The censors were raising hell but it was all swell publicity. The house was packed.

Porter arrived backstage just as Gilda Gray and the chorus girls were launching into a wild shimmy in the "Ubangi" number. He noticed that Blanche Williams, Harlow's black maid, was standing alone in the wings, watching. Her eyes were sad – and a bit angry. Porter walked up to Blanche and put his hand on her shoulder.

"Gilda and her girls aren't worth your little finger," he said.

*

He finally had a few private moments in Harlow's dressing room. It was the first time he'd seen her since the rather spectacular kiss she'd provided him Friday night. She was dressed in her evening gown, ready for her 9:15 P.M. stint, and seemed moody.

"You might have tipped me off you'd be tagging Marino," said Harlow, standing in front of a full-length mirror. "He showed up here this afternoon and raised a terrible stink."

Porter imagined that, despite all the adulation, Harlow was tiring of her three-times-a-day gig on Loew's stage, especially in a week that would climax with her wedding. She perused herself in all her regalia in her mirror with expert scrutiny but no apparent vanity. She looked sexy as hell and Porter wondered anew why

Paul Bern, the jackass, was mourning the loss of his animal-loving porno queen, and fighting to keep his screaming prune-faced harpy in the city by the bay.

"You make up your mind?" asked Porter. "About the lady in San Francisco? The one whose name you dare not speak? 'She goes or I go,' remember?"

"If I can live with her existence," Harlow said poutingly, sitting at her makeup table, "you should be able to."

"24 hours," said Porter. "She or me."

"You'd really run out on me?"

"Sure."

She lit a cigarette and Porter noted the Fatimas. He also noticed Harlow's Mitsouko. He figured he'd be seeing the same brand of cigarettes and smelling the same brand of perfume when he visited Annie later tonight.

They were silent and the mood was heavy. Porter took the rabbit's foot from his pocket and held it before her. "By the way, look what I got."

For the first time during Porter's visit, she smiled. "That's swell," Harlow said, sounding almost touchingly pleased. "Say…Would you like to stay and see my act? I smile and wave even better than last week."

"We'll talk later," Porter chuckled. He put on his hat and placed the rabbit's foot back in his pocket.

"Can I ask you a question?" said Harlow.

"Fire away."

"Are you dating that girl who was with you Friday night? Maggie?"

"We go out for ice cream now and then," said Porter. "Now, can I ask *you* a question?"

"Do you want to know if platinum blonde is my natural hair color or if I ever wear underwear?"

"I want to know if it's dawned on you yet that you're Jean Harlow. And that you can run your own life."

Harlow looked at Porter, then back at her reflection.

"I am who they tell me I am," she said, still looking in the mirror.

Chapter Twenty-Nine
Falcon Lair

Tuesday, June 28, 1932

Porter knew the basics about Falcon Lair, but had never had the slightest urge to see the abandoned dump.

The address was 1436 Bella Drive, on the west side of Benedict Canyon. He turned left onto Cielo Drive and drove up into the hills. Bella Drive was on the right. Deer watched the car from the darkness under the trees – Porter saw their glowing eyes. Coyotes thrived in Benedict Canyon, howling in the night, and Porter wondered if this was their mating season as the creatures' calls eerily sounded.

He reached the top of Bella Drive and saw a large gate with portals, each reading:

Falcon Lair

To the side of the gate was a Mediterranean-style house with a round stained-glass window. It was the gatehouse. The real splendor was behind the iron, unlocked gate.

The old Valentino estate rambled down a hillside to a building that resembled a baroque medieval mix of castle and monastery. Floodlights illuminated the center tower, its entranceway flanked by two tall cypress trees, and there was a flag raised above the tower's roof. A light played on the fountain in the center of the courtyard. It no longer spouted, and the foul residue water in the fountain was mostly dank and green.

There were other outbuildings, tall trees framing the main house, the lights of Benedict Canyon to the south and east creating a magnificent, starry backdrop. Porter, sensing decay about the place, walked down the hill to the courtyard.

*

Nobody appeared to be here, despite the lights, but there was a large black Doberman, chained to a post by the main door. When the dog saw Porter, it barked furiously and lunged at its chain.

Porter recognized the dog – the highly-strung, apparently hungry Helen.

"What's the matter?" Porter asked the dog. "She cut you off?"

The tower's flag fluttered in the night breeze and the whole place seemed like an old, forsaken DeMille set. The dog barked more viciously, and then…

"Helen!"

The voice came from above, and the dog stopped barking, whined and sat. Annie Spry was standing at a cranked-open, second floor, diamond-paned window in the tower. She wore a dark, slouch hat, cocked over one eye, and the room behind her was dimly lit in flickering candlelight.

"Welcome to Falcon Lair, Sailor Boy."

Annie up at the window, Porter down in the courtyard…it reminded him of *Romeo and Juliet's* balcony scene. *What blackmailer through yonder window breaks*, he thought.

He could see the bodice of her severely tailored dress, with a white corsage pinned to it. The dog looked up intently and the voice from the window was soft and seductive.

"You're very handsome tonight, Mr. Down."

Porter said nothing. The figure at the window lifted a glass of wine.

"Care to join me? The vintage comes from Valentino's own cellars."

"No."

"Afraid I might drug you…then have my wicked way with you?"

Porter shook his head. *Jesus*, he thought.

The shadowy figure drank. The stars were bright and the coyotes bayed in the hills. "Do you know the legend of Falcon Lair, Mr. Down?"

"I bet I'm about to hear it."

"Well, once upon a time, Rudolph Valentino created this beautiful place as a gift for the woman he loved, Natacha Rambova… dancer, writer, designer. She'd helped create the Valentino mystique and he always wore her slave bracelet. Of course, Natacha was born Winifred Shaughnessy in Salt Lake City."

"Don't you hate phony women?" said Porter.

"I knew them both, personally. Valentino prepared all of this for Natacha...the boudoir, the wine cellar, the fountain...the stable below, where he'd imported stallions. He named the showplace *Falcon Lair*, because Natacha was preparing a film for him, *The Hooded Falcon*. But she didn't want *Falcon Lair* – or *him*. Rudy moved here all alone. The following year, he died. And tonight, at Hollywood Memorial Cemetery, Rudy rots... with Natacha's slave bracelet on his wrist."

"What's Natacha up to these days?" asked Porter.

"She conducts séances in Pasadena, the silly cunt," replied Annie.

"Sounds like quite a gal," said Porter.

"The power of love is all around here," said Annie, and her voice had a fierce mockery. "Can't you *feel* it here *this very night*?"

She raised her glass as if in a toast and drank. "Nobody lives here anymore," said Annie. "Everyone thinks Falcon Lair is haunted. But the current owner, a valued client, allows me to use this hallowed spot... for special occasions."

The figure came closer to the window, peering down at Porter. The coyotes howled again.

"Come up," said the seductive voice. "Tonight's a premiere. Just follow the candles."

*

Porter was inside Falcon Lair now, following lit candles to a staircase. The surviving furnishings were heavy, Italianate. There was a large, ornately framed painting of a woman Porter presumed to be Natacha Rambova, wearing a turban.

The candles led him to an upstairs theatre. Two candelabra glowed on either side of a movie screen. The chamber had the impressive columns and balustrades of an opera house and Porter could make out a painting on the high ceiling – a mural of a sheik and his lover under a star-filled desert sky. He immediately noticed the smell of perfume in the room...*Mitsouko*... then Annie appeared deep in the room, in the shadows by one of the candelabra.

"Please be seated. I believe the middle row is best."

Porter sat.

"Valentino naturally furnished his own theatre," said Annie, now blowing out each candle one by one. "This screening room could have accommodated all the greats of Hollywood tonight. I resisted. This premiere is just…for…*you!*"

With each of her three final words, the dark figure blew out the three remaining candles. The room was in total darkness. And then suddenly came a piercing cat yowl. Porter jumped, and then heard laughter and the clicking of high heels.

*

A projector suddenly came to life from a booth in the rear. It was the first time Porter realized somebody else was here, beside Annie. The projectionist, he figured, was probably doubling tonight as Annie's bodyguard.

The screen lit up with the silvery spectral light, the numbers counted down, and Porter scowled as he saw the title:

AS
Productions
Presents
THE WEDDING NIGHT OF
JEAN HARLOW AND PAUL BERN

The piano music soundtrack sinuously tinkled under the credits, playing "I Wanna Be Loved by You," popularized by Helen Kane, the "Boop-boop-a-doop" girl. The scene came up – a shot of Bern's actual home, filmed from atop the crest in Benedict Canyon. One could see the lights in the windows and Porter realized AS Productions must have secretly dispatched a cameraman and crew to Easton Drive to get an actual night-for-night shot.

The love nest of the Platinum Blonde Bride and the Father Confessor Bridegroom! read the silent film's title card.

The scene was a bedroom. Languishing on the bed in a long shot was a platinum blonde, wearing the same Harlow cheesecake costume "Jeanie" at the MGM cathouse had worn – short black velvet jacket, black stockings and black heels. The piano music played and Porter recognized that "Harlow," adorned in the black lingerie and platinum wig, was Annie Spry.

The Blushing Bride so wants to please her Lover on this Magical Night! read the card.

The camera moved in slightly closer. Yes, it was the feline face, but the artistry of Annie's impersonation was amazing. Her figure appeared as voluptuous as Harlow's, no doubt, figured Porter, due to her miracle-working, flesh-tinted body stocking, worn under the costume. *She'd almost fool me, if I didn't know better*, Porter admitted to himself.

"Harlow" reached into an ice bucket on the bed table with tongs, selected an ice cube, pulled down the front of the jacket, and luxuriantly proceeded to press the cube against each of the body stocking's rubber nipples. *Yeah, the story got around from* The Public Enemy, thought Porter.

Mr. Bern, in the privacy of his bathroom, performed his own pre-love-making ablutions…

There was a flash shot of a balding, pot-bellied, mustached man squatting on a toilet. Porter heard male laughter from the projection booth.

Miss Harlow – now Mrs. Bern – wonders, "What is keeping that man?"

There followed a little comic showcase for "Harlow" – yawning, scratching…. selecting a chocolate from the bedside candy box after gouging several in search of a favored flavor…greedily licking her fingers…adjusting her stockings…playfully snapping her garters against her thighs. Annie, who he'd noted was left-handed, was pre-dominantly right-handed in the film, just as Harlow was. Annie had done her research, thought Porter, and had carefully studied her subject's nuances and mannerisms. The film was all the more horrible for the undeniable skill and timing of the player who acted it.

Will he ever come out???

At length "Harlow" knelt in the bed, turned her ass to the camera, showed off the tops of the stockings and the bottom of black panties, reached for something hidden under a pillow, pulled out a movie magazine with Jean Harlow adorning the cover, sat back against the headboard, and gawked narcissistically at the magazine.

At last, the Bridegroom enters the boudoir,
the glorious arena of love…

"Bern" came into the bedroom from the bathroom, wearing a robe. The plump, mustached, milquetoast character actor playing the producer posed forlornly as "Harlow" kept eyeing the magazine. The groom finally pantomimed clearing his throat and the bride looked up, tossing the magazine out of the scene.

"Harlow" knelt again in the bed, smiling, winking lasciviously, and wiggling a finger to lure her lover…

The Platinum Vamp turns up her siren act…
She kneels to the Father Confessor…

There was a close-up of "Bern," tugging nervously at his mustache.

Is he playing hard-to-get… or does he have a <u>secret</u>?

Porter watched the players on the screen – this cat-faced Jean Harlow from Hell, and the comic Paul Bern, who probably was third runner-up for the sissified school principal in an *Our Gang* comedy. Sweat was running down Porter's face. "Harlow" winked and coyly wiggled her finger again, then finally gave up the "siren act," put hands on hips and shouted, "Get the hell over here!" – Porter could read her lips. "Bern" waddled over to the bed, "Harlow" smiled teasingly, and then she pulled open his robe with a flourish…

And lo and behold!

There was a close-up of "Harlow's" shocked face, a "Boing!" sound effect, and another close-up – this one of a large leather dildo strapped about "Bern's" hips. "Harlow" began laughing hysterically, falling back on the bed, kicking her legs in the air, pedaling them as if riding a bicycle. The hysteria infected "Bern" who, now spastic with humiliation, shed his robe and stood naked except for the dildo.

Oh, what a LOVER!

The piano soundtrack seductively played a harem girl dance as "Bern" wiggled like a belly dancer. It thunderously pounded the *William Tell Overture* as he pranced about, "riding" the phallus as if it were a horse. It antically offered Laurel and Hardy's *Cuckoo Song* as he skipped around the room. At length "Bern" approached "Harlow" and the bride reached teasingly for the groom's dildo, squeezing the "balls" – and the dildo shot water into "Harlow's" face.

He bought the DELUXE model!

As "Harlow" sputtered, Porter stood up and, in the light of the film on the screen, hurried from the dark theatre, down the candlelit stairs, and out to the courtyard. He desperately needed fresh air.

*

Ten minutes had passed.

Porter sat in the courtyard, on a marble bench to the right of the entranceway. The night was hot, he was sweating, and he'd taken off his jacket and rolled up his sleeves. Annie Spry sat facing him, legs crossed, a yard away on a marble bench to the entranceway's left, smoking a Fatima, holding the black Doberman Helen on her leash. The can of film rested against the tower steps.

Her blouse and corsage were white, her hat, stockings, and heels black, her dress a dark burgundy. She looked, Porter thought, rigid, almost prim, fashionably professional.

"You'll have to excuse any flaws," said Annie. "It was written, filmed, and scored quickly. There was little time for finesse."

"A question," said Porter. "Are you madly jealous of Harlow? You smoke her brand of cigarettes...and wear her choice of perfume."

"It was part of my research for my performance. I'm smoking a Fatima and wearing Mitsouko tonight in honor of the premiere."

"Like hell. You were smoking a Fatima and wearing Mitsouko the first night we met."

"It's sweet that you noticed and remember."

Porter grinned tightly. "You think anybody who sees that filth is dumb and/or blind enough to think you're really Harlow?"

"And I was expecting flattery," said Annie. "You know people will accept the illusion. They'll believe what they want to believe."

"As if anybody cares," said Porter, "about what a bottom-of-the-barrel smoker shows."

"You know Goddamn well they'll care," said Annie sharply. "These impersonations tap right into all the Hollywood gossip about your two famous friends. Once my film's circulating to my world-wide clientele, the rumors spread, and fiction becomes fact. The public will *prefer* it that way. Harlow and Bern will be a dirty joke… the two biggest sex freaks in Hollywood history."

The panting Doberman, excited by the rising emotion, suddenly pressed her head up against her master's pubic area. Annie snapped her fingers and the dog instantly moved away.

Porter regarded them both. What she said sounded crazy, but was right. Most of the movie-going public believed Virginia Rappe had died in 1921 because Fatty Arbuckle had raped her with a Coca-Cola bottle. There wasn't a shred of evidence to support it and two juries had acquitted him of her murder, but Arbuckle remained an ostracized monster. He wondered if the "AS Productions" library featured a smoker called *Fatty, Virginia, and the Coke Bottle*.

"Okay. What do you want, Annie?"

Annie tossed her almost extinguished cigarette. "Paul Bern's annual MGM salary is $75,000. Jean Harlow's $65,000. Add them together, throw in a $10,000 bonus for my style and élan, and I demand $150,000."

"They don't have it."

"An advance will do for now. Tonight is June 28th. I want $15,000 before midnight of July the second – Paul and Baby's wedding day. Another $15,000 by August the second…the remaining $120,000, by September the second. No advance by the July date and 50 prints of *The Wedding Night of Jean Harlow and Paul Bern* start circulating in select U.S. cities and as far away as Berlin and Paris… at popular prices."

"I have a counter-offer," said Porter. "Here it is. You're asking *us* to pay *you* $150,000 by September the second. Now…if, instead, *you* pay *us* $150,000 *and* fifty cents by September the first, I won't tell your Nazi German buddies that Annie Spry is 43-years-old, and has built her career on whorehouse doubles."

Annie casually lit a fresh cigarette. "I see, Mr. Down. You've been doing legwork investigating me. How darling of you."

There was hostility in her voice. The Doberman, sensing it, began to growl.

"Listen," said Porter. "You and your stunt gals can go on filming your sex epics. I don't give a damn if you go to Berlin and start 'Ball-Buster Productions'...but I suggest strongly you not try to do it with my friends' money."

"Fuck you," said Annie.

"You've fallen in love with yourself, or rather with your own movie creation," said Porter. "And you're so jealous of Harlow, you've decided to go for her throat. You hate her because she's everything you dreamed of being – she's a major star, and you're a freak in 'zoomimic masochism' smokers. Poor Annie."

The dog growled ominously. "Not yet, Helen," said her master.

"'Helen,'" said Porter. "Why the hell didn't I think of it before? 'Helen' was Harlow's character's name in *Hell's Angels*!"

The growling dog, hearing its name repeated, glared hungrily at Porter, jaws salivating. Annie smoked her cigarette. Porter noticed her hand was trembling, despite her attempt to appear unruffled.

"Go home, Annie," said Porter. "You look a little drawn."

Annie's eyes suddenly sparkled, as if she realized she held an ace. "Maybe," she said, taking a deep drag on her cigarette. "But on my worst days, and from my worst angles...I still look a whole fucking lot better than your dead wife does tonight."

Porter went for her.

"*Helen, go!*" shrieked Annie, standing and releasing the dog. It attacked, roaring, its teeth bared and mouth frothing. On its hind legs, the dog was nearly as tall as Porter, and at his throat. Porter slammed the dog with his arm and while he deflected its jaws from his neck, the teeth tore into his left forearm. Blood sprayed as he charged past the Doberman and toward Annie.

"*Helen!*" screamed Annie, retreating. "*Go! GO!*"

The dog leaped again, now at Porter's back, and both he and the dog fell. The dog slavered on Porter's neck and was about to bite deeply into it when somebody fired a shot from an upstairs window. It barely missed Porter, but Helen yelped and was still.

"Helen!" shrieked Annie.

A second shot fired, passing just inches from Porter's face. He vaguely made out a man at the window. Realizing that both shots had been meant for him, Porter got to his knees, pulled out his pistol, fired, and saw the man fall back into the room.

It was suddenly still.

Porter, kneeling on the ground, glanced at the dead dog, then at Annie, now without guard dog or armed bodyguard. Her eyes took in Porter, then the dead Helen, then the window where the bodyguard had fired and fallen, and then Porter again.

"Helen's dead," she said brokenheartedly, then viciously snarled "It's your fault!"

Annie suddenly screamed and wildly threw herself at Porter, her nails going for his eyes. Her cat face, with its eye shadow, false eyelashes and lipstick, was very close to him, and he smelled the overwhelming scent of Mitsouko as she cursed at him and spat in his face.

Despite his wounds, Porter caught Annie, his violence barely in check as he shook her by her shoulders like a rag doll. He knew if he lost a shred of self-control, he'd snap her neck.

"Party's over, Annie," he said through clenched teeth.

Porter grabbed her by the waist, felt the stiff girdle through the dress, and threw her over his shoulder. She screamed hysterically, battering his back and kicking as he staggered to the fountain and, raising her above his head, threw her face-first into the foul, green water.

"Drink it, you sick bitch," said Porter.

After a moment she rose from the pool, gagging and breathless. Porter pressed her head again under the stagnant water, held it there a moment, and then turned and walked away. He caught his breath, hearing her splashing and coughing behind him, and looked up again at the window where the man had fired. No one was there. Feeling the full impact of his wound, he picked up his hat, staggered over to the entranceway to get the film can, and turned.

Annie had emerged from the fountain and collapsed against its wall. Her dress was ripped, her silk stockings torn, she'd lost her hat, her hair was drenched. Her mouth was bleeding and she gasped for air, trying to speak. Porter picked up his jacket and the film can and put it under his arm.

Annie looked mournfully at the dog's carcass. Then she got to her knees and, on all fours, crawled across the courtyard and collapsed crying on the dead dog.

"No, Helen," she keened. "No, no, no!"

She raised her face towards Porter, who paused to look down at her. He shook his head and began walking out of the courtyard.

"You *cock!*" Annie shrieked. "*You stinking, fucking cock!*"

Porter continued his march from the courtyard. "You'll *pay*," wept Annie Spry. "You stinking, fucking *cock!* You'll *pay!*"

Porter kept walking in intense pain, fearing he might pass out from loss of blood or, if the bodyguard was still alive, be the target of another bullet. He tried to staunch the bleeding from his arm, aware of the coyotes howling again. Annie was still sprawled by the dead dog, and her voice rose hysterically into a scream, filling the courtyard.

"You'll die! *You'll fucking die!*"

In his deepening pain, Porter thought the woman's hysterical screams and the coyotes' mating cries were echoing together, deafeningly and nightmarishly in the canyon. The night seemed a sordid, terrible fantasy.

It was a true "AS" Production.

Chapter Thirty
Approach of the Nuptials

Wednesday, June 29 through Friday, July 1, 1932

On Wednesday night, almost exactly 24 hours later, Porter was on the eastern side of Benedict Canyon, standing on the little bridge over the stream at the Easton Drive house, leaning on the wooden rail. His stitched and bandaged forearm hurt like hell.

The film had to be shown, not explained, and the only place possible was the privacy of the couple's house. The producer, of course, had a projector and a screen in his home. Harlow had come to Easton Drive this Wednesday night from the 9:15 P.M. appearance at Loew's, and her chauffeur awaited her down at the gate in the limo. Porter had sat with Bern and Harlow tonight as they'd watched *The Wedding Night of Jean Harlow and Paul Bern*, three nights before their actual wedding night, and he'd witnessed their sense of cruel, horrible violation.

Porter shared with them the demands of Annie Spry. Bern seemed surprised, but his patented Father Confessor look of stoical tolerance revealed no revulsion. Harlow wept.

"She really looks like Jean Harlow," she said, almost in awe, and began crying again.

What they had seen shocked and frightened them deeply. Porter kept thinking that Annie should be frightened too: If Bern and Harlow went to Mayer and Eddie Mannix, MGM's thug brigade would be on the march and Annie Spry, within days, would belong to the ages. She'd also soon be dead if Harlow went to Longie Zwillman. It would be, Porter had to admit to himself, the most direct and permanent way of handling the problem.

It would also be murder.

Porter was impressed that the couple had the decency to mention neither of these possibilities, although they must have occurred to them. He was also surprised that Bern and Harlow both appeared to rely solely and totally on him for the help they so desperately needed.

*

He explained the counter-blackmail idea, said he was confident in its potency, and admitted they'd have to play a waiting game to see what Annie would do. If she communicated with him or them again, Porter promised to fight her with every weapon at his disposal.

"You two have to promise me you're prepared for whatever happens," said Porter.

He'd stepped outside to give them time to discuss the situation privately. Porter had been furious at times with both of them, and honest in his threat to abandon the case if Harlow didn't confront Bern about Dorothy Millette. But now, standing outside the fairy tale house on the little bridge in the dark forest, high in this lonely canyon, the lantern lights in the trees, the starlight on the little pool, he felt trapped with them in some mad enchantment. He couldn't leave. What was happening was evil, almost preternaturally wicked. The world offered a complex worship to those who provided their fantasies. Valentino, whose file he'd reviewed today after his visit to Falcon Lair, had said audiences often made gods out of stars only for the sadistic joy of tearing them down and stomping them to dust.

And unto dust the audience shall return as well, thought Porter.

These two sad, frightened people needed him. He looked again at the sky and instinctively touched the talisman of St. George and the Dragon that he wore always.

There was a sense of righteousness in the battle now.

*

The wedding was to be an informal affair, held at the Club View Drive home of Harlow's parents on Saturday night, July 2, 1932. The bride and groom had to tend to the many details of the wedding while simultaneously meeting all duties at MGM. It was a day and night schedule, with Harlow still making three-a-day personal appearances at Loew's through Friday night.

The Thalbergs and Selznicks had received wedding invitations. Bern's brother Henry and his wife were *en route* from New

Rochelle, New York, and his sister, Friederike Marcus, was also to attend. Bern had asked John Gilbert to be his Best Man. Harlow, to avoid hurting any feelings, had no Maid of Honor.

Porter Down's involvement with the couple on Thursday – after they'd agreed to his terms Wednesday night – was rather marginal. They were appreciative if visibly nervous, still shaken by what he'd shown them. Porter noted that Irene Harrison, surely via the directive of her boss, even received him that day with a basic civility. The couple wanted Porter to provide his own special security at the wedding ceremony, in addition to Metro's usual task force.

Although the names were not mentioned, there was the unspeakable thought that Dorothy Millette and/or Annie Spry, maybe in all her Harlow finery, might show up as party crashers. On Thursday night, Porter met Maggie for dinner at Santa Monica Pier and afterwards, walking the beach, they discussed this danger. Maggie was following up on every lead she could find.

"I have a feeling this wedding might never happen," said Maggie.

*

Friday, July 1, presented a magnificent sunrise. There was great excitement that beautiful morning at MGM, for this was the eve of a wedding of two people the studio "family" saw as virtual royalty. The commissary boasted a sense of festivity, almost pageantry, especially as Bern and Harlow entered together, hand-in-hand, at precisely noon. They received a thunderous ovation and shook hands with not only stars, producers and directors, but with many of the grips, technicians, and basic "commonality" that served them. Mayer was at his table, and he regally watched the "family" as they cheered the bridal couple.

Porter Down, in his tweed suit, observed the idolatry from his solitary corner table. Then Bern ushered Harlow outside to a limo. She had to be on time for her 1:00 P.M. *Red-Headed Woman* personal appearance at Loew's.

*

After a solitary lunch, Porter left the commissary. Outside, a telegram boy was shouting, "Western Union for Patrick Killarney." Porter tipped the boy and wondered who the hell was sending him a telegram. He opened and read:

URGENT WE MEET AWAY FROM MGM STOP MAJOR DISCOVERY STOP COME TO HIGHLAND BY THREE MAGGIE.

*

Porter arrived at Maggie's Highland Avenue apartment just after 1:30. Maggie answered the door, exhilarated.

"I couldn't risk talking to you at Metro," she said, closing the door behind them. "The walls have ears there. Porter...Dorothy Millette is Paul Bern's common-law wife!"

"Says who?"

"They were together for years. I called New York – the Academy of Dramatic Arts. Bern attended there and an old teacher of his remembered Dorothy. He said she'd lived for years at the Algonquin in Manhattan. The teacher claimed Dorothy was Bern's wife. And he says he believes Dorothy spent time at an institution...or as he put it, an asylum."

"Go on," said Porter.

"Porter, is there any way we can stop this wedding? It's virtual bigamy. And from what you saw of this woman that night in San Francisco, and considering her medical history, she might be dangerous."

"We've got about 30 hours," said Porter, "to scrap this farce."

"You might have help," said Maggie. "I traced Bern's brother Henry – he lives in New Rochelle and is supposed to arrive with his wife in Los Angeles by train today. He likely knows the truth. Maybe he's come out to stop the wedding himself."

"Great work, Maggie. Will you stay put? I'll need you later, but I'm not sure where yet."

"I'll wait for your call."

Porter hurried out of the apartment building. *Bern, you son-of-a-bitch*, he thought.

*

Porter arrived at Bern's office about 2:15. "He's gone to meet his brother and sister-in-law," said Irene Harrison. "Once they're settled in at the Ambassador, he'll be back here."

The Ambassador, thought Porter. *Longie Zwillman...*

"In case I miss him," asked Porter, suspicious of a stonewalling, "give him a message for me." He took a piece of stationery from the desk and Irene's fountain pen and scribbled:

DM – Your common-law? PD

He stuffed it into an envelope, also taken from the desk, licked it shut, and handed it to Irene. "See he gets it," said Porter, and he was gone.

*

Porter, reaching the Ambassador at 3:00, had just missed Paul Bern. He asked to talk with Henry Bern on the house phone. The man who answered sounded stuffy and annoyed. "I don't speak to reporters," he said.

"My name's Porter Down and I'm a security agent for your brother and his fiancée," said Porter hurriedly. "If you don't believe me, call him, but you and I need to talk."

"We need to do nothing of the kind."

"The topic is Dorothy Millette."

There was a click. Porter wasn't certain if Henry Bern had heard the name or not. He called the room again and there was no answer. He made for the lobby exit – he'd have to go back to MGM and find Paul Bern now…

"Hey, Porter!"

He turned and saw Longie Zwillman, fresh off the elevator. The mobster held his hat and a leather travel case. Nick Kirk and two subsidiary bodyguards carried suitcases.

"I was expecting a call from you," said Longie confidentially.

"Everything's fine, Longie."

Zwillman touched his nose. "I smell trouble and it stinks. If I keep smellin' it, I might still toss out a line or two in my own investigation."

The mobster, of course, had a masterful poker face. *If Longie knew about Millette, he'd grind up Bern into sausage*, thought Porter. *And probably her too.*

"I'm flying east tonight," said Longie Zwillman. "Gonna' stay awhile. Anyway, tell the blushin' bride I'm sorry I won't be at the wedding to get a piece. And I don't mean the cake."

"Maybe you'd catch the garter," smirked Porter.

Longie touched his chest. "With what I got in this locket," he said, "I don't need a fucking garter."

*

Porter telephoned MGM. Bern wasn't at the office. Irene Harrison thought he'd gone to confer with Judge Yankwich, who'd officiate at the wedding, and might go home from there.

Yes, Irene told Porter, she'd given him the envelope with Porter's message. He'd opened it, read it and made no comment. Porter believed the secretary was telling the truth.

Carmichael answered the phone at the Bern house at 4:30 and said his employer wasn't there. Porter sensed a stonewalling. He decided to bide his time a bit. If he couldn't get to Bern, he'd see Harlow, and tonight there'd be no mystery where to find her... Loew's State Theatre.

*

The stage show following *Red-Headed Woman* ended at 9:15 P.M. and Harlow made her grand entrance onto the Loew's stage. The audience cheered her both as a movie star and as a bride on the eve of her nuptials. She smiled, waved, threw kisses and appeared altogether radiant.

Porter stood in the wings on one side of the stage with Maggie, whom he'd called to meet him at Loew's. As he'd suggested, she'd dressed for the kill, wearing a snug dark suit and looking every inch the vampy reporter. They could see Marino Bello and Mother Jean in the opposite wings. Bello smiled and Mother Jean waved wildly to her daughter as if sending semaphore. At last, the curtain came down slowly, and Harlow struck a final pose and stood motionless in the spotlight. Her smile vanished the instant the curtain hit the floor. The house lights came up and Harlow looked into both wings, seemingly confused as to whom she wanted to see, or avoid. She finally went to her mother and stepfather stage right. Porter noticed that both of them kissed Harlow on the lips.

*

"Ah, the desert gumshoe," said Bello after Porter crossed the stage.

"This is the reporter, M. S. York," said Porter, indicating Maggie. "She wants to interview you and Mrs. Bello for an exclusive."

"Yes," smiled Maggie smoothly. "Let's go somewhere private, where we can talk."

Bello and Mother Jean left immediately with Maggie, who took them to a far corner. Porter gripped Harlow's arm. He walked her past backstage well-wishers and infiltrating fans and ushered her into her stage left dressing room, locking the door behind them. One of Strickling's publicity people saw them go inside and knocked at the door. "Miss Harlow, are you OK?"

"Leave us alone, please," called Harlow. "Keep anyone away from the room." She sat at her vanity, crossed her arms and legs, and looked Porter in the eyes.

"Our mystery lady with no name might be Bern's common-law wife, apparently spent time in an asylum, and is possibly dangerous," said Porter. "The wedding's off."

"I know all those things," said Harlow softly, with both a tinge of shame and a definite defiance. "And the wedding is on."

"You know all that – including the common-law wife news? When did he tell you?"

"Last night. The night after we saw the…the…"

"Did you finally learn her name?" asked Porter. "Because I'm going to tell you. It's…"

Harlow covered her ears like a scared and angry child. "Dear Dorothy," she whimpered. "He just calls her 'Dear Dorothy.'"

"Put your hands down!" ordered Porter, and she did. "So, you know about her long history with Bern? And her mental illness?"

"Yes!"

"Holy hell," ranted Porter, his voice an angry whisper. "Why don't you invite 'Dear Dorothy' and 'Annie Spry' to be bridesmaids? Or have you already, for God's sake?"

"Stop it!" wept Harlow.

It took her a moment to recover. When she did, there was a desperate force in her voice he'd never heard.

"What Paul and I are facing is terrible. At this point we think the only thing we can do is be a friend to each other. We need you to be our friend now too."

"A friend doesn't let you marry a bigamist. Or a man who, by most accounts, doesn't have the right to marry anybody anyway."

"Yes," said Harlow softly. "I know all about that as well."

Porter looked at her closely. "You're sitting there tonight – Jean Harlow, world-famous movie star – telling me you're going to marry a man who's twice your age, has a common law wife who's spent time in an asylum, has a potential blackmailer who wants his and your salary for the next year…and is probably sexually dysfunctional?"

Harlow again looked him in the eyes but said nothing. "Damn," said Porter. "This, in its own crazy way, just might be the greatest love story in history."

"If we call it off," said Harlow, "we're surrendering. The people trying to hurt us win. We *can't* surrender now. Paul and I can only face all this if… we're both together."

"Listen," said Porter. "Tomorrow night, the judge will ask if anyone knows any reason why you two shouldn't …"

"No!" said Harlow, standing. "No, please don't do that. It would be horrible."

"You're both walking into a pit," warned Porter. "Don't do it."

"Porter" said Harlow, close to him, "that day you and I met we discussed that speech from *Hamle*t. About love and the 'cue for passion' and how real-life people can't show love sometimes while actors can. Remember?"

"Yeah, so what?"

"Well, what I show onscreen isn't love or passion – it's phony and I know it, and I'm a phony and I know it. What I'm doing now for Paul feels more like real love to me than anything I've done in the pictures. It's kindness, it's caring, it's… a *promise*. It's helping somebody who I believe really does care for me, despite everything. I know I'm crazy, but this somehow makes me…happy. Please don't take that away from me."

Her eyes were sad, pleading but still defiant. There was a knock at the door. "Miss Harlow?" It was Blanche Williams.

"Just a minute," she called. She wiped her eyes and moved even closer to Porter, taking his hand. "Do we have a promise too?"

"I'm a fighter," he said. "I won't stand by and see you marry a bigamist."

Harlow squeezed his hand, hard. "Please," she said, her eyes sad and pleading. "After the wedding, you can go. You don't have to worry about the blackmailer. You're free to go...and you never have to see me again."

He looked at her, frowned and nodded almost imperceptibly.

"May I kiss you goodbye?" she asked.

Porter turned his back on her, opened the door and walked out. Blanche walked in with more flowers, including a gigantic bouquet from the absent Paul Bern. Other well-wishers crowded into the room and thronged at the door, and everyone made a fuss over Bern's floral tribute. Marino and Mother Jean joined them in a din of laughter and celebration as Porter made his way to Maggie, waiting for him at the stage door.

*

On King's Road, a limousine pulled up in front of Billee's at precisely 11:00 P.M. The Madame was expecting its arrival.

That morning, Billee had received a call from a new client. The man said he represented a certain party who wanted to engage Billee's "Jean Harlow" for the weekend and a trip up the coast. Billee imagined the "certain party," aware Harlow was marrying Paul Bern Saturday night, wanted to have his own fantasy "nuptials" with his own "Harlow."

Always cautious, and ever-reluctant to let her girls work outside the house, Billee had originally said no. Then the man on the phone offered $1,000 in cash, pre-paid, for a 24-hour assignation – 11:00 P.M. Friday, when he'd pick up "Jeanie," to 11:00 P.M., Saturday night, when he'd return her to King's Road. Billee, thinking it a hoax, laughed and hung up. Two hours later, a uniformed chauffeur had knocked at the door and offered her an envelope containing $1,000 in cash. Billee had reconsidered.

As the grandfather clock struck eleven in the Tudor-style brothel, the chauffeur knocked again at the door. "Jeanie" was packed and ready. Billee hugged her as "Jeanie" went off to earn this remarkable payday.

The chauffeur opened the limousine's back door. "Jeanie" slid inside and was surprised to see nobody was there. The chauffeur started the limousine, U-turned at the top of the hill, and headed down toward Sunset Boulevard.

Chapter Thirty-One
The Wedding

Saturday, July 2, 1932

The wedding was the informal yet epic event everyone expected it to be.

MGM security was at full force early Saturday evening as hundreds of curious fans and reporters gathered outside the house. The Thalbergs and the Selznicks ascended the Club View Drive stairs. Marino Bello smiled like a buccaneer and Mother Jean posed like the star she'd always wanted to be. Best Man John Gilbert looked thin and wan but bravely grinned, realizing this was the only truly pleasant publicity he'd had in three years.

Porter, his own one-man security squad, stood on the outside front stairs. He looked somber in his navy-blue suit. The P.I. kept an eye out for anything and everything, including the unthinkable, but Annie Spry and Dorothy Millette were not in evidence. He felt a bit of apprehension when he saw Bern's sister, Friederike Bern Marcus, who had the look of a frumpy Greek oracle and for a moment reminded him of Millette, although Millette was considerably more attractive.

Henry Bern, taller and balder than his brother, had a dead-serious expression, although his wife appeared pleasant. The justice of the peace, Judge Yankwich, had an owl-like face and a startled, nervous manner, as if he were about to do something reprehensible.

Porter had asked Maggie to be on call if he needed her for an emergency. Otherwise, serving on security tonight was Porter's final task on the case. Harlow had made a choice. He had no expectation of expressing his personal farewell to the bride or groom. His job had been to get them safely married. Within hours, they would be.

Maybe, thought Porter, who had a strange instinct that something was wrong.

*

Around 8:00 Howard Strickling approached Porter. "Jean wants to see you," he whispered.

"Why me?"

"She didn't say. Will you come with me?"

Strickling smiled professionally as he led Porter into the house and up the stairs, determined not to betray any anxiety to the guests. He knocked at Harlow's door.

"Come in," she answered faintly.

Porter found himself in the flower-filled boudoir of Jean Harlow, who was weeping as she sat at her vanity. The brave defiance of the previous night was gone.

"Please go, Howard," she said. "And close the door." Strickling obeyed.

Harlow stayed at her table. Her hair was brushed and fluffy, her makeup light, her bridal dress white. She looked to Porter softer, fairer and considerably younger than she did on the screen, possibly due to her tears. He remembered again that she was only 21-years-old.

"I'm scared," said Harlow, dabbing her eyes. "I keep seeing that person, in that movie...dressed up as Jean Harlow."

"You have a whole house of people here tonight," said Porter, "who wish you well."

"But tonight, we go up to Paul's house," said Harlow. "I'm afraid up there."

She was crying more intensely now and the words came out in a rush.

"I've had nightmares about that person... She's up there in the canyon...and comes out at night, dressed up as Jean Harlow..."

"Stop it," said Porter.

"And comes after me, and wants to kill me, and bury me in the woods..."

"Stop it!" repeated Porter.

She was trembling and weeping and he placed his hand firmly on her shoulder. She put her hand on his. "Will...will you stay there tonight?" she asked.

"You mean at Bern's house?"

"Yes... Please?"

Porter was silent for a moment. "You gotta' be kidding," he said finally.

"Please. Blanche will be there."

"Yeah, but I'm sure Mr. Bern doesn't want another man in that house...not tonight."

"You could stay with the Carmichaels. Or by the gate...or on the ridge. Please! As long as I knew you were nearby."

She began sobbing again and tightened her grip on his hand. There was a knock at the door. "Baby?" chirped her mother.

Harlow looked up helplessly at Porter. "I can't stop crying," she whispered, pitifully and desperately.

The bride-to-be was falling apart before his eyes. He wondered how in the hell she'd make it through the ceremony under the gaze of all the guests downstairs. Mother Jean knocked and called again.

"Baby? Baby!"

"In a minute," Harlow called. She looked up again at Porter. "*Please?*"

"I'll be there," said Porter, softly and uncomfortably. "I'll...I'll drive up and keep watch on the ridge... if that'll help you tonight."

"You promise?"

Porter nodded. Harlow released his hand, stood, and thanked him in her own instinctive way – she kissed him fully on the mouth. He took his handkerchief, wiping away her lipstick on his lips and teeth and her tears on his face before opening the door. As he exited, Mother Jean breathlessly entered.

"It's time!" she announced joyously as Porter closed the door.

*

On his way down the stairs, Porter passed John Gilbert, *en route* to get Paul Bern. Porter had not seen Bern since the previous noon in the MGM commissary. He knew Bern had read his message but there'd been no response. Bern was sequestered in another bedroom, alone now, staring at a "gift" that had arrived in the mail from San Francisco that morning. It was the picture of Bern and Dorothy Millette that Porter had seen that night at her apartment. Dorothy, in the tiniest lettering, had written "Liar" on it over and over again, so many times that the words almost obliterated the picture. The only area untouched by her pen was her pair of eyes, which now stared at Bern from the defaced photo.

As Gilbert rapped at the door, Bern placed the picture in his inside coat pocket.

*

At 8:30 the groom appeared, distinguished in his dark double-breasted suit, a flower in his lapel, wearing his tight-lipped grin. The bride, of course, was beautiful, and smiled convincingly as she made her entrance. Porter realized she really was a hell of an actress.

The ceremony was brief. Judge Yankwich asked the inevitable "If any man or woman knows any reason…" question, and Porter quietly moved outside on the front steps. A few moments later, he heard applause and cries of congratulations.

"God help us all," said Porter.

*

In Malibu, Luke Foster was fiddling with the radio, trying to tune in any ships at sea when he heard a high-powered car pull up by the pier and stop with shrieking brakes. Before he could get on deck, the car roared away.

Luke saw a large bundle on the pier, wrapped in a blanket. He pulled back the top, saw the corpse, turned away, and vomited.

*

The after-wedding reception at Club View Drive was effusive and gave signs of lasting a good while. Porter policed the grounds. He was in the back area, taking a break and sitting on the patio, where he'd first met Harlow, when a cop found him.

"Mr. Down? Come with me. We got a message for you on the car radio."

Porter hurried to the car. The voice was faint and scratchy. "Porter Down? This is Deputy Sheriff Bloom in Malibu. A woman's body was dumped about an hour ago at the pier where you've been staying. Luke Foster found it."

Christ, thought Porter, a chill running up his back. "Do you have an I.D. on the body?"

"Not yet," responded Bloom, "but she's young, she's blonde…and she's a hell of a mess."

*

Porter immediately ran into the house and grabbed the telephone in the lobby. Nobody seemed to notice. He dialed Maggie York's number. She answered on the fourth ring.

"Thank God," said Porter.

"Porter? Is that you?"

"Get up to Malibu, fast," said Porter. "There's been a murder…a body dumped at the pier. I can't take the time to loop into Hollywood and pick you up. Move!"

*

Several police cars and the morgue wagon blocked the pier at Luke's Marina. Porter arrived just after 11 P.M. He passed the well-fed Deputy Sheriff Bloom, the covered corpse and the other cops, and went directly to Luke, who was sitting on the deck of *The Frederick*.

"You okay, pal?" asked Porter.

"I'm okay, Porter," said Luke, clearly shaken.

Porter approached the body. "Let me see her."

"Get ready," said Bloom.

It was a double shock. First, the woman's throat had been cut and the face had been severely battered. Second, the resemblance to the Jean Harlow he'd just seen an hour ago was frightening, despite the pummeled face. The corpse even wore a white wedding dress, very similar to what Harlow was wearing tonight; the press had published photos of the wedding gown after Harlow had selected it. This one, however, was drenched in blood.

"Luke says he found the body dumped here about 10:15," said Bloom.

On the same night Harlow and Bern got married, thought Porter. He looked carefully at the corpse, and then said, "I think I know this woman. Let me look at her right ear."

Bloom nodded. Porter looked. He touched the torn lobe. "Jeanie," he said.

"Who?" asked Bloom.

Porter removed his wallet and looked inside for his card from Billee's. He found it and handed it to Bloom. "You or one of your guys call this number. Ask if 'Jeanie's' there. If she's not, tell Billee we think we know where she is."

A cop went into the shack to make the call. Porter remained kneeling beside the corpse.

Annie did it, he thought. It was Annie Spry's revenge for Tuesday night. It was her way of letting Porter know she knew where he stayed, and that she had paid muscle...she'd clearly relied on pros to stage this murder. Annie had hired the girls at Billee's for her movies, and she knew "Jeanie." And he'd have bet big that although the muscle committed the murder, Annie had directed the slaughter, loving every Goddamn minute of it.

The bitch might have just cut her own throat, thought Porter.

The cop emerged from the shack. "Billee's hysterical. Sounds like her girls are too...I could hear 'em wailing in the background. Billee says 'Jeanie' left last night on a trip with a client. I've called West Hollywood Police to go to Kings Road and calm them down."

A car pulled up at the beach and Porter saw Maggie, getting out of the car and running toward the pier. He met her at the blockade, walked her past the body and directly to the trawler, where Maggie hugged Luke.

"It'll all be okay, honey," she said.

"Look after Luke tonight," said Porter. "Take him back to Hollywood with you. Get him some food. Sit with him if he can't sleep."

"Of course," said Maggie, still hugging the young man. "What are you going to do?"

"I've got a Goddamned promise to keep," said Porter.

*

The reception had lasted until after midnight. Paul Bern finally took his bride home to 9820 Easton Drive. Blanche Williams and the Carmichaels, not at the wedding, greeted the new lady of the house and discussed the reception to be held there tomorrow afternoon.

Meanwhile, Porter, who kept his promises, and who also feared there might be another atrocity tonight, parked at the top of

Easton Drive. He took a flashlight and walked up the steep slope and along the ridge. His forearm hurt like hell and the bandages on it itched this hot summer night. He removed his hat and jacket, loosened his tie, and opened his collar.

He looked down at the Bavarian hideaway, its lit lead glass windows, its candlelit lanterns hanging on the trees. Now and then he heard voices and a bit of laughter. The stocky Carmichael and his corpulent wife eventually made their way back down to the servant quarters, extinguishing the lanterns on their way. After a time, the house lights went out downstairs.

Porter sat under a tree, looked down at the "love nest" where a dim light burned upstairs in the window of what he presumed was the master bedroom. It was a site that was on the minds of millions of prurient people tonight, the subject of countless bawdy jokes, the inspiration for innumerable private fantasies. Then, at the window, he saw a face. It was Harlow – the platinum hair was a giveaway. It seemed to Porter that she was looking up at the ridge, as if wondering if he were really there, as he'd promised.

Porter turned on his flashlight and blinked it twice. She put a hand to her lips, as if blowing him a kiss, and then her face disappeared from the window.

Throwing me a kiss…on her wedding night, thought Porter.

He placed his pistol beside him on the ground under the tree, and then saw again in his mind the bloody corpse in the bridal dress at Malibu. Porter wished he were chasing Annie Spry right now, but he'd given the cops what they needed to know. If he caught Spry tonight, he'd rip her to shreds. He was in enough legal trouble as it was.

He looked down at the house and its one lit window. Then the light went out. The dark house was silent, its sloped roof and turret shining under the starlight.

It was going to be, Porter knew, one hell of a long night.

Part Three
The Baby

Chapter Thirty-Two
Phone Call

Friday, August 26, 1932

The summer of '32 presented a rich season of gossip at MGM.

Garbo was on strike in Sweden. John, Ethel and Lionel Barrymore were co-starring for the first (and last) time together in *Rasputin and the Empress* – and proving why they all had reputations for being difficult. Boris Karloff had come to MGM on loan from Universal to star in *The Mask of Fu Manchu*, portraying the sinister Fu, complete with Myrna Loy as his nymphomaniac daughter and a bevy of outlandish torture devices.

Joan Crawford solemnly told a reporter, "I shall walk off at the climax. No, just before the climax. I want to do some really fine things to be remembered by, and then I shall say goodbye, thanks a lot, it was lovely." Meanwhile, MGM officially terminated its contract with John Gilbert the last day of July. Ten days later, Gilbert married Metro starlet Virginia Bruce, then suffering as the heroine in another Metro horror show, *Kongo*.

MGM had suffered an embarrassment with the July Broadway premiere of the notorious *Freaks*. Determined to top Universal's *Frankenstein*, Thalberg had allowed horror specialist Tod Browning to direct this saga of a circus diva who marries a midget for his money...only to have the vengeful sideshow folk mutilate her into a squawking "Chicken Woman" after they discover her vile plan. Filmed with real circus "freaks," *Freaks* was a livid disaster, and some audience members had reportedly fled the theatre in hysteria at the West Coast preview.

Louis B. Mayer was actively campaigning for the re-election of Herbert Hoover. L.A. was excited to be hosting the Olympics. And MGM's eyes were still on the newlyweds... not so much Gilbert and Bruce as Bern and Harlow. Bride and groom had clocked in Tuesday, July 5, having hosted a reception at Easton Drive the afternoon after the wedding, having had no honeymoon and only the 4th of July to extend their marriage weekend. Harlow was set to start shooting *Red Dust* in August, with co-star Clark Gable replacing John Gilbert and with Victor Fleming directing.

Porter Down, meanwhile, was back in Twentynine Palms.

*

Investigation had revealed that Annie Spry had taken a plane to Europe the morning after "Jeanie's" body had been dumped at Malibu. There was no direct connection that she'd ordered the execution, but Porter was confident that Annie had been responsible, as well as dispatching her bad boys to dump the corpse at the marina. At any rate, there'd been no more foul play and by mid-July, Porter figured there was no longer a threat. Meanwhile, he'd stayed on guard at the marina whenever Luke was there and not out at sea.

On Wednesday, July 6, four days after the wedding and while Porter was still in L.A., Howard Strickling had personally delivered Porter's MGM payment. Mayer was so pleased that the marriage had proceeded smoothly without any evident incident – "Jeanie's" execution apparently didn't count as an incident – that he'd paid Porter for the full four weeks, even though Porter had informed him he was leaving a week early for other concerns... mainly, Luke's safety. Mayer had also paid the promised bonus and even told Porter to keep the Ford.

It had also been on July 6 that Porter had attended the funeral for "Jeanie," whose real name, he'd learned, had been Susan Peerce. The funeral had taken place at the chapel of the Strother Mortuary, 6240 Hollywood Boulevard, where the inquest had occurred the previous day and where Porter had been associated on other murder cases. A very emotional Billee had attended, as had her "Garbo" and "Crawford" attractions. Porter thought both young whores looked fresh, natural and not at all spooky without their MGM-style makeup and ritualistic costuming.

He and the three women had been the only attendees at the funeral.

*

Come Sunday, July 17, Porter had arrived back home in Twentynine Palms and the next day hired a contractor to install his pool.

The contractor also expanded the Yaqui Crest adobe house, adding two more rooms, dressing up the interior a bit, and improving the plumbing. Porter did some of the work himself and even bought some new furniture, including a five-foot-tall radio.

Porter also hired a mechanic in Twentynine Palms to finetune his Spad. At the same time, he had him make a modification: the addition of a second cockpit in case Porter ever needed to accommodate a passenger.

There was still a big stash left over and Porter, not trusting Depression banks, hid it in a metal tool chest behind a few adobe bricks in the house tower.

*

This Friday afternoon, August 26, Porter was in his biplane, *Timber Wolf*, nose-diving over the desert, his passenger's flaxen hair flowing under her leather flight helmet. It was Maggie York's third visit to Twentynine Palms since mid-July and her first ride in the new passenger cockpit of the biplane. Porter veered back up into the cloudless blue sky, circled his house, and landed smoothly on the sandy flats below the crag.

"Perfect landing, skipper," shouted Maggie over the roaring engine.

Maggie had stayed on at MGM until two weeks ago as an undercover starlet, keeping her eye on the Bern and Harlow situation, funneling most of her information to O'Leary back at LAPD. She shared with Porter what little credible observations she'd seen or learned, such as the rumor that Bern now carried a pistol wherever he went, and that he'd slapped Harlow for flirting with a taxi driver.

She'd also kept tabs on the Dorothy Millette and Annie Spry dangers. Millette was reportedly confined to the Plaza in San Francisco and Maggie wondered if Millette were in deep denial. Spry remained presumably in Europe. Maggie had run regular surveillance at the house in Castellammare, but nobody was there. Meanwhile, unanswered correspondence and orders to AS Productions were accumulating at the company's Santa Monica post office box. None of the usual production staff had heard anything from "Miss Spry," who they presumed, was negotiating for her dream studio in Berlin.

Porter had a gut feeling they'd hear from her again…and soon.

For the most part, Maggie and Porter tried to forget the nightmare. She'd taken a few days off from LAPD to be with him at Yaqui Crest. They'd become intimate, making love the previous night on the deck and under the stars.

*

This afternoon, as he brought the plane up near its hangar, they removed their leather helmets and goggles and climbed out of the cockpits, both wearing shorts and t-shirts in the dry 100-degree heat. They strolled over to his new pool under the Joshua trees, an area Porter had dubbed his "Oasis." Neither one wanted to walk up to the house to get their swim suits.

"I haven't skinny-dipped since I was a kid in Nebraska," laughed Maggie.

*

They were full and content after a meal of barbecued steaks and salads made from Porter's home-grown lettuce, tomatoes, and grapes. As they watched the stars appear in the desert twilight, the telephone rang.

"Is this Mr. Down?"

"Yep."

"This is Blanche Williams."

It was a surprise. Porter had heard nothing personally from Harlow, Bern or anyone at MGM since his pay day a month-and-a-half ago. He suspected trouble.

"Miss Harlow and I are near your house, I think. We're off the highway…a place called Pancho's."

Pancho's was a rowdy cantina, maybe a half hour south of Twentynine Palms. Porter imagined the riot if Jean Harlow came strolling in there with her black maid. "Are you inside at Pancho's?" asked Porter.

"No sir. Baby in the car and I in the phone booth."

"Stay right there. I'm on my way."

*

Porter and Maggie arrived at Pancho's in his truck. Cars filled the parking lot – it was nearly 9:00 on a Friday night, the cantina's busiest time of the week. Off to the side of the building they found Blanche's Chevy and saw her face through the windshield.

"I don't see Harlow," said Porter.

He and Maggie greeted Blanche, who indicated the car's back seat. There, curled up with a scarf over her hair and sunglasses despite the darkness, lie a sleeping Jean Harlow.

"What's goin' on, Blanche?" asked Porter.

"She been workin' so hard on that new movie, sir. Baby's exhausted. They gave her the weekend off and she told Mr. Bern and me she wanted to drive here and see you."

"Is there trouble with Mr. Bern?"

Blanche hesitated. "Yes, sir. I think so."

"OK. You follow me back to my place. Maggie, you go with Blanche." Maggie climbed into the back seat, placing Harlow's head on her lap.

*

The wind had picked up during the drive to Twentynine Palms. Tumbleweed blew over the highway and Porter saw wildlife, mostly foxes and coyotes, foraging food. He couldn't decide if their eyes bright in the headlights reminded him of Annie Spry's or Marino Bello's.

Probably both, he thought.

When they reached the top of Yaqui Crest, Harlow was still soundly asleep in the back seat. "Was she awake at all?" asked Porter.

"No" said Maggie. "But she talked a little in her sleep."

"What did she say?"

"Something about a baby. And a couple times she said, 'She's coming.'"

Porter's efforts to rouse the sleeping woman failed and he finally lifted her from the car, noting several empty bottles on the car floor. He carried her into the house as Blanche and Maggie followed. Harlow was soaked in sweat and her skin looked gray. She sighed and moaned again as Porter took her into his bedroom and placed her on his bed.

"I'm calling a doctor," said Porter. "And while we wait for him, Blanche, I need to ask you some questions."

Suddenly Harlow stirred on the bed. "She's coming," she sighed, tossing in her sleep.

*

Harlow had fallen back to sleep. Porter, Maggie, and Blanche sat out on the deck under the stars. The host had lit an old railroad lantern on the deck and they were drinking Coca-Cola.

"I saw hooch bottles in the car, Blanche."

"Yes, sir. Baby been drinking."

"Stop calling me 'sir.' You used to call me 'Porter.' Is she fighting with Mr. Bern?"

"Yes. Last week they fight about the house. Baby don't like it, never did like it. She's talkin' about selling it and them movin' in with Mother Jean and Mr. Bello. And Mr. Bello wants to sell the house and invest the money in his gold mine."

"Are they fighting about anything else?" asked Porter.

"Yes…Porter. I think so. But I really ain't sure about what it all means."

"She mentioned a baby," said Maggie.

"Yes," said Blanche softly. "She talks about that a lot …sometimes in her sleep."

"She also said, 'She's coming,'" said Maggie. "Does she say that in her sleep a lot too?"

"No," said Blanche. "Just this past week."

*

Dr. Bernard Otts had lived most of his 72 years in Twentynine Palms. He resided contentedly on his avocado ranch, made house calls any time of day and night, and knew what he liked and didn't like. He liked to talk medicine. He cared nothing about movies. He admired Porter Down.

Arriving that night at Yaqui Crest around 11:30, Dr. Otts looked like an old, fat Dutch burgomaster in his wire-rim glasses and too-snug three-piece suit. He hustled his rotund body up to the deck, brandishing his black bag and peering over his bifocals at Porter, who took him inside the house.

"There's a sick lady in the bedroom," said Porter. "She's Jean Harlow."

"Who?" asked Dr. Otts.

Porter wasn't sure that Dr. Otts was serious, but he knew he wasn't impressed.

"She's asleep," said Porter. "Might be exhaustion. Or too much hooch. Or both." Porter lowered his voice. "Check for bruises. And you might look for any signs of sexual abuse."

Dr. Otts nodded and promptly waddled into the bedroom.

*

A half-hour later, Dr. Otts emerged from the room, came out on the deck, peered again over his glasses, cleared his throat and beckoned Porter to follow him down the drive to his car.

"Exhaustion, definitely," he said briskly and clinically when out of earshot of Maggie and Blanche. "The alcohol doesn't help. No bruises or cuts. No sign of sexual abuse or abnormal penetration."

"So, she'll be OK if she gets some rest?" asked Porter.

"I don't know." Dr. Otts stopped and looked owlishly at Porter. "Is she a client of yours?"

"Yeah."

"She's very restless," said Dr. Otts. "She said something in her sleep about somebody coming. I gave her a strong sedative at midnight. She'll sleep soundly, maybe as long as 18 hours."

"Okay."

"She awoke long enough to complain of severe migraines. It could be just a hangover. Or it could be a sign of early kidney failure."

"What makes you think that?"

"Her face is puffy, her body's bloated, and her skin's slate gray. That particular shade of gray usually signals one of two things. The patient's either on the verge of kidney failure, or a corpse."

"Tough to determine that just from a bedside visit, isn't it?" asked Porter hopefully.

"Maybe. Maybe not. I've only been a doctor for 45 years, you know."

"If she has kidney failure, what can she do to get better?"

"Nothing. She'll be dead in five years. Should I send you the bill for this visit?"

Chapter Thirty-Three
Travel Plans

Saturday, August 27, 1932

Porter, shaken by what Otts had diagnosed, made his way up to the house as the doctor drove down the hill. He found Blanche sobbing on the deck and Maggie comforting her. For a moment he feared she'd somehow overheard what the doctor had guessed. "Blanche?" he asked tentatively.

"Blanche is supposed to be the godmother for a friend's baby tomorrow," said Maggie.

"She can go back," said Porter softly. "You and I can handle this."

"That's what I told her," said Maggie. Blanche was hesitant but, assured by both Porter and Maggie that they'd take very good care of "Baby," she finally agreed to return in the morning to L.A. She also eventually accepted their insistence that she take the guest room – Porter and Maggie would spend the August night on the deck.

"Thank you, both of you," said Blanche tearfully. "This…this been so sad a time." She began to go inside, and then turned at the door. "Oh…please. I gotta leave the light on in Baby's room all night. She doesn't like to be alone in the dark."

*

Blanche had retired after unpacking Harlow's bag and arranging her various items in the bedroom and bathroom. Porter and Maggie sat on the deck. He didn't tell her Dr. Otts' grim prognosis.

"The 'she's coming' can refer to Spry or Millette," said Maggie. "After all, Millette's not going to be content to hide in San Francisco forever. Porter…I have an idea."

"Shoot."

"We never got any answers about Millette. Henry Bern and his wife went back to New Rochelle without ever responding to our questions. We know virtually nothing more about the Millette situation than we did almost two months ago."

"You want to call Henry Bern?"

"No. I want to go to New York and do some exploring."

"You're talkin' 2500 miles. Metro will never approve the expense."

"I can work around that. A special MGM mail plane leaves L.A. every Wednesday and Saturday night for New York. It takes off at midnight and, even with the three-hour loss, gets into New York City by the following midnight. The object is to get major correspondence and contracts to the Manhattan offices as early as Friday morning and no later than Monday morning. Sometimes with approval, they take a passenger."

"You think Whitey Hendry will approve? After all, you're no longer a starlet there."

"If he doesn't approve, I'll be a stowaway. Blanche is leaving early morning for L.A. Maybe I can leave here late tomorrow afternoon and if Harlow's feeling well enough, drive her back with me. Then I'll pack for the trip and fly east tomorrow night. There's a Wednesday night MGM plane from New York to Los Angeles too. I'll fly back on that one."

They were both silent. "If Miss Harlow's not well by tomorrow night," asked Maggie finally, "are you willing to baby-sit her alone? Would that be too... awkward?"

*

Blanche Williams left early in the morning after rousing Harlow long enough to get her to the bathroom and back to bed. Maggie York prepared to leave about 5:00 P.M. and also got Harlow to the can before the star collapsed back into bed and fell into a deep sleep.

"If she's up by eight, I'll drive her back tonight," said Porter. "It'll soon be 18 hours since Otts gave her the sedative. It should be wearing off."

He walked Maggie to her car. "Good hunting in New York," he said.

"I'll call you as soon as I learn anything," said Maggie.

They kissed and Maggie drove away. Porter looked back up at the house, sensing trouble.

*

Harlow wasn't awake by six. Porter made a chicken stew, using carrots, potatoes and beans he'd grown in his garden and a chicken from his own coop. It smelled delicious, if he thought so himself, and he hoped the smell would rouse his guest. It didn't.

At sunset, Harlow was still asleep. Porter watched the desert change colors and the stars emerge in the pink and then black sky. There'd surprisingly been no call from Bern or the *Red Dust* unit manager at MGM. He knew the studio must be having fits about Harlow's absence and presumed Bern had told them to leave his bride alone. Still, it was telling that *he* hadn't called himself.

Porter put on a pair of shorts and went down to the pool for a brief dip. The night grew chilly and the wind picked up. When he came back to the deck about 9:30 P.M., he heard the shower running in the bathroom. It ran a long time and after it finally stopped, he heard movement inside his room.

He sat on the deck, figuring if she wanted to see him, she'd come looking for him.

Chapter Thirty-Four
Saturday Night Date

Saturday, August 27, 1932

"Ohhh... *There* he is!"

Porter at first thought she was flirting with him. When he turned, he saw Harlow was standing on the deck, looking in the pen and cooing at Long John. She had put on Porter's white cloth bathrobe, she was barefoot, and her albino hair was still wet.

"He's adorable!" she said of the rabbit. "Can I hold him?"

"He's skittery," said Porter. "He might jump away. If he falls, he could hurt himself. I'll hold him – he's used to me – and you can pet him."

"That'll be swell."

Porter, bare-chested and still in his swimming shorts, lifted the one-legged jackrabbit and placed it on his lap. Harlow pulled up a folding chair and sat in front of him, admiring the rabbit and stroking its fur. Her famous hair was only inches from Porter's face and he had a view of her breasts inside the loosely sashed robe. He noted she'd applied her Mitsouko.

"I saved some stew for you, if you're hungry," said Porter.

"I'm not, but that's sweet," said Harlow.

"You haven't eaten in at least a day-and-a-half," said Porter.

"I'm fine," said Harlow. As she petted the rabbit, her fingers touched Porter's hands.

"It's kinda' late now to drive you back tonight," said Porter. "But I'm ready if you are."

She grinned. "Are you that anxious to get rid of me?"

"Tomorrow's Sunday," said Porter. "And I don't have any peroxide, Clorox, Lux flakes or ammonia in the house."

She laughed. "Feel free to tease me. I like it better than when you're grumpy. Anyway, it looks like you're stuck with me for your Saturday night date."

Harlow grinned at Porter. When he didn't return the grin, she gently and curiously probed with one finger the area where the rabbit had lost its leg. "Did it take a long time for him to get better?"

"A little while."

"Was he a better patient than I am?"

She touched the area again and Long John tried to jump. "Oh! I'm so sorry, Toots," said Harlow to the jackrabbit as Porter took it back to its cage.

"He's OK," said Porter. "He just gets jittery when he's admired for too long."

"I bet you do too."

Porter didn't respond. Harlow stood and went to the deck rail. The solitary palm tree over the house was swaying in the night wind, which also tugged at Harlow's robe. Porter sat again and looked at her. She'd regained some of her color, her face wasn't as puffy, but she still wasn't at her best. Nevertheless, even without any makeup, even with her hair wet and unstyled, even in this dumpy robe, she was phenomenally sexy.

"I've never seen so many stars," she said. "And I love the wind up here."

"We need to talk about what's happening," he said curtly.

"Do we?"

"You said, 'She's coming.' Do you mean 'dear Dorothy'?"

"What do you think?"

"Quit the game and give me an answer."

Harlow kept looking at the stars. "Yes," she said finally.

"When?"

"Soon. Maybe next weekend… Labor Day weekend."

"And you're hoping I come back?"

She looked at Porter. "No. I'm begging you to come back."

"Cut the vampy I'm-so-helpless act."

"You know I can't act."

He looked at her eyes in the starlight, seductive and ringed in black, but it wasn't makeup. It was that natural darkness he'd noticed before and he thought again of Otts' grim diagnosis. He felt attraction to her overt sensuality and sympathy for her vulnerability and knew right now he should be feeling neither.

"OK," said Porter. "If I come back, and the lady from San Francisco shows up, your husband sees her. You don't. He and I confront the situation honestly. No MGM payoffs, no Eddie Mannix dirty deals, no Howard Strickling magic tricks. You might be looking at an annulment."

"Plenty of reasons for that," said Harlow cryptically.

"You better be ready for anything."

"I am…if you're with me."

"Can it," he said firmly.

The night wind blew more sharply now, rustling and bending the palm tree, wafting the smell of her perfume toward him. She shivered.

"It's cold out here," she said.

She slowly walked toward Porter, her eyes intently on him. Suddenly she was in his lap. She kissed him passionately, her mouth open and warm, her hands rubbing his bare chest, the Mitsouko all around him.

"No," he said.

Harlow stood, totally assured in the only arena in which she felt completely secure. The robe was fully unsashed now and she moved so it fell from her shoulders to the floor of the deck. She stood in the starlight, reaching for Porter's hand and leading him into the house.

Chapter Thirty-Five
West and East

Sunday, August 28 through Wednesday August 31, 1932

The next morning, Porter and Harlow left the desert in *Timber Wolf*. He sensed he'd need the biplane once back in L.A. and he could always borrow one of the jalopies that Luke tinkered with at the marina. Also, in the air, there was no way they could talk to each other.

Come morning he'd made some hasty plans to pay a nearby rancher to feed Long John and the livestock during his absence, and told Harlow they were flying back. She didn't seem overjoyed to take a plane ride but she didn't protest.

Porter's mind was racing. The sensations of the night – the feeling of her in his arms, the bed drenched in their passion – had him in an emotional vice that he now resented bitterly. Even in the air he could still smell the Mitsouko, emanating from his passenger who sat in the cockpit behind him.

Harlow wore her scarf and sunglasses, and nobody recognized her when they landed at the Malibu airfield. A taxi took them to the marina. Luke was out fishing and Porter figured it was better for the boy that Luke never knew that the Platinum Blonde had stood on his dock and even used his bathroom.

He took one of the jalopies and they began the long ride to Benedict Canyon. They were both silent, but Harlow several times stared at him, as if demanding he look at her, talk to her. He did neither.

By mid-afternoon they drove up Easton Drive and he unloaded her two bags. The cockeyed Carmichael, in his white servant's jacket and formal black pants, took the bags while his wife's plump face curiously peered through the screen window on the second floor of their quarters.

Harlow removed her sunglasses and looked at Porter. There appeared to be a small grin of victory – yes, she'd seduced him to coming back to Los Angeles. But her eyes were sullen, because they saw the anger and resentment in his.

"See ya'," he said brusquely.

She watched the car pull away, and then followed Carmichael, like a child returning to a reformatory, up the 75 steps to her home and her husband.

*

Settled again at Luke's marina, Porter looked out at the sunset over the Pacific, cursing himself for what had happened, for having broken a cardinal rule. How could he have been so damned stupid...even if she was, for Christ's sake, Jean Harlow?

And he felt he'd betrayed Maggie.

*

Maggie York had arrived in New York City 12:05 A.M. Monday, August 29, found an all-night restaurant, had a turkey sandwich, checked into the Algonquin, got seven hours of sleep, and went immediately to work.

She called the Academy of Dramatic Arts professor who'd told her on the phone in July about Bern and Millette, and he agreed to see her, again validating that Dorothy had been Paul's common-law wife. The doddering oldster gave her three more names to contact and while two of them turned out to be dead, the one living contact also agreed to see her, although he was more guarded than the garrulous professor.

Come Monday evening and Maggie found several Algonquin house staff who all knew Dorothy Millette, claiming she'd lived there for years and had only left last spring. All remembered her as reclusive and suggested Maggie call a former manager for more information. The man was cold to her query and quickly hung up on her.

Maggie slept like a baby Monday night and, following a Tuesday breakfast of eggs and pancakes, was eager to resume the chase. The professor had said he'd heard the rumor that Dorothy had at one time entered the Blythewood Sanitarium in Connecticut. Maggie was dressed in her favorite blue outfit and felt bold and brassy as she planned to take a cab to Grand Central Station and board a train to Greenwich. Then a towering, big-nosed man in an expensive suit suddenly approached her in the lobby.

"Good morning, Miss," he said in a deep but gracious voice, tipping his hat. "It's a beautiful day."

"It is," smiled Maggie. *Great suit, bad toupee*, she thought.

The man moved to her side and took her arm. "I beg your pardon?" she demanded.

"Keep walkin', Miss," he said.

The quick, smooth, forceful manner in which Nick Kirk had whisked her out the door and into a waiting limousine, its back door held open by another large, well-dressed man was, Maggie thought nervously, a genuine art form. The door slammed briskly beside her and as Nick got in the front next to the driver, Maggie looked at a large man beside her in a very expensive suit. He removed his hat and his full, close-cropped hair glistened with tonic.

"Don't worry, Miss York," said the man. "You're perfectly safe. My name is Abner Zwillman. Welcome to New York City."

Maggie recognized the name, both from the headlines and from what Porter had told her. The man's calm manner was reassuring but his size was intimidating. "What do you want?" she asked and the car began to move. He gave no answer.

"I'll scream!" promised Maggie.

"Be my guest," chuckled Longie. "We're soundproof. The outside hears nothing inside and the inside hears nothing outside."

"Are you 'taking me for a ride'?" asked Maggie scornfully, although she truly was frightened.

"Yeah...a *nice* ride. See, I got a call last night. My caller tells me that a lady from L.A. is here, asking lots of questions about Paul Bern and Dorothy Millette."

Maggie suspected the Algonquin's unfriendly former manager had blown the whistle on her.

"Don't worry, Miss. I'm just here today to save you time. Yeah, we're going for a nice ride. To places in this city. New Jersey, Delaware and Connecticut too. I call it the 'Paul and Dorothy tour.' We'll stop for lunch. You'll have a good time. And you can tell your pal Porter Down all about it."

*

It was after 7 P.M. Tuesday when Maggie, after her 11-hour tour of sites in four states, arrived back at the Algonquin. Zwillman's limo had dropped him off in Harlem on the way back for unspecified business and she wandered into the Algonquin, escorted to the door and through the lobby by Nick Kirk. He tipped his hat and said good night to her at the elevator.

Maggie was almost numb after what she'd seen and learned. She actually wanted no supper. In her room she undressed and ran a bath, feeling a need to wash away the day. She put on her nightgown and sat silently for a long time. Finally, she picked up the telephone.

"I want to make a call to Los Angeles, please," Maggie told the operator.

*

Porter Down had stayed in Malibu since Sunday evening, fishing with Luke. It was Wednesday night now…August 31.

Dorothy Millette was due from San Francisco sometime this coming weekend. He'd been stubbornly waiting for Bern to call him. Last night, Maggie had phoned him with her explosive news about Bern, Millette…and Longie.

Porter, stir-crazy, couldn't delay the inevitable any longer. He was just about to head for town to see Bern when the phone rang.

"This is Irene Harrison," said the voice on the line. "Mr. Bern needs to see you as soon as possible. It's an emergency."

Chapter Thirty-Six
The Father Confessor's Confession

Wednesday, August 31, 1932

Porter was to meet Bern at MGM at 9:30 P.M. Of course, since he had flown to L.A., he had had to borrow one of Luke's old jalopies. The gateman, suspiciously regarding the decrepit automobile, insisted on calling Bern's office before admitting him. Irene Harrison gave the green light.

The August night was hot and it felt odd to Porter to be back at MGM, which seemed unusually still. He knew Harlow was on the *Red Dust* soundstage, the company working nights to make up for her recent absence. There was no need to go see her and he didn't. Porter was heading for the Lion Building when he heard a voice.

"Sweet *Chrrrrrist*, look who it is!"

The small figure, staggering in the middle of the dark street, wore a dirty, pale three-piece suit and a homburg hat at a sharp angle. He was unshaven, had a cigarette dangling from his mouth, cocked his head like a rooster, and was obviously plastered.

"Behold!" he cried, dramatically pointing at Porter with his walking stick and slowly approaching him. "It's Leo the Lion's Sacred Savior!"

Porter recognized the man…John Barrymore. He figured Barrymore had heard rumors of his previous adventures with Harlow and identified him by his sailor's cap.

"Rejoice, for he has come!" shouted "the Great Profile," proclaiming in a voice tailor-made to intone Shakespearean lines. "To ransom our souls from Hollywoodus-in-Latrina!"

Maggie had told Porter that Barrymore had been drinking heavily and required supervision. He reached Porter, slapping his hand on his shoulder. The star's eyes reminded Porter of the eyes in stained glass windows of the saints, and in photographs of serial killers.

Barrymore let loose with a cackle, then wandered on, the smell of whiskey wafting behind him, waving his walking stick...drunkenly amok in the MGM streets. A moment later, two men, apparently Barrymore's keepers, came running, obviously looking for him.

*

Paul Bern's office was the only one in the Lion Building with a light on this night, and the door was open to circulate air. Irene Harrison was standing with her back to Porter as he entered the office, absorbed in her filing, and at first, she wasn't aware he was there. He looked at her, admiring her rather nice fanny, and remembering a rumor that had come his way – that the puffed-up Irene was actually Bern's sado-maso mistress, who could get him hot in ways his movie star wife never imagined. Porter's imagination flared up again and he envisioned Irene in a boudoir, waving a baton in one hand and whipping the hell out of Bern with the other, all to the strains of *Stars and Stripes Forever*. Somehow the imagery was very vivid and when she finally turned and saw him with a small, surprised gasp, he almost blushed.

"Good evening, Mr. Down." The secretary said it surely with no affection, but with what might have been a touch of respect. "Mr. Bern is in his office."

Through the door Porter looked at the man behind his desk, which was hopelessly cluttered with red ink-annotated pages of various script drafts. Bern was not at his distinguished best this evening, his face ashen, his scalp showing through his thinning hair, looking at least ten years older than he had the first night Porter visited him at his home two months ago. His eyes were almost as dark-circled as his wife's.

"Thank God you're here," said Bern, his tie still taut at his neck, although he'd draped his jacket this warm night over his chair. "I've learned...that this Sunday..."

"You're having company," said Porter. "Company who's stayed with you before at all these addresses." Porter took a paper from his pocket, unfolded it and dropped it on Bern's desk. On the paper were addresses of homes Bern and Millette had shared in New York City, New Jersey, Delaware, and Connecticut. Porter had written them down during his call from Maggie York. The last address on the paper was *Blythewood Sanitarium, Greenwich, Connecticut*.

Bern paled even more but said nothing. Porter indicated Irene Harrison, who'd returned to her desk. "Is it OK she hears what we say, or should I close the door?"

"You may leave it open."

"These addresses," said Porter, "come from possibly the most powerful mobster in the U.S. today. Among many other franchises, he runs 40% of the contraband that comes over the Canadian border. It seems he still has a vested interest in Jean Harlow."

"Yes," said Bern, lighting a cigarette. "One of my dear wife's more celebrated former admirers. His soubriquet is 'Longie,' I believe?"

"Don't start," warned Porter. "No time. We're in a hell of a mess."

Bern glanced at Porter, his tiny grin grim. "My apologies, sir. Yes, we need to talk. Not here. I trust Irene implicitly but I've come to fear my own office might be, as the crime world calls it, 'bugged.'"

The man's paranoia surprised Porter, but considering Eddie Mannix, maybe it was valid.

"I know a safe place to chat," said Bern. "Come with me." Bern stood and took his jacket. It weighed heavily in his hand and Porter saw the reason. The lining had a sewn-in holster and the handle of a revolver was visible.

"Shall I wait for you, Mr. Bern?" asked Irene.

"No," said Bern. "You go home."

"Very well," said Irene. "Good night, Mr. Bern. Goodnight, Mr. Down."

*

Bern led Porter down the hallway, out a window, across a fire escape and over a maze of catwalks, two stories above the streets and alleys of MGM. Porter looked across at the water tower and the soundstages. He gazed down at the set/prop/wardrobe workshops below, some still lit up as the craftsmen and craftswomen labored late into the night. He wondered if Barrymore's "keepers" had found him yet.

"Don't consider jumping," said Porter, only half-kidding.

They continued over the catwalks until Bern reached what appeared to be the top floor of a warehouse. He took a key Irene had given him from a locked drawer, unlocked the door, and put on a light. Inside was a virtual drawing room, complete with antique furniture, plush velvet armchairs, floor-to-ceiling draperies, a marble mantle fireplace, and a baby grand piano. The walls were walnut and a large screen dominated one end of the room.

"This is Irving's private screening room," said Bern, locking the door behind him. "He told me today he'd recently had the room checked by our technicians for any invasive spying. It's probably as close to a foolproof sanctuary as you'll find in Los Angeles tonight."

Porter looked at the elaborately posh, exquisitely tasteful furnishings of Thalberg's *sanctum sanctorum*. This was where the producer mercilessly scrutinized every MGM movie, assessing the potency and allure of his stars, ordering retakes after decreeing that Norma Shearer looked cock-eyed in her death scene in *Smilin' Through*, and that Conrad Nagel's toupee looked phony in a swamp sequence in *Kongo*. Porter had heard a rumor that Garbo's ass had looked too fat in her hootchie-kootchie dance in *Mata Hari*, and that Thalberg had reshot the whole damn sequence with a double; here's where the producer would have made that delicate decision.

This was where "the Boy Wonder" exalted and protected "More Stars Than There are in Heaven" but there was more involved here than actor vanity. It was where a corporate artist calculatingly fashioned the MGM product, inspiring fantasy that assured unprecedented worldwide success. Yes, it actually made sense that MGM would make this chamber a fortress. After all, it was Thalberg's genius, even more so than Mayer's steel trap business sense, that made the difference in Hollywood between an $8-million-dollar profit and seemingly hopeless bankruptcy.

There was a bar, of course, and Bern was preparing drinks as Porter took in the chamber. The producer handed the detective a glass and a bottle of Coca-Cola. "I recall you're partial to Coke," said Bern. "So is Irving. He drinks several bottles a day for energy. Please make yourself comfortable."

They sat across from each other beside the unlit fireplace. The room was cool this hot night, almost cold. "Are you surprised by the room's temperature?" asked Bern. "It is cooled by cakes of ice behind the wall. Fans blow over the cakes through the vents. Irving uses the same technology at his beach house."

"Stop talking about Thalberg," said Porter, "and about room temperature."

"Yes, I'll get to the point," said Bern, sipping his drink. He looked especially small in his large chair. When he spoke, his voice, still smooth and cultured, had a softness and sincerity that Porter had never before noticed. "My dear sir, I once expressed sympathy to you regarding the death of your young wife. I assured you empathy if you ever felt a need to discuss that tragedy. Please assure me of empathy as I begin my story."

"Okay. I'm empathetic."

It took a moment for Bern to begin. "My mother, Henrietta Levy, was a remarkable woman," he said finally. "We were very close…indeed, *too* close. My mother was ill, Porter. Mental illness marks my family. My mother once warned me she'd never survive if I married."

"Go on."

"I met Dorothy in 1911. It was at the American Academy of Dramatic Arts in New York. I was only 21 years old. She had left her husband and wanted a career in the theatre. Eventually he divorced her. By that time, we had been together for several years."

"And did you marry then?"

"No." Bern paused and drank again. Porter noticed the man was perspiring despite the ice-cooled room.

"Dorothy, too, was…ill. I could never take her to my family. I could only take her to certain friends. What you saw in San Francisco is not a recent aberration, sir. I know how terrible it is to witness one of her episodes. She was – is – terribly possessive. She and my mother were much alike. Of course, Dorothy was a Gentile. For years, I kept our secret from my mother. But she finally learned the truth. And she kept her promise. Twelve years ago, next month, aware of Dorothy's place in my life, Mother leapt from an embankment and drowned herself."

Bern's eyes were wet. "I'm sorry," said Porter in all sincerity.

"It destroyed Dorothy," said Bern, his voice distant. "She felt responsible. She developed a religious mania. She spoke constantly of suicide, of trying to find my mother in Heaven. Many nights I had to restrain her."

The Sacrifice, Porter remembered.

"Now it was destroying me. So, I did what I thought was best… in 1922, I committed Dorothy to the Blythewood Sanitarium in Greenwich."

"Then what did you do?" asked Porter.

Bern's face was filled with guilt. "I…I left for Hollywood."

Porter finished his Coke. He took it upon himself to get up and get a fresh bottle. "How long was she institutionalized?"

"Only months. She despised being in the sanitarium. They wrote me how she cried and screamed. I relented and authorized her release. When she left, she settled at the Algonquin. I paid all her expenses. I saw her whenever I was in Manhattan but…the visits made me sick."

Porter sat again across from Bern. The man was shaking. It was as if by pieces he was melting down, gradually losing his cultured veneer.

"Last May, Dorothy decided to move to San Francisco," said Bern. "I arranged for her new home at the Plaza. I haven't been to see her. My last visit at the Algonquin had been too…unsettling. My relationship with Jean had been going on for two years when Dorothy decided to come to the West Coast. I didn't know what to do, so…"

"So, you improvised," said Porter. "Never told Harlow about Dorothy until you had to. Never told Dorothy about Harlow until you had to. Meanwhile, you had that cockamamie script idea…"

"She's worse now," said Bern. "She's demanded stardom. Jean is a star, so Dorothy wants to be a star. She desired a script that handled her religious issues. The only other option I had was to commit her again and I simply can't bring myself to do that."

"So what will you do," demanded Porter, "when she shows up Sunday and starts squawkin' about starring in *The Sacrifice*? And featuring Harlow in her supporting cast as Salome, or whomever? And claiming she's your rightful wife?"

The dime slot grin emerged. "I'll do what my mother did, and what dear Dorothy has long threatened to do," said Bern, slowly removing the revolver from his jacket and placing it on the coffee table.

The dramatic impact Bern hoped for wasn't achieved – Porter had seen the gun in his office – but Porter knew the man was serious. Movies were filled with suicides. They handily resolved love story crises. Bern had a mother who'd committed suicide, a common-law wife who'd wanted to commit suicide, and a job where he doctored scripts by providing suicides. It was *de rigueur* in his life and work.

"Suicide will probably invalidate your life insurance," said Porter.

"I don't really care," sighed Bern.

"A couple questions," said Porter. "Have you said anything to Mannix about Dorothy…or do you have any reason to believe he knows about what's happening?"

"I've said nothing to Mr. Mannix, nor to Mr. Mayer. Nor even to Irving. He's aware I'm in distress, but doesn't know the details."

"Next question. You love to suffer, right, Mr. Bern? Because if you take my advice, I just might make you a very fulfilled man."

Bern wasn't capable now of a comeback. He fully believed in his own tragedy and tears and sweat ran down his face. "What do you mean?" asked Bern weakly.

Porter picked up the pistol, examined it, and emptied the bullets. "First, we get ready for our 'Welcome Dorothy' party. When she comes-a-callin', you'll meet her at your house, or Jean's house, or whoever the hell now owns the house. I'll be close by. Harlow will be miles away. You look Dorothy in the eyes and tell her the truth – that the papers aren't lying about there being a new Mrs. Paul Bern, this one with a marriage license…that there's no MGM spectacular coming up called *The Sacrifice*…that there's no starring role of any variety in Dorothy Millette's future. If she takes all this reasonably, she can go back to San Francisco, and you can assuage your profound guilt by continuing to pay her way through life."

Bern's face was pale. "And if she doesn't respond 'reasonably'?"

"You and I together take her back to San Francisco. We stash her back in her room and you call a press conference. You admit Dorothy Millette is your common-law wife and that marrying Jean Harlow was a virtual act of bigamy. We get a doctor, or several of them, to judge if Dorothy belongs in an asylum and if they say so, off she goes. And you announce that under these circumstances, you're pursuing an annulment."

Bern actually shivered. "The studio would fire me."

"Fired, you'd still have a pulse."

"With no job or money, I couldn't afford to support Dorothy or pay for a sanitarium."

"Your pal Thalberg... maybe he can help you. Worse comes to worse, you do what most people in this country are doing – take it a day at a time."

Bern wept.

"Look, Mr. Bern. I can think right off the bat of three people who'd like to load this gun and empty it into you. Annie Spry, for one, ever since we called her bluff on her blackmail. Marino Bello, if he figures he can't get his hands on your money any other way. And most dangerously, Longie Zwillman. He knows all about you and Dorothy, and frankly – if you don't do what meets Longie's particular code of honor – you might not have a chance in hell."

Bern glanced at the gun Porter held. "Perhaps I should save him the trouble."

"Oh no," said Porter, his anger rising. "All over way too fast. See, this way, Hollywood's Father Confessor gets to suffer not just for one instant while a bullet fries his brains. He gets to suffer for days, weeks, months, years, privately, professionally, losing his wife, his job, his dignity, aiming those sad puppy dog eyes at all the photographers who want shots of the poor little MGM has-been schnook, maybe landing a job on Poverty Row proofreading scripts for Saturday matinee cowboy movies if you change your name, possibly living to be 100-years-old and waking up every morning and going to bed every night as one of the biggest jokes in Hollywood history. How can you resist it?"

Bern had wept during Porter's harangue but now he became still. "Perhaps, Mr. Down," he finally said very softly, "you should review the definition of the word 'empathy.'"

Porter had to laugh. His ire subsided. "Think about what I said. It takes guts and there's sure in hell more honor than suicide. Break away from this trap. There probably are some people in this town who'd respect you for what you'll do. At any rate, if you want my help, and if Jean wants my help, it's the only way to go."

He handed the gun back to Bern, who slowly placed it back in his jacket.

*

"Another thing," said Porter as he and Bern made their way back to his office across the catwalks. "I've had a funny feeling lately that we're going to hear from Annie soon."

"I've heard nothing from that woman," said Bern. "If I do, I'll tell you." A moment later, he turned to Porter, his face in the night shadow.

"I never thanked you for accommodating Jean last weekend and for bringing her home."

"You're welcome," said Porter.

"I trust that, during her stay, she didn't…you didn't…."

He broke off, turned away and silently resumed his way over the catwalk.

*

Porter drove back to Malibu, wondering if Paul Bern would find the courage to do what Porter had demanded he do. Yes, the man was in grave danger. As Porter had said, Annie Spry, Marino Bello, and Longie Zwillman all had motives to kill him. Bern, in his own mind, had motives to kill himself. But Porter had intentionally left out another suspect in talking to Bern, although this one might be the most dangerous: Dorothy Millette.

Chapter Thirty-Seven
Impending Visit

Thursday, September 1 through Saturday, September 3, 1932

Maggie York took the Wednesday night MGM mail plane back from New York City. Porter was at the airport when she arrived after 9 P.M., Thursday, a bit faded from the nearly 24-hour flight and still slightly shaken by her Tuesday adventure with Longie Zwillman.

"You look like hell," said Porter.

"You always know what to say to a girl," grinned Maggie. "Whoever decided to try to pass you off at MGM as a poet?"

*

Porter drove Maggie to a diner, then to her apartment. He filled her in during the driving about the impending Millette Sunday night visit, Bern's family history, and his suspicions about Annie Spry's imminent comeback.

"Where are Bern and Harlow tonight?" asked Maggie.

"Home. Having dinner with Willis Goldbeck, one of the writers on *Freaks*. I think Bern's trying to persuade him he's not washed up in Hollywood."

"Bern's a sweet man, actually," said Maggie.

"The sweetest," said Porter.

He waited for Maggie to come forth with remarks about Longie Zwillman, but she'd been mysteriously silent on that topic. It was only as they neared her apartment building that she touched on the subject.

"Abner Zwillman said I should say hello to you," she said finally.

"What else did he say?"

"He said the two of you have a 'history,' as he called it, but wasn't specific. He also asked me to tell you he only began researching Dorothy Millette after his people told him you'd left the case in July."

Porter nodded.

After a pause, Maggie said, "I wouldn't have guessed that you and he are…acquainted."

"Are you impressed or disappointed?" Longie was a slick dude, but from Maggie's tone, he'd have bet disappointed.

"Neither, really. Just…puzzled."

"Well, puzzle about it later. We have a hell of a holiday weekend on tap with dear Dorothy coming to call. And Longie – excuse me, Abner – might know more about it than I do."

"Maybe he does," said Maggie. "From what he told me, he was due to arrive in L.A. by plane earlier today."

That could mean everything or nothing, thought Porter.

"Our problem is suspects," said Porter. "Zwillman wants Bern dead because Longie once had a fling with Harlow. He told you about it, didn't he?"

"No, but I guessed."

"Marino Bello likely wants Bern dead to get his money. Dorothy Millette might want Bern dead because she's a scorned woman. Same, in a way, with Annie Spry. And Bern meanwhile wants himself dead because he's obsessed with suicide."

"You're missing a suspect," said Maggie.

"Who?"

"Jean Harlow. Maybe she wants Paul Bern dead more than anyone."

*

Porter escorted Maggie up to her room, carrying her bag. "Would you like a Coke?" she asked.

"No. We better get some sleep and stay fresh."

Maggie paused. "I never asked. Was there any…trouble…getting Harlow back to Beverly Hills from Twentynine Palms?"

For an instant they looked into each other's eyes and neither liked what they saw.

"No," said Porter tightly. "Good night." They didn't kiss goodbye.

*

Porter was back at the marina. It was after midnight but he was wide awake and the Pacific wind was cold as he sat on the trawler deck. Some animal had washed up on shore nearby and died, a large animal, judging by its rank smell, maybe a seal.

The phone rang shortly after one.

"Hello, Sailor Boy."

The voice was soft, feminine and taunting, and although a bit slurred, Porter recognized it instantly.

"Annie," he said. "You know my private phone number. I feel violated."

"So nice to learn you've rejoined the party," said the voice.

"Why are you back, Annie?" asked Porter. "The deal in Berlin fell through? You didn't titillate the Teutons?"

"I've been keeping tabs on your girl Friday," said Annie. "Just like *she* was keeping tabs on *me*. That nice, blonde, *big* girl. I believe her name is Maggie?"

"Let me guess what happened in Berlin," said Porter. "You couldn't find any Deutschland whores to double you and the producers saw you naked."

"How does Maggie taste in your bed?" asked Annie.

"What do you want, Annie? You sound plastered."

"I want precisely what I demanded originally. Otherwise, 50 prints of *The Wedding Night of Jean Harlow and Paul Bern* are ready for rental. I might just invite Paul and Baby to the new gala premiere...this time with a packed house. I'll be in touch very soon to make arrangements."

"Sober up, Annie."

"Good night, Sailor Boy. Give that nice, blonde, *big* girl a kiss for me...a *French* kiss. Tell her I..."

Porter hung up. Yes, he'd sensed this coming for weeks. He knew Annie knew the location of Luke's Marina. And she had contacts with underworld assassins.

He woke up Luke in *The Frederick*. "Luke, we might have a dangerous situation. The woman responsible for the murder of the girl whose body was dumped here in July is back in town. I want you to sail out a few miles and stay there tonight and every night till we find her."

"Should I go now?" asked Luke.

"Yeah," said Porter. "Right now."

Luke obediently prepared to set sail. Porter went to the shack, got a Coke, sat on the deck of *The Phoebe* and thought about how

Fate had brought Annie Spry back into his life just in time for Labor Day Weekend…and a visit from Dorothy Millette.

*

Because of Monday being the Labor Day holiday, MGM staff planned to work long hours Friday, Saturday, and Sunday. Jean Harlow acted in *Red Dust* with Gable and Bern worked on a story treatment for *China Seas*.

On Friday morning, Porter drove to Castellammare. As he'd anticipated, and as Maggie had told him, there was nobody in the house where he'd been the guest of Annie Spry two-and-a-half months ago. Nevertheless, he had a gut feeling somebody had been there recently, at least briefly…maybe Annie since returning from Germany?

He met O'Leary at the Santa Monica Post Office, learning that someone had picked up all the accumulated mail for AS Productions over a week ago and had closed out the box. Almost 20 more pieces of mail had come over the past couple days and Porter and O'Leary retrieved them before the post office had returned them to senders. They were all rental orders for pornography and several pieces were from Europe.

From there, Porter and O'Leary went to the Beverly Hills Bank, where the manager showed them the receipts that revealed Anne Cynthia Spry had withdrawn almost all the money in the AS Productions account, and her own personal account, at various times during the first half of 1932, the last withdrawal in late June. The remaining combined sum in both accounts: $64.55.

"She's wanted for the murder of Susan Peerce," said O'Leary to Porter as they left the bank. "She's hiding somewhere…and she's desperate for money."

*

Saturday morning, Porter visited Bern in his MGM office. "Should we talk in signals?" asked Porter, half-joking and closing the door behind him.

Bern, perspiring in the morning heat, took a note pad, scribbled for a moment, tore off the message, and handed it to Porter:

Studio chauffeur will deliver Sunday circa 10 P.M.

"That's swell," said Porter, tearing up the note. "I have more great news for you."

He told Bern about the re-emergence of Annie and the renewed threat of blackmail. Bern began sweating even more profusely than he had been. Porter reassured him that O'Leary and Maggie were on Annie's tail.

"Then her people will send out that film!" said Bern.

"Worry about that some other weekend," said Porter.

Just then Irene buzzed Bern. "Mr. Thalberg and Mr. Mayer need to see you, Mr. Bern. Mr. Mayer's office. It's regarding the *China Seas* project."

"Please excuse me, Porter," said Bern, rising, straightening his tie. "You may feel free to relax here. I hope I won't be long." He took a copy of the treatment and he was gone.

However, Bern's meeting did run long and Porter left the office without seeing him again. He thought of visiting the *Red Dust* soundstage and checking on Harlow, but decided to skip it. Porter would bet anything that, although Bern had told him about Sunday night's impending visit from the prune-faced looney, that he hadn't told Jean.

Chapter Thirty-Eight
Temper Tantrums

Saturday, September 3, 1932

Saturday night, Porter, restless and hot-headed, drove to the Ambassador Hotel. He had to see Longie Zwillman, and it was best to do it now…and confront the dragon in his lair.

He dressed in his brown suit and arrived about 11:00. The hour was calculated: Longie drank and partied on Saturday nights and was usually shit-faced and loose-lipped by this time. Guests packed the Ambassador, and Porter used the house phone to reach the Zwillman penthouse. There was music and raucous laughter in the background as Nick Kirk answered the phone. Porter identified himself and asked for Longie, who took a while to pick up the receiver.

"What do you want, ya' fat-assed bastard?" chuckled a jolly and obviously drunk Longie.

"I need to see you. I'm coming up."

"Bullshit. You can't do that. Most of the fine ladies up here got their clothes off. The one next to me does, anyway." Porter heard a female giggle shrilly. "I'll come down," said Longie. "See you in the lobby."

Porter hung up. Suddenly he saw a small man in a dark suit and with a protruding forehead and a receding hairline making his way through the crowd toward the lobby men's room.

"Oh, Jesus Christ," said Porter out loud.

*

Porter followed and found Paul Bern standing at a urinal. He took position at the partitioned urinal beside it. "All right," said Porter. "And you're here tonight because…?"

Bern looked up startled. "Oh! Oh, my. Actually, Porter, it's a private matter and…."

"Longie Zwillman," said Porter, "is on his way down to the lobby right now from his penthouse. If he sees you, he's gonna' figure I brought you to him on a platter. Drain it fast, jackass, and follow me outside."

Bern finished, washed his hands and rushed out behind Porter, trotting through the lobby and outside the Ambassador. "Alright," said Porter. "You got 30 seconds to explain to me why, of all the places tonight in Goddamn Southern California to take a piss, you just took one at the Ambassador Hotel."

"I had no idea Zwillman was here, Porter," said Bern hurriedly. "I came because my friend Bernie Hyman, a fellow Metro producer, is having a clandestine meeting with a starlet, whose name is … well, never mind her name…"

"Will you answer my question?" snarled Porter.

"Bernie and his lady needed a third party to make their rendezvous appear innocent. I dined with them at their bungalow to establish they weren't there alone."

"And they're in the bungalow now? Just the two of them, screwing like rabbits?"

"Well! I can't say…"

"Where's your wife right now? Did you leave her alone?"

"No. She's staying the night with her mother. Bello left tonight with Clark Gable on a fishing trip to Catalina. I had hoped to go to Freddie March's tonight – he's hosting his birthday party – but Jean announced she was going to Club View Drive. She has an early call at the studio tomorrow and it's closer for her…"

"Stop bullshittin' and get the hell out of here," said Porter. "Give the valet your ticket and have your chauffeur drive you home. Fast."

Bern scurried to the valet and Porter headed back into the lobby. He shook his head – even tonight, on the eve of what might be the most devastating night of his life, with a common law wife about to visit him and a blackmailer on the loose, Bern was moaning over missing a birthday party and still playing the "Father Confessor" for a producer and starlet with hot pants.

The man's a disaster, thought Porter.

The lobby elevator door opened and Longie Zwillman emerged, sporting a tailored beige double-breasted suit and a yellow paper party hat tied under his chin. Nick Kirk was with him and he looked stinko – Longie, not Nick.

"Porter, ya' chunky fuck," grinned Longie.

"Step back in the elevator, Longie. Now."

Zwillman, surprised, stepped back into the elevator with Nick and Porter. The three men filled the elevator and there was no room for the uniformed elevator operator, whom Nick promptly tossed out into the lobby. The door closed and Nick worked the buttons.

"Miss York tells me you had a field trip together in New York," said Porter.

"Yeah," growled Longie as the elevator ascended. "Classy gal. Right, Nick?"

"Very classy," said Nick.

"Smart too, right Nick?" asked Longie.

"Very smart," said Nick.

"Leave her alone, Longie," said Porter. "And leave Harlow and me alone too."

"Why ya' beefin'?" demanded Zwillman. "You checked out of MGM two months ago. It's a free country, Down."

The elevator stopped at a floor and two well-dressed couples began to board. "Stay the fuck off!" barked Longie. The women gasped and Nick pressed the button to close the door.

"I'm warning ya', Longie," said Porter. "Keep the hell away from Harlow, Bern, Maggie, Millette... and me."

"You're warning me?" bellowed Longie. "You tellin' me how to run my life all of a sudden? You my fuckin' nanny? You never noticed I do *what* the fuck I want, *when* the fuck I want, *how* the fuck I want?"

"You're shitfaced, Longie."

"Yeah, I'm shitfaced." He seemed suddenly to notice he was still wearing his paper party hat and tore it off, crumpling the hat in his huge hands. "Maybe it's time I taught you a lesson, Down. Maybe I'll do somethin' to show you I don't give a shit for you givin' me warnings! Maybe pick a name from that list you just gave me. Maybe..."

"Longie," said Porter, "You touch Harlow, Bern, or Millette, and I'll personally blow the whistle on you. You touch Maggie, and I'll kill you."

The elevator landed in the lobby again and Nick pushed the open button. "Porter," he said, politely but firmly, "I think you better get out now."

"Fuckin' right," said Longie.

"Be a good boy, Longie," said Porter. "Bye." He stepped out of the elevator.

"Good boy?" roared the red-faced Longie. "Good boy? Fuck you, Porter! FUCK YOU! FUCK…!"

Nick Kirk, aware of the scene Longie was making, hit the button and discreetly closed the elevator door.

Chapter Thirty-Nine
Hiding Place

Saturday, September 3 and Sunday, September 4, 1932

Porter glanced at his watch. It was after 11:30.

As he drove away from the Ambassador, Porter wondered if Paul Bern, after his "Father Confessor" duty that night, had called (or would even think to call) his "dear wife" at Club View Drive to be sure she was safe. It occurred to Porter he better call her himself.

He stopped at a phone booth. Claudette the maid answered at Club View. No, Mrs. Bern wasn't there. She was still at the studio, claimed Claudette. She volunteered the information that Marino had left that night for a fishing trip with Clark Gable to Catalina, that Mrs. Bello expected Mrs. Bern to spend the night with her at Club View, and that Mrs. Bern should be there momentarily.

Porter drove to MGM. It was almost midnight. He parked at the *Red Dust* soundstage. The lights were still on but only a skeleton crew was there, cleaning up from the day's shoot and preparing for tomorrow. The studio would work Sunday to make up for the Labor Day holiday on Monday. "We stopped for the night a half-an-hour ago," said a technician. "Baby and her maid might still be in her dressing room."

There was a rowdy gang of revelers at the MGM dressing room complex. Porter had removed his coat, tie and snap-brim hat as he walked up to the building and saw the group was moving in and out of Joan Crawford's second floor quarters. The lights were out in Harlow's first floor dressing room. Porter looked for Harlow amidst the laughing, drinking folk who, Porter presumed, were celebrating Saturday night and the Labor Day weekend.

Porter stood at the bottom of the stairs. "Can I help you, handsome?" called out a female voice on the balcony. It belonged to Joan Crawford, who held a drink and a bottle.

"Lookin' for Jean Harlow," said Porter.

"Won't I do?" flirted Crawford. "I can be a better hooker than Harlow any night of the year." She put down the bottle, hiked up her skirt and showed her legs. Her gang whistled and cheered. For Porter, at the base of the stairs, the view was especially provocative.

"No thanks," deadpanned Porter. "I was hoping for something a little fresher."

Crawford picked up the bottle and threw it at him. She barely missed.

*

A studio car was parked nearby, and Porter saw a uniformed chauffeur leaning against the car and smoking a cigarette. He was a lanky Cockney nicknamed Limey – Porter had met him on the lot a time or two. "You by any chance waitin' for Harlow?" asked Porter.

Limey nodded.

"Where is she?" asked Porter.

"Cripes, man, I don't ask questions," said Limey.

She wasn't at the soundstage or in her dressing room. Porter had an idea where he might find her. He looked at his watch. It was 12:10 A.M.

*

It was very dark on MGM's Lot Two, with only a few pilot lights burning. No one was at the gate. Porter made his way to the *Tarzan the Ape Man* dock set. Sure enough, there was Blanche Williams' Chevy and Blanche herself, on the lookout outside one of the little thatched huts. Porter approached quietly and gave a little cough. Blanche jumped, turned and saw Porter.

"She in there?" asked Porter, pointing at the nearest hut.

"Yes," said Blanche. "She's very bad, Porter. Nights like this… they be the worst."

Porter saw the urgency in Blanche's face. "Stay on guard," he said, ducking into the hut.

Harlow was huddled in the corner, barely discernible in the shadow, even her platinum hair almost totally suffused in the blackness. "Why have you come?" said the slurred voice from the dark corner. "You don't care."

"I'm here, aren't I?" demanded Porter. "Squatting in here in the dark with you? Smellin' your boozy breath after midnight?"

"Did Paul send you? Did Mother send you?"

"Paul thinks you're at Club View. Your mother expects you there any minute."

Porter could hear the shadow drinking, he guessed from a bottle. "He doesn't want me at the house this weekend," said Harlow.

"I wouldn't want a stinko wife around either when I'm having company," said Porter.

"You go to hell," said the shadow. "And take his 'company' with you."

Porter moved a bit closer. "How much has he told you?"

She was silent.

"I'm sure you'll be staying at Club View again tomorrow night," said Porter. "That's when we expect the ever-charming you-know-who."

The shadow stayed silent. "I want to see her," she said finally.

"Like hell you do," said Porter. "You stay at Club View. Let Paul and me handle this."

"What will you do?" she asked.

"Paul hasn't discussed it with you?" asked Porter.

"He's just told me to stay away."

The bastard, thought Porter. *He probably has second thoughts about coming clean.*

"I've got a plan," said Porter. "Trust me."

The shadow squirmed in the corner, the platinum hair becoming radiant in the darkness – almost, thought Porter, as if the hair were there by itself. He heard her drink again. "They take everything away from me, you know," she said. "They never let me have what I want."

"Cut it out," said Porter, with his old allergy to self-pity. "You have fame, money, and beauty. And you're a hell of a lot better off than most…"

"They took my baby," she said.

"What?"

"My baby. They took away my baby. Chuck and I were going to have a baby, and they made me…they made me kill it."

She began crying. Porter knew "Chuck" was Charles McGrew, her first husband.

"You mean… an abortion?" asked Porter softly. "Who made you do that?"

"Mother and Marino. They made me kill my baby."

Even in the darkness, he could tell she was trembling. "I wanted my baby," she wept. "My whole life would be different if they'd let me have my baby…"

She began sobbing. After a long moment, Porter moved, sat beside her, and reluctantly put his arms around her in the blackness. Her weeping increased, almost hysterically, her sobs deep and heartbreaking. She shook and he held her tightly and the smell of Mitsouko was all around him.

"I'm sorry," said Porter as she wept in his arms, almost like a child herself. "I'm sorry."

Chapter Forty
Pick-Ups

Sunday, September 4, 1932

The bastards, thought Porter. *The miserable bastards.*

It was well after 1:00 A.M. now and Porter was on his way back to Malibu. He and Blanche had driven Harlow from the back lot to Limey and his waiting studio car on the main lot, and she was probably at Club View by now. He still felt the sensation of holding her in his arms. He'd said very little to her, all the time simply holding her, feeling the great depth of her sorrow. Yes, she'd been drinking, but it was way beyond that.

Mother Jean and Marino…how could those self-centered bloodsuckers ever have allowed room in Harlow's life for a baby? Nor did Porter envision any bundles of joy on Harlow's horizon. From what he knew of Paul Bern, there was sure in hell no chance of the patter of little feet at 9820 Easton Drive. And adoption probably wasn't going to be high on the wish list of an epically neurotic man, so set in his damned ways that he didn't even want a kitchen in his house.

Yeah, the Platinum Blonde Bombshell wanted to be a mommy. It seemed too pat to be true. And her boozing and maternal meltdown were coming at one hell of a lousy time, on a weekend when she might have to be the strongest she'd ever been in her life. Yet Porter didn't resent her. He'd felt and heard her agony. It was shattering and gripped him with a profound sympathy.

Despite his resolutions, Harlow was haunting him all over again.

*

Porter was back at the marina by 2:00. At about 4:00 A.M., the phone rang again. He guessed it would be Annie Spry. He was right.

"Ready to make arrangements, Sailor Boy?" she asked.

"Yeah," said Porter, in no mood for banter. "Your funeral arrangements."

"You listen to me…," said Annie.

"No, *you* listen to *me*," snapped Porter. "You're finished, Annie. You're wanted for the murder of Susan Peerce – 'Jeanie' to you – and for the intended blackmail of Bern and Harlow. You stick your neck out from under that rock where you're hiding and LAPD, the MGM gangster squad, Longie Zwillman's world-class hit men, and me, will all be there in an instant to cut it off. And you know what? *I'll* be there first."

For a moment, there was silence. Porter thought he heard whimpering. When the voice finally spoke, it was cracked, but vicious and bitter.

"Down…If I have to *kill* somebody to stop *you* laughing at me… then by Christ, *I swear* I'll do it!"

The ferocity had its effect. Now Porter was silent.

"*You'll die!*" howled the voice. "You'll all *die!* You, and Bern, and Harlow, and that sow you're fucking…big, blonde Maggie. *You'll all die!*"

Porter slammed down the phone.

*

Although it was after four in the morning, Maggie answered on the second ring.

"Maggie…It's Porter."

"Are you alright? Your voice sounds strange."

"Yeah. Listen… I could use your help tomorrow…actually later today. Are you busy?"

"No. I've been waiting to hear from you."

"I got a call from Spry. We have to be sure she doesn't get it into her insane skull to come to Easton Drive anytime tomorrow. Could you just keep an eye on her house for me…and if she shows up there, and if she leaves at any time try to follow her?"

It was, of course, a ruse. Porter, spooked by Annie's threat, wanted Maggie to leave town but knew she'd be insulted and defiant if he did. The last place Annie would be this weekend was at the house at Castellammare and Maggie would be safe on surveillance there while still thinking she was helping the cause.

"Sure," said Maggie. There was a pause. "Porter?"

"Yeah?"

"I…I'm sorry if what I said about Harlow upset you."

Her voice was sincere with no petulance. "Don't worry about it," said Porter. "Get some rest. Stay safe. We'll talk again when this is all over."

"You stay safe too. Bye."

"Bye."

Porter went out to sit on the trawler and look at the ocean. He felt much better having talked to Maggie but sensed terrible danger.

Chapter Forty-One
Countdown

Sunday, September 4, 1932

6:00 A.M. Sunday. Porter, who'd slept little, watched the dawn from the deck of *The Phoebe*.

Meanwhile, Maggie York, after a restless night, dressed, made herself breakfast, and by 7:00 A.M., was on her way to Castellammare to work surveillance at Annie Spry's house.

As she drove out Sunset Boulevard, Longie Zwillman stirred in his bed at the Ambassador Hotel, his eyes squinting shut against a horrible hangover. The dyed platinum blonde showgirl beside him nestled her naked body against his.

"Good morrrr-ning!" she cooed.

"Shut up, you stupid twat," he grumbled.

*

Noon. The crowd around the Plaza Hotel in San Francisco looked like a fashion parade, the women in their Sunday gowns and bonnets, the men in their suits and hats, many with boutonnieres in the lapels. Grand cars drove by the fashionable Union Square area, but the limousine that parked before the Plaza at the very stroke of twelve was especially impressive. A small crowd gathered to see who would emerge from the hotel and board the exquisite car. There was some disappointment when the passenger proved to be a small, plump, moon-faced, middle-aged woman, almost teetering in her especially-made high heels, unimpressive despite the expensive red ensemble and the hat cocked over her now cut and tinted reddish-blonde hair.

"She's nobody," said a surly someone in the crowd.

The woman heard the remark and smiled superciliously. These silly, gawking people weren't *en route* to re-unite with the great love of their lives...and about to begin a life of film stardom! The uniformed chauffeur held her travel bag with one hand and opened the car's back door with the other. Moments later, the limousine was on its way to Los Angeles and the passenger tried to relax for the eight-to-ten-hour drive, already uncomfortable in the new corset she'd purchased for the visit. Paul had always liked her in red and the way she wore this hat, which she'd kept all these years.

She opened her purse, took her compact and studied her reflection. The hairdresser had assured her the new style and rinse made her look ten years younger, and she didn't miss her tresses – MGM would provide her wigs, after all, for her biblical role. She raised the hem of her skirt, looking at her own legs and the dark stockings she'd selected to make her thick legs look more slender.

Then she removed a Bible from her handbag and began reading.

*

1:00 P.M. Paul Bern lay in his bed with his special-ordered books from the Dora Ingram Bookshop.

Jean Harlow, after working a half-day on *Red Dust*, drove herself to Easton Drive. Bern, who had told her to stay at Club View Drive through Monday, was angry to see her. The Carmichaels will later claim they heard Bern shouting and that Harlow, leaving, had said tearfully, "He wants me out of here." Harlow drove back to her mother's house, leaving Bern free to meet his visitor tonight without his wife on the premises.

*

By 6:00 P.M, Maggie York had spent nearly ten hours parked atop the Castellammare colony. There was no car in view at Spry's home, nor any evidence that anyone was in the house. Now and then Maggie had looked away at the Pacific view, eating the peanut butter crackers and candy bars and drinking the root beer she'd brought along for her lunch and dinner. She'd also made one excursion down to the beach to use the public bathroom.

Maggie was angry. She figured Porter has sent her on a wild goose chase. Spry was obviously in hiding, probably far away, and Porter had sent Maggie here, she realized, to keep her safe.

Bored and restless, she decided to break into the house. She got in easily. The house was mostly bare, stripped of its furnishings, and she found nothing incriminating until she looked through a full waste basket upstairs. There were several envelopes, rubber-banded together, from MGM's publicity department. All were empty. There was also the top half of a torn letter, clearly from an ardent fan of Annie's films. The fan offered to lease his (or her) vacation home to Annie if she ever "wanted to get away from it all." The bottom half with details was maddeningly missing, but the fan did mention the basic location of the house.

San Luis Obispo, read Maggie. It was a seaside town, about 190 miles north of L.A.

*

Porter Down arrived at Easton Drive, as scheduled, at 7:00 P.M. As it was going to be a hell of a long night, he'd dressed comfortably in his sailor suit. He found Bern already showered and dressed in a dark blue suit and tie, although his guest probably wouldn't arrive for three hours. The host was watching Carmichael setting up a small portable bar by the pool.

"Everything as planned?" asked Porter.

"As far as I know," said Bern. "Jean is spending the night at Club View. The Carmichaels have their orders to stay in their quarters after 9:00. They'll call up here when the car arrives. Isn't that right, John?"

"Yes, sir," said Carmichael, and shambled away inside the house.

"By the way," said Porter. "No news yet of catching Annie Spry. She's still on the run."

"Oh God, *that* creature," said Bern. He was perspiring and mopped his brow with his blazer handkerchief. "You don't think there's any chance of *her* trying to contact me tonight? With everything else we need to worry about?"

"Who knows?" shrugged Porter, relaxing in a chair. The birds were singing in the trees, the smell of the wildflowers filled the air, and the sun was setting over the hills of the canyon.

"You know, you have a nice place here," said Porter. "Or Harlow does."

"Do you think Dorothy will like it?" asked Bern.

"She better not," said Porter.

*

Eight P.M. had come and gone. Maggie York, having returned to Hollywood, had packed her bag and decided to make the four-hour drive to San Luis Obispo tonight.

"If a Mr. Down calls," Maggie told the clerk at the lobby desk, "please read him this note. It explains that I might be out of town for a few days."

Meanwhile, at Club View Drive, Jean Harlow, tiring of Mother Jean's prattle, had her mind on the events this night on Easton Drive. She asked the maid, Claudette, to make her a drink. When Claudette delivered the drink, Harlow demanded the bottle.

*

8:45 P.M. Carmichael, aware of the gravity of this night and solemnly silent, made his way down the 75 steps, lighting the candles of the lanterns that hung from the trees. He then entered the servant house as ordered, keeping vigil for the limousine that was expected sometime in the next hour or so.

Night fell over Benedict Canyon. A coyote howled in the hills, but its cry went unanswered.

*

An hour passed. Porter and the hyper-tense Bern continued their vigil by the pool. Several candlelit lanterns provided the minimal light. Porter spun his sailor's cap on one finger. Now and then, he mentioned the bright stars or the natural forest scents, but Bern was mostly silent. Nor did he take Porter's suggestion to pass the time playing cards, chess or checkers.

"I'm going to use the little boy's room," said Porter. "You won't want me flushing the toilet after your guest shows up."

"Perhaps I should go as well," said Bern. "You may use the master bathroom upstairs."

Porter hadn't been inside the house since over two months ago, three nights before the marriage, when he'd shown Bern and Harlow Annie's movie. Drawing his eyes to the first-floor beamed ceiling was a large mural – too large to place on the house's book-lined walls, hence its fixture on the angled ceiling. It was a painting of various MGM celebrities – Harlow, Norma Shearer, Joan Crawford, Irving Thalberg, and more, all in Elizabethan garb and festively gathered at a dining table.

"Impressive, isn't it?" asked Bern. "It was my wedding gift to Jean. A young Russian artist painted it to my specifications."

Porter picked out a few more faces. "Is that lusty wench on the end Irene Harrison?"

"Yes," said Bern. "I believe Irene was quite honored to be included."

Porter shrugged. "I wouldn't want all those faces looking down on me," he said.

Bern nodded dourly. "I don't believe that Jean was very pleased by it either."

*

The grandfather clock chimed 10:45 P.M. The two men had returned outside to their post by the pool. Porter thought he heard a car down on Easton Drive. A moment later the phone rang and Bern rushed back inside the house to answer it. He emerged, his voice high and strained.

"That was Carmichael," Bern said. "My God, she's here!"

He sighed, and then started down the steps and toward the gate. Porter stood by the house and a moment later, heard the limousine heading back down Easton Drive. He moved into the house and from an upstairs window saw Bern emerging from the trees, in the lantern light, crossing the footbridge, gallantly escorting a woman by the arm, Carmichael following and carrying her bag.

Porter noticed the woman's tippy-toe walk in her built-up high heels.

Chapter Forty-Two
The Audition

Sunday, September 4 and Monday, September 5, 1932

Porter's post was in a small garret above the master bedroom. Its window offered a view of the pool area.

Carmichael had returned to the servant quarters. From the garret window, Porter could see and hear Paul and Dorothy by the patio and pool, the lady sporting her new look.

That don't-I-look-younger carrot-top-hair-do does nothing for you, Dottie, thought Porter.

The couple small-talked pleasantly. They smoked. They had two or three drinks from the portable bar. Dorothy's voice was soft and dry, her laughter arch – a sophisticated admirer like Bern might have called it "tinkling." Bern seemed controlled but nervous, also laughing gaily, as if auditioning for a Noel Coward play. From what Porter could hear, they were reminiscing a bit about New York (or "New Yawk," as Dorothy pronounced it), and comparing notes about West Coast weather. Eventually Bern invited Dorothy to enjoy the pool.

"You may go right upstairs and change to your swimsuit," said Bern in a suddenly loud voice, to be sure Porter got the word.

Porter heard Dorothy's high heels on the patio and she went into the house and up to the bedroom. He heard her sighing and wheezing a bit, and after some time he heard her going down the stairs and saw her re-appear on the patio, stuffed into a rubber-paneled bathing suit and carrying her white silk bathing robe over one arm. Bern told her how charming she looked, and then came upstairs to change into his swimming trunks.

A few moments passed. Porter peered out the window and thought he saw a shadow by the door. He strained to see if Bern was now with Dorothy at the pool, but he could only see Dorothy. After a moment Bern appeared and Porter figured the shadow he'd seen had been Bern's as he stood by the door.

Probably making a last-minute adjustment of his trunks for optimum effect, thought Porter.

A moment later he saw Bern ease himself into the pool. Dorothy sat on the edge, dangling her feet in the water.

*

It was, Porter realized, after midnight. He continued keeping watch from the garret. They were both still bullshitting down there, doggy-paddling in the pool, now and then laughing self-consciously, their voices affected, the lantern light illuminating the area so he could see their faces.

The night dragged on. 12:30. 12:45. They were out of the water now, standing by the pool, having another drink. Dorothy's phony, obnoxious, tinkling laughter rose again in the night. Several times she called Paul "darling." Now and then, Porter thought he heard a bump in the house, but figured a weird structure like this one made all variety of middle-of-the-night sounds as the temperature cooled.

"Oh, darling!" he heard Dorothy tinkle.

Porter looked at his watch. 1:05 A.M. The coyote howled again in the hills. Porter peered out at the stars and the night and then down again at the pool area. He could see Dorothy, her newly styled and tinted hair still dry and coiffed, as she'd never dipped below her neck in the pool. He could see Bern, his bald spot showing through his wet hair, potbellied in his trunks, also holding a glass. Yet something was different now. It was in Bern's manner, the way he stood close to her, the way he'd softened his voice. The forced conviviality had lessened and a sense of sympathy was in play.

With increasing anxiety, Porter watched what followed.

Dorothy seemed to be dismissing whatever Bern was saying. She directed Bern to sit and after he was settled with a fresh drink, she put on her robe and went around to the other side of the pool. The effect she had created was almost as if he were her audience, seeing her on a stage or a screen.

"Watch, darling," he heard her say.

Then, after a moment of stillness, she began to pose. It was as if she were striking moods, each one fervently dramatic. She held her arms out at her side, allowing the robe to separate and drape around her. The effect was almost angelic. Bern sat entirely still and now Dorothy fell to her knees, raising her hands as if in prayer.

The Sacrifice, thought Porter, and he felt the hair rise on the back of his neck.

She blessed herself, making the Sign of the Cross, her face freakishly transfigured, playing a holy heroine, 20 years too old for the role, grotesque with her tinted hair and gaping eyes. Now, she began to sing – what sounded like a hymn – in a weak and quavering soprano.

O sacred head surrounded, by crown of piercing thorn...

The hymn sounded like a dirge, and her voice was ludicrously off-key. Bern clutched his glass. Dorothy kept performing. The coyote howled in the hills, as if mocking her pathetic singing.

And now she stopped singing and stood. Dorothy looked across the pool at Bern and, like some seducing witch, took off the robe and pulled down the front of her bathing suit, exposing her sagging breasts. After a moment she came slowly around the pool. With some effort she removed her suit entirely, shoved it away with her foot, and now leaned into Bern, sitting on his lap, passionately kissing him.

"I rest for all eternity," sighed Dorothy, "in the arms of my beloved Savior."

Bern pushed her away and stood. "No…. *No!*" he shouted.

As Porter watched, Bern, repeating "no" over and over, wiped the sweat from his eyes as Dorothy stood a few feet from him, silent and staring. Then Porter heard it. It was that rising whine that reminded him of both a child and an animal, the keening sound he'd heard in San Francisco after Dorothy had discovered the ruse that had gotten him into her room.

Good God, thought Porter.

Now the cry escalated, mad, warped, approaching hysteria. Having failed her audition as both star and lover, Dorothy, naked, livid, and mortified, stamped her tiny bare feet like an angry child, pounding at Bern's chest the way she'd pounded at Porter's.

"Liar!" she screamed. "LIAR!" And now she slapped his face.

"Stop!" shouted Bern, gripping his glass so tightly that it broke into pieces and cut his hand.

"LIAR!" she shrieked again and slapped him viciously again.

"*GET OUT!*" Bern bleated, his voice almost as distorted and chilling as hers.

Dorothy Millette screamed in rage, again and again. Porter realized it was sure in hell time for him to descend from his hideaway, and then suddenly sensed a silence. He looked back out the window and saw Bern and Millette both staring to the side, looking toward the landing by the front door.

To their shock, and Porter's, Jean Harlow came into view.

"Just wanted to see my competition," she said.

*

Harlow was dressed in white tennis top and shorts, and her voice was slurred.

"Sounds like you're both having a swell time," she smirked.

Dorothy's face contorted. She ran to get her robe.

"Poor girl," grinned Harlow. "Imagine your embarrassment."

Dorothy pulled her robe around her naked body, returning to the side of the pool toward Bern and Harlow. Bern, dazed, looked alternately at Harlow, Dorothy, and the pool. The coyote yammered in the hills as if laughing at the dark comedy scene. And now, Dorothy's whine rose again.

"Whore!" yowled Dorothy at Harlow. "Whore!"

"Slap me, granny," said Harlow, "and I'll scratch your eyes out."

"Stop it!" shouted Bern.

"Whore!" screamed Dorothy. "WHORE!"

"*Stop it!*" shouted Bern again. "*Dorothy, get out of my life!*"

Dorothy looked at Bern, shuddering at his words that echoed in the canyon. Then, tears running down her face, she charged Harlow, aiming with her little fists, and Bern grabbed her and restrained her. Suddenly all three noticed a new player joining the scene.

"Nobody move a muscle," ordered Porter.

Dorothy Millette gasped as she recognized him from her apartment. She pivoted toward him, raised her tiny fists again and then, standing beside the pool, she fainted.

Chapter Forty-Three
The .38

Monday, September 5, 1932

An hour had passed since "Dear Dorothy's" swoon at Easton Drive. Porter had taken command of the situation.

He'd required some time to revive Dorothy. Now, still naked under her bathing robe, she sat silently by the pool. Harlow sat on the front door step. Porter took Bern inside and had him telephone MGM to arrange for a limousine to take a "passenger," as Bern discreetly put it, to San Francisco as soon as possible. The studio promised to alert a chauffeur and have the car there within 90 minutes.

Porter came back outside and ordered Dorothy to change back into her clothes – her wet bathing suit still lie on the patio – and prepare to head home. Drained by her fit and her faint, Dorothy silently and obediently went inside and upstairs. She passed Harlow at the door and neither said a word.

"Why'd you come here?" Porter asked Harlow.

"I live here," she said.

"Your breath smells like a distillery," said Porter. "You drove up here drunk as a skunk?"

"So what?"

"Never mind. Stay out here by the pool while she dresses."

"It's cold out here and it's my house. I'll go sit inside."

She did, sitting sullenly in the living room on the fireplace hearth. When Dorothy came downstairs, after taking a long time to dress, Porter immediately took the visitor out by the pool.

"Don't move from this spot," he said.

The woman sat in a folding chair, silently looking up at him, her face round and anguished in the starlight.

The married couple sat by the fireplace. Bern, who'd put on a robe over his swim trunks, sat in a chair. Harlow, in her tennis suit, sat on the hearth, her bare legs crossed and her arms folded.

Neither spoke. The "More Stars Than There are in Heaven" MGM mural, with the stars in Elizabethan finery, gazed blithely down upon the scene. Porter entered.

"We'll talk upstairs, Mr. Bern."

"Very well." Bern and Harlow looked at each other for a moment, and he weakly went up the steep steps.

"Can I trust you to stay where you are?" Porter asked Harlow. "No wandering outside? No girl talk with dear Dorothy?"

"Go to Hell," said Harlow, but she grimly nodded.

Porter went upstairs and found Bern seated in the dressing room, facing a tall, wooden closet. He'd removed his robe and looked shrunken and somehow malformed in his trunks. Suddenly he squinted and tears flooded his face. A sob escaped and he covered his mouth. Porter regarded the man more so than ever before with a sense of pity.

"What do I do?" cried Bern, almost in a whisper.

"You do what we planned. The car will be here from MGM soon. We'll leave with Dorothy and get her back to San Francisco. In a day or two, you call your press conference and admit the virtual bigamy and the planned annulment. Meanwhile, you get Dorothy back in an institution. We all saw proof tonight that's where she belongs."

"I'm ruined," said Bern, weeping. "In every way a man can be… I'm ruined."

"Oh, I don't know," said Porter. "You had two ladies down there, a blonde and a redhead, both ready to catfight over you."

"This isn't funny, Porter." He paused, wiped his eyes. "Actually, I suppose it *is* rather funny. A comedy…isn't it?"

"Yeah," said Porter. "Hilarious. Anyway, you're doing the right thing. The honorable thing. I know that and you know that."

Bern nodded and then gave one of his patented ironic grins that Porter had come to know all too well. "Well, Porter, as you said…I suppose this is all a dream-come-true for a self-professed masochist."

"How do you top it?" asked Porter.

"What about Jean tonight?" asked Bern. "I…I can't face her with this…"

"I'll fill her in," said Porter. "She's still too drunk to drive. She'll sleep here tonight. I'll tell the Carmichaels to take care of her after we go. You can telephone from San Francisco and tell her what to expect. The important thing now is to get the hell out of here."

It was an instinctive sensation. Even with the two female adversaries apparently willing to stay in their respective corners, Porter had a strange sense of danger. He was very anxious to get off the property.

"I'll…I'll leave her a note," said Bern.

"Write it fast," said Porter impatiently. "We'll give it to Carmichael and he can give it to her in the morning. By that time, we'll be near San Francisco."

Bern opened a Morocco-bound notebook on his dresser and took a pen. His grin was sad, self-mocking, but oddly sincere as he wrote in haste:

Dearest Dear/
Unfortunately this is the only way to make good the frightful wrong I have done you and to wipe out my abject humiliation/I love you.

Paul

Bern reviewed his words, wiped a tear from his eye, and added a hurried postscript:

You understand that last night was only a comedy

He handed the notebook to Porter, who read the message and handed the book back to him. "Yeah," said Porter. "Last night was a laugh riot. Now get dressed."

Bern stood in the dressing room he and Harlow had shared for their 65-day marriage. There seemed almost a grave reverence about him, as if he were aware he'd probably never be in this place again after this night – after all, he'd gifted his wife the house. Rather than give the notebook to Carmichael to deliver, Bern decided to place it against Harlow's perfume bottle on the dresser. His hands were trembling and as he did so, he accidentally knocked over the bottle. Only a small pool of the Mitsouko spilled, but its scent suddenly filled the room. Porter remembered the rich, sensual smell was one of his first sensations the day he met Jean Harlow.

Hollywood's "Father Confessor," now about to make his own confession to the world, looked again at Porter, his eyes filled with loss, sadness, and bravery. Porter nodded, and then glanced out the window, down at the pool and the forlorn figure of Dorothy Millette.

Then suddenly a masked figure crashed from the tall wooden closet and, in barely an instant, grabbed Paul Bern around the neck and fired a .38 revolver into his right temple. The bullet and a spattering of Bern's brains exploded through his left temple and the body fell to the floor.

Chapter Forty-Four
Aftershock

Monday, September 5, 1932

The figure immediately fired a second shot, aimed at Porter, who dived to the floor, intentionally overturning the tall dresser closet. The bullet went out the window and as the figure aimed again, Porter shoved the closet toward his attacker. It hit the figure squarely, knocking the killer down the steep steps as Porter heard the two women screaming below.

The dresser now blocked the steps and Porter's only exit was the window. He opened it, looked down and saw the killer darting out the door. Porter jumped the 10-feet, landing directly on the assassin just as the gun fired again, the bullet barely missing Dorothy Millette.

The figure fought like a hellion and it took all of Porter's considerable strength to subdue him. The assassin clubbed Porter with the revolver, stood, and aimed the .38 at him on the ground, but he was too late. Porter had pulled his derringer from his pocket and fired. There'd been no time to aim and the bullet struck the figure's face. Blood spurted out of the mask's eyeholes and the killer, falling back into a bush, was still.

Porter quickly examined the body and found a holster strapped against the right lower leg. He pulled a handkerchief from his pocket, picked up the .38 and wedged it into the killer's holster.

*

Porter looked over at the unharmed Dorothy. She was standing, her tiny hands almost coyly covering her mouth as she realized she'd just seen a man shot to death and had almost been shot herself. Then she collapsed back into a chair by the pool.

Harlow, thought Porter.

He tried to keep focus, rushing back into the house, shoving his derringer back in his holster. Harlow was on the stairs, frantically striking at the overturned closet that blocked the upper steps.

"Paul!" she screamed. "*Paul!*"

Porter finally shoved the closet away and he and Harlow each regarded Bern's corpse, clad only in his bathing trunks, crumpled in the corner, almost in a sitting position, his bloody head resting against the wall. Harlow opened her mouth as if to scream but no sound issued and Porter held her tightly as she surrendered to hysteria. The strength of her small body was surprising and Porter rocked her as he held her.

Millette, thought Porter.

"Don't move," ordered Porter, helping Harlow to a seated position on the floor. He now hurried downstairs and out the door, just in time to see Millette running madly down the path and over the footbridge. Porter began pursuit but she was well ahead of him and probably due to hysteria, surprisingly fast. As she ran the heel snapped on one of her shoes. She nearly fell but kept running, hobbling and scuttling like a goblin, appearing and disappearing in and out of the light and darkness as she ran past the lantern candles. Finally, she stopped, removed both shoes, and resumed running in her stocking feet, disappearing under the trees and toward the gate.

"Stop!" Porter shouted.

The MGM limousine had arrived, boarded its passenger, and revolved at the top of the hill. The car started down Easton Drive and Porter leaped in front to stop it. Limey, the cockney chauffeur, was alarmed by the sudden appearance of Porter, whom he didn't recognize.

"Drive!" Dorothy shrieked. "Fast!"

Limey, spooked by the mad screams of his passenger, nearly hit Porter as the car tore down Easton. The limousine skidded into Benedict Canyon Drive, speeding south to Sunset Boulevard.

Bern was dead, Harlow was hysterical, and Dorothy Millette was on the loose. As a P.I., Porter had had better nights.

*

He had to think fast and further mistakes were not an option.

Porter knocked at the servants' house and enlisted the dazed Carmichael into service, telling him Bern was dead. They made their way up to the house where Harlow was still crumpled on the floor, shaken and weeping. Carmichael gaped at the body and Harlow listened fitfully as Porter took her by the shoulders and communicated some grim facts.

"Paul's dead," he said. "There's no use calling an ambulance. Understand?"

"Yes," shivered Harlow, barely audible.

"Also," said Porter, "his killer is dead. You're safe, for now."

Harlow nodded and wept.

"I'll provide the police Paul's body," said Porter, "and his killer's…but not now."

Harlow stared at Bern's corpse, her eyes wide and haunted.

"Meanwhile," said Porter, "you have to do what I tell you."

"Alright," whimpered Harlow.

Porter decided he'd take her back to Club View Drive. He had doubts about removing her from the premises but to leave her here with the body, even with Carmichael nearby, could give her a breakdown…and there might also be a second killer in the vicinity. If so, the killer might want to shoot Porter, possibly Harlow, but probably not Carmichael.

He'd drive her back in her car to her mother – a loony, but probably the person she should be near now. Porter and Carmichael went outside and extricated the killer's corpse from the bush and Porter removed the mask. It was a young man, his body taut and strong, the face mutilated by the bullet Porter had fired into the eyes. They carried the corpse behind the house, and Porter told Carmichael to stay with the body, indeed, not to let it out of his sight, until Porter returned.

"Don't touch the body," said Porter, "and if anybody gets here before I do, don't let anybody else touch the body, or that pistol."

*

It was after 3:30 A.M. Porter left Carmichael guarding the killer's body and walked the widow down the stairs to her car. Many of the candles in the lanterns had burned out during the night and the stars were the primary light. Still, there was enough of a glow for him to see near the gate Dorothy Millette's damaged shoe, which she'd dropped in her race to the limousine.

Porter picked it up. There was a faint light in an upstairs window of the servants' house and Porter saw Mrs. Carmichael's fat, frightened face staring down at him and Harlow. Harlow's car was parked at the gate. Porter moved his car up into the woods, got Harlow into her car, tossed Millette's shoe into the back seat, and started the engine.

*

Harlow shivered and trembled as they drove away and Porter wished he had a blanket to wrap around her.

"I'm not sure when we'll talk again," he said. "Can you understand what I'm about to tell you?"

She sniveled and nodded.

"Bern and I had planned to take Millette back to San Francisco. If she were diagnosed as ill as she appeared, he'd have committed her to an institution, would have announced his common law marriage, and pursued an annulment."

Harlow nodded again but remained silent.

"He cared about you and…he had courage," Porter forced himself to say. "He left a note for you at the house, explaining that… sort of."

*

The aftermath at Club View Drive was all he had expected. Mother Jean was almost as hysterical as her daughter and both women fell into each other's arms onto Harlow's bed.

They wept and wailed for some time, and Claudette the maid, looking very un-French at 4:00 A.M. without her spit curls and Gallic makeup, did what Porter told her to do: she brought Jean and Mother Jean each a glass of bootleg whiskey.

"You two have to stay quiet," ordered Porter, "and say nothing to anyone. With luck, I'll have this situation under control around eight this morning. Understand?"

Mother Jean nodded. "I have to go to the bathroom," she whimpered.

Porter nodded and Mother Jean left the bedroom. She quietly descended to the study, opened her private address and telephone book, and dialed Howard Strickling.

"Oh, Howard," she sobbed. "This is Jean Bello. The most horrible thing has happened…"

*

After Mother Jean returned to her daughter, Porter asked to use the phone. He called O'Leary's home. There was no answer. It was Labor Day Weekend. Had Jim possibly gone away with his family?

The women were hysterical again upstairs. Without Marino in the house to provide fascist but at least masterful control, Porter was reluctant to leave Club View Drive. Claudette was too hellbent on getting dressed in her ooh-la-la French maid costume and making herself up to be of any assistance.

Another half-hour passed. Porter thought of Blanche Williams. She had her own home, although she spent many nights at Easton Drive with Harlow. Mother Jean provided Blanche's number and Porter reached her by telephone.

"Oh, poor Baby!" wailed Blanche.

Porter said he'd await her arrival. He was restless, thinking of the two bodies up on Easton Drive, figuring Carmichael wouldn't be worth a damn if there was any trouble of any kind, fearful the butler might phone the police himself…or MGM.

As the first light of Labor Day approached, and Porter kept watch for Blanche Williams to arrive, he had no idea that, thanks to Mother Jean's telephone call, the MGM powers – Louis B. Mayer, Irving Thalberg, Eddie Mannix, Howard Strickling, and various minions – were already on a mission to Easton Drive. They were angry, frightened, desperate – and about to concoct a lasting rewrite on an infamous night in Hollywood history.

Part Four
"Frightful Wrong" and "Abject Humiliation"

Chapter Forty-Five
Labor Day Morning

Monday, September 5, 1932

It was just after dawn when a cab dropped off a fired-up Porter Down at the entrance to Easton Drive – a full hour later than he'd hoped to return. Blanche Williams had arrived at Club View Drive in tears, after a delay caused by car trouble. Porter's continued calls to O'Leary's house had all been unanswered. Even getting a cab early on Labor Day morning had been problematic.

He'd decided that, back at Bern's house, he'd call LAPD, and make up his mind to trust the detectives who arrived. As he walked up Easton Drive, he saw several cars. Guards were already at the gate. He recognized them as MGM cops.

"Son of a bitch," he said.

*

Porter gave his name to the guards. They seemed to know who he was and admitted him. He ascended the 75 steps. He saw the triumvirate of L.B. Mayer, Eddie Mannix and Howard Strickling awaiting him, and the wraith-like form of Irving Thalberg standing by the pool. He ordered the shrieking Mayer to let go of the lapels of his shirt. When Mayer had slapped him, he'd slapped him back.

They entered the house, sitting in the living room by the cold, unlit fireplace. Strickling got Mayer a glass of water. Porter smelled the Mitsouko upstairs and the rank stench of death.

"There was another woman here," said Mannix. "The servants said so. We found a woman's wet bathing suit by the pool – looks like it was designed for a damn rhinoceros. Definitely not Jean's."

Porter kept a poker face. He'd forgotten about the bathing suit last night.

"Carmichael tells us the woman was from Bern's past," said Mannix.

"Carmichael was supposed to be keeping his mouth shut," said Porter.

"Just tell us what you know," said Mannix.

"Alright," said Porter. "This is it in a nutshell. Yes, a lady from Bern's past had come to confront him. Harlow showed up too... drunk. An assassin shot Bern, I shot the assassin, the other woman took off, and I drove Harlow to her mother's. Have you called the cops?"

"Whitey Hendry and the boys are upstairs now," said Mannix.

"I mean the real cops," said Porter.

"I remind you that Whitey is police chief of Culver City, not just MGM," said Mannix.

"And I remind you the corpse isn't in Culver City, but Beverly Hills," said Porter.

"What's this woman's name?" demanded Mannix. "And where in the hell is she now?"

"I'll tell you when the police get here," said Porter.

"You got a hell of a wait," smirked Mannix.

Porter sprang up the stairs. Husky, blonde-haired Whitey Hendry was kneeling on the floor, flanked by two other men. Bern's body, only hours before leaning against the wall in an almost-seated position, was now flat on the floor, on his stomach and naked. The swimming trunks were nowhere in sight. The face was turned toward a photographer, who was gauging the light for the picture. The room, which at the time of the murder had just a faint scent of Mitsouko, now reeked with its smell. Porter noted the almost empty perfume bottle which had been half-full last night. The wooden walk-in closet, into which the killer had fired bullets, was gone.

And just below Bern's hand was a .38 pistol.

"Son of a bitch," said Porter slowly.

He rushed downstairs and outside, Mannix and Strickling following, hurrying around the pool and past the silent Thalberg. Porter saw Carmichael and his wife standing, like school children disciplined to stand in the hall, where the killer's body had been.

It was no longer there.

"Son of a bitch," Porter repeated.

"We don't know nuthin'!" said Carmichael loudly, like an over-rehearsed grade school child saying his one line in the class play.

"Nuthin'!" echoed Mrs. Carmichael.

"You let these bastards bully you?" asked Porter. "Helped them move the body?"

"We don't know nuthin'," repeated Carmichael mournfully. His cocked eye looked at Porter while his good eye looked away.

"Funny what corpses can do up here," said Porter. "One gets up, finds a .38, takes off its swim trunks, pours perfume all over itself, and curls up on the floor. Another one just Goddamn disappears. Weird, ain't it, Eddie?"

"Swell work, Down," said Mannix. "Maybe we should just forget you were here last night. Maybe you should forget it too."

Then Porter remembered – Bern's own .38 pistol…the one he'd told him he kept in his bedroom drawer. These bastards had probably done a quick examination of the room and found it. They'd wedged the pistol into the corpse's hand. Meanwhile, the corpse outside and *that corpse's* .38 had been taken away by the MGM squad.

The registration would I.D. the gun in his hand as Bern's. Yep… MGM was staging a suicide.

"Come back inside, Porter," said Strickling, looking warily at Thalberg, crumpled mournfully on a bench by the pool. "Please. Hear us out."

They went into the house. Thalberg remained by the pool. Porter kept standing. Mayer said nothing. He sat there like a passive god, listening, observing, but oddly distant.

"Jean's not takin' the rap on this," said Mannix.

"Why should she?" said Porter. "I can prove she's innocent."

"I don't mean that," snarled Mannix. "That dead little son-of-a-bitch up there made a fool of Jean. Married her while he already had a woman stashed away…maybe the woman was his wife. Imagine the horselaugh if word gets out that Metro's number one sexy star walked in on her bigamist husband!"

"That isn't what happened," said Porter. "And if it was, do you think that matters now?"

"Fuck yes, it matters now," said Mannix. "Believe you me, Jean's not getting the laugh. Bern, the pansy asshole...*he's* getting the laugh."

"You see," said Strickling, "it's p-part of our mission of p-protecting Jean. It's too late to protect Paul..."

"Shut up, Howard," said Porter. "Let Eddie tell it. This all seems to be his brainwork."

"No, it's Howard's too," said Mannix, more in compliment than blame. "Bern died of shame. A suicide. He was impotent. Don't believe me? Go upstairs. Take a peek at his pecker – it's the size of a baby boy's. And take a look at the note he left about his 'humiliation.' For Christ's sake ...The only way he could bang Jean was by wearing a damn dildo!"

Porter felt a chill. "Who showed you that film?" he demanded.

Mannix actually paled. "Who showed *you*?" He paused. "That blackmailing bitch...Well, if you saw it, why the hell didn't you *do* something about it?"

"I did, back before the wedding," said Porter. "When did *you* see the film?"

"Only last week," said Mannix. "I sent the bitch word we wouldn't pay her a dime and if we ever heard from her again, we'd find her and squash her like a bug."

Porter realized Annie Spry had perhaps hoped for double-dipping, getting money from both MGM and the Berns.

"And you actually believed what you saw in that smoker?" asked Porter.

"I knew it wasn't them, of course," said Mannix, "but it's just what the rumors have been sayin,' even before they were married."

"So, let's see if I got this right," said Porter. "You saw that film. Last night Bern's murdered while another woman is here. You remember that film. Corporate policy becomes that Harlow's more valuable to the studio if the world thinks she's what she was in the smoker...a ball-busting floozy. And you're here this morning, ready to lie to the world that Harlow humiliated Bern into stripping naked, pouring her perfume all over himself, and blowing his brains out, rather than..."

"Rather than tell them she's a dumb, peroxide blonde phony whose husband cheated on her, yes, Goddamnit, 100% right," said Mannix.

"God help us," said Porter, looking at all three men. "MGM. The dream factory. And this is the dream you're selling the world. A Goddamn sex freak nightmare."

"Give it up, Porter," said Mannix. "News of a hit man might cause investigation of mob connections at MGM. That's not happening. Just tell us what you know and then go the hell back to the desert. It'll be worth your while...right, L.B.?"

Mayer said nothing. He nodded agreement almost imperceptibly.

"So, hoodlums don't meet the MGM standard," asked Porter, "but ball busters do?"

"We like our story," said Mannix, allowing himself some dark humor. "So will the public. And, after all...Howard's 1932 motto is that MGM's 'All out for sex.' Right, Howard?"

"Eddie, please," sighed Strickling.

Porter turned. He went outside to Thalberg by the pool, took the "Boy Wonder" by the arm, briskly escorted the frail man into the house and sat him next to Mayer.

"Mr. Thalberg," said Porter, "a man who gave a hell of a lot of sweat and blood to your company, and who was your personal friend, was murdered last night. Your pals here are weaving a conspiracy to disgrace him, meanwhile concealing a body, distorting crime evidence, withholding information from the police, and…"

Thalberg doubled over in his seat. He covered his face and began sobbing. His emotion seemed to stabilize and strengthen Mayer.

"Irving," he said. "Irving!"

Mannix looked embarrassed by Thalberg's weeping. "OK, Down," he said. "Tell us. Who is this woman who was here…and where is she now?"

Porter looked into Mannix's eyes. "Jesus," he said, and immediately hurried out the door and down the steps, heading for the car he'd parked up in the trees the previous evening. They watched him go from the door.

"I bet I know what's on his mind," said Mannix. "Anyway, we need to get hold of Bern's secretary. She'll know the bitch's name and address."

There were footsteps above and Whitey Hendry stood on the stairway. "I think we'll be foolproof," Hendry announced. "Just give us a few more minutes." He returned upstairs.

"Let's go home," said Mayer, standing, now in control. "Mr. Carmichael knows he's supposed to claim he discovered Bern's body about four hours from now. We'll all be here again early afternoon, supposedly for the first time today."

He looked down at Thalberg, pale and bowed, still weeping in his chair.

"It's for the greater good," said Mayer profoundly. "We can't allow three sick degenerates to destroy an international corporation and hurt *all our people*! It's for the *greater good*, Irving! Don't you *understand*? It's for the *greater good!*"

Chapter Forty-Six
Suspects

Monday, September 5 and Tuesday, September 6, 1932

Porter's job now was to find and save Dorothy Millette.

Limey's limousine had picked her up at three and she couldn't be back at the Plaza Hotel in San Francisco before eleven. There was no way to contact her in the meantime. He might be able to get to San Francisco by his plane close to the time she would get there by car. Labor Day could work in his favor – MGM was closed until 6:00 A.M. tomorrow. Mannix would be awaiting the returning Limey, who wouldn't be back until late tonight and considering the holiday, might even stay overnight somewhere between San Francisco and L.A.

Of course, if Zwillman was behind this execution – and that was Porter's best guess – then Longie surely had his own contingency plan. Dorothy Millette might already be good-as-dead. Still, Porter had to do whatever he could.

He reached the airfield in Malibu at 7:45 A.M. He ran to a pay phone and again tried calling Jim O'Leary. Again, there was no answer. In the City of Angels, "Doc" was the only cop Porter fully trusted. He dared not confide in another.

*

Over the ocean in *Timber Wolf*, Porter reviewed what had happened. The killer in the closet ...was he a hit man sent by Longie? The bastard had plenty of motivation – his jealousy, the recent rumors that Bern was slapping Harlow around, his awareness of Dorothy Millette's existence, and his drunken but no doubt sincere promise Saturday night to Porter:

Maybe I'll do somethin' to show you I don't give a shit for you givin' me warnings…

But, if the killer had come from Longie, how had he learned about Millette's visit?

Or was the killer hired by an enraged Annie Spry, after both Porter and Mannix refused to arrange blackmail?

If I have to kill somebody to stop you laughing at me, then by Christ, I swear I'll do it...

But if the killer was Spry's man, why didn't he shoot Harlow... and why did he try to shoot Millette, of whom Spry presumably knew nothing?

Or was it Marino Bello's idea:

I love my wife and stepdaughter like a tiger and I will protect them like a lion...

If so, why would Bello kill Paul Bern, now his family's major source of revenue?

Then he realized ...Harlow. The assassin took no shot at her. She already owned Bern's house and would presumably inherit his estate. Her hysterics convinced him, but she was, after all, an actress, tutored in the art by the finest coaches in Hollywood.

Why had she driven to Easton Drive in the middle of the night? Had Harlow actually come to Easton Drive to witness three executions – Bern's, Millette's, and Porter's?

*

Porter landed in San Francisco about 1:00 P.M. He called O'Leary, who answered. The family had just returned from an overnight Labor Day weekend trip to his in-laws in Pomona. O'Leary said he'd rush to Easton Drive.

"I'll be at Bern's house within an hour," promised O'Leary. "Give me the phone number where you'll be."

Porter told him to call the Plaza Hotel's main number and ask for Dorothy Millette's room.

*

A taxi delivered Porter to the Plaza at about 1:45 P.M. He asked for the manager and showed him his MGM employee badge. "I believe Miss Millette, in Room 625, is in trouble," he said. "Take me up there. Get a bellboy you trust to come with us and bring a tool that can break a chain lock."

They rode the elevator to the sixth floor. The manager knocked at Room 625. There was no answer. "You better unlock it," said Porter.

The manager turned his key. The several chain locks were in place and at Porter's order, the bellboy took the metal clippers kept for emergencies and severed the chains. The manager and bellboy stood in the hallway as Porter entered the room. He followed the sound of sobbing and gently opened the bathroom door.

The first thing he saw was Dorothy's other shoe on the floor. Her red dress, white corset and dark stockings were draped over the side of the bathtub and her little red hat was in the tub itself. Then Porter saw Dorothy, clad in a robe and on the floor beside the toilet. The room reeked of vomit and when the woman looked up at Porter, she shivered.

"You've come… to kill me," she stammered, her croaking voice hoarse, her eyes wild and terrified. She lunged over the toilet, was sick again, and then began softly weeping.

"No," said Porter. "No. I'm here to save you…but you'll have to do exactly what I say."

Dorothy nodded, then vomited her stomach lining.

*

By nightfall, the death of Jean Harlow's husband was America's number one news story. Porter sat in 625. It was 10:00 P.M. now. O'Leary had been in contact by phone, reporting what little inside information he could glean. He'd arrived at Easton Drive just as the first waves of detectives had replied to Thalberg's belated call, but hadn't been allowed on the premises.

"They're stonewallin' me," O'Leary said to Porter.

*

Shortly after 11:00 P.M., a drawn but defiant Irene Harrison sat solemnly and stubbornly at her work desk. She'd spent Labor Day at the beach with a friend and had returned home after 9:00 P.M. to find Mannix's minions waiting for her. They'd driven her directly to MGM, basically holding her prisoner in Bern's office, where she told them nothing. She was now observing a cursing Eddie Mannix and two of his thugs brutally ransacking the office, searching for any information about Bern's mysterious female visitor.

Irene stayed heroically silent, even as Mannix vowed that Mayer would fire her and the studio blackball her. Finally, he emerged from Bern's office, having smashed open a locked file cabinet, holding several carbons of typed letters.

"Alright," he said to Irene. "Who the hell is Dorothy Millette?"

*

Just before 11:30 P.M., a bellboy delivered a late "Extra" edition newspaper outside Room 625, knocking on the door to signal its arrival. Porter grabbed the paper, which presented a front-page photo of a crowd milling around the guarded gate on Easton Drive. The ghouls were gathering and Porter read the lies already carved in black and white – for example, Carmichael had claimed he discovered the body about 11:30 A.M.

The studio had slipped up here and there. Thalberg claimed he got to the house around 1:00 P.M. but didn't call police until after 2:15 P.M., which indicated a cover-up, but these were the first takes on the tragedy. Surely MGM would finesse details in the upcoming days.

Meanwhile, "dear Dorothy," finally falling asleep, snored and moaned in her bed.

*

As midnight approached, Longie Zwillman sat on his balcony at the Ambassador Hotel, sipping a cold beer and reading the late Extra editions coverage of Paul Bern's death. Nick Kirk, also enjoying a beer, sat across from Longie, observing his boss chuckling at the inept, contradictory coverage. Nick chuckled too.

It's as if he's reading the funny papers, thought Nick with admiration.

"Not any mention of a certain lady in San Francisco," smirked Longie. "Perhaps this situation needs your personal attention, Nick. You always enjoy visiting San Francisco, don't you?"

Nick sipped his beer and nodded. "Very cosmopolitan," he said.

*

Shortly after midnight at Club View Drive, Marino Bello, having returned from his weekend trip, looked at the late edition and decided to bask in the spotlight once more before going to bed. He strolled down the steps at 12:30 A.M. and suavely met a posse of reporters.

"Is it true," asked a brassy female reporter, "that you encouraged your stepdaughter to marry Paul Bern for his money?"

Bello glowered. "I have more money than Paul Bern ever had in his life," he lied.

"Is it true you have mob connections?" she persisted.

Bello, proud of that fact, knew he couldn't show it. "Shut your filthy mouth," he said.

*

It was nearly 1:30 A.M. in San Luis Obispo. Annie Spry was celebrating. The news that erupted today would be grist for her movies for years to come. She'd sent one of her bodyguards for the late editions and he'd returned with three different newspapers. All reported Bern had been found nude. All featured a photo of what was called "the suicide note."

Annie looked out at the view of the Pacific. No one else, she proudly thought, could make a film based on this scandal like she could. Hell, the first part — what could play as the flashback to their wedding night — had already been shot! She'd start writing the continuation of the script tonight.

Wearing only a pair of black silk panties, she sat at her typewriter, sipped a glass of bootleg gin, smoked a Fatima, and grinned as she starting pecking at the keys.

Chapter Forty-Seven
The Aftermath of the "Suicide"

Tuesday, September 6 and Wednesday, September 7, 1932

It was just after 5:00 A.M. that the phone rang in Dorothy Millette's apartment. Porter, nodding beside the phone in the living room, answered it.

"Who are you?" demanded an angry female voice.

"Who are *you*?" asked Porter.

"I'm Irene Harrison. Is that you, Mr. Down?"

"Yep."

"Is Dorothy there?"

"Yep."

"Listen," said Irene, her voice more angry than afraid. "I stalled them as long as I could…as best I could. They know about Dorothy."

"Who knows?"

"Eddie Mannix and his gang. They hammered at me almost all night!"

"Are they coming here?" asked Porter. "Do you think they'll send somebody here?"

"I'm thinking they will. That's why I called."

"Thanks for the tip, Irene. We'll be out of here as soon as I can get Dorothy together."

"Where are you going?"

"Damned if I know."

*

Ninety-minutes later, while Dorothy was showering, Porter was on the phone with O'Leary in L.A.

"What's your plan?" asked O'Leary.

"It was to toss Dorothy in my plane and deliver her to you personally at the Malibu air field," said Porter. "But the very mention of flying in a plane gave dear Dorothy the dry heaves."

"What's your new plan?"

"The only policeman in California, other than you, that I trust is Pete Ambrose, a retired cop in Sacramento and a hell of a good guy. I just got off the phone with him. Millette's agreed to go with me to Sacramento and Pete will hide her in a private hospital under an assumed name with day-and-night security. Meanwhile, I'll get back to L.A. and you and I will get out the true story."

"How ya' gonna' get her to Sacramento?" asked O'Leary.

"Steamboat," said Porter. "It's her idea, and maybe the safest way. How's Harlow?"

"Under a doctor's watch. Complete breakdown. Her mother and Bello are with her at their house."

"I bet it's a circus."

"A three-ringer."

"What's the latest rumor?"

"Bern killed himself due to being a sexual failure. Or, and this one's the dark horse for now…Harlow killed him for the same reason."

"Nobody seems to know about Dorothy Millette?"

"Not yet. Hard to tell what Zwillman and Mannix know. We're taggin' them.... they're both still in town. We don't know where Annie Spry is."

"I'm not letting Millette out of my sight until Pete meets us in Sacramento," said Porter. "I'll get a train back to San Francisco and fly to L.A. within 48 hours. Meanwhile, keep an eye on things, Doc. Try to insinuate yourself into the case as much as possible."

"You bet I will," said O'Leary. He paused. "Porter…we both know MGM took a stand on this yesterday. We both know they don't want this hysterical woman making them liars in front of the whole world. And we both know they don't want you to be helping her."

"So?"

"So…Watch out, fella."

*

A steamboat called *Delta King* would leave at 9:00 P.M. that night from San Francisco and reach Sacramento the next morning at seven. Porter and O'Leary both confirmed with Pete Ambrose that he'd be at the Sacramento dock Wednesday morning.

Porter had thought off and on through the night about Maggie. With Dorothy still preparing to go, he decided to phone Maggie, not to detail his plan, but mainly just to hear her voice.

The clerk was cordial and read the message Maggie had left for him. "On the case alone for a while. Be back soon." Porter figured she'd realized he'd sent her on a wild goose chase and was now doing things her own way.

He admired her spunk, but was worried about her.

*

After Porter got off his call with the clerk, he called down to the Plaza's front desk and asked to speak with the manager. He was nervous about staying in 625 since that was the first place anyone would look if intending harm to Dorothy Millette. He explained that Miss Millette had been ill the previous night and asked if they could accommodate her in another room while her suite was being cleaned by the housekeeping staff. The manager assured him that Miss Millette would be perfectly comfortable in room 530 while housekeeping freshened her suite.

Porter thanked the manager and also asked if the bellboy Timothy was on duty this morning. When told he was, he asked the manager to send him up as soon as possible.

Porter was waiting for Timothy outside the door of the suite when he arrived.

"Oh no!" said Timothy, recognizing Porter.

"This is an easy one," said Porter. "When the stores open, get me a change of underwear, a suit, shirt, tie, socks, shoes, and a hat with a low brim – also a small travel bag. Here's a list of my measurements and enough money to buy everything I've asked for. I'll see you're handsomely tipped when you bring me what I've requested. Oh, and we'll be in room 530."

"*She's* not in there, is she?" asked Timothy warily.

"Yeah, she's in there," answered Porter. "Now scoot!"

Timothy "scooted."

*

They'd moved into room 530, Timothy had come through with Porter's change of clothes, and the day had passed uneventfully. Porter had crammed the clammy sailor togs he'd worn the past two days and nights into the travel bag Timothy had brought, dressed and was ready to leave at 6:00 P.M. By that time, Dorothy entered the room, having dressed and tended to her hair in the bathroom. She wore a white dress and hat, similar in style to the red dress and chapeau she'd worn to visit Paul Bern. The color seemed significant to Porter.

Still casting herself in The Sacrifice, he thought.

Dorothy saw the morning edition of the newspaper that Porter had picked up outside her door. He silently cursed himself for not having discarded it as she grabbed the paper and quietly read the garish headlines.

"We need to go," said Porter.

"Wait!" said Dorothy.

She stood perfectly still, reading the purple prose reports that, between the lines, made out Paul Bern to be sexually deformed. She studied the sexy pictures of Harlow and briskly but obsessively read each account. And she read the "suicide" note from Bern to Harlow, a picture of it again reproduced, and saw the words "frightful wrong," "abject humiliation," and "You understand that last night was only a comedy."

"'Only a comedy,'" she read aloud, and began sobbing uncontrollably.

*

Porter and Dorothy left the Plaza Hotel fifteen minutes later, him carrying her suitcase and his travel bag.

Dorothy spoke barely a word. She seemed subdued, somber, seemingly fatalistic. Porter imagined how brutally the "…last night was only a comedy" line had devastated her.

"'Dearest dear,'" she suddenly said after a long silence. "He called her his 'Dearest dear.'"

*

At 7:00 P.M., they were at the dock. Porter purchased their tickets. It required no registration and he paid in cash. They would share the same room.

Dorothy and Porter crossed the gangplank, Dorothy tippy-toeing in her white pair of specially-adjusted high heel shoes. Porter carried her suitcase and his own small bag. The new hat shielded his eyes.

They found their room on the top level of the boat. Dorothy promptly walked out to the railing, as if embarrassed by the intimacy, and Porter stood beside her as she stared silently back toward the twilight of San Francisco.

Night fell. At promptly 9:00 P.M., the *Delta King* pulled away from the dock, blasting its horn. Meanwhile, two large men at the rear of the crowd had just missed the boat. They stood very still as they watched it pull away, chugging into the night current of the Sacramento River.

*

More shocking Hollywood news reached the *Delta King* that Tuesday night. Another Hollywood celebrity had attempted suicide, but failed: Jean Harlow.

The word circulated through the dining room and into the dance hall and Dorothy Millette, revived from her silent reverie, was hungry for details. Porter persuaded one of the officers to allow him to call O'Leary on the steamboat's radio while Dorothy stood quietly by.

"Here's the story," said O'Leary. "Buron Fitts, the D.A., went for the headlines today and announced he'd indict Harlow for murder. Mayer and his big boys went to Club View Drive. I managed to squeeze in as one of four detectives present. Mayer told Harlow she had to support the story of Bern's impotence or risk lookin' at a murder charge. She refused. He got tough. She got hysterical. Suddenly she ran to the balcony – she sure looked ready to jump to me – but Mayer got to her first. He restrained her. We all did."

"Jesus," said Porter.

"Of course, L.B. claims he tackled her all by his lonesome. As I was leavin' the house, Mayer was telling reporters he saved her from, and I think I'm quotin' accurately, an 'attempt to follow her husband into eternity.'"

"Has she made a statement?"

"No, but it hardly matters. The impotence story is totally out of the bag. The saga goes that Bern was a deformed sex freak. Tonight, there's even a rumor out that he was a hermaphrodite."

Longie Zwillman, fanning the fire, thought Porter.

"It's become a sex and horror story – the Platinum Blonde in the claws of a pervert who could no longer handle his shame. It's bad. Really bad. Stay safe, Porter."

The ship's officer politely terminated the call. Dorothy looked questioningly at Porter.

"She's having her problems," he said. "But she's OK now."

Dorothy's large eyes were bitter. She'd obviously hoped for worse news.

*

The music had played in the dining room of the *Delta King* until well past midnight. A young couple had danced until the man, tired and seemingly angry, left the room. The willowy woman, perhaps tipsy on bootleg liquor, danced alone, even after the musicians had retired for the night, swaying elegantly in the dimly lit dining hall to imaginary music.

Dorothy Millette had watched her intently through a deck window. "She seems like a ghost," said Dorothy.

So do you, thought Porter, but he said nothing. Dorothy claimed she couldn't sleep. She'd haunted the upper and lower deck all evening and Porter, growing confident that they'd safely escaped any pursuers, nevertheless stayed by her side. He glanced at his watch: almost 1:00 A.M. The lone dancer finally ceased her solitary performance, departing for her room, and a steward turned off the few lights still burning in the dining hall.

Dorothy refused to return to their room. She and Porter continued walking the decks, the night air growing colder, the scent of the fruit trees along the shore perfuming the steamboat, the stars growing brighter in the black sky. At 1:30 A.M. *Delta King* docked at Rio Vista, dropped off and took on a few passengers, and then resumed its voyage. It was 2 A.M., then 2:30.

Why won't she sleep, wondered Porter. *What the hell is she thinking…or anticipating…*

Time passed. It was nearly 3 A.M. They hadn't seen another passenger or even a steward for over an hour. Dorothy Millette's anxiety concerned him. It was the desperate, instinctive dread he'd seen in soldiers before combat, the musky anxiety he'd witnessed in prisons on the nights of executions.

Delta King sailed under Painterville Bridge and Porter looked at the bridge's lights and total lack of traffic at this hour. The wind sighed and a chill was in the air.

"Are you cold?" asked Dorothy, and her moon eyes were bright and fearful.

He did feel the chill. They walked to the end of the top deck. Again, Porter noticed how bright the stars were, how pungent the fruit trees were, how cold the night was becoming. And then, as they made the turn, two large men bounded from the shadows. Their surprise attack and strength slammed both victims against the wall and as Porter swung, he heard an oddly familiar sound – the high-pitched wail he'd heard the first night he'd met and surprised Dorothy Millette. As he fought, he saw her from the corner of his eye, suspended in the air, and then she was gone.

He reached inside his jacket for his gun, then felt a knife thrust into his side. The two men were on him now, and the knife wound gushed as he tried to keep from blacking out.

Then he suddenly sensed he was falling, and cold water closed around and over him.

Chapter Forty-Eight
Walnut Grove

Wednesday, September 7, 1932

Lt. Jim O'Leary had expected the call to come by 7:30 A.M. At 8:00 he telephoned the docks at Sacramento. Yes, the *Delta King* had arrived on schedule an hour ago. He'd just hung up when he received another call.

"This is Pete Ambrose," said the caller. "Porter Down and the lady never got off the boat."

*

Later this Wednesday morning, Tallulah Bankhead heeded the summons to visit L.B. Mayer in his office. Mayer tried to woo Tallulah into replacing Harlow in *Red Dust* and, hoping to appeal to her dramatic nature, acted out Bern's shame-inspired suicide.

"Go to Hell, Louie," said Tallulah, and walked out.

Mayer was delighted, however, with the loyalty of Dr. Edward B. Jones, a studio physician vacationing in Honolulu, who'd cabled Mayer as soon as he learned of Bern's death:

I understand the motive and will leave at once to testify for you and Miss Harlow if necessary.

The studio made this message public and also revealed that Bern had consulted Jones shortly after his marriage to Harlow. The quote leaked by the studio cited "a lack of domestic relations." Jones vowed to reporters in Honolulu, "There isn't any doubt that Bern's death is suicide," despite the fact that he was over 2,500 miles from the corpse.

Crowds still milled outside Club View Drive, held off by LAPD and MGM security, desperate for a peek at the cloistered widow. A mob also hung out by the locked gate on Easton Drive. MGM dispatched guards there too and, for the sake of good public relations, even provided snacks and beverages for the morbidly curious. The studio charged all expenses against the estate of the deceased.

*

After 48 hours of success that seemed almost divinely sent, MGM finally took a potential hit, and from a surprise source.

Henry Bern, the dead man's brother, arrived in L.A. Wednesday after a two-day flight from New York. In stop-overs he'd read the newspaper inferences about his brother's impotence and sexual deformity. Exhausted by his trip but righteously outraged, he vowed to reporters he'd refute the horrid rumors.

"My brother was previously morally married," he protested. "I shall reveal the name of the woman shortly."

Mayer clearly had other ideas. Howard Strickling intercepted Henry Bern and took him directly to Club View Drive to meet with Mayer and Harlow. This time O'Leary was not present, nor was any detective as the widow, bereaved brother, and studio head met behind a locked door. From outside the room, Mother Jean, Marino Bello, and Claudette the maid could hear both men shouting and Harlow sobbing.

*

Walnut Grove, a tiny town known for its forests of walnut and oak, occupied both the east and west banks of the Sacramento River. Connecting the two sectors was the first cantilevered counter weight bascule drawbridge – basically a see-saw – built west of the Mississippi River. Among the approximately 500 residents was a sizeable Japanese settlement. Lumber, fishing, and raising pears were the primary commerce.

On this afternoon, Porter Down awakened on the grassy eastern shore, feeling the sun through the towering trees. He looked up, tried to move, felt the intense pain from the knife wound, and crumbled back into the grass. He remembered vague sensations of being in the river, fighting to retain consciousness, trying to swim in the darkness despite the pain, but it all seemed a distant nightmare.

Then he remembered his pistol. The derringer was not in its holster. Had it fallen out in the river? Had the attackers taken it?

At the moment, it didn't seem important. It was exhilarating simply to realize he was alive, smelling the forest and the river, hearing the birds, seeing the rays of sun through the boughs. He tried to rise once more but fell again and, exhausted by his pain and ordeal, lapsed back into unconsciousness.

*

The press hovered outside Club View Drive, desperate for Henry Bern's promised revelation. The man finally emerged in the early evening looking ashen, almost violated, the sweat glistening on his bald pate.

"Certain complications make it impossible for me to give a statement," he said. "Please don't ask me what they are."

An MGM car took him to the Ambassador Hotel. Beaten down by his air trip, Mayer's bullying, and Harlow's hysteria, Henry Bern, in the privacy of his room, ordered a room service supper and then placed a long-distance call to the Plaza Hotel in San Francisco, asking to speak to Dorothy Millette.

"Miss Millette has checked out," said the Plaza desk clerk.

Henry Bern, fearing the worst, suffered diarrhea all night.

*

Jim O'Leary was in contact with the police chief in Sacramento. He advised him of the disappearance of Porter Down and Dorothy Millette and the significance. He asked for a search to begin as soon as possible, but the chief reminded him of the daunting job it would be to cover over 80 miles of water and coast between San Francisco and Sacramento.

"We'll keep this quiet as long as we can," promised the Sacramento police chief. "And we'll start tonight with a search. But from what I see in the papers, the dead man's brother is promising to shoot his mouth off. This won't be a secret for long."

"Probably not," said a weary and distressed O'Leary.

He sat by his phone and thought of what had transpired. Had MGM foreseen the complications that had erupted, they surely would have told the truth, buried Bern, figured the hell with Millette, and hung Harlow out to dry. Instead, they had lied in their panic and now the lie had gone too far. As he'd suspected, Mayer and Mannix weren't protecting Jean Harlow anymore; they were protecting MGM, a monstrous corporation with mob connections. Mayer was even emotionally righteous about it all, believing he was defending "his people."

Anything, O'Leary realized, could have happened. He strongly suspected MGM was behind all this mayhem. He'd nail the bastards if it took the rest of his life.

*

The sun was setting by the time Porter Down finally got to his feet. A rowboat piloted by two Japanese fishermen saw the man standing by the waterline, wearing a torn suit, muddy and stained with blood. He waved to them for assistance. They rowed to shore, helped him into their boat, and headed for the town dock.

One of the fishermen took him to his tiny cottage, where the fisherman's wife tended to his knife wound. It was jagged, deep and hurt like hell, but clearly wasn't life threatening. The woman put a poultice upon the wound and bandaged it delicately but securely. The man and woman also served him some cooked fish and Porter thought it delicious.

It was night now and the fisherman rowed Porter under the drawbridge to a general store on the west side of Walnut Grove. The proprietor asked few questions and turned down Porter's money when he offered it for the use of the store phone. He reached a joyful Jim O'Leary in L.A. O'Leary asked Porter to call the Sacramento police chief to let him know he was alive.

"This isn't a crank call, is it?" demanded the chief.

"If you took the bags from Millette's room on *Delta King*," said Porter, "and I'm sure you have, open my bag. There are white clothes, a cap and a pea coat in it."

"We've opened them already," said the chief. "You're right. I'll have a man down there as soon as I can."

"Send my clothes along," said Porter, regarding his mud-and-blood-spattered suit. "I'm sentimental about 'em."

*

A Sacramento detective named Bob Meservey, along with a Sacramento uniformed policeman named Ralph Considine, showed up at the general store around 11:00 P.M. Wednesday. Sacramento Police had flown them down in a private plane and the general store proprietor had picked them up in his car at the nearest airfield, ten miles away. Meservey, a handsome, solid man with thick, black marcelled hair and a mustache, met Porter on the store front porch, where Porter was relaxing in an old rocker, looking at the stars over the river. The detective gave Porter his bag of clothes. Porter promptly changed to his sailor togs and tossed his suit with its mud and bloodstains into the trashcan. He changed to his canvas shoes but put the new pair he'd been wearing into his travel bag.

"I understand you have a lot to tell me," said Meservey. "I'm all ears."

The two men moved inside the general store and as Officer Considine kept watch, Porter quietly gave the detective the number one sex and crime story in the USA. Meservey took no notes. He knew he wouldn't forget any of it.

"We found a pair of women's shoes behind a chair on the deck," said Meservey.

"High heels with special lifts?" asked Porter.

"You bet."

"They were Millette's. Left there by the killers to look like suicide."

"We'll do what we can to find the body. Any chance she survived as you did? "

"She didn't impress me as a strong swimmer."

Detective Meservey told Porter about Henry Bern's L.A. arrival. "My guess is we can keep Millette's name quiet for 24 hours tops. Meanwhile, the chief would like us to bring you back with us... although it might be better if we got you to the nearest hospital."

"Neither idea appeals to me," said Porter wryly. "Listen…for now, until we bait the trap, plan to go public tomorrow night with the Millette suicide theory. Also, I've told you everything. I feel fine. Where's the nearest train station?"

Chapter Forty-Nine
Coroner's Inquest

Thursday, September 8, 1932

Thursday was the date for the coroner's inquest. It began at 10 A.M. at the Daniel-Price Mortuary where Bern's body rested. Jean Harlow was excused from the inquest. Her appearance, read a note from a doctor, "would gravely endanger her life."

Henry Bern, who was expected, didn't show.

Testifying at the inquest were Marino Bello, who'd already refuted charges that he was after Bern's money and now claimed the marriage was happy; John and Winifred Carmichael, who recited the script MGM had provided them; and Irving Thalberg, who failed to explain how he'd got to the house at 1:00 P.M. and didn't call police until after two. The coroner, awed by the "Boy Wonder," didn't pursue it. Thalberg also confirmed Bern's handwriting on the "suicide note." Blanche Williams merely admitted Bern's deep moods. The testimony of the detectives who'd answered the call from Easton Drive on the afternoon of September 5, built a case for suicide.

Saved for the climax was coroner Dr. Frank Webb, who had performed Bern's autopsy. Webb had the showcase role of proving or disproving the now round-the-world saga that Paul Bern was a sexual Quasimodo.

Q. Find any deformities?

A. Only as stated, slightly underdeveloped.

Q. What was that?

A. Sexual organs showed slight underdevelopment – I would correct that. I would not say "underdevelopment." I would say undersized. They were developed normally but undersized.

Q. Were they of such a character to indicate impotence?

A. No sir.

It was far from the hermaphrodite tale or the sexual deformity saga, but it was enough. "PHYSICAL DEFICIENCY," read a

Los Angeles Record headline. The jury decided a verdict: "Suicide, motive undetermined." Lt. Jim O'Leary, present at the inquest, looked at Louis B. Mayer, who'd observed the proceedings.

Mayer was poker-faced, but the poker face glowed.

*

Still, Mayer's script was not foolproof. Also on Thursday, the *Los Angeles Record* ran a headline that gave the MGM powers a chill:

ESTATE LEFT TO MILLETTE GIRL IN 1920

The news had not come from the beleaguered Irene Harrison, who'd stoically reported the past three days to Bern's office despite having nothing to do there, nor from Henry Bern, who stayed huddled in his Ambassador room like a kicked dog, nor from the Sacramento police, who were still sitting on the story. It came courtesy of Paul Bern's lawyer, Henry Uttal, in New York City. The attorney had known Dorothy personally and described her as "a very pretty woman, very intelligent."

"They came to my house often, and I knew her as Paul's wife," Uttal told the press. "All his other friends knew her as his wife also."

Uttal claimed he'd received a letter from Bern regarding his marriage to Harlow about a week after the wedding. He'd assumed Dorothy Millette was dead. The cat was out of the bag now, O'Leary realized, and the whole country would be looking for Millette…a massive army of a manhunt. Meanwhile, Detective Meservey had alerted fishermen to be on watch for the body of a woman in the Sacramento River.

Late in the day, Henry Bern, aware of Uttal's announcement, festering after Mayer's demands he keep his mouth shut, and ashamed of himself for not attending the inquest, angrily emerged, summoning up the courage to embrace the press. Reporters swamped him in the Ambassador lobby.

"Yes, my brother Paul was morally married to a woman named Dorothy Millette," said Henry Bern timorously, soaked in perspiration, blinking at the popping flashbulbs. "And they had a tragic affair."

"Where is this woman?" demanded a reporter.

"Is it true your brother suffered from a physical deficiency that doomed his marriage?" shouted another.

Henry winced. "No comment. I promise to have more to say very soon."

He fled and holed up again, sick in his hotel room bathroom. Considering what might have happened to Dorothy, Henry wondered if perhaps he should keep quiet. A few moments later the phone rang and an anonymous caller suggested, profanely and threateningly, that he do just that.

*

Porter Down had no phone book address in San Francisco – his place of residence was officially listed in California records as Twentynine Palms. However, he was now at his old top floor quarters at *The Lorayne* in San Francisco. Porter figured any assassins looking for him, or for evidence of what he knew about Jean Harlow, Paul Bern, and Dorothy Millette, would learn about this address. The question was how long it would take for them to get here, or if they'd been here already.

The two men who struck on the *Delta King* would have arrived in Sacramento Wednesday morning. It was now Thursday night. Porter, sitting in the darkness in his quarters atop *The Lorayne*, had found the rooms undisturbed and figured he'd give the two men, or their compatriots, until dawn to show up.

After that, he couldn't waste any more time before heading back to L.A.

*

Porter sat with a pistol he'd taken from his apartment safe and an 18" piece of pipe he'd taken off the room's radiator. It was 9:00 P.M. now. He'd been at *The Lorayne* since late morning, after the freight train had delivered him to San Francisco. He was hungry and his knife wound was beginning to hurt like hell again. Then he heard the door open from the stairwell.

Heavy footsteps emerged, and then grew silent. Two large shadows fell across the smoked glass window of his door and one of the shadows jiggled the doorknob. Porter stood with the pistol and pipe and silently moved to a corner.

Come right on in, boys, he thought.

A moment later, the shadow easily picked the door's lock and the door slowly opened. The two men entered and Porter instinctively knew they were the same men from the steamboat, even though he'd had no good look at either assailant, and even though these men were in darkness. There was a weird, inexplicable familiarity about them, and Porter felt his anger rise as each man took a gun from a holster under their coats.

"Sure in hell looks empty, doesn't it?" mumbled the shorter man.

"Yeah," said the taller man. "I tell ya', I knifed him straight through while you were still jostlin' with the pruneface. There's no way in hell he swam…"

Porter sprang from his hiding place with his pipe. He knocked the guns from both men's hands and then swung the pipe like a club, pounding each man separately and squarely in the face. Blood spurted, they hit the floor, and Porter, resisting the urge to shoot them both, instead raised the pipe and brought it down again and again, breaking each man's knees.

"Bastards!" he hissed. "Goddamned bastards! Who sent you?"

One of the men was unconscious. The other began vomiting in his pain.

"I said who the hell sent you?" demanded Porter, hitting him again.

The man yelped. "Maginni…," he moaned, and passed out.

"*Who?*" asked Porter, not recognizing the name. He dragged each man outside the room and into the hallway, grabbed their guns and pulled open their coats. He frisked their pockets.

Inside one of them was his derringer.

He ran back into the room, put on his pea coat and cap, and made a quick and anonymous call to the police. Then he locked the door, scooped up the pistols and headed down the stairwell, leaving both men crippled and unconscious.

Porter was now armed with four guns.

*

The stairwell opened both to the lobby and the rear alley entrance. Porter wondered if the duo upstairs had reinforcements in the lobby. He took a peek.

There was one man in the lobby, seated so Porter saw him on profile, and he recognized him immediately. It was Nick Kirk. He was sitting there with his swell suit and broken nose and bad toupee, flirting and joking with the platinum blonde receptionist. She flirted and joked back with the man who was Longie Zwillman's "executive officer," "chief secretary" and number one bodyguard.

Longie, thought Porter. *Goddamn Longie.*

Porter exited into the alley, ran a block, and waved down a cab. At the airfield he grabbed a hot dog and Coke, ate and drank on the run, got a fistful of change, and called Longie Zwillman's number at the Ambassador Hotel in Los Angeles. Longie wasn't available and an underling took Porter's message.

"Tell Longie to meet Porter Down at the Malibu air field," said Porter. "I'll be there by 4 A.M. If I'm not, tell the bastard to wait for me. He knows better than to stand me up."

Porter hung up. With four pistols stashed in his belt and under his pea coat, he went to his biplane and was soon in the air, wide awake and mad as hell. He knew damn well Longie could have a firing squad at the field ready to blow him away the instant he got out of the plane, but it didn't matter. If Zwillman was after him, it was only a matter of time. He'd never be safe. He wasn't about to spend his last days and nights hiding like a rat. He might as well confront it all now.

This was probably it, but by God, he'd go down fighting.

Chapter Fifty
San Luis Obispo

Thursday, September 8, 1932

Maggie York had been in San Luis Obispo for nearly 72 hours, and since late Monday night. Her reporter's gut feeling had alerted her that Annie Spry was in this seaside town, 190 miles north of L.A. The scrap of paper in Spry's house had been her only clue.

Since her arrival, evidence had accumulated slowly. The citizenry of the seaside town, charming with its wharf and pelicans and harbor seals, was determined to protect privacy. Also, Annie Spry, Maggie knew, might have appeared here in any number of disguises. But on Tuesday, she'd visited the post office and, via cleverly and charmingly phrased inquiries, had learned that large crated boxes of film equipment – apparently a camera and boxes of lighting apparatus – had arrived here recently. The post office clerk, realizing he'd said too much to the attractive blonde investigator, gave no more information.

It took two more days to find the delivery man who'd driven this equipment to its purchaser. When she asked him if he'd tell her the address, he declined, but reflexively looked toward a hill by the ocean. There was a house up there. When Maggie drove to the site, she saw a drive leading up to the house, behind a locked gate. It was similar in its Spanish style and ocean view location to Spry's house in Castellammare.

*

Tonight, Thursday, near midnight, Maggie returned to the site. She left her car a distance away and eventually managed to slip around the gate. She walked up the hill, parallel to the drive, staying in the shadows.

There were lights in the house. Maggie figured she only had to peer into a window and see the movie equipment – and/or Annie – to pinpoint the woman she personally believed to be behind the murder of Paul Bern. If Spry were there, Maggie would return, phone Porter in L.A. and keep tabs on Annie until she was apprehended.

The windows were too high. Maggie found a chair on the small veranda facing the ocean, and moved it into position. She removed her shoes and stood on the chair, looking through the windows, into the room. Spry wasn't in the room, nor anyone else. There were, however, two large movie cameras. Lights, arcs, coils. A microphone on a small boom. The room was a modest but functional film studio.

Maggie lowered one leg to descend from her perch and hurry back down the hillside. Suddenly a man emerged from the shadows, roughly knocked her off the chair and yanked Maggie to her feet.

Chapter Fifty-One
Night Flight

Friday, September 9, 1932

Now Porter believed he knew the real story.

Harlow had told Longie about her misery with Bern and the upcoming visit from Dorothy Millette. She'd mentioned Bern had a gun. Longie had promised his former paramour he'd eliminate her weasel of a husband and his wacky common-law wife. And when Harlow learned that Porter would be there, Longie had told the hit man to rack up *three* victims.

Had Porter not been so fast with his gun, the killer, after shooting Bern, would have killed Porter and Millette. Then the murderer, using Bern's .38, would have made Bern's death look like suicide. Millette's body and Porter's would probably have disappeared for good – Longie's guys were artists at that. There was probably a second man in the woods prepared to help dispose of the bodies, and who'd fled after Porter had shot the killer.

What taunted Porter most was that Harlow had come there, casually reeking of booze and Mitsouko. Had she wanted to witness the executions? Was she curious to see the corpses? Was she willing, thought Porter bitterly, to give the killer a quickie for having performed his task so smoothly?

I was a fool, thought Porter. *A Goddamned fool.*

*

Porter's Spad touched down a few minutes before four. While *Timber Wolf* taxied, he saw a large limousine parked to the side of the Malibu landing strip. Porter tore off the leather helmet and goggles, jumped from the plane, winced at the pain of his knife wound and headed for the car. He felt his arsenal of pistols, gripped two of them, and figured he just might be about to die in a blaze of glory.

He saw the chauffeur emerge, open the back door, and the imposing figure of Longie Zwillman get out in dark overcoat and hat. The chauffeur closed the door and moved behind the car.

"Alright, Down," said Longie casually. "Why'd you get my ass out here on this fuckin' cold night…?"

"Shut up, Longie."

"Good thing I brought along something to keep me warm," said Longie, opening the limo's back door. He indicated a naked woman in the back seat. She giggled and coyly covered her breasts as Porter glanced at her. Zwillman laughed and Porter kicked the door shut.

"Tell me how you've handled Paul Bern's death, Longie."

"You mean other than cryin' all week?"

"You told me you'd stay out of this."

"I did."

"Like hell. You sent one of your boys to Easton Drive Sunday night to kill Bern, Millette, and me. When she and I got away, you sent two of your boys to San Francisco to kill us. When I got away, you sent *three* of your boys up there to kill me…one of them Nick Kirk."

"So Millette was at Bern's house?" asked Longie. "And she's definitely dead?"

"Yeah, pretend you never knew," said Porter. "What did Harlow give you, Longie? Another dyed quiff hair for your locket?"

"Are you drinking again, Porter?"

"Can it, Longie. I saw Nick in the lobby. He's probably called you from jail that two of your thugs are on the permanent disabled list with pudding for kneecaps."

"Yeah, Nick called me. From his room at the Saint Francis. He called to say he had gone up to your room to see if you were there and if you were okay, and found two shitheads outside your office upstairs with their knees broken. They claimed that you'd worked both of them over with a pipe. Nick waited a few minutes, giving you time to get away from wherever you were by that time, then called the cops to pick up those two broken-kneed assholes."

"And you're gonna' lie to me they weren't *your* assholes?"

"Hell no! Nick was there because I'd sent him to check up on you. You'd disappeared after Bern died. I figured you were in trouble and ..."

"You're breakin' my heart, Longie. Tell me you're not workin' with MGM on this Paul Bern-Was-a-*Her*maphrodit*ee* epic, spoon-feeding them all the shit they want to hear...a Louis B. Mayer/Abner Zwillman spectacular."

"You're fulla' bullshit, Porter. Nick found out those two clowns worked for some half-ass wop gangster wanna'-be in the Bay area."

"You're a liar, Longie."

"The hell I am. Maybe Mannix and Orsatti ordered the hit men from the wop, or maybe your sweet-smellin' pal Bello did. Maybe *all* of them did. Nick says the wop's name is Maginni."

Maginni, the name mumbled by the one gunman, remembered Porter.

Zwillman looked at Porter and shook his head.

"You fuckin' ingrate! You still don't get it, do you? I tried to kill you? Asshole! Listen, I didn't do shit to Bern. If I'd known that shriveled-up common-law wife of his was in L.A., I wouldn't have killed her – I'd have let her loose! Seein' and hearin' her scream to the reporters while she reduced both Bern and Harlow to fuckin' laughing stocks would have been a hell of a lot more fun than blowing the little creep's brains out. And as you should know, Porter...*my* guys don't make mistakes on jobs. Considering what's happened, whoever sent that guy to Harlow's house sent an asshole...and *is* an asshole."

Porter had no comeback. Zwillman regarded him, his face angry and mournful.

"We're through, Down. We had a history. I wanted to be sure you were OK. I thought you called me tonight because you needed help. But no. You think I'm the big fuckin' bogeyman, so fuck it. Handle this mess yourself. You and me are done!"

"Shut up, Longie."

"Yeah, I'll shut up. And when a new team of killers shows up, sent by Mannix, or that grease ball Bello, or whoever gives the order to put a bullet through *your* brains, I'll come to the funeral.

I'll be curious to see how the undertaker disguises the bullet hole in your head."

Longie Zwillman got into his limo and the car drove away into the night.

*

Porter, saddled with the sinking feeling that Longie had told him the truth, walked the mile-and-a-half in the purple pre-dawn light to the marina. Luke was still out fishing.

The wound hurt like hell and Porter removed the bandage the Japanese woman had applied. He waded out into the surf and let the cold ocean water wash against the cut. He crudely applied clean bandages he found in the marina shack, drank a Coke for breakfast and called O'Leary at home.

"Listen Doc," he said. "Use whatever you have to use, but get me a place on the security force at the funeral today… where I can see the faces of the mourners and they can see me. I wanna' see who looks like they're seeing a ghost."

He paused a moment, then called Maggie's hotel. No, replied the clerk, she had not returned this past week. No, there'd been no further word from her.

Porter wondered where she was. He was worried.

Chapter Fifty-Two
The Funeral

Friday, September 9, 1932

The papers of Friday, September 9 blazed the latest news in the Harlow/Bern scandal. "PHANTOM BEAUTY MISSING FROM BOAT," headlined the *L.A. Record*, rhapsodizing that "Dorothy Millette, beautiful phantom from the past life of Paul Bern, suicide bridegroom of Jean Harlow, has vanished – probably into a watery grave."

It was the second blast, exploding even before the body from the first event had been buried or, in this case, incinerated. Detective Meservey had waited to release the suicide account until Thursday night, as promised.

Porter had shaved, showered and dressed in his navy-blue suit from MGM for the funeral. Longie's tantrum had convinced him the true killers came from either Mannix, Bello or, as a dark horse, Annie Spry. If Harlow actually had the decency and the post-bereavement courage to deny vehemently the sex freak tales and acknowledge the Sunday night visit from Dorothy Millette, this still could eventually blow up in the faces of Mayer and Mannix, especially if Bern's brother had the guts to champion her. And both broken-legged assassins, now in custody, would eventually go on trial, tell their story, and reveal their connections.

Today, however, the eyes of the infatuated world would be on the platinum blonde widow. Supported over the next week or so by Porter Down, Henry Bern, and those two jailbird cripples, Jean Harlow could truly be a ball buster...and it would be MGM's turn, or Marino Bello's, or Annie Spry's, for "abject humiliation."

*

Henry Bern, wan and pale, exhausted from his gastrointestinal sieges, angry at himself for having failed to be forceful, was anguished by what he'd read in the morning paper. Once again, he dared to face the press. They were waiting to pounce on him in the hotel lobby.

"What can you tell us about this Dorothy Millette?" howled the reporters.

"I believe poor Dorothy is dead," he replied miserably.

"Was Millette aware of your brother's physical deficiency?" demanded a female reporter.

A cacophony of voices deafeningly echoed the question. Henry Bern merely shook his head and, once again, terrified by what he faced, retreated to the elevator and his room, ill and shaken. He knew he couldn't face his own brother's funeral.

*

The funeral was set for 2:00 P.M. at Grace Chapel at Inglewood Park Cemetery. The day was hot and sunny and Porter arrived at 1:00 P.M. A mob the newspapers later estimated at 750 already milled outside the quaint chapel, with its gray stone steeple and California-style orange tile roof. Inside, flowers swamped the casket, so plentiful that they spilled outside the chapel and onto the lawn.

"It's the greatest profusion of flowers in the history of Hollywood funerals," an undertaker proudly told reporters.

Grace Chapel was small, with ten pews on each side. There would be only 50 invited mourners. Thousands of fans, too late to gain entry near the chapel, filled the streets outside the cemetery. The LAPD, along with Inglewood and MGM security, kept the crowd inside a safe and respectable distance from the funeral site.

O'Leary had scored again. He assigned Porter to the steps right by the door, where he'd see everyone enter. Limousines filed by the chapel and celebrities arrived as if it were a premiere.

The limousine bearing Harlow arrived and parked by the side of the chapel, near the "private" family entrance, but nobody emerged yet. The widow and her personal entourage would be the last to enter the chapel.

Howard Strickling visited the limousine, then confidentially approached Porter and spoke in a hushed tone. "I've told Jean you're here so she wouldn't be startled if she saw you," he said. "She's very grateful you've come."

"Swell," said Porter.

The crowd of Who's Who mourners already nearly filled the chapel. A prelude dirge sounded from the organ and the gothic music, along with the ongoing parade of stars and spectacle of flowers, stirred the crowd that the security forces held at bay.

A very drawn Irving Thalberg arrived, accompanied by Norma Shearer. Then came Louis B. Mayer, and a respectable step behind him, Eddie Mannix.

"Hi there, boys," grinned Porter.

A poker-faced Mayer glanced at Porter for only an instant before entering the chapel. Mannix took a longer look. The two men stared right into each other's faces. If Mannix had sent the two thugs to Porter's room, he surely knew by now the failure of their mission. He revealed no emotion, but his eyes were cold as he removed his hat and followed Mayer into the wake.

"Jean will enter now," said Strickling to Porter. "You'll want to change your post."

Porter moved to the side of Grace Chapel, joining other security men at the family entrance.

*

It was a macabre circus, and the widow Harlow its center ring star attraction. She now emerged from the limousine, naturally adorned all in black, complete with hat and veil.

The crowd sighed at the sight of her, as if in awe, and then became deadly, respectfully still.

She appeared genuinely sorrowful and frightened, so much so that Porter felt some guilt about his suspicions. She moved slowly and supporting her were Marino Bello, sporting sunglasses, and writer Willis Goldbeck. The crowd shifted, pressing toward the side of the chapel. Then, as the widow made her way to the steps, a weird, spine-tingling sound arose from the mob, like the chant of a baseball crowd emotionally anticipating a home run. As Harlow reached the door the cheer finally exploded, and Porter worried the crowd might break through the security and rush her.

Harlow's haunted eyes suddenly looked at Porter and lingered. Then Bello, who'd noticed the glance, whispered to her and they entered the chapel. Porter and the other guards followed them inside, closing and locking the chapel doors.

*

The widow sat in a small anteroom that concealed her from the crowd. Bello, Mother Jean, and Goldbeck sat with her. Porter stood behind them.

Paul Bern's body lie in an open, flower-bedecked casket. After the organ finished its dirge, actor Conrad Nagel, MGM star, distinguished in his dark suit and blond toupee, delivered the eulogy, later quoted in the *L.A. Record* as follows:

> *Dear Paul, we've tried in our poor way to gather the love we have and send it on to you. It is more difficult for us than for you, and extremely difficult for one dear to you. Because we loved you so much, we love her and stand ready to help in every way possible. We're better for having known you, Paul. God speed, and, as you always said to us, 'We'll be seeing you.'"*

John Gilbert was crying, Irving Thalberg sobbing bitterly. Although the assemblage could not see Harlow, they heard her weeping from the anteroom.

Rabbi Edgar Magnin recited the Hebrew prayer for the dead, the Kaddish. Then Friederike Marcus, the frumpy sister of Bern who, at the wedding in July had reminded Porter of Dorothy Millette, began crying and shrieking.

"Where is he?" she screamed, *"Where is he?"* – even though the body was only a few yards away from her.

She wailed, and Porter thought of the madness that reportedly plagued Bern's family and his "dear Dorothy." Friederike's rising screams reminded Porter of Dorothy's strange keening, and for a moment a fanciful but frightening sense hit him: Dorothy's ghost had come to the funeral and taken over Friederike's body to express its lament.

Jesus, he thought.

The organ soon drowned out the cries of the dead man's sister and Louis B. Mayer personally led Jean Harlow to see the body a final time, Bello and Willis Goldbeck behind them. She wept, nearly fell, and Bello and Goldbeck faithfully held her as they moved her back to the family room.

The service was over, but the organ still played and the coffin remained open. Rabbi Magnin invited the mourners to view the body. However, with Harlow about to depart the church, the real show was over and only two people accepted the Rabbi's invitation. One was Silent screen vamp and Bern friend Jetta Goudal. The other was Irene Harrison. Both women wept at the bier.

*

During the service the security forces had made a major error. They had relaxed the formations keeping back the crowds. The mob had rushed to the chapel, the vast majority of it now tightly flanking the family entrance, where the widow would depart.

Harlow's veil had covered her face, but at the request of the press, she'd moved it so it flowed down behind her hat. This way, the photographers could take pictures of her face. As Harlow came outside, there were many people so close they could almost touch her.

The police and guards rushed into action, forming a corridor for the widow to reach the limousine. It was a horrible, mob ugliness such as Porter had never witnessed, and he joined the men at the security line. Young women holding fan magazines, their eyes mad with excitement, sighed, moaned and sometimes screamed.

"We love you, Jean!"

"Did YOU kill him?"

All the while the organ dirge played inside the chapel, and Porter felt the danger swell as near-hysteria festered. The crowd powerfully rammed again the phalanx of security men.

"Stay back, Goddamnit," said Porter through clenched teeth.

Suddenly Porter was aware of a woman across from him, to the other side of the widow. She had platinum hair and wore a black dress and hat similar to Harlow's. Sunglasses covered her eyes, and she'd moved her veil to imitate the way Harlow now wore hers.

The Harlow wanna'-be lunged against the linked arms of the security forces to behold the genuine Harlow herself.

"Murderess!" she sighed, and then screamed almost rapturously, "MURDERESS!"

Her cry rose over the crowd and many women in the mob screamed. Porter saw Harlow wince as if someone had slapped her, and Bello and Goldbeck now rushed her the remaining short distance into the car. The crowd shifted and thrust again, and the woman in black fell back into it.

The celebrity mourners, leaving by the front entrance, were relieved to see the crowd had moved to the side of the chapel and hurried to their cars. Then a disembodied voice came over the public address system.

"Ladies and Gentlemen…Please…Inglewood Park Cemetery has decided to open the chapel to the public so you may pay your respects to Mr. Paul Bern…"

The crowd roared triumphantly, the remaining mourners ran like hell to their cars, and the widow's limousine departed the cemetery.

*

The public viewing, Porter realized, was a damn lousy idea, especially considering the body-robbing threat. Yet Inglewood had thought it an emergency necessary to control the mob and now it was too late to stop it. At Howard Strickling's request, Porter joined three other security men by the bier as the curious lined up by the front entrance.

Having seen the body at a distance from the family room, Porter took time now to look at Paul Bern's corpse. It appeared waxy and artificial, despite what surely were the best efforts of the undertaker and MGM's own makeup specialists. And no, he could see no evidence of a bullet hole at the body's left or right temple – remembering Longie Zwillman's bleak promise regarding Porter's own prospective wake.

The crowd silently passed the bier and now Porter noticed the Harlow copycat in sunglasses, black hat and cascading veil, in line and nearing the casket. For a moment he feared she'd try to touch the corpse, but instead she simply snapped off the head of a flower atop the casket. Porter glared at the creep, figuring she'd morbidly preserve the flower in an old book, or perversely carry it in her panties until the petals disintegrated, or whatever. She regarded him through her sunglasses for a moment, grinning faintly before she passed on her way. Only after she was gone did he feel the tingle of possible recognition.

Annie...

Porter left his post, hurried outside, but couldn't find her in the crowd. After several minutes of searching, he went back into the chapel.

Chapter Fifty-Three
Paternal Affection

Friday, September 9, 1932

Howard Strickling needed witnesses to the cremation, due to threats that the body would be stolen. Porter thought again of Longie.

I'll hang the hermaphrodite's body from the HOLLYWOODLAND sign, he'd said that day at the Ambassador.

Porter declined to be a witness. "There actually are some things I refuse to do," he said to Strickling, who promptly rustled up two other witnesses. The casket was taken to the cemetery crematory with its tall and ominous chimney.

The possible sighting of Annie Spry had advanced the credibility of a body-snatching caper, but now this was another potential horror averted. Of course, she could still steal the ashes, but that would yield no secrets about the "sexual deformity." Porter, relieved, began departing the cemetery when an undertaker approached him.

"Mr. Down? Mr. Marino Bello would like to see you."

"I thought he left," said Porter. "In the limo with his stepdaughter."

"He's returned and is by the lake. He'd like to speak with you privately."

*

Inglewood Cemetery's Lake was down the hill behind Grace Chapel. As Porter approached it, he saw two men lakeside. One of the men was Bello. The other had the imposing look of a bodyguard. Bello swaggered his way to Porter and extended his hand. Porter didn't shake it.

"Why aren't you still with your stepdaughter?" asked Porter.

"Harlean needs time with her mother," said Bello. "And I need time with you."

Bello looked around the quiet cemetery, now free of its mob. Black smoke was curling from the crematory chimney. Bello led

Porter some distance away from the bodyguard, removed his sunglasses and took out his gold cigarette case.

"We can talk here. Cigarette?"

"No."

Bello lit up, his bodyguard keeping watch against any interruptions or eavesdropping on this impromptu conference.

"Mr. Down, I understand you are still peeking and probing into the death of my Baby's sorry excuse of a husband. I'm going to save you a great deal of trouble. I'm going to name the man responsible for his death." He dramatically paused, dragged on his cigarette, and blew the smoke through his nose.

"And I assume," asked Porter impatiently, "you're going to tell me this sometime today?"

"Eventually. It's crucial we first understand each other. More so, it's crucial you understand Harlean."

"Talk fast."

Bello seemed to relish the chance to tell his story. "During the two months and three days that my stepdaughter was married to Paul Bern, I learned two things. First, he was by no means the man to fulfill Harlean's most passionate needs. Second, he was not, as you put it that night in Mexico, 'royalty.'" He sucked at his cigarette. "In fact," Bello said viciously, "he was a fucking pauper."

"What about the house he gave to Harlow? Which she allegedly signed over to you?"

"Mortgaged. Almost for its full amount."

"His $1500-per week salary?"

"Squandered. Given away. Who knows where? You tell me."

Bello calmed a bit. "He could not provide for Harlean sexually or financially. He was a phony, a fraud, a failure as a man in every way."

"He gave her confidence as a movie star," said Porter. "He transformed her from an industry joke to a respected attraction."

"Ha!" snorted Bello. "Harlean's attraction is her beautiful body. It is all she needs. At any rate, we had plans when they married. Bern's misrepresentation destroyed those plans. I naturally could not leave Harlean in the hands of a sick man who had virtually no property or penis."

The black clouds were hanging over the crematory. Porter tensed at what Bello was saying.

"I have warned you of my contacts. Last Saturday night, Clark Gable and I went to Catalina for recreation. This conveniently placed me out of town for what I had planned to happen Sunday night. You see, I'd learned that Bern's San Francisco woman would be paying a call."

"How did you know?"

"Harlean tells her mother everything. Her mother tells *me* everything."

"And I ruined your hit man's evening?"

"You killed him. Harlean told me that herself."

The thought finally hit Porter. "Life insurance," he remembered. "Bern had told me that he was taking out life insurance…"

"$85,000 worth. My suggestion."

"You son-of-a-bitch."

"I argued it was the least he could do, considering how little he possessed. Bern passed his physical eight days ago and signed the policy."

Porter looked even more intently into Bello's eyes. "You knew from Harlow that I'd be at the house that night, didn't you? Your hit man went up there with *three* targets…Bern, Millette, and me."

Bello shrugged like a man caught cheating at penny-ante poker. "My original plan was to make it appear that Bern had killed himself. You and Millette were to disappear altogether. Meanwhile, I was prepared to cast suspicion on your chum Zwillman…"

"Sure," said Porter. "And while Longie fought a murder rap, you'd cozy up with whatever mobster moved into his territory – maybe the same mobster who provided the hit man."

"The $85,000 would have paid off all of Bern's debts," said Bello, "and still have left us more – for a rainy day, if you like."

"Only Harlow showed up that night unexpectedly," interrupted Porter. "I saved Millette's life. MGM has bought or contrived a coroner's verdict of Bern's suicide. The coroner's jury accepted it. That cancels out any murder suspects, probably invalidates the insurance policy, and leaves you and Harlow nothing but debt."

"Perhaps," shrugged Bello with a smile. "But the story is wonderful for us! Is it not so? Look how it has happened! Harlean will be a bigger star than ever. Bern is dead. Millette, according to the morning newspapers, is dead too. She had worried me. I was negotiating her death, but she saved me the trouble and drowned herself."

I was negotiating her death.... she drowned herself, thought Porter.

"You're telling me," said Porter, "you never sent any little pals of yours to San Francisco? Pals who will have to carry out all their assassinations from now on out of wheelchairs?"

Bello's hooded eyes were confused. Porter could tell he knew nothing of what happened either on the *Delta King* or at Porter's San Francisco apartment.

Bello ordered the hit on Bern and Millette, thought Porter. *But Mannix ordered the job on Millette and me...*

He realized Bello was still crowing. "The $85,000, whether we collect it or not, is nothing, compared to what Harlean will earn in the next two years. She is now the most famous star in the world. Everyone worships her for the sensational tragedy she has inspired, and the one she will survive. And I require no sponsor. She's all the power I'll ever need." He flicked his cigarette toward a gaggle of grave markers and smiled.

"Hollywood is famous for its happy endings...is it not, Mr. Down?"

"What if this isn't the end?" asked Porter. "What if Henry Bern tells all he knows?"

"You didn't see him at the funeral, did you?" smirked Bello. "He's so shocked by Millette's death he couldn't even come to his own brother's wake. He telephoned his regrets this morning …and the news that he's going home. He is no match for Mayer or me and he knows it. He's of his brother's sickly pansy blood."

"Then try on this for size," said Porter. "You just said you know that Longie Zwillman is my 'chum.' What makes you think I won't tell him what you told me about possibly setting him up for Bern's murder, and that he'll be serving you as sausage?"

Bello beamed, as if Porter had demanded he show his ace card. "Harlean has just survived, quite miraculously, a terrible shock and tragedy. Another so soon on its heels would kill her, at least professionally. Surely *you* wouldn't want to be responsible for my death... and her breakdown?"

"She wouldn't waste a single tissue at your funeral," said Porter.

Bello preened. "You wouldn't say that," he said, "if you had seen her last night... as I held her and comforted her in my arms."

"You're a bald-faced, baldheaded liar," said Porter.

"You're a poor, jealous man," grinned Bello.

"You're telling me you took advantage of your own stepdaughter's grief to..."

"I took advantage of nothing. It has always been so. Ever since I married Harlean's mother five years ago."

"I still say you're a damned liar."

Bello reached into his suit pocket and handed Porter a small envelope. Porter opened it to find snapshots of Harlow, who looked barely 16-years-old, posing naked on a bed. One of the pictures featured Bello, also naked and on the bed with her.

"Did Mother Jean take this shot?" asked Porter, trembling with rage.

"No," grinned Bello. "But she has seen the pictures. Among other things, the possibility they might circulate discouraged her from divorcing me two years ago."

"And you actually carried this filth with you to the funeral today?" demanded Porter.

"They are both mine, mother and daughter," said Bello, casually lighting another cigarette. "I love them like a tiger, I protect them like a lion, and last night I loved *and* protected Harlean. So touching and so passionate in her sorrow."

He chuckled sympathetically.

"The silly girl thinks she's a fake, you see. A phony. The sexy 'Platinum Blonde,' yet she could not make a man out of Bern. She blames herself for so much of the unhappiness in their farcical marriage. In her eyes, she is a bigger phony than *Bern* was!"

Bello gave his startling hyena laugh. He puffed his cigarette, blowing the smoke from his nose.

"She was...so grateful to me for my reassurance. She was magnificent..."

Porter, feeling almost ill with rage, clenched his fists and walked away.

"I imagine," called out Bello, "Harlean told you her sad story about the aborted baby. We had no choice. After all, although she was married to McGrew at the time, it was possible, you see, that I was the father."

Porter turned, approached Bello, and with all his might punched his face. Harlow's stepfather fell back, stumbling and splashing into the edge of the lake. The massive bodyguard sprang into action, soundly hitting Porter twice, once right where his knife wound was. Porter gasped in pain, but rage was on his side and he pounded the bodyguard three times in the jaw, the third punch knocking him unconscious as he fell. Bello crawled from the lake and Porter grabbed the lapels of his suit, jerking him to his feet and looking wildly into his eyes.

"Now you repeat after me," hissed Porter. "I'm a Goddamned liar."

Bello shivered, blood and water trickling from his mouth. "Say it!" shouted Porter.

"I am a Goddamned liar," said Bello.

Porter wanted to believe he saw admittance in the man's eyes as well as fear and threw him to the ground. He saw the envelope of snapshots in the grass, picked them up, and tore them to shreds. Bello, crumpled on the ground, watched Porter. He raised himself up to his knees.

"I have negatives and other copies, of course," he said with effort.

Porter turned and kicked him in the mouth.

"I could beat you to death right now," said Porter. "If I ever hear you've talked again about those pictures or shown them to anybody, I swear to God, I'll kill you."

Only now did an Inglewood undertaker, leaving the chapel, see the two figures sprawled by the lake. He began hurrying down the hill as Porter began walking up it. Bello determinedly raised himself up on one elbow, his face and suit splattered with blood.

"You'll always remember what I showed you," he gasped.

"Shut up," said Porter, still walking, the blood staining his shirt from his aggravated knife wound.

"Ha!" shrieked the beaten Bello, kneeling by the lake. "I knew it that first day. She has bewitched you too!"

Porter kept walking, clutching his bleeding side as he spat on the ground.

Chapter Fifty-Four
The Weekend

Friday, September 9, 1932

Jean Harlow, movie star …and a sexually abused teenager and young woman.

What Porter had sensed Harlow saw as her only bargaining agent in this life – her sexuality – apparently extended to her own stepfather. Marino Bello probably rejoiced in taking the sordid responsibility for advancing her fears and promiscuity. Even now, as one of the world's most adored Hollywood attractions, she was too insecure and frightened, at least according to Bello, to refuse his advances. Especially now, as she felt a failure for not rousing Bern's manhood... and saw herself as a total fraud as an actress and a woman.

The one real hope for justice now, Porter realized, was Henry Bern.

*

"Tell me what happened," said the bald and sallow Bern.

Porter had come to the Ambassador after visiting a clinic and having his knife wound dressed. The doctor who treated him was alarmed by the wound, the loss of blood, and Porter's rising fever, and strongly suggested he enter a hospital. Porter refused. His wound stitched and re-bandaged, he'd stopped at a clothing store, bought a new shirt, and headed to see Henry Bern.

It was now after 7:00 P.M. Bern had finally and reluctantly agreed to see Porter, only after he'd sent a note up to his room, writing that he'd been with both Paul Bern and Dorothy Millette when they were murdered. Bern's bags were already packed. Porter spoke of the attack on Easton Drive and the one on *Delta King*.

"It's that Marino Bello creature, isn't it?" asked Bern.

"He claims he'd arranged your brother's death, and had hoped to arrange Dorothy's," said Porter. "He'd probably had gunmen tracking her, but it looks like MGM got there ahead of him. I want justice, Mr. Bern... for your brother and Millette."

Bern paused, and in a mannerism reminiscent of his dead brother, pinched his temples. "Mr. Down, since I have arrived here two days ago, I have seen Evil as I never knew it existed."

Henry had his brother Paul's sense of the dramatic. With the fustian Henry, it came out more awkwardly but at least as sincerely.

"Paul and Dorothy are both murdered. That monster Mayer will never admit the lies he told, and the crimes he either planned or allowed to happen. Nor will Bello. And I don't expect there will be any passion for justice pursued by my sick, pathetic sister-in-law."

"I admit it'll be a hell of a fight," said Porter.

"No, Mr. Down. There will be *no* fight. Considering what has happened this past week, I'm probably fortunate to be still alive myself. I'm going home to my wife in New Rochelle. I shall never speak publicly of these events again. I thank you for your information. It has given me some degree of closure and I'm grateful."

Henry Bern stood and offered his hand. "Goodbye, Mr. Down," he said with finality.

*

Porter, his fever rising, drove into Hollywood to Maggie's apartment. The desk clerk reiterated that she was still away. Porter demanded her room be opened to check that she was all right. No one was there and everything was in order.

As he drove back to Malibu, the images from the funeral haunted him, and he could hear Bello's crowing voice as he spoke of the abortion. Porter could never let himself believe it. He felt pity for Harlow more so than disgust, and disgust for himself for feeling pity for her.

Perhaps Bello was right...maybe Harlow had truly bewitched him.

Right now, he didn't care. He thought over and over again of Maggie. Where had she gone? Where was she now? Arriving in Malibu, Porter phoned her apartment house he'd left only an hour ago. No, Maggie had not returned.

"I have to find Maggie," he said to himself.

The visions from the funeral came back...Bello's smirking face... Annie Spry in her Harlow wig and widow's weeds. Yes, it must have been her at the bier...there was no doubt of it.

She has Maggie, he suddenly thought. *Spry has her...*

It was after 10:00 P.M. Luke was out fishing on *The Frederick*. Porter stood on the deck of *The Phoebe* and looked out at the ocean. His fever spiked, his face was flushed and the knife wound hurt like hell. He sat on the deck, dozing off, having a nightmare. When he was a boy, Porter had dreams about fighting a three-headed dragon. The dragon was back in tonight's dream, and each of its heads had blonde hair – Harlow's platinum blonde hair, Annie's ash-blonde hair, and Maggie's flaxen blonde hair. He had a sword, and he was trying to decapitate Annie while not harming Harlow or Maggie...

Porter awoke. The phone was ringing. He stumbled to the shack and grabbed it.

"I could have reached out and touched you at the funeral today," said Annie Spry. "You looked so handsome, I wanted to."

"Where's Maggie?" demanded Porter.

"Right here with me," said Annie. "She's about to become a movie star....in the latest AS Production."

"I'll kill you if you hurt her."

"Shut up, Sailor Boy. This time I hold the aces. You'll see this film only after I've slaughtered your sow. I'll be in Europe, and you can bury what's left of her...if you can find the pieces."

Porter choked in anguish.

"So," ordered Annie. "This will be the second of your beloved ladies whom you failed to protect. Maybe you can bury her next to your wife. Save time commuting to the graveyards."

"Annie...God damn you, Annie..."

"By the way, I'll be in the movie too, in case you want to watch it in your underwear. *Au revoir*, Sailor Boy. After what I'm doing tonight, I bet you'll be the brawniest guy in the madhouse. Nighty-night."

The phone went dead. Porter staggered off the trawler, almost delirious with fever and rage, onto the dock. He grabbed keys from the shack and, oblivious to the fact that he had no idea where Spry and Maggie were, headed for one of Luke's jalopies. He had to find Maggie...save her....

Blood seeped liberally from his bandages, and after having gone almost three days and nights without sleep or food, he collapsed, falling face-first into the gravel.

Chapter Fifty-Five
"Dorothy Millette's Ghost" – A Horror Movie

Friday, September 9 and Saturday, September 10, 1932

Maggie lie on a bed in a glaring spotlight, the klieg lights mercilessly shining on her from tower pole arcs. She was wearing the Jean Harlow pin-up costume of black velvet jacket, black stockings, and high heels. She wasn't wearing the Harlow platinum wig that Annie Spry had worn, and her own blond hair was tousled and damp with perspiration.

Ligatures bound her wrists to the brass rods of the headboard. The almost blinding light made everything else in the room nearly black, but she could see silhouettes. A large film camera was aimed at her, and there was a monolithic generator, a microphone hanging from a boom to the side of the bed, and other equipment. Now and then, a man's head peered over the camera – there were two men in the room, both of them eerily silent.

She took in what she could see, feel, hear, smell. The blazing white light and ominous dark shadows. The torturous heat from the lights. She heard the thunderous, slapping surf of the ocean, far below the cliff. And she smelled herself...forced to wear, along with the costume, a perfume that was luxuriant and familiar.

It was, she realized, the perfume that Harlow always wore...Mitsouko.

*

She hadn't seen Annie Spry since being apprehended. The two men had taken her to a room and locked her inside it. They took turns bringing her food and water and escorting her to the bathroom, where she was allowed to use the toilet under the watchful eyes of her escort. She estimated that about 24 hours had passed since she had come here.

Then, one of them had brought her the Harlow costume.

"Miss Spry wants you to wear this," he'd said gruffly, and left.

Both men had then escorted her to the "set" and the bed. Maggie realized Annie had clearly been planning to make a different film tonight, with herself as Harlow – hence the costume. Now she was creating an improvised vehicle to take advantage of Maggie's presence.

As the men tied Maggie to the bed, she saw to the side of the set a closed door and light seeping from under it. Music was playing...a recording of an opera that Maggie didn't recognize. One of the men checked the equipment and then tapped at the closed door. He mumbled something.

"Thank you, Mack," called a pleasant voice from inside the room.

It's her, thought Maggie.

The second man came beside the bed and tested the tightness of Maggie's ligatures. Then he rapped at the closed door and spoke in a low voice.

"Thank you, Sam," said the voice, soft but clearly audible.

Mack and Sam took positions behind the equipment. Maggie was perspiring on the bed. The opera record played behind the closed door.

*

Time passed. Everything was silent, but for the record and the pounding ocean surf. Maggie, unable to move, was feeling increasingly claustrophobic. She was afraid she might scream. And then, from the corner of her eye, she saw light bleeding out into the dark room as the door opened a sliver.

"Good evening, Maggie," said Annie Spry. She didn't emerge. There was only her voice.

"I'm sorry if you're uncomfortable," said Annie, her voice soft, almost breathless. "But undoubtedly, you look very attractive. At any rate, never fear. I plan to be patient...and gentle."

Mack and Sam, behind the camera, sullenly watched the scene.

"You've undoubtedly been reading the newspapers about that tragic Millette woman," said Annie. "How could we both not?" She gave a girlish laugh. "How the public adores its Hollywood tragedies! Yet, oh, so sad. The papers today claim she drowned herself...or...someone drowned her..."

Maggie tried to see Annie through the partially opened door, but could only glimpse a figure moving.

"The poor lady," said Annie. "The agony... Losing her man to a much younger woman. Yes, Paul Bern was a fetishist – don't I know! – who couldn't fuck, or handle money, and was probably a psycho... but he was *her* Paul. And he cast her away for a tawdry, out-of-the-bottle blonde. Such is the way of the world... isn't it, Maggie?"

Maggie yanked surreptitiously at the ligatures that strapped her hands to the bed.

"Poor Dorothy...The papers write that no one has found her corpse. She's been in the river for four days and nights. Did you know, Maggie, that a body decomposes quickly when it's in water?"

"Stop," said Maggie.

"How nice to hear your voice finally!" said Annie. "Anyway," she continued, "poor Dorothy, in the river, all the while her skin sloughing off, scaring the hell out of the fish. I fancy her cadaver dreaming, fantasizing, how she desires revenge...on that woman who stole away her Paul...."

"Stop!" cried Maggie.

"A horror movie!" exulted Annie. "They're so popular these days! *Dorothy Millette's Ghost*. It will be an uncensored thriller about the ghost's vengeance on Jean Harlow! An AS Production!"

The door opened suddenly. A new record began playing, Rubinstein's sad, mournfully beautiful *Kamennoi Ostrow*. Maggie shut her eyes, then looked in spite of herself as a dark form emerged from the room and moved toward the foot of the bed. The figure was all in blackness, then finally, stepped forward into the light.

Annie Spry stood horrifically adorned as a rotting corpse, soaking wet, as if just retrieved from the river. The newspapers had only run a grainy head and shoulders portrait of Millette from years before, but Annie had properly guessed Dorothy's hair had been red, and the wig she wore was long, drenched, and hung over her shoulders. Her skin, pale with a green cast, seemed in places to be putrescent, actually peeling away. Maggie knew Annie was a master at makeup, but this was almost unspeakably horrible. She wore a pale, sashed burial shroud, wet and clinging to her body.

"I'll be Dorothy," said Annie. "You, of course, will be Harlow. "

She moved beside the bed. "You're so perfectly cast. You have such soft, white skin," and she teasingly traced her finger with its sharp nail down the plunging neckline of Maggie's black velvet jacket. Water dripped from her wig and shroud onto Maggie, who jerked her body away. Annie leaned in close to her neck and sniffed the Mitsouko

"You smell so luscious," giggled "Luscious Custard."

*

The camera began filming, the microphone having swung into place. Annie sat beside Maggie on the bed, and began ad-libbing the plot.

"Oh, don't be scared, darling!" she said "Dorothy will be gentle. Doesn't everyone call you 'Baby'? Well, Dorothy will call *you* 'Baby'…and play with you…as if you're just a little baby!"

Maggie suddenly strained upward from the bed, but the ligatures were still too strong, yanking her back onto the mattress, on her side, facing Annie. Despite her efforts, tears formed in her eyes.

"Don't cry, Baby!" cooed Annie. "Dorothy is going to make sure you have fun. Don't all babies love to be tickled?"

She revealed she was carrying a sharp stiletto knife.

"Maybe right here, just behind the ear," said Annie, clearly intending to remind Maggie of the cut ear of the dead whore "Jeanie." "Kootchie-coo?"

She slowly dragged the knife down behind Maggie's ear, the blood trickling down Maggie's neck. Now Annie reached over, playfully ripping open Maggie's jacket, down to her navel.

"Wheee!" Annie laughed, playfully touching the knife's tip back and forth to Maggie's breasts, and reciting:

> *Eeny, Meeny, Miney, Mo!*
> *Which nipple will be first to go?*

Maggie stifled a whimper. Mack and Sam looked at each other a moment, and Sam grimly shook his head.

"Dorothy has a big surprise for you, Baby!" said Annie. "Now, open your eyes."

Maggie defiantly kept them shut.

"Open your eyes, Baby," ordered Annie.

Maggie refused.

"Open your damn eyes!" shrieked Annie. "While you still have two eyes left to open!"

Maggie trembled and opened her eyes.

Annie stood at the foot of the bed. She held something cylindrical and leathery in her hand. Maggie realized it was a phallus.

"This is prized memorabilia," she grinned, "from my film *The Wedding Night of Jean Harlow and Paul Bern*. I don't know if you ever saw the movie, but I'm sure Porter Down told you all about it. You surely remember this item! I might be in the mood later for you and me to engage in a little… experimentation."

Maggie clenched at the headboard. Her eyes flashed and her body heaved with anger and defiance. She shook her head in denial, thinking how damaged Porter would be if he ever saw this film, if he ever learned what Annie did to her.

She couldn't let this happen.

*

Kamennoi Ostrow swelled reverently as Annie strapped on the dildo and hovered over the bed. "Now, before anything else… I want you to scream. Baby is having a nightmare, and Dorothy will come and… console her, shall we say."

"Go to hell!" spat Maggie.

"Scream!" shouted Annie, kneeling beside her on the bed, slapping Maggie's face.

"No!" cried Maggie.

Annie climbed on top of Maggie, straddling her, slapping her again. "Goddamnit, bitch! *SCREAM!*"

Annie, Mack, and Sam were unaware that Maggie had been steadily rubbing the ligatures against a burr in the headboard. Her right arm was free now….and she suddenly slammed Annie's face, throwing her off balance so that she fell off the bed.

It was Annie who screamed as she crashed against a pole holding an arc light. An immediate chain reaction saw the pole falling against the other pole, both capsizing to the floor and the hot klieg lights exploding with a spray of sparks and glass. Within seconds, the canvas draperies on the floor ignited.

"Fire!" shrieked Annie.

The knife was still on the bed. Maggie cut the remaining ligature binding her left hand, kicked off the high heels, and escaped the room.

"Get her!" screamed Annie.

Mack and Sam tried to clamber over the fallen equipment to get their guns and pursue her. Annie, seeing the flames already licking at the canvas sheets in the hotbox room, realized the imminent danger: the severe combustibility of the camera's cheap nitrate film.

Annie ran out of the house, and saw Maggie was nowhere in sight. She rushed down the steps to the patio, hysterically throwing herself into the pool to escape the fire. Her suspicions were accurate. Within a minute, there was an explosion and the house erupted into flames. A heavy chunk of tiled roof landed in the pool, nearly striking Annie's head as she bobbed in the water, dressed in her shroud and wig, screaming in fear and nearly insane anger.

*

It was almost 3:30 A.M. when Luke Foster returned from fishing and saw flashing police lights at the pier. A pair of medics and two policemen were loading Porter Down into an ambulance, having found him unconscious in the gravel.

Maggie, having escaped the burning house in San Luis Obispo, had flagged down a passing motorist who gladly picked up the blonde woman in her black fetishist attire. His hopes were dashed when she insisted he drive her to the town's police. Meanwhile, the fire department had arrived at the scene of the fire and the police joined them to search for Annie and her bodyguards. They'd found Sam dead, a victim of the fire, but Mack and Annie were gone.

Instinctively fearing that Porter was in grave trouble, she'd asked the San Luis Obispo police to contact the Malibu police and dispatch cops to Luke's pier. It was a good thing she had. Porter had nearly bled to death.

*

On Saturday afternoon, Longie Zwillman swaggered into the hospital in Santa Monica. He took the elevator upstairs and went directly to Porter Down's room. He already knew the room's number.

Porter was asleep and looked like hell. Maggie, having been driven to Malibu by the San Luis Obispo police, sat in a chair beside the bed. She wore a hospital gown, had a bandaged ear, and had been treated for several minor injuries.

"We meet again, Miss York," said Longie, removing his hat.

Maggie was silent.

"Is he gonna' make it?" asked Longie.

"Yes," said Maggie softly.

"I know all about what happened last night," said Longie. "As you know, I've got my sources."

Maggie nodded slightly, as if she weren't surprised. "The police between San Luis Obispo and L.A. are looking for her," she said.

Zwillman looked at her a moment, then at Porter, then again at Maggie. "When your friend wakes up," he said, "tell him I dropped by. Tell him not to waste any time and energy planning to go after Annie Spry. It'll all be resolved within a week. I'll see to it. Tell him my services are on the house."

Longie Zwillman nodded to Maggie, put on his hat and left the room.

Chapter Fifty-Six
Lake Arrowhead

Sunday, September 11, 1932

Lake Arrowhead is 80 miles east of Los Angeles, in the San Bernardino Mountains. The September night was cold and the moon, a few nights from being full, had risen over the lake.

It was after 10:00 P.M. Mack was rowing his passenger with two suitcases to a guest cottage perched on a spit of land jutting out into the lake. It was the bodyguard's final job for Annie Spry.

Mack looked at the woman across from him in the rowboat, a dark coat draped over her shoulders, a high-crowned hat cocked over one eye. Yeah, working for her made Mack feel like a sex creep himself. Spry dressing up like a corpse – and what she wanted to do to that poor girl – it had all been almost too much to ask, even for the cash the cat-faced bitch had promised to pay. He was actually glad for the fire, even if Sam, who was his pal, had died in it.

But Mack was really ending his work for Annie Spry for a different reason: He had the instinctive feeling that the cops, or somebody, were on their tail. Since late afternoon, Mack had the sensation somebody was watching him. Tonight, after getting back, he would be taking off for Mexico...fast.

*

His passenger sat silently in the rowboat, looking at the moon and the lights in the windows of the cabins and cottages along the lake and in the hills. She shivered. This was the first stop of her escape plan. Tomorrow a contact would pick her up and take her to an airfield. From there to New York...from New York to Berlin.

Hopefully, the wealthy Nazi producers who'd previously negotiated with Annie for her services, would still be interested, despite the fact that she'd be arriving in Berlin without the money from Porter Down that was to have paid her way into this new partnership. She feared their interest had cooled. As they had told her on her last visit to Berlin, she wasn't a young woman anymore...

and had to expect to finance part of this new arrangement. Now she was basically broke, but still would need this contract in order to provide protection from the American authorities, who would assuredly come looking for her.

It was all Porter Down's fault...and Maggie York's. They'd destroyed her plans...and she knew that Down would surely be on her tail if he had to chase her all over Europe.

The pigeon-toed mother-fucker, thought Annie.

*

They'd reached their destination. Annie stood on the dock. Mack put on the cottage lights and carried the bags inside to the upstairs bedroom. Annie handed him an envelope with payment, watched as Mack promptly rowed away, and then went inside and locked the door.

She started up the steps, exhausted from the recent days and nights with hardly any sleep, from the rigors of her escape, from the torment of her defeat. She felt sick and dizzy, tripping in her high heels. Anxiety gripped her and she trembled, allowing her coat to fall off her shoulders and down the steps behind her. She gripped the rail, got herself up to the bedroom, removed the heels, opened the French doors and stood out on a little balcony that offered a view of the moonlit lake. After a moment she went back inside, removed the hat, then the dress, and then peeled off her stockings and girdle.

Annie unpacked her bags and ran a bath. She still wore her makeup and false eyelashes as she eased herself into the bathtub, soon falling asleep in the warm water. She had the nightmare that had plagued her during the past year: Her skin had sloughed off her body as she bathed, and she was a skeleton sitting in the bathtub, the water filled with skin and hair and blood.

"NO!" shrieked Annie, bolting upright in the bathtub, gasping... alone. She felt her face and hair. She was still whole. Yes, it had been a nightmare...for nothing horrified her as did aging...

"And eventually dying," she whispered to herself.

Only one thing had saved her from total despair. Sex...or her nightmarish burlesques of it.

*

She emerged from the bath, regarding her naked body in the bathroom mirror, pushing back the strands of her dyed hair, now limp and thinning. Yes, she'd have to wear a wig all the time very soon now. She took from her bag a long, white silk negligee, put it on, and returned to the bathroom mirror, refreshing her makeup, brushing her hair, enjoying this private show of vanity, wondering if she could trust anyone, when the time came, to bury her expertly made up and beautifully coiffed and dressed. Meanwhile, tonight, she'd sleep this way.

She went to the large, plush bed, so puffed up there was a footstool to help her ascend into it. She thought again of Porter Down, Jean Harlow's "Knight in Shining Armor," and Maggie York. Someday, perhaps, she'd find a way to get her revenge on all three of them.

She stepped on the stool and pulled back the covers. There was a piece of stationery, very feminine, and scented with Mitsouko. She clawed at it and read:

Say your prayers, Annie

She stared at it for a long moment, her fear spiked and she ran to the balcony.

"*Help me!*" she screamed.

The bedroom door burst open behind her. Powerful arms attacked her, one hand covering her mouth as the other lifted her by the waist. There were two well-dressed men behind her, one of whom ripped the silk negligee off with one hand, and both of them then tossed her through the air, across the room and onto the bed.

Both men looked at the naked, gasping Annie. One man mockingly wolf-whistled.

"Looks like a sweet little pussycat, doesn't she?" said the second man.

Annie, writhed and whimpered on the bed, backing against the headboard. And now, a third well-dressed man came up the steps. It was Nick Kirk.

"Hey, let's show some respect," said Nick, tipping his homburg and showing off his new, almost undetectable toupee. "We're lookin' at the famous 'Luscious Custard.' Remember…from the smokers?"

"Get out!" cried Annie.

"You made a mistake, glamour girl," said Nick, sitting in a chair across from the bed, placing his hat in his lap. "You upset a pal of ours…Mr. Porter Down. He doesn't know we're here tonight, doing him this favor…but he will."

The two other men were removing their coats. Both had a pistol housed in a shoulder strap and both removed several knives from their pockets. Annie, in her many sex fantasies, had actually imagined such a violent death. Now, with execution imminent, all she felt was terror.

"For starters," said Nick appraisingly, "maybe one of those cat eyes."

Annie, fighting hysteria, lost. She pissed the bed, screaming so wildly that her dentures fell out. And as the terror and madness totally consumed her, she suddenly arched her hand like a cat's claw, crinkled her eyes, and gave her loudest, wildest cat screech.

The three men just laughed at her. "Okay, boys," said Nick. "Let's play 'skin the cat.'"

Annie Spry's cat cry became a yowl, and finally a scream, as the midnight moon lit the sky, reflecting romantically on Lake Arrowhead.

Chapter Fifty-Seven
Wrap-Up

Monday, September 12 through Friday September 16, 1932

On Monday, September 12, Jean Harlow returned to MGM and *Red Dust*.

"How are we going to get a sexy performance with *that* look in her eyes?" lamented director Victor Fleming to *Red Dust* co-star Mary Astor.

The next day Harlow shot retakes of the notorious scene in which she bathed nude in a rain barrel and said a line that formerly had amused her:

"I'm La Flamme, the gal that drives men mad!"

Her eyes suddenly had their haunted look and she gazed out past the lights and into the soundstage darkness. "I don't have to say that, do I?" she asked softly.

*

Two days later, Wednesday, September 14, Porter Down left the hospital, ahead of schedule. He and Maggie had dinner together, then walked the beach at Santa Monica under the full moon. Maggie removed her flats and walked in the surf.

They didn't discuss how eager Porter was to learn, via the men he'd crippled in San Francisco, who'd sent the assassins to kill him and Dorothy Millette. Also, as far as he knew, Annie Spry was still on the loose. Police hadn't located her and there'd been no communication from Longie Zwillman.

Porter was determined to find her.

*

Late that night, Detective Meservey telephoned Porter from Sacramento with major news: fishermen had found the body of a woman in the Georgiana Slough near Walnut Grove. Meservey described it as "terribly decomposed."

The detective had called the manager of San Francisco's Plaza Hotel to make identification. Would Porter come too?

Come dawn, Thursday, September 15, Porter was flying north in *Timber Wolf*, arriving in Walnut Grove before noon. Meservey picked him up and drove him to the morgue. The cadaver, after a week in the river, was pitiful to see. Both Porter and the Plaza manager agreed that the recently tinted blonde-red hair, framing the remnants of the face, was a major cause for affirmation. Porter also recognized the tatters of clothing as looking like those he had last seen on Dorothy Millette.

"I got word the MGM lawyers are galloping up here like Attila the Hun's army to kill this story," said Meservey. "You know they're going to fight for a suicide verdict."

"Yeah," said Porter.

"There was $38 in her purse we found on the boat," said Meservey. "Looks like she's heading for a Potter's Field grave."

"Ask the MGM lawyers for a donation," said Porter.

A call came for Porter from L.A. It was Jim O'Leary.

"Bad news, fella. Both our crippled assassins are dead. Throats slit in the bathroom at San Quentin."

*

Flying back from Walnut Grove that night over the Pacific and under the full moon, Porter reviewed the case.

The two men who'd killed Millette and had tried to kill him were dead. Someone outside the jail had sent in the order. Neither Harlow nor Henry Bern had the guts to fight.

The irony of it all was that although the saga of "Dear Dorothy" Millette had finally become news, nobody gave a damn. The world preferred the MGM-concocted saga of a madly frustrated Paul Bern, so humiliated by platinum bride Jean Harlow that he finally stripped one forlorn summer night, penned a suicide note, poured her Mitsouko perfume over his naked body, and fired a bullet into his brain.

Actually, it was more ironic than that. For all he knew and all he'd been through, Porter couldn't swear on a Bible about the innocence or guilt of anyone involved. Bello might very well have told him what he did because he was an egomaniac asshole who wanted any excuse to show off his dirty pictures. Annie Spry actually had more smarts and stronger motivation to have arranged an assassination. And while it sure seemed to Porter that Mannix was guilty of the attack on the *Delta King*, there was, again, no real evidence. Did ex-bouncer Eddie really have the brains, skill, and contacts to have arranged this hit, and actually get away with it?

What Porter had learned about Bern and Harlow might have been only the tip of the iceberg. There might be enough sex blackmailers and gangster boyfriends out there, Porter realized, to have a damn annual reunion.

It was basically over. He just wanted to get the hell away from it all. There was just one more job. He'd track down Annie Spry, even if he had to chase the bitch all over the world.

*

Friday morning, September 16th was hot. Porter had assisted Luke with the previous night's catch, helped load the truck and after Luke drove away, returned to his maps. Maggie, who'd been staying at the Marina with them, had driven to the market.

Porter was on deck, charting an airlines course to Europe, specifically to Berlin, which is where he predicted Spry would flee. He wore only his sailor's cap, a pair of shorts, and a bandage that circled his stomach, dressing his cut and keeping it from infection. As he sat on the trawler, he saw a limousine pull up to the dock, parking next to the *Luke's Marina* sign. A pick-up truck was behind it.

The chauffeur opened the limo's back door and an ebullient Longie Zwillman emerged, wearing a new, tailor-made grey suit with matching snap-brim hat. A bodyguard got out of the passenger door.

"I got a new suit!" Zwillman shouted to Porter.

"You drove all the way up here to tell me that?" asked Porter.

Zwillman chuckled and strutted down the dock, followed by his bodyguard. "I hear your lady's been staying here," said Zwillman.

"Yeah, so what?" asked Porter.

Zwillman placed his foot up on the stern of *The Phoebe*. "What plans you got?"

"Europe," said Porter grimly.

Zwillman chuckled again and shook his head. "Listen. I got you a present. You and the kid…Luke." He looked at his bodyguard. "Bring that present here, OK?"

The bodyguard went to the bed of the pick-up truck.

"You got a good thing here, Porter," said Zwillman. "Why not invest more of your time at the marina? Good change of scenery from the desert. Farm there, fish here. Relaxing work. Hookin' seafood day and night. You catch lobsters? I'd buy all my lobsters here, whenever I'm in L.A."

The chauffeur, bodyguard, and truck driver came forward, lugging what looked like an old ship's figurehead. It was a woman with bare breasts, large painted eyes, and lanky hair colored an ash blonde.

"We said once we were both pirates, remember?" smiled Zwillman. "Well, here's a present fit for a pirate…and to fit onto your fishing boat."

The men placed it on the edge of the dock, stood behind it, and smirked. Porter looked at it, and them, with an instinctive hunch.

"Now, it ain't an antique," said Longie, strangely pleased with himself. "*Looks* like an antique, a fuckin' old antique, but it's all new. Made of wood and ballast and mortar…plus a secret ingredient."

"What secret ingredient?" asked Porter suspiciously.

Zwillman rapped on the figurehead's head. "Sex creep cadaver," he said.

The bodyguard, chauffeur, and truck driver all laughed, then turned and walked back to the car and truck. "Jesus Christ," said Porter, staring at the figurehead's face.

"Yeah," said Zwillman, "Annie's in there. Every bone in her fucked-up body – or what was left of it, after Nick and the boys caught up with her. This is her eternal reward. And I just saved you the cost of a fuckin' trip to Europe."

Porter stared at the figurehead's face. "It even looks a little bit like her."

"Like Annie?" snorted Longie. "Not in that twat's wildest dreams. Annie never looked that good in her life."

Longie removed his hat and placed it over his heart. His tone took on that of a eulogist. "Farewell, Annie," he orated. "Ya' see, this way, in death, you'll always be like you were in life. In other words, you'll always smell like fish."

Porter was silent. "Holy shit," he said finally.

"Anyway," said Zwillman, "all's well that ends well. Now take your eyes off those Goddamn plaster boobs and follow me."

Zwillman chortled, climbing up into the trawler. There was no need for this confidentiality, but it was a Longie ritual and Porter followed.

"You notice Nick didn't come out with us today," said Longie. "He thinks you might be mad at him for beatin' you to the punch with Annie. You know what a sensitive guy he is."

"Yeah," said Porter. "I'll send him flowers."

"Oh, one more thing," said Longie. "Come here. I want you to see something."

Zwillman walked to the bow of the trawler. He removed his hat, loosened his tie, and unbuttoned his collar. Then he reached inside, took his gold locket with the Harlow relic, and broke the chain as he snapped it from his neck. He looked significantly at Porter and then, with a pro-football star's power, threw the locket far out into the ocean.

"See ya, Porter," said Longie Zwillman.

Chapter Fifty-Eight
Farewell Cruise

Friday, September 16, 1932

Luke had taken *The Frederick* out for fishing. Porter and Maggie took *The Phoebe* out for a late dinner and a talk they both knew they needed to have.

They'd packed sandwiches and a carton of Cokes. The stars were bright and they sat aft, looking at the lights of the coastline.

"Anything you need to tell me?" asked Porter finally.

"Yes, it's about time I did," said Maggie. "My brother's having trouble running the farm in Nebraska. I think I better go home for a while and help him." She paused. "I think...he has a drinking problem."

"Then he needs you," said Porter.

"While I'm there," said Maggie "I'm going to try writing a novel. And don't worry – I won't make you a character in it, tempting as it is."

"You better not," said Porter.

He knew her depth of feeling for him. He also knew her ambiguity of emotions. When he'd told her that Zwillman had caught and killed Annie – without details – he'd sensed her mixed feelings...that a horrible woman was dead, but that she'd been murdered by a gangster. This was Porter's world. He doubted she'd ever be comfortable in it.

"If you think I'm making the right decision," said Maggie, "I'll tell Lt. O'Leary tomorrow."

"Yeah," said Porter. "Go help your brother. Kick his ass, fix up the farm, and write your novel."

"Then I will," said Maggie. She paused and her eyes were wet.

"I'll write you letters...lots of letters," said Maggie. "Maybe later...I'll come back."

They were both silent for a while. Then she leaned over, kissed him, and they were in each other's arms.

Chapter Fifty-Nine
A broch tsu dayn lebn

Tuesday, September 20 through Monday, September 26, 1932

It was Tuesday, September 20, 1932, fifteen days after Paul Bern's death, six days after Dorothy Millette's body had been found, and one day after Maggie York had left for Nebraska.

Porter Down had an appointment. To his amazement, Louis B. Mayer's office had called the marina and left a "request" that Porter meet with Mayer at 9:00 A.M. at MGM. He was pleased to receive it. There were a few choice things he'd like to say to L.B.

He went dressed in his sailor togs, just as he'd been when he'd reported to Culver City back in June. As he strolled across the lot to the executive building, he saw a woman in the distance whom he recognized by her marching band strut. She was on her way to the mailbox. It was Irene Harrison.

Porter approached her. "Hi 'ya," he said.

"Well, Mr. Down," said Harrison. "I didn't expect to see you on these premises again."

"It'll be a quick visit. I figured you'd have cleared out of here by now."

"Actually, I've given my two weeks' notice. I'm going to work for Mr. Bern's old friend, Sally Rand."

"You gonna' be a fan dancer too?" winked Porter.

"No," said Harrison, resisting a grin. "Her secretary. I'm filing everything in Mr. Bern's office, and then I'll be leaving MGM."

"Well, good luck," said Porter. "And swell job stonewalling the big boys here. I was impressed properly."

"Thank you," said Harrison, taking his hand and giving it a firm handshake. "And…thank you too for all you've done. I have a feeling you've had adventures these past weeks that I can only imagine."

"Maybe. Bye."

"Goodbye." And Irene Harrison marched away. Porter watched her for a moment, whistled a line or two from *Stars and Stripes Forever*, and headed into the executive building.

*

A secretary led Porter into Mayer's office, and then exited. Mayer stood behind the desk, firmly yet placidly. Flanking him on his left was a stone-faced Eddie Mannix. Nobody extended a hand but Mayer did invite Porter to take a seat. As he sat, so did Mayer and Mannix. Mayer regarded Porter a moment.

"Our company, I can say with confidence, has weathered this recent storm," said Mayer. "Miss Harlow is back to work on *Red Dust*. Her popularity seems only to have increased. Miss Millette, according to the authorities, has taken matters into her own hands. We feel certain that the decisions we made on this situation were all for the best."

Mayer seemed innocent as a newborn babe. The mogul patiently awaited Porter's reply. There wasn't one.

"It appears," continued Mayer, "that you have no intention of pursuing this matter, or making any unnecessary revelations to the press."

Porter shrugged. "No point, really."

"Exactly!" beamed Mayer. Mannix folded his thick arms and frowned suspiciously.

"I have only one question, and then a proposal," said Mayer. "The question. As a man who understands the world so well, why…" – Mayer paused to chuckle – "…why did you feel compelled to defy me and try to be the champion of some lost soul? Some mad woman?"

Porter looked intensely into Mayer's eyes. "A lost soul mad woman needs champions too," he said. "Especially if she's basically harmless, outnumbered, and facing hopeless odds."

Mayer, eyes gleaming, emotionally pounded his fist on his desk. "Can you tell this man was a war hero?" he crowed to Mannix. "Do you hear his idealism? And this brings me to my proposal. Porter, I need a man with your principles, your courage. For all our differences in a very dark hour, I've always respected you. As such, I want to make this offer to you in front of Mr. Mannix: that you be Leo the Lion's special troubleshooter. It will be a full-time position, at a salary higher than ever paid to a security expert at any studio, with all the benefits you request. There will be no formalities in the job or required hours. You'll receive a full 52-week employee package, but need only work when we need you."

"No kiddin'?" asked Porter.

"Oh yes!" said Mayer. "I recruit the best of everything for my company. You're the best man in your field. I want you with Metro-Goldwyn-Mayer."

Mayer paused. "God is good to me, Porter. He has saved me, my studio, and my people in this dark hour and given me many blessings. You're one of them."

He stood, an Old Testament patriarch of a movie mogul, solemnly offering his handshake on the deal. Porter, languishing in his chair, didn't take it. Finally, Mayer, beet red, slowly sat. And now Porter stood.

"Louie," he began, "you've allowed Eddie here and his goon squad to present one of your own stars – a mixed-up, unhappy girl, abused from her dyed platinum hair to her red painted toenails – as a balls-smasher whom the whole, hung-up-on-sex world can take to its heart. She ought to be in a hospital right now. Are you actually proud she's back to work on a movie set?"

"L.B." interrupted Mannix, "Do we have to...?"

"Good ol' Eddie," said Porter, eyeballing Mannix. "So just how big was the brick you shit when you learned I didn't drown in the Sacramento River?"

"L.B.," chuckled Mannix, his eyes dark, "maybe you should be offering Porter a job writing screenplays."

"The Bulldog," sneered Porter. "A canine clown. Oh, and by the way...where did your boys ever dump that hit man's body you found at Easton Drive?"

"You'll sure in hell never know," smirked Mannix.

"Yeah, and I'll never be able to prove what I suspect," said Porter. "As far as Millette's murder – and I have a feeling both you boys know damn well it was murder – maybe you two are innocent. I can't prove you are or aren't. But you're both sure in hell guilty of covering up Paul Bern's murder, slandering one of your most devoted employees, and bullying a sad, sick, scared girl so you wouldn't lose a cent on your investment."

"Down," growled Mannix, "so help me…"

"Shut up, Eddie," said Porter. "And as for you, Louie. No, I didn't do what I did for you, or for Leo the Lion, or for Garbo and Gable, or for some ass-scratchin' usherette at a Hoboken theatre. I tried to help Dorothy Millette simply because she needed help and it was the decent thing to do."

"Get out!" shouted Mayer, standing dramatically.

"You told me back in June, Louie," said Porter, "that the decay always comes from within. Well, it's sure ripe in here."

"*A broch tsu dayn lebn!*" Mayer snarled. "You know what that means? It means 'your life should be a disaster!'"

"I'm still workin' on matzo ball," said Porter, turning his back and exiting the office.

*

Porter decided he'd spend the rest of the week helping Luke with his catch, then fly home the following Monday. Saturday evening, after they'd returned to the pier from a steak dinner – they were damned tired of fish – the phone rang in the shack. It was Detective Meservey from Sacramento.

"Reading the papers down there?" asked Meservey.

"Avoiding them like the plague," said Porter.

"Well," said Meservey, "the news got out about Dorothy Millette's pauper's grave. We heard from two of her sisters."

"They're paying for the grave?" asked Porter.

"No," said Meservey. "They're suing Harlow for half of Bern's estate."

"I wish 'em all the luck they deserve," said Porter. "His estate's just a pile of debt. Harlow will be paying it off for a long time."

"Yeah, the joke's on them," said Meservey. "Anyway, here's the interesting part. We got a call today from somebody who *did* offer to pay for Millette's grave. Guess who?"

"Aimee Semple McPherson?"

"No. Jean Harlow."

Porter had no comeback. After a moment of silence, Meservey continued.

"Yep. Miss Harlow's gonna' pick up the tab. A plot at East Lawn Memorial Park up here in Sacramento."

"Interesting news," said Porter. "Thanks."

*

Come Monday morning, Porter drove to Santa Monica for an early lunch with O'Leary. In their previous discussions, the LAPD lieutenant shared Porter's conclusions: Annie Spry had arranged the murder of "Jeanie" and the dumping of her body at Luke's Marina; Marino Bello had sent the killer to Easton Drive to murder Bern, Millette, and Porter; and Eddie Mannix had sent the killers to murder Millette and Porter, tracing them to the *Delta King*. The two men didn't talk about these topics today.

"Say, fella," asked the lieutenant, "did I ever thank you for that 'commission' you paid me back in July…for my having set up your deal at MGM?"

"Yeah," said Porter. "Only about ten times."

"It got us a new roof. Paid tuition for the girls for the next two years. And…" O'Leary winked, "I bought Charlotte a mink coat for her birthday."

"Goin' Hollywood, Doc?"

"The rest I put aside for a rainy day," said O'Leary. His mood grew serious. "Thanks, fella. I'm sorry for all the grief this one caused ya.' I only wish we'd known back in May what we know now."

"Forget it," said Porter.

Chapter Sixty
Flying East

Monday September 26, 1932

In Malibu, Porter gathered and packed his few belongings. Luke told Porter that, based on all the money he'd paid him the past year, they were now 60/40 owners of the marina. The kid looked so hurt when Porter declined that he finally agreed to take 10% of the future profits. After all, he could always put it into an account and give it back to Luke sometime.

If Luke refused, what the hell…he'd donate it to another of his favorite charities: The Porter Waldo Down Retirement Fund.

*

At the airfield, Porter offered his hand and after Luke shook it, the kid hugged him and hurried back inside the car, ashamed of his tears. Luke stayed in the car to watch Porter take off. *Timber Wolf* ascended and Porter gave Luke thumbs-up as the Spad soared into the east.

The flight was pleasant, the scenery beautiful, and Porter landed on the strip below his house shortly after 4 P.M. He checked on Long John and the chickens and turkeys – everything seemed fine. Then he drove his truck into town, arriving at the Twentynine Palms post office just before it closed. Among the letters were two from Maggie. There was also a black-trimmed envelope, the kind one would send to acknowledge a condolence. Porter noted the return address:

1353 Club View Drive
Los Angeles, Calif.

*

Porter unpacked at the house, barbecuing a steak for dinner. He walked down to the "oasis" under the Joshua trees, but the evening air was brisk and he stayed in the pool only briefly. The night became cold and windy and he built a fire in the hearth, glad to be home, relaxing with a Coke.

He enjoyed the fire, glancing at the flames and the shadows they cast on the Indian painting on the tower ceiling. The flickering shadows made the painted eagles seem to fly and the painted spirits to dance, and Porter enjoyed the show. He listened to the radio for a while, and come 11 P.M. he read Maggie's letters. They were full of affection and her characteristic humor and energy. All seemed to be going well at the farm – her brother seemed open to help, and she'd started work on her novel.

"I miss you very much," Maggie wrote in both letters.

Porter read each letter twice. He decided it was time for bed. Then he remembered the last time he slept in his bed, Jean Harlow had shared it with him.

He hadn't opened her envelope and had considered tossing it into the fireplace. For a time he'd succeeded in putting it from his mind but now, late in the night, his curiosity returned. Porter took the letter from the table and went out onto the deck. He stood by the rail, lit the lantern, took his penknife, and slit open the envelope. As he did so he felt foolish for his hesitation; the contents were probably just a pre-printed thank-you-for-your-kind-expression-of-grief card. However, he'd never sent her any expression of grief.

What he extracted, however, was a hand-written note. It bore a slight scent of Mitsouko and it read:

> *Dear Porter,*
> *Thank you – for what you did do – and what you didn't do.*
> *I hope you will read this letter even after you realize it's from me. Marino told me what he told you and showed you.*
> *Please believe that what he told you about my baby – that he was the father – is a lie. I swear it.*
> *I wish I could swear what else he told you is a lie, but cannot. You have every reason to hate me – although you probably don't as much as I hate myself.*
> *Please forgive me. You must be so disappointed in Jean Harlow. I wanted you to admire me and like me and I know how terribly I have failed.*

A favor – please don't throw away the rabbit's foot I gave you. I'm sure you don't want it anymore but somehow, I'll be glad to think you've kept it. Please.

I am so sorry.

Love,
Me

The wind blew the swaying palm tree and Porter looked out at the night and the stars. He didn't read the letter a second time, placing it back in its envelope.

Epilogue

September 18, 1933: Jean Harlow married Hal Rosson, her cinematographer from *Red Dust* and 1933's *Bombshell*. Reporters thought the diminutive, mustached, 38-year-old Rosson looked as if he could have been Paul Bern's brother. They separated May 5, 1934, after less than eight months of marriage, and subsequently divorced.

September 26, 1935: Mother Jean divorced Marino Bello. She cited his mining scams and testified, "The man truly acted as though he were a maniac." Bello demanded a divorce settlement that took all the money Jean Harlow had saved – $22,000.

September 14, 1936: Irving Thalberg died of pneumonia at his Santa Monica beach home. Jean Harlow attended the funeral. Louis B. Mayer, long jealous of his colleague, was said to have murmured at Thalberg's funeral, "Isn't God good to me?"

June 7, 1937: Jean Harlow, age 26, died at 11:38 A.M. at Good Samaritan Hospital in Los Angeles. Cause of death: kidney failure.

*

There had been considerable gossip after Jean Harlow's death that there would be no viewing of the body. The sudden ravages of kidney failure had been truly horrific; her body had bloated hideously, and the doctors had shaved her head, planning to drill holes in the skull to relieve the swelling pressure.

Still, there was a viewing at the Pierce Brothers Mortuary, on Washington Boulevard. Pierce's master morticians and the MGM makeup wizards laid out Jean Harlow in a blonde wig and a pink negligee that she'd worn in her latest picture, *Saratoga*. MGM would complete the film with doubles for her body and voice.

The funeral was set for 9 A.M. on Wednesday, June 9, at the Wee Kirk of the Heather at Forest Lawn Memorial Park in Glendale. On Tuesday night, the eve of the funeral, the celebrity crowd gathered in the "Tennyson Room" of Pierce Brothers and reverently filed by the body, surrounded by profuse flower displays and resting on a chaise lounge with a gardenia in its hand. William Powell, widely regarded as Harlow's fiancé (but who'd resolutely failed to marry her), wept uncontrollably. Several people noted that Powell, his receding hairline exposed without his hairpiece, actually resembled Paul Bern, Hal Rosson, and Marino Bello.

An epically grieving Mother Jean stood like a statue of the bereaved Madonna, and Marino Bello returned briefly into Mother Jean's life for his stepdaughter's obsequies.

That night, as the mourners passed by the corpse, Porter Down, wearing the brown-striped suit MGM had provided him almost five years before, brought up the rear of the line. He was in L.A. on a case and had decided, reluctantly and only at the last minute, to pay his respects. As he approached the corpse, he thought that despite all the makeup artistry, the dead woman looked far older than the Jean Harlow he remembered from the sad summer of 1932. Although he hadn't actively followed her life since, he knew it had been a roller coaster.

He looked at her, and remembered. How she'd worn a swimsuit at their first meeting to impress him, even though there was no pool at Club View Drive. How she'd tearfully begged him to stay on the hill at Easton Drive on her wedding night to Bern, as she was terrified that Annie Spry was "in the woods" near the house.

Poor lost girl, he thought.

He remembered the two of them in each other arms at Yaqui Crest, her beauty, their passion. Her dazed horror the night she saw Bern's body… Her terror at Bern's funeral as the crowd had moved in on her. And he remembered the note she'd sent him after it was all over:

> *You must be so disappointed in Jean Harlow. I wanted you to admire me and like me and I know how terribly I have failed.*

Porter said a quick prayer, and with no desire to see Bello, Mother Jean or the others, made for the door.

"Porter?"

He recognized the voice before turning around, even if it had only said one word. It was Clark Gable. The star shook Porter's hand. "It's good to see you, but not in these circumstances," said Gable.

"Yeah," said Porter.

"Listen" said Gable. "Some of Baby's friends are planning a tribute tonight. I can't be part of it – the press would distort it – but maybe you'd want to be." He led Porter into a corner of the room, where anonymous faces crowded. Porter recognized a seated woman. She was Blanche Williams, Harlow's personal maid.

"Blanche," said Gable, "you remember Porter Down?"

Blanche's large eyes looked up admiringly at Porter. "My, yes," she said softly. "Thank you for coming, Mr. Down."

He took her hands. "Porter, remember?" he said.

"Excuse me," said Gable. "I'll let you both talk." He returned to his companion that evening, Carole Lombard.

"Baby liked you, Porter," said Blanche, her eyes moist. "She never forgot you. She'd bring you up now and then. She told me more than one time, 'I gave that man a rabbit's foot.'"

Porter reached in his suit coat pocket, removed the rabbit's foot, and showed Blanche the lucky piece. "You kept it," said Blanche significantly. "For some reason, she always wondered if you kept it."

"Yes. I kept it," said Porter. "In fact, I always carry it." He placed it back in his pocket.

Blanche suddenly began crying. "Baby was so sad, Porter," she sobbed. "Most of the time I know her...she was so sad."

Porter stood silently as Blanche composed herself.

"Tonight, we're having a tribute to Baby," said Blanche. "The manager here said he'd let some of us stay. See...the Baby always said... she didn't like to be alone in the dark. You remember?"

"I remember," said Porter.

"After tomorrow," said Blanche, the tears running again, "she'll always be alone in the dark." She paused and wiped her eyes. "Will you stay too?"

"Yes."

A few minutes later, the family and famous members of the crowd dispersed outside to the waiting limousines, the inevitable curious crowd gawking and applauding. The manager indeed allowed the small group of technicians, makeup crew, costumers, and others who genuinely loved Jean Harlow to stay. MGM security took posts near the body as the management locked the doors and reverently dimmed the lights in the Tennyson Room.

In the shadows, Porter Down sat beside Blanche Williams, lowered his head in private thoughts, and silently joined the vigil.

The End

Author's Note

This, of course, is a work of fiction.

The characters of Jean Harlow, Paul Bern, Dorothy Millette, Marino Bello, "Mother Jean" Bello, Abner "Longie" Zwillman, Eddie Mannix, Louis B. Mayer, Irene Harrison, Blanche Williams, Howard Strickling, Irving Thalberg, Henry Bern, Friederike Marcus, John and Winifred Carmichael, Whitey Hendry, Willis Goldbeck, Warden James B. Holohan, Anita Loos, Dr. Frank Webb, Dr. Edward B. Jones, Henry Uttal, Rabbi Edgar Magnin, and Judge Yankwich are based on the author's research, and dramatized accordingly. So are the "cameo" appearances of Mary Astor, Lionel Atwill, Tallulah Bankhead, John Barrymore, Joan Crawford, Florence Eldridge, Victor Fleming, Clark Gable, Charles Gemora, John Gilbert, Jetta Goudal, Gilda Gray, Carole Lombard, Fredric March, Conrad Nagel, William Powell, Irene Mayer Selznick, Norma Shearer, Lupe Velez, Johnny Weissmuller, and Cornelius Vanderbilt Whitney.

All the other characters are fictitious.

The dates, times and revelations related to the deaths of Paul Bern and Dorothy Millette are all based on the actual events, although these deaths (still officially ruled "suicides") and their details remain a 90-year-old mystery.

Among the real-life events that figure in this novel:

Jean Harlow's abortion during her marriage to Charles McGrew is factual and reported by her most in-depth biographer, David Stenn, in his book *Bombshell: The Life and Death of Jean Harlow* (New York, Doubleday, 1993). She deeply regretted having had the procedure.

Rumors of Harlow's sexual relationship with Marino Bello dogged her for much of her career. Famed columnist Mark Hellinger even publicly addressed them (and wrote he didn't believe them) in October of 1932, a month after Paul Bern's death.

Abner "Longie" Zwillman, who saved Harlow's career in 1931, reputedly spoke coarsely of Harlow in his later years. A pillar of

"Murder Incorporated," he was found hanged in his home in West Orange, New Jersey, on February 27, 1959, and officially ruled a suicide. His death came shortly before his scheduled appearance before the McClellan Senate Committee hearings on organized crime. The suicide verdict is a controversy, and famed mobster Lucky Luciano claimed Zwillman was assassinated due to his potential as a government informant. Luciano also claimed Zwillman's killers trussed him up like a pig before hanging him.

Marino Bello died in 1953 at the age of 70, was survived by his third wife, and is buried in the Graceland section of Forest Lawn Memorial Park, Glendale. Mother Jean died in 1958 at age 67 and is entombed in the "Jean Harlow Room" in the Sanctuary of Benediction at Forest Lawn, with her daughter. The marble room with stained glass ceiling was purchased by William Powell, Harlow's lover at the time of her death, and had three crypts, presumably for Harlow, Mother Jean, and Powell. However, Powell married a starlet in 1940; after his death in 1984 at age 91, he was buried at Desert Memorial Park in Cathedral City, California, next to his son, who had committed suicide in 1968. The third crypt in the Jean Harlow Room remains unoccupied.

Eddie Mannix stayed a power figure at MGM and died in Beverly Hills in 1963 at the age of 72. His legacy includes notoriety for allegedly ordering a "hit" on actor George Reeves, TV's *Superman*, whose 1959 death by gunshot was officially ruled a suicide. The story goes that the aging Mannix was enraged by his wife Toni's longtime affair with Reeves; the film *Hollywoodland* (with Bob Hoskins as Mannix) explored this saga. Mannix is entombed at Holy Cross Cemetery in Los Angeles.

San Quentin Prison was the only jail where executions took place in California, and still take place today. Hanging was the form of execution from 1893 to 1937. The hanging there of one Effie Abigail McCoo in 1932 is entirely fictitious.

The "bestiality" episodes described in the films *Tarzan the Ape Man*, *The Sign of the Cross*, *Blonde Venus*, *Island of Lost Souls*, and *King Kong* survive in the prints available on DVD and Blu-Ray. Fictional character Annie Spry, of course, had nothing to do with them.

In researching this novel, the author has visited many of the sites described in this book, including the Paul Bern/Jean Harlow house in Benedict Canyon (at least the basic area – the house is privately owned and entry to the grounds protected by a locked gate); the remnants of Falcon Lair (the main house bulldozed in 2006, also in Benedict Canyon); the former MGM Studios in Culver City; the former Mack Sennett Studio in Echo Park; the city of Twentynine Palms and its surrounding area; the Castellammare colony in Santa Monica; and Grace Chapel in Inglewood Cemetery.

Besides David Stenn's *Bombshell: The Life and Death of Jean Harlow*, I'm grateful to the books *Jean Harlow*, by G.D. Hamann (Filming Today Press, Hollywood); *Deadly Illusions: The Murder of Paul Bern*, by Samuel Marx and Joyce Van Der Veen (Random House, New York, 1990); and *Harlow in Hollywood: The Blonde Bombshell in the Movie Capital, 1928-1937*, by Darrell Rooney and Mark A. Vieira (Angel City Press, Santa Monica, CA, 2011). Helpful too was *MGM: Hollywood's Greatest Backlot*, by Steven Bingen, Stephen X. Sylvester, and Michael Troyan (Santa Monica Press LC, Solana Beach CA, 2011). Also, an ironic thanks to the late Irving Shulman, who presented the "dildo story" as a fact in his controversial best-seller, *Harlow: An Intimate Biography* (Bernard Geis Associates, distributed by Random House, New York, 1964).

The novel's interpretation of the "Dearest Dear..." note, left by Paul Bern the night he died, is totally created by the author.

For all its factual material, this novel, again, is a work of fiction, and the reader is to approach it as such.

- GWM, January, 2023

Made in the USA
Columbia, SC
27 May 2023

9303a0df-1dba-413a-87a0-f4d0ca96a5f7R03